Advice from the Wicked

a novel by

Glen Pitre

ISBN-978-0970138354

COVER DESIGN by the author, with waves borrowed from the famous Katsushika Hokusai woodblock print; a woman borrowed from an early 1900s New Orleans Blue Book brothel advertisement; and the boy and his mount adapted from a photo I took of my nephew who dropped by as I was installing an eleven and a half foot (taxidermied) alligator into a museum.

Côte Blanche Productions, inc.
720 Mandeville Street, New Orleans, LA 70117

www.CajunMovies.com

for Michie

Other works by Glen Pitre

Air Racers
American Creole
Belizaire the Cajun
Cajun Country
Cigarettes & Nylons
Country Roads of Louisiana
The Crawfish Book
Eddie Robinson: Coach
En Bas du Bayou
La Fièvre Jaune
Floating Palace
Flood Streets
The French Quarter by Night
Good for What Ails You
Great River
Haunted Waters, Fragile Lands
The Heart of India
The Home Front
Huit Piastres et Demie!
Hurricane on the Bayou
In Quiet Night
Les Raconteurs de la Louisiane
Life in Balance
Lights, Camera, Pirates!
The Man Who Came Back
Memories of Terrebonne
Rescuing the Treasure
The Scoundrel's Wife
Time Served
Top Speed
Treasures of the Tunica
Willie Francis Must Die Again
Wings Over the Wetlands

Lesson I

TELL-TALE SIGNS OF ONCOMING DISASTER

Men already tipsy, women in their finest homemade skirts, and hordes of restless children crammed the cottage. Sawhorse tables sagged under piles of oysters and pots of fricassée. A ring of beaten gold slipped onto a delicate finger, symbol of the ill-starred union that would forever rob that poor girl of any lasting happiness. It was to prove even less pleasant for her bridegroom.

Did he realize his peril? Not a bit. Besotted by love and homemade wine, he saw no further than the party at hand and the wedding night ahead.

And the bride? Beaming, nervous, dazzling in the sapphire-colored dress she'd sewn herself, she would've laughed at or argued with or banished outside as drunk and unruly anyone who forecast her marriage might turn out less than long and happy. But secretly she knew — she must've known — that such optimism was desperate, hollow, credible only if she rejected the warnings of her substantial powers of clairvoyance.

The hard truth was, in just a few hours, barely seventeen and not a full day past her wedding, she would already be a widow.

And I would be to blame.

Maybe it's best the groom didn't know what the bride wouldn't admit. Wisdom comes at a price; smart to purchase on the installment plan, a little at a time. Following that logic, neither should we hurry into *my* role in this whole sad affair. I'm ten for ten breaking the Lord's Commandments, seven for seven chalking up Deadly Sins; much you will learn from studying my misdeeds, but precious instruction can't be rushed.

So let's back up a bit. Say, twenty-four hours. We can meet a few villagers who will themselves attend the wedding, each playing a part in the crisscross of guilt and innocence. To make the puzzle more challenging, we'll start with an apparently inconsequential man at a seemingly insignificant moment. His name: unimportant also, since almost no one knew it. Anyone who called him anything used a mean-spirited childhood nickname, "Touloulou."

It was a late September evening in 1893. Mosquitoes buzzed. Sheep-head Bocage, a strikingly unhandsome fellow, stood in his door and counted seventeen cents into Touloulou's callused hand, payment owed for digging the pit for Sheep-head's new privy. Touloulou peeked inside at the fishermen hooding their cards around a table covered with scrap sailcloth. He recognized Achille Cheramie, the brawny lug who the very next evening would be marrying the girl Touloulou had heard experienced mystical visions; except the visions gossip probably wasn't true, Touloulou decided, else their little village of Chenière would be overrun with pilgrims like Lourdes or Guadalupe.

"Shoddy send-off for your last night of freedom," admitted Placide Guilbeau as he topped off Achille's glass from a bottle of Old Saratoga. "We should hoist sail for Grand Isle."

When the buck-toothed boy, Philo Leboeuf, snickered, Touloulou understood what was being suggested. On Grand Isle a couple of whores kept cribs, mostly for tourists but with special rates for locals who could bring them fish in winter after the tourists went home.

Achille said, "Touloulou, want to sit in, save me from these tomcats?"

Any other night Touloulou would've declined, but that afternoon he'd excavated the earthenware crock that held his life savings. The pennies just collected brought his fortune to eighty-six dollars and twelve cents. Enough, finally.

Letting these men see his money was foolish. Touloulou knew that even as he limped in, lifted the bulging flour sack from inside his shirt, and loosed its drawstring. Foolish, but men like Achille sailed out every day with no fear of sinking or capsizing in a gale. Touloulou wanted just once to impress them and this might be his last chance.

Money spilled onto the table. The fishermen gaped. "*Maudit!*" said Achille, picking up the most valuable coin in the pile, a $5 half-eagle. Touloulou pinched the gold piece out of Achille's fingers. Win or lose, he didn't intend to risk his shiny Lady Liberty.

Another evening, Touloulou might've found the men playing poker or euchre, but tonight they dealt *bourré*, a risk-taker's game where losses swiftly befell the reckless or unlucky. Minutes in, suffering *bourré* on a big hand obligated Touloulou to ante sixty-seven cents for the next pot. That's about what a Chenière fisherman got for a topped-off bushel of shrimp, netted by hand, cleaned, headed, and delivered to the floating cannery at Little Temple. Around the table, Touloulou noticed, laughter had died away.

Too impatient to wait for good cards, Philo burnt through his meager stake but stuck around to re-fill glasses with Sheephead's rye whiskey. When nobody'd take his ill-tempered, one-eyed cow as collateral, Placide also retired from the game. Still the pots grew. Most often, Achille raked them in, Achille who by now had his sleeves rolled up and his shirt halfway unbuttoned. Because the room was warm, Touloulou wondered, or to show off his fisherman muscles? And if the latter, was it vanity? Or a warning not to question his astonishing luck?

Touloulou composed several silent prayers to the Blessed Virgin to dam his river of low trumps and useless off-cards, but

She did not intercede. He kept playing anyway, at first because he couldn't bear to have these men think him cowardly. Later, as the maw of poverty gaped wider, he stuck out of frantic need to win back what he'd lost. All his plans depended on that money. Despair swirled around him like gunsmoke.

"Damn!" Touloulou cursed as Achille, winning the night's largest pot, snatched the five-dollar piece from it, kissed the likeness of Lady Liberty, and buried the gold coin in his pocket. Drunk on rye and good fortune, he invited them all to his wedding the next evening, his wedding to a girl maybe touched by God, which, Touloulou supposed, might explain Achille's extraordinary run of cards.

~

The next afternoon, Touloulou tested the fire in the big outdoor oven he'd built for Victorine, who owned the general store. Shaped of clay, this *fourneau* was a lumpy, imperfect creation that would only last a few years, yet it could hold heat for hours, long enough to render crusty brown the batch of vanilla tarts Victorine had been hired to bake for Achille Cheramie's wedding, the order paid for with money Achille had won off Touloulou.

As he raked crackling hackberry coals, Touloulou wondered how much of his cash Achille had left. Where might Achille keep it? And what would he himself be willing to do to get it back?

~

Forty feet from where Touloulou endured the oven's heat, Victorine Guidry, a wealthy widow, age twenty-eight, gathered saliva, puckered her lips, and spat into a pot of bubbling yellow pudding. She awaited a pleasurable frisson. It didn't come.

Even secret retribution needs a witness, Victorine decided. Some man to laugh so she could smile back coyly. With her willowy figure, haunting eyes, and overflowing cash box, Victorine might've had her pick of male companions. She considered that no great achievement: most every roughneck in these marshes, single or married, would happily flop into any bed if open arms waited. Cajun or Creole, Croatian or Sicilian, Houma Indian or *Américain,* all randy as goats. Victorine could hardly imagine one worth inviting onto her mahogany four-poster.

Through the window she peeked at the handyman tending her backyard oven. Touloulou had the almond-shaped eyes of a Filipino and he limped, but he said his prayers and finished his chores and lacked the imagination to ever cheat her.

How dull.

Curse Achille Cheramie.

As Victorine let the curtain slip, her stirring spoon bumped a Mason jar. She watched it fall, fall, fall, then shatter on the floor like a broken taboo. The fragrance of vanilla assaulted her as she stooped to rescue the dark, finger-like pods. Around them, shards of jar glistened. Mixed into the custard, glass slivers might go unnoticed, she realized, perhaps until late when wedding guests home in bed would wake with bellyaches they would at first put off to too much food and liquor. How many would die? Would she be caught? Victorine didn't think Louisiana hanged women, at least not often. She savored the image of tonight's bride, a course, illiterate fish-gutter, spitting blood onto the dress she'd spent weeks sewing from the three-and-a-half yards of garish imitation penang Victorine had sold her.

Glass might be too obvious.

Sliding the pan to the edge of the stove, Victorine left the smells of the kitchen for the merchandise-filled store that took up most of her house. On a top shelf a red pasteboard box advertised, "For Rodents." Victorine wondered how bitter it tasted and whether she should grind another vanilla pod into the custard.

~

Ding-da-ding the bell jingled as twelve-year-old Zeph Leboeuf entered the store. When she saw whom it was, Victorine greeted him in French.

"I want to buy a lantern," Zeph announced in the same

language.

He awaited her surprise. A lantern cost almost a dollar, a sum few boys his age could ever stockpile. Instead, "Table lamp or railroad type?" was all she said, climbing down the ladder, a red box tucked against her bosom.

"To hang from the mast so Achille's new wife can spot us when we work late on the bay," Zeph said. It was the perfect gift. He was proud to have thought of it, till he noticed how the store mistress was scorching him with her scary eyes.

"You think wasting money on wedding presents will help get you a partnership in Achille's boat?" she said.

Well, what if he did? What business was it of hers?

~

To Zeph's left, whitecaps rifling Caminada Bay made the spindly masts of fishing boats sway and dance. To his right, past the mangrove scrubland, angry waves broke against the driftwood tangle lining the Gulf of Mexico beachfront. Just as well Achille's wedding tonight had kept their boat moored, Zeph thought as he walked along their low-lying spit of isolated coast past the gardens and pastures and unpainted cottages that comprised Chenière.

Madame Victorine was sure a grouchy one. Maybe 'cause she was octoroon. Or so people whispered. She didn't look Negro to Zeph, not even one-eighth Negro. The lady was paler than he was, he thought, especially after his summer working in the sun.

They'd almost missed the season. Achille hadn't bought the boat till May — heaven knows where he got the money. Heaven knows where Achille got so much money this morning, a handful of which he gave Zeph, back pay long overdue. Achille was lucky like that. Only twenty-six, already owning his own boat. And catching a girl so pretty and sweet-natured to marry. Zeph would listen in when she and her sister Clo or whoever else was chaperoning would come visit as Achille and Zeph worked on salvaging the old boat, spending June scraping and sanding, July patching and painting, early August tarring net and dipping canvas. Zeph's shoulders still ached from days unbroken even in the worst noon heat, evenings when driftwood fires barely offered light to see or enough smoke to chase off mosquitoes, short nights when his dreams cadenced to the *clunk, clunk, clunk* of a caulking hammer.

Worth it opening day though, when they hoisted their red sail: Achille Cheramie, Chenière's newest captain, and young Zephirin Leboeuf, who'd earned his berth as deckhand, and who would one day, he was certain, become Achille's partner.

~

"Why in the world?" Zeph asked.

Achille shook his hair out of his eyes. "Don't distract me."

Carrying the new lantern out the rickety catwalk over the water, Zeph had found Achille on their boat barefoot and busy like always, cuffs rolled up, palmetto-straw hat tossed aside. Zeph had expected his captain to be mending net or splicing rope, killing time till his wedding. Instead Achille was doing the damnedest thing: drilling a hole through a five-dollar gold piece. Round and round went the auger, screwing a deep wound into the ear of Lady Liberty. Zeph had never even touched a coin of such value as Achille was ruining now.

Achille flashed that look that always promised mischief. "Broad daylight. I can see fine."

Zeph chuckled and set the lantern down. "My wedding present," he explained.

"Should be saving your money," Achille said, his powerful hands surprisingly nimble as they fingered gold shavings into a tidy pile.

"I'll earn more money," the boy chirped. "We both will. Right from this deck."

When Achille offered no smart-alec reply, Zeph detected something amiss. "Won't we?"

~

Hiding under an oilcloth, Philo Leboeuf heard his kid brother's question hang. Why didn't Achille answer? Get it over with.

The end of shrimping season meant moving on to better money oystering, but that took muscle. Achille was six foot four with shoulders broad as a stallion's, but little Zeph didn't have the brawn to work a pair of oyster rakes. Six years older, Philo was plenty strong. Top of that, with the older sister hitched to Achille, Philo could marry the younger sister, Clo, making the two men family. So Philo taking over Zeph's deckhand job made perfect sense.

'Course, when Philo first explained it, Achille laughed, saying Philo might find Clo too much a handful. Well, what made Clo's big sister so perfect? Philo did enjoy watching that kind of glide in how she walked, but so what? Clo walked pretty spicy too and had even bigger *tétons*.

Philo heard *tang, tang, tang,* a hammer on metal, and wondered what Achille was doing now. He wished he could see. The air was getting stuffy under the tarpaulin.

"They working on the schoolhouse today?" Achille asked. Philo stuffed his hand into his mouth to keep from laughing. How *that* must pepper Zeph! Over the summer, volunteers had started building Chenière its first school. A teacher from Grand Isle even held a few classes under a shade tree, giving the children a taste. To Zeph, Philo knew, it tasted like rancid lard.

"I can count on my fingers," Philo heard Zeph say. "Scratch an 'X' for my name, same as you, Achille. And when we sell our oysters in New Orleans, I'll figure out which markings mean 'saloon' by the time I'm old enough to go drinking in one." Achille chuckled, breaking the rhythm of the *tang, tang, tang.* Zeph kept talking. "You mention school to rile me, but you're not mad at me. What you are is scared, Achille. 'Cause of getting married."

"I'm not scared," Achille shot back, "but marrying changes things. So I been thinking—"

At last, thought Philo, here it is, but then came "*pock, pock, pock*," like a yard hen. Philo could picture his brother, fists tucked into armpits, pecking at imaginary corn. *Pock, pock, pock!*

"I'm not chicken," Achille protested, but he was laughing.

Achille's hearty laugh was always something to see, but Philo didn't want to picture those perfect teeth now. I taught Zeph the chicken dance, he lamented. Well, Achille better tell the boy. He'd promised. True, not the first time they talked, with those cracks about Clo running Philo ragged. But Achille sure promised when Philo brought it up again, after catching Achille lit up on liquor and in such a good mood walking back from last night's card game.

To Consider

Yes, the same card game where the crippled handyman Touloulou lost, if not his shirt, at least his meager fortune. If I've led our narrative in a circle, it's to make this point: you can't unmask evil by tracking a straight line. Evil doesn't follow a single thread. It exists as fabric, scrabbling over and burrowing under itself, snaking and slithering in all directions simultaneously.

The good news: by diligently examining its weave, one *can* frequently unravel the foul cloth, occasionally even re-stitch those twisted fibers into something prettier.

The bad news: despite this lesson's title, oncoming disaster rarely offers obvious, telltale signs, at least not until it's too late. To re-purpose bad into good you must learn to parse elusive clues and ambiguous omens.

Wouldn't you love the skill to render null the wicked things that fate or other people sometimes do to you? Let alone the worse things you too often do to yourself?

If so, keep reading.

Lesson II

A NUPTUAL CASE STUDY

"Give me your hand," Achille said.

"My palm's sweaty."

How silly, he thought; wonderfully silly. He took her hand, squeezing. The crowd fell silent. The bride's stepmother, Eune, and godmother, Da-Dool, together laid a broomstick on the floor in front of the couple.

Achille had wanted a Catholic wedding. He wasn't devout, but his bride was, and a priest in brocade vestments, chanting Latin nobody understood, was so impressive. Father Premeaux visited their village only rarely though. Achille couldn't wait.

"Ready?" he whispered. She nodded, emerald eyes anxious but her smile wide. There existed something in that smile — warmth it offered, delights it hinted, dreamy mysteries it promised — that made him forget other women existed.

"*Un, deux, trois*," they counted, then jumped a short, public hop that Achille was sure would transform his life.

Landing shook loose her hair, an elaborate topknot ringed with curls that her sister Clo had constructed, calling it high fashion. Achille didn't know boo about fashion and suspected Clo didn't either, but it was pretty. As his bride pinned back her yellow-brown curls, he imagined how later she'd look still prettier with her hair brushed out for bed.

From his pocket Achille unfolded a handkerchief, revealing something hidden there. He loved surprising her and this was a big one. For a moment she didn't breathe.

"Don't you want it?" he teased.

Still she couldn't voice an answer. Slipping the ring onto her finger, he realized he hadn't gotten the size right. Maybe nobody would notice.

"We said, 'no ring,'" her words finally gushed, "at least not right away because we couldn't afford it with so much to buy for your house, I mean our house, with me moving in and your boat with oyster season starting, we said it, we agreed, yet here's a ring—"

He loved how her thoughts flowed out through her musical voice like clear, rushing water, how tears could roll down her cheeks as she wore the brightest smile.

"—a real gold wedding ring like city women in fancy feathered hats wear and it's the most beautiful thing I ever owned and it must've cost a fortune, way too much, and I know you put thought into it because you had to have ordered it weeks ago from some faraway jeweler—"

She seemed not to suspect he'd made it himself that very afternoon. Maybe everybody else would be fooled too. He'd tell her eventually, he supposed. Not tonight.

"—or else snuck to New Orleans in your boat to pick it out when I thought you were shrimping so little Zeph must've been in on it, both of you, you're bad, yes, bad, and I love it, the ring I mean, love it so much and I love you too, Achille Cheramie, and now you're my husband for the rest of our lives and I'm so happy I can't stop blubbering."

The more she wept, the more the crowd laughed. Achille raised her arm like a boxing victor so that everyone could see the ring. "My wife deserves every pretty thing and I'll wrestle any man who says different!" he hollered, then swept her into a kiss that drew raucous applause from every person there.

Well, everyone except Achille's new father-in-law.

~

Bride and groom were pulled here, there, then apart for kisses and congratulations. Had he not been so tall, she'd have lost sight of him.

"Lemme see, lemme see," said Clo. She examined her sister's ring. "Fits loose."

"He had to estimate size, to keep it a surprise."

The ring wasn't the smooth circle it should've been, Clo saw. "Not exactly round either."

"The latest style, obviously. Yap-yap all you want, Clothilde Marie Gaspard. You won't spoil it for me. Nothing's going to spoil tonight."

Clo smiled. "Notice how drunk your bandleader is?"

~

Léon's cousin's job was to drone rhythm; Léon, Jr., tapped the beat on a triangle hammered out of an old hay rake; but when he was halfway sober it was Léon Dantin's fiddle that kept people dancing. Léon was savoring the dregs from a quart of homemade wine as the bride approached.

"Remember, start with *The Waltz of Unending Love*," she said.

Léon rosined his bow. "That one's too syrupy. How about *No Escape from Heartache*?"

"To dance to at my wedding?"

"And the rest of your life." Léon saw color rise in her face. It made her even prettier. Why couldn't his wife look like that? Why was Achille so lucky? People whispered the girl could tell things about you that you didn't know yourself, but if so, why couldn't she see Achille for what he was? Thanks to bullying from Da-Dool, who Léon never should've married, if not for their kids, fine kids, all eight of them, from Léon Jr. to mischievous little Tellia, who, well, anyway, because of Da-Dool, 'cause she was godmother to the bride, here was Léon playing Achille's wedding for free. Free! Even though all morning long Achille had been scattering cash around the village.

The bride was talking. "*Unending Love*," he heard her say again. "It's the perfect song and my wedding has to be perfect."

Léon wondered what Da-Dool would say if he refused to play at all. "Because Da-Dool can't make me any more miserable than she does already," Léon said, answering a question he belatedly realized the bride hadn't asked. Fresh envy and old grudges swept through his brain, crackling with lightning like summer squalls over Barataria Bay. He'd let the bride have her "*Unending Love.*" She'd discover what a fairy tale it was.

~

After one perfect waltz, an hour of up-tempo reels and polkas left dancers fanning themselves and bickering over seats. The wedding couple two-stepped on, swirling past improvised tables overflowing with seafood jambalaya and guinea hen gumbo. Achille's windfall had bought three hams and nine fried chickens. Next to pitchers of milk from Placide Guilbeau's one-eyed cow sat what remained of Victorine Guidry's delicious (though perhaps lethal) custard tarts.

As he held his bride close, Achille decided that all the money he'd thrown into this party was well spent. He had the finest boat, the biggest wedding, the sweetest bride in Chenière. If he also had the Reaper stalking him, well, at least he didn't know it yet.

~

From a corner, friendless, Jerome Chabert watched the newlyweds dance. He'd been engaged once, but the girl broke it off after his blackouts started.

The blackouts had ruined his life. All those hours he couldn't account for, coming once or twice a month, had beget rumors that he was a *rougarou.* Jerome didn't swallow the notion that a man could periodically change into a large dog, let alone change back again. He especially refused to credit that he himself while thus transformed had slaughtered several of his neighbors' chickens, including a prize Spanish rooster that Sheep-head Bocage still hounded him to pay for. The torn clothes and feathers or muskrat entrails he'd sometimes find around him when he woke from his blackouts Jerome put off to cruel tricks played by mischievous boys.

Jerome suspected he'd been invited tonight to prove that Achille was afraid of nothing; Achille, so handsome his grin could melt a candle, now whispering some sweet nonsense into his bride's ear, then squeezing toward the back door through the crowd bestowing him adulation. Achille lived life like it was a story, an adventure tale, with himself its trickster hero.

The bride was more complicated. When Jerome arrived and everyone reacted how he knew they would, the bride took pity. Jerome didn't like being pitied but loved what she'd done next: kissed his cheek like he was a favored guest. "Cousin Jerome," she'd greeted him so everyone would hear, though he was Achille's cousin, not hers. What made her so gracious? Especially since, he'd seen in her green eyes, she was as afraid of him as the others were.

Jerome decided now might be a good moment to thank her, bestow his congratulations, to offer help should ever she or her family need it. He pushed off from the wall, excusing himself as he nudged through the crowd. People flinched as they saw who touched them. The small commotion drew attention even in the noisy room. Jerome's eyes met the bride's. "Don't alarm my guests," her expression pleaded. "I hate to ask this of you, but I do."

Jerome gave her a smile that he hoped didn't reveal too much sadness and went back to leaning against the wall. He'd find some other time, some other way, to thank her.

~

"Where's your groom?" Clement Gaspard asked his stepdaughter.

"Gone pee," she whispered. "He's coming right back so don't start."

"Nothing to start. Done now. My girl's seventeen, hard-headed, wouldn't wait."

"Look around," she said. "These people, this food. I thought I'd have only close relatives sharing a redfish, but at the very last minute Achille turned our little family wedding into this magnificent affair. Admit it. I married a magician."

"Your magician's only trick was frittering today the money he won gambling last night."

He saw a flicker of surprise. So Achille hadn't told her. She toyed with the ring floating loose on her finger. "Last night?"

"Something wrong?"

She shook off her mood. "*You'll* think so, 'cause I'm going to make you dance."

Gaspard was a clumsy dancer and didn't enjoy proving it but couldn't refuse at her wedding, even a wedding to a man she was too good for. He took her in his arms and tried to follow the beat, counting steps and dodging elbows.

"Hey, you've been practicing. You're pretty good," she said, an outright lie. Despite her smile, he could tell something bothered her. Maybe a headache coming on. Maybe one of *those* headaches.

"Does Achille realize you see things?" Gaspard asked. "Things to come?"

Her smile disappeared. Gaspard understood mentioning her visions would cut deep, but from tonight on she was beyond his protection. This dance might be his last chance to tell her everything he never knew how to explain.

"You have to let him know about your premonitions. So that when you start seeing stuff, he doesn't go all loony thinking his wife's loony and—"

"Just dance, Papa." As she said it, she took control. He felt himself manhandled this way then that and realized his movements were now on the beat with the music. The world wasn't a dance floor, though. Every bright day brought after it a dark night. She was too young to know how men could seem strong but be weak.

"Every time it happened, when you saw stuff, bad stuff, and later it came true, we always let you pretend it was coincidences. Maybe that was wrong. But if you're old enough to tie the knot, you're old enough to stop pretending. So tell me, you truly see roses blooming always ever after for you and Achille?"

"Who on Earth sees roses always blooming?"

"I did," Gaspard said. "After you and your sister came into my life, I did."

The bride chewed her lip. "Papa, you're silly as a sea gull and you make me so mad though I love you anyway and I don't know how Mama put up with you so long."

"I don't either."

She chuckled. "To answer your question, yes, roses *will* always bloom for Achille and me, year in, year out, every day of our lives because I'm going to make, excuse my language, *damn* sure they do."

~

A year earlier, when he'd decided time had come to choose a wife, Achille had walked Chenière one end to the other, sniffing every rose bush in the village. From the most fragrant he took a cutting and planted it next to his back steps where, when grown, its perfume would block the odor of his outhouse. A wise man chooses a wife with a sensitive nose. Such a woman can smell a weather change in time to gather hanging laundry, or recognize when yesterday's fish is better for garden fertilizer than family dinner, and she could always detect the scent of another woman on her husband. Knowing that, he would never be tempted to stray.

Achille's rose bush was now tall enough that its thorns pricked him when he backed into it. He squinted in the moonlight trying to make sure Touloulou carried no weapon. No, the handyman's clenched fists were empty.

"Give me back my eighty-six dollars and twelve cents," Touloulou repeated.

"The money's gone," Achille said. "Go inside, eat something, dance with a pretty girl."

"You know I can't dance."

Of course. Touloulou's left leg was a few inches shorter than the other, an affliction since birth. His nickname, "Touloulou," meant fiddler crab in the local French. Achille vowed to remember the infirmity in future but knew there was no point apologizing now. "I've got to go," Achille said. He pointed at the outhouse.

The cripple raised his fists. "Not till you promise to pay back every penny."

"You saying I cheated you?"

"I *need* that money."

"I need to piss."

Touloulou hobbled after Achille, catching up near the pile of fresh shells smelling of the salty bay. Wedged into the cypress top of Achille's shucking table were an oyster knife and hatchet. Achille stopped when Touloulou grabbed the hatchet.

"For years I took any job nobody wanted," Touloulou lamented. "Never lit candles, wore second-hand clothes, ate nothing but cornmeal mush."

Achille eased backward. "Even with your leg, you could've made decent money fishing."

Touloulou swung the hatchet. Achille dodged. Touloulou swung again. Achille scooted toward the table, plucked up the oyster knife, feinted a jab, then maneuvered so the light spilling from the house would silhouette him.

"Best you get home," Achille said. "Gladiating like this ain't proper for a married man."

"My plans, all my plans, go down the well without that money," Touloulou moaned.

Achille heard someone behind him. Did Touloulou have an ally?

No. Women's voices. Laughing. Not the sound of danger, except the threat of his wife finding out he was knife-fighting at their wedding. He risked taking his eyes off Touloulou.

Helping Widow Falgoust down the steps was his wife's godmother, Da-Dool Dantin. Nothing Da-Dool witnessed would go unreported, Achille knew. He turned to face her, figuring he'd see it in her expression if Touloulou lunged for him. Would that give him time to defend himself? His heart raced.

"What you doing out here, Achille?" Da-Dool demanded.

He waggled the oyster knife. "The two of us were thinking to shuck a few more."

"Two? Seems your help ran off."

Achille spun. The hatchet lay on the ground.

"Too late to hide now, Achille," cackled Da-Dool as the women entered the outhouse. "Your fate was sealed by that wedding ring, which everybody but that love-blind girl can see wasn't store-bought."

To Consider

Da-Dool claimed Achille's fate was sealed. At that point, was it?

I've introduced nine wedding guests who, whether they knew it yet or not, were to be my accomplices in the death of Achille Cheramie. You see, most crimes comprise not only actions but also *failures to act*; connivances of the consciously malicious, sure, yet also collusion of persons unwitting, uncurious, uncautious, or unwilling to get involved. Even the deceased bears some responsibility for his own demise (though I recognize it seems churlish to assign him blame when I survived and he didn't).

As we return to the party and the upcoming tragedy, carefully follow the nine above-mentioned wedding guests. See if you discern a precise moment when the death of the beautiful bride's new husband became inevitable, the moment when his fate really was sealed.

Lesson III

STEPS TOWARD A FOUL PLAY

"Where'd you chase him?" Clo asked. "I want to waltz with him."

"*I've* barely waltzed with Achille. Léon plays quick-steps whenever he sees us together."

That made Clo laugh. Her poor big sister. Pious as a nun, and just as innocent. "While I dance with Achille, you grab…" Clo scanned the crowd. "Jerome Chabert! Oh, also, important, swear, tomorrow you tell me everything about it."

Sheep-head Bocage squeezed by, sloshing gumbo from his bowl. The bride dodged bits of falling okra. "About dancing with Jerome?"

Clo rolled her eyes. "No! About…" She hugged herself and pursed her lips into a succession of noisy kisses.

"Behave," pleaded the bride.

"The first time might hurt," Clo continued, "but pretty soon you need it like air and food and water."

"Clo, don't pretend you know anything about it."

"More than you, which isn't much. Your forehead's wrinkly. Not getting a headache? One of your spells?"

"No spells on my wedding night."

"Awful if one came right when you two were—"

"Hush," the bride hissed.

"Well, if not a spell, you're still acting grumpy. Maybe you need food. Try the custard tarts. I don't know what Miss Victorine put in them, but their taste will send you to Heaven."

As Clo let a two-step pull her toward the dancing, Philo Leboeuf stepped into her path offering a buck-toothed smile. "Let's kick up some dust, Clo."

He was nothing to look at, but what could a girl do when she lived in a small town?

"Know the Monkey Glide, Philo? It's what everybody's dancing in New Orleans."

"You never even been to New Orleans," Philo scoffed.

His remark, though true, was ill-mannered, Clo decided, so she brushed past him. Philo pursued. "Okay, okay, I'll dance like any monkey you want."

That did not sound like an apology. "This one's spoken for," Clo said.

He put his hand on her arm. "By who?"

Such impertinence: unforgivable. She paused. Peered into his eyes. Took a deep breath which swelled her breasts, daring him to glance down at them. Her dazzling smile bludgeoned him, piercing flesh, cracking ribs. "Who will I be dancing with instead of you?" she cooed. "With your little brother, Zeph."

~

The store mistress, Victorine, watched the bride glide toward her. If the younger sister captured the eye first, this one invited a longer gaze. Taller, with ample curves but on a leaner frame that time would be kinder to. Curly hair that flashed hints of gold. Achille's new wife carried a slice of custard tart.

"Wanted to make sure you got some," the girl said, offering the saucer.

"I tasted while baking. Please, you enjoy." Victorine indicated the seat next to her, which even in the crowded room had stayed empty all evening. She expected polite refusal, but the bride sat. The girl had brought a fork for Victorine but now put it aside and picked up the pastry with her fingers.

"Mm, lots of vanilla," the bride said after she bit in. Victorine hid her smile.

"I wanted to thank you for loaning Achille the money to fix his boat," the girl went on. "If you hadn't, we might not have been able to get married."

Victorine stiffened. "If you want another loan—"

"No! And if we did I wouldn't ask at our wedding where you'd feel cornered."

She seemed genuinely concerned that Victorine think well of her. Under the fisherfolk ways, a passable lady might lurk, Victorine allowed.

"But I do want to ask a favor, a huge favor." The girl paused to scoop stray custard from her lip. Victorine wondered if the suspense was intentional. "If we're blessed with a child, would you be its godmother?"

Victorine was surprised, an emotion she rarely enjoyed. "You wouldn't give that honor to your sister?"

The bride laughed. "Clo hasn't grown up yet, and might never." She grew serious. "My whole life I'll wear an apron smelling of fish. Fine. I'll have a good husband, a happy home. But I'd love to think my son or daughter might learn about the world out there and—"

"—and you believe, with no children of my own, I'll open my strongbox—"

"It's not about money," the bride said. "Children need a guide. Look around this room. Good people, but even the ones who crossed the world to come here picked it *because* it was tucked away. You're only here because that store ties you down."

Victorine observed the children dancing without shoes, the gossips in patched skirts, the men with untrimmed mustaches who thought themselves prosperous if they had a ten-dollar gold piece buried near their steps. The pretty fishwife was not as stupid as she'd thought, Victorine decided.

The French the girl spoke was so Cajun-accented, it'd be mocked in New Orleans, barely understood in Paris. She'd done a competent job making her wedding dress but possessed no real artistry as a seamstress. Clearly she'd never been taught proper table manners. Yet as the bride swiped her plate for crumbs and licked her fingers clean, she exhibited a certain feline grace. Victorine imagined this girl and Achille grappling as lovers later tonight and knew that before the days of novelty were over, this young wife would develop whatever wiles she needed to hold her man.

Victorine thought about how that afternoon in her kitchen she'd carefully spooned a precise quantity of strychnine from the red pasteboard box and ground nine extra vanilla pods to hide its bitterness; but how, just before adding it to her custard tarts, she instead handed the measuring cup to Touloulou to spread the powder along her garden fence to poison rabbits.

Here, watching the new bride enjoy her sweet confection, Victorine wondered if she'd made the right decision.

~

When finally Achille was able to unleash it, the stream of urine brought immense relief. When he'd finished and shook himself dry, Achille stared down at the penis in his hand.

"Big night," he told it. His penis did not reply.

Buttoning up, Achille stepped into the yard.

Whump. Someone shoved him into the outhouse wall. A fist slammed his stomach. As Achille waited for air to re-enter his lungs, his crouching attacker threw another punch. It stung Achille's ear.

Light from the house fell on his assailant. Not crouching, short. Not Touloulou, a boy. His deckhand. "*Maudit* Zephirin Leboeuf! Back off or I'll smash your head!"

"*Try*," said the twelve-year-old, kicking Achille in the knee, drawing a yelp. "Philo said he's taking my place on your boat!"

"*Maudit* Philocles Leboeuf. That's still just talk."

"Why even talk? He's my brother, I love him, but Philo's dumb as a post. Maybe he's stronger, but I'll catch up. Life's long, Achille. You didn't marry that gal inside to trade her off after one season."

"Zeph! My wedding! Can we hash out your future some

other time?"

Embarrassed, Zeph shrugged acquiescence. "All I want is to be just like you, Achille."

Achille sighed. Grinned. "Well, who could blame you for that?"

Zeph was right, Achille knew. Life's long. Always better to look beyond tomorrow. Starting up the back steps, he dabbed at his injured ear, relieved to find it wasn't bleeding.

~

Inside, Achille felt the floor shaking with the rhythm of a mazurka. Hand after hand clapped his back. He spotted his bride. His expression froze. She was chatting with Victorine.

When he'd needed a loan to refit his boat, Achille had realized Victorine granted him mighty generous terms. Later, he'd pretended to misunderstand her hints that his debt would be forgiven if he made her a marriage proposal. He wouldn't have invited her tonight except he hadn't expected her to come.

Achille's rejection of Victorine wasn't over the octoroon rumors. She didn't look any part Negro to him, and if she was, he didn't care. There stood another problem. She could read. Read whole books, speak high-sounding French and proper English, do arithmetic, run a business. She was smart, willful, and capable of weaving webs around almost anybody. His wife was clever too but in a different way. If he'd married Victorine, how soon before she tired of him? So he rejected her as he'd rejected Clo, who when nobody was near was even less subtle about her attraction. In his bride he sensed constancy the other two lacked.

He would hurry over before Victorine ladled God knows what sweetly worded poison into his beloved's ear. Ask his wife to dance so it'd not seem like he just meant to break up their conversation. But hurrying over might be a perilous journey in a room packed with well-wishers, strewn with hazards, and haunted by the lurking specter of his own imminent mortality.

Achille had taken only three steps when a hand touched his arm. Clo. Lord, she was pretty. "Come dance, Achille. You'll have all night with my sister. Now, dance with me."

~

"Waaaaaa!" wailed Tellia Dantin, the three-year-old daughter of the bandleader Léon and his wife, Da-Dool. Playing tag through the crowd with her cousins, who said she was too little but they were wrong, Tellia had gone running fast and bumped right into Jerome Chabert, who because he was a *rougarou* sometimes turned into a big, mean dog, and who last week had eaten Tellia's mama cat's kittens, and who Poppee said might eat her too if she ever walked down to the bay alone without permission. Where was Poppee? She heard his fiddle playing the finish of a song but couldn't see him through the people. Or Mommee? Nowhere, neither. Everywhere skirts and pant legs. Then Tellia recognized Tante Clo, because Tante Clo wore the prettiest dresses. Tante Clo would protect her.

Tellia dashed toward the splash of color that marked the bride's sister.

~

"We'll dance later, I promise," Achille said to Clo, then he took his next step, still looking back, perhaps because Clo was so lovely, perhaps to not seem rude. Either way, he didn't notice Tellia dashing for the safety of Clo's skirts. Like Achille the girl was glancing back so she didn't see him in her path.

The collision occurred. Tellia tumbled, unhurt; kiddies are indestructible at that age. But when Achille tried to hop over her, his knee — the one Zeph kicked — didn't respond briskly enough, so he saw that while he would not fall on Tellia, he would instead fall on his face, there in public, at his own wedding party, and nothing he could do would prevent it.

Worse, at the same moment, Léon Dantin stepped from the improvised bandstand for yet another drink he shouldn't have. As his youngest daughter screeched and Achille went flying, startled Léon dropped his fifth of muscatel. The bottle shattered, its bottom becoming a circle of jagged peaks that looked like the Italian Alps in a stereopticon picture Victorine had once showed Achille, standing very close as she did.

Though he lacked schooling, Achille possessed an instinctive grasp of odds (which often helped playing cards) and a sailor's understanding of geometry. Estimating point of impact, Achille decided chances were eight-maybe-nine in ten that the green glass Matterhorn rising from the puddle of wine would slice his throat and start him bleeding at a rate no one at the party, nor in all Chenière, nor even on Grand Isle if he lived long enough to be carried there, would be able to stanch. And on his wedding night! How unfair, how unfair.

To Consider

I previously confessed my guilt for Achille's death, but as I haven't yet properly introduced myself, let's lay my culpability aside for a moment. Of the nine wedding guests I did introduce, which share blame for Achille's unhappy situation? The coquettish sister? The rambunctious child? The inebriated fiddler?

Or does the fault lie with occasionally-canine Jerome Chabert, for frightening the kiddie? With the mercurial store mistress, Victorine, for conversing with the bride? With Clémence Gaspard, who might've done more, even he would've admitted, to keep his stepdaughter Clo's flirtatious charm and curvaceous beauty from habitually outrunning her common sense and good manners?

"But none of them *intended* Achille any harm," you complain? Okay. What about Touloulou? His brandished hatchet rattled Achille when later extra presence of mind might've saved him. Or Zeph? Didn't Zeph kick the knee that subsequently failed to prevent the fall? Was it in fact a lethal kick, no less fatal because its deadly result arrived some time afterward?

One might even argue the foul play began when Philo — peeved that Clo had danced with Zeph — announced that Achille had given him Zeph's deckhand job, thus spilling the beans that roused the wrath that inspired the attack that spurred the kick that bruised the knee that succumbed to the stumble that launched Achille toward horrible, gory death.

"But it was *an accident*," you say? No one's fault? Then answer this: what is an accident if not the intersection of random chance and inescapable destiny surrounded by people who did not prevent it? So let's ask again, which one's to blame for Achille falling on that bottle?

But that's entirely the wrong question.

What Happened Next

With animal quickness that seemed, yes, supernatural, to those who witnessed it, Jerome Chabert perceived the danger, dove from his spot leaning friendless against the wall, and wrenched Achille to safety.

"You saved my life," Achille said. To the crowd he repeated, "Jerome saved my life!"

A community that routinely receives both life and death from the sea learns to appreciate irony. Thus everyone took delight that of all people Jerome had saved Achille. Men clapped his shoulder. Women offered him dessert. He drank up their kindness like lemonade yet knew that in their eyes he remained a cursed killer of chickens and maybe, one day, a killer of people too.

For Further Consideration

Since Achille escapes the broken bottle, do our nine at-minimum-partially-guilty parties suddenly become innocent? Without confession, without atonement, without lifting a finger?

Only fair, you say, seeing as the evil has been thwarted?

But evil can never be defeated, not permanently. Re-purposed, sometimes, yes. But defeated? At best, you dodge it in the short term or beat it back temporarily. Let me provide an illustration. Say you're walking through the park. Overhead, a flying pigeon shits. If you're observant and quick you sidestep so the falling crap misses you. Failing that, you're shat upon, find a fountain and clean your lapel: damage contained. But neither alternative prevents you from being shat upon again the very next day. Even if you snatch a stone and throw it true and kill the offending bird, there's always another pigeon needing to void its bowels.

So Achille didn't die upon the broken bottle, but he did indeed die not so very long afterward and each of those same nine villagers played a part in his death. As well as myself, of course, as you will soon learn.

Meanwhile, later that night, the bride was learning a few new things herself.

Lesson IV

HUMAN SEXUALITY vis-à-vis UNTIMELY DEATH

It burned. Heavens, it burned. Achille was rasping her insides out.

He'd started gently, kisses and caresses like butterfly wings, his rough fisherman hands like velvet as they discovered parts of her she'd barely explored herself, touching and stroking till her nook grew moist, then wet, then drenched and begging to be entered. He'd put himself inside her; tenderly; deliberately; quarter-inch by quarter-inch, pushing aside the folds of her flesh so slowly she thought she'd die of anticipation.

That was before. Now a very different Achille was thrusting into her hard, fast, and with such passion she had to clutch the bedpost to keep from sliding across the mattress. He was a steamboat, huffing, puffing, pushing waves aside, intent only on his destination until, suddenly, he stopped moving. Held his breathe. Lifted his weight off her with his powerful arms. She saw the muscles of his jaw clench, hard as steel.

"What's wrong?"

"Too soon," he said.

"Too soon?"

"To finish."

Did she want him to finish? She wasn't sure. It didn't burn as much now. She wanted him to enjoy it and regretted that she didn't understand more about what she could do to give him pleasure. It wasn't something she whispered about with her friends the way Clo did. She wished she could enter Achille's mind, the way he'd entered her body, to see herself as he saw her, and find out what he would like her to do.

Achille started back moving, slowly like in the beginning, except not quite. His breathing was deeper, his arms more rigid now. Achille, her Achille. His hand snaked under her bunched nightgown, the heat of his touch rippling over her flesh. His palm found her breast, his fingers her nipple. Oh, nice! As was his stroking, in and out, in and out. It didn't burn at all anymore though he was again picking up speed. She felt an unfamiliar yearning, an intensity of desire she'd never dreamt hid within her. Surrendering to it, she let Achille guide her, as if up a mountain, a mountain like in picture books, higher and higher. Take me up the mountain, Achille. Take me.

When Achille's moment came — no man can hold out forever — she hadn't quite reach hers, but it was all so new she didn't know enough to be disappointed.

~

After a short repose, they did it again. Ah, newlyweds!

~

Bodies entwined but passion spent, whispering softly she promised she'd be a good wife. He swore he'd be a good husband. She'd be his strength. He'd bring her joy. She'd never ask anything he could not give. Alas, intruding on their dove-like cooing was a headache she recognized as foreshadow of a premonition. She'd felt it earlier, at the wedding. Her papa had noticed, as had Clo.

Now, so did Achille. He studied her frown. "You're sad?"

"No." Sad wasn't it. More annoyance. Occasional waking nightmares had plagued her since childhood, messy, scary things, useless for predicting exactly what would happen, only that it'd be bad. Her "look-ahead spells" had come up a few times during Achille's courtship, but she'd always changed the subject, and he'd let her. What if he thought they made her too strange? Unfit to be his wife?

"Something's bothering you," Achille said.

"What happened to your ear?" she asked.

She saw surprise in his eyes. "Nothing."

Married just a few hours, already she could tell when he was lying. He'd spoken too fast. Glanced away as he said it. His left ear was red, scraped, like he'd been fighting. She'd noticed it earlier. He was lying and part of her was excited by that. She'd married a man who would try to keep secrets from her. Secrets were puzzles. Easter eggs to hunt for, something hidden to seek. With this man life would not be dull. She pinched his ear.

"Ow!"

"Want to tell me how you bruised it?"

"Our wedding night. We going to talk about *ears*?"

"Our wedding night," she repeated, letting the words dance on her tongue. She held out her hand. "The truth. How much did you pay for this ring?"

He chuckled. "Five dollars even." A straightforward answer but also another puzzle.

"Hungry?" he asked. Slipping his arm from under her, he climbed out of the mosquito netting, buttoning his long johns, heading for the kitchen. She regretted the loss of his touch.

Reaching for her rosary, she kissed the crucifix. Weeks might pass before Father Premeaux arrived to sanctify tonight's union along with any confessions or christenings accumulated since his last visit. In the meantime, to be sure Heaven blessed her new marriage, she'd be diligent with her rosaries.

"I believe in God, the Father Almighty, Creator of Heaven and Earth," she started, then the premonition hit.

~

Jerome Chabert pounced. She stifled a scream, shifted away, but in each direction a new beast attacked. A tabby cat, its claws bared. A brindled cow, its horns sharp. Even a swamp hare looked fearsome.

The image shifted. Someone covered in blood cried out. A face she recognized but couldn't place. Maybe the blood was her torn maidenhead, the start of womanhood, the blood of life. Or maybe death. Judging from its vividness, not gentle death. Not the death of a stranger.

She shook her head to clear it, instead saw other visions, more jumbled. She recognized the cripple who did odd jobs, Touloulou. He hugged a cross, except on the crucifix wasn't Jesus, it was Achille. She fought the image, but it was like swimming against a torrent. She tried to concentrate on the cheerful whistling from the next room, the scent of Achille on the pillow, the sweet ache in her sex; but she could no more cut short the spell than an epileptic could curtail his seizures, or Jerome Chabert stop his transformations.

A choir sang of fear in languages she couldn't understand. Then another picture. Achille again, in a boat with little Zeph, only Zeph was steering, not Achille. Squawking chickens bobbed on the water. Achille was bleeding. Bleeding that wouldn't stop. She never saw herself in her visions, but shouldn't she see herself now? She was his wife. If she were there she could stop the bleeding. Then it seemed Achille mustn't be hurt after all because he was sailing through the air. Clo was there, flying too. Shouldn't she be flying with them?

Then it was gone. All of it. She was back in the bedroom, tangled in the sheet, heart racing. She'd seen Achille in the vision but was telling herself it couldn't have been about him. Couldn't possibly. If he appeared in it, it was because he was her whole life now. Tragedy would touch someone else. Perhaps the poor cripple, Touloulou. Or young Zeph, but she hoped not; she liked Zeph.

When Achille came back from the kitchen, she tried to stop trembling, closing her eyes so he'd think she was sleeping. His weight created a depression in the mattress she could have rolled into but didn't. His hand touched her side, an invitation, warm. She longed to embrace him but was afraid if she did, she might weep. Instead, she clutched the rosary so tightly the tiny figure of Jesus bruised her palm.

Getting no encouragement, Achille's fingers moved away.

Within moments his breathing assumed the regularity of sleep.

His bride was wide awake, but she refused to analyze her look-ahead vision. What good would it do? It made no sense, none at all. Instead she concentrated on recalling every detail of the marvelous physical act they'd performed. Twice! She'd learn to be a good lover, she vowed, because obviously Achille enjoyed this... this... *screwing!* Ha! The word almost made her laugh aloud. They'd screw often, have children, grow old together, spoil their grandchildren. Her life with this man would froth with passion, brim with laughter, she swore it. Her premonition was a false echo, stirred by bridal nervousness, nothing to worry about. That's what she made herself believe.

~

Dawn painted a gold sliver where the bedroom shutters met, enough to illuminate Achille's smile. The smile inspired a kiss. Kissing led to touch, touch to renewed desire.

Achille sat up. "Where are you going?" she asked, alarmed.

"Just clearing the deck." Thrusting arms and bending legs, he peeled out of his long johns and was naked. Having a man so naked so close seemed even newer and stranger than anything they'd yet done. She wondered if she should remove her own gown, go naked like him. Before she could decide, Achille bunched it up around her waist and tried to push in. She mewed discomfort. He retreated.

"Try again," she urged.

He readjusted. The thing still sat not quite right so she reached down and took him in her hand. Was that proper, she wondered? She liked the heft of the thing, its warm, living firmness as she positioned it at her threshold. "Now," she whispered. With a roll of his hips Achille was in. Along with the rush of sensation she felt pride at having successfully placed the bird upon the nest.

Achille began rocking in and out, gentle swaying like a lugger's deck on a balmy day. She joined him, moving her hips, with each thrust pulling him deeper, her body welcoming each extra bit of him as she listened to his soft moans.

There'd been times in her life when she knew she was attractive, to Achille most of all, but to other men too. This was different. What she sensed in Achille was need, a need she possessed the power to fill. She didn't know all she could or would ever do with that power, but it was hers to call on, and if she wasn't careful she knew it might make her drunk as sweet wine.

Her arms encircled his lean sides, marveling at his smooth skin; at his powerful muscles coiling and uncoiling as he worked to give her pleasure; at how his buttocks dimpled each time he stroked into her. Then, for a while, she stopped thinking at all.

She saw him smiling and realized that her own eyes had grown glazed, staring at nothing. Meanwhile he'd watched her. Making sure of her enjoyment. What a wonderful man. She'd known she loved him with her heart. Now she understood there were other parts where the bond could be as strong. Lifting her head, she kissed him. Without breaking rhythm, lips devoured lips. Without breaking rhythm, their breath mingled. Without breaking rhythm. Not letting him break rhythm.

She felt herself wanting more. Her hands raked his back, urging him on. Their movements grew faster. All she asked for, he gave. And more, and more, and more. She offered herself up, his to take, to carry away, up, up. Suddenly, oh! She was there! Where mountaintop meets Heaven. A feeling she'd never known before, as if God was touching her down there. Rapture spread through her body. Meanwhile Achille kept driving in, aware of her pleasure but jealous of his own pleasure too. Driving and driving. Wouldn't stop. Couldn't stop. She didn't want him to stop. Not ever.

And that's when I showed up.

~

It was necessary to describe the couple's erotic explorations because they inform the events which followed. If it quickened your pulse, go drink a dipper of water. I now intend to reveal myself and expect your full attention.

~

Bed timbers creaked like a schooner in a gale. The bride's moment passed; chasing it came her husband's. His eyes rolled. His breath stopped. Semen spurted.

On the threshold I tensed, preparing to spring out.

Achille thrust again, a second spurt. Still I waited, a thief in the night.

Again his penis erupted. Unable to hold back any longer, in that third gush of would-be sons and daughters I came shooting out of his testicle sack, surging up his urethra, leaping from his glans: a single cell with a muscular tail, plunging toward Life with boundless vigor.

I remember it like it was yesterday.

Mostly I recall… *swimming.* Swimming like my life depended on it, which, in fact, it did. Conception may be a holy miracle, but only one sperm gets to enjoy it. Thus, fratricide defiles the uterus worse than in any Ottoman sultan's court. I witnessed a thousand casual murders and, okay, committed several myself. Breaching a cell with a well-aimed jab. Bashing a neighbor into a deadly pile-up. Nipping a tail to leave a rival rudderless.

Did I feel badly about it? No. A fundamental milestone of wickedness is that moment we decide that any given person or people is somehow inferior to us, thus allowing us to lord over them, beat them, swindle them, even end their miserable existence, all without undue recourse to moral scruple. By our simple act of opinion, we make the other more akin to the cockroach than ourselves, and who but the holiest Hindu feels badly about smashing a cockroach? Swimming along, I smashed every cockroach I could.

Another early lesson was that beauty can trump physical strength as easily as an ace takes a deuce. Here's how I learned it: I was spawning up the birth canal, set to smash another cockroach, when I got a good look at my victim. I pulled up short, canceling the casual homicide (or, more accurately, spermicide) that I'd up to then flawlessly executed. Why?

Because she was gorgeous. Through her translucent membrane, I detected what Drs. Stevens and Wilson have since begun calling the X chromosome; if she made it to the egg, she'd become a daughter. I observed the elegant stroke of her tail, the sensuous ripple of her cell wall, chromosomes writhing temptingly within. As if swimming required less effort of her, leaving time to attend to her beauty and allure.

With a snap of my flagellum I shook off this dangerous reverie. What annoyed me wasn't that I found her attractive — I'd just murdered several of my brothers; a little latent incest was hardly going to shock me. What was scary was that I'd let her charms distract me. In the race to conception, apart from the occasional tie we acknowledge as fraternal twins, no prize goes to second place.

Coming in the third spurt of the third copulation within a few hours, I began at great disadvantage. My existence functioned merely as biological insurance policy, as if some Swiss actuary had ordained provision be made just in case mishaps befell each of the twenty million sperm secreted before me. I won't blame anyone, anything, or any circumstance for the malicious character I possess today. Like a diabolical Daniel Boone, I blazed my own trail to wickedness. That said, I often wonder if that first unlucky draw of cards jinxed me from the start. If I'd not had to cut so many corners and sabotage so many rivals to reach Mother's egg, would I have turned out a better man? Or at least a less deadly companion?

To Consider

Human beings clothe sexuality in myriad costumes. Matrimonial relations as quasi-sacramental rite. Coitus as biological imperative. Copulation as agreeable sport. Fornication as sin of choice for those lacking self-restraint. Athletic fucking as proof of one's manhood, womanhood, approaching adulthood, over-seventy-but-still-got-some-left-in-me-hood.

Yet despite tortured rationalizations, the act's zoological root purpose (if you'll pardon the pun, the mixed metaphor, and of course the indelicate subject) is to plant a seed. For Father and Mother, I was that seed, the only one of millions sown to germinate. Since I'm the single living result of their passion, don't I also bear the burden of its other consequences? If Achille died for love, isn't it fair to say I slew my father?

True, Achille wasn't entirely blameless nor his bride completely idle. Your next lesson will inventory victims' typical mistakes, of which getting lulled by great sex is hardly least common.

And those nine villagers? What portion of my guilt should they share, you wonder?

Again, you're asking the wrong question. What makes you think they'll even be around to share it? Did I ever say that Achille Cheramie would be the only one to die?

Lesson V

VICTIMS' COMMON ERRORS

The fiddler Léon Dantin was first to notice — an accident of circumstance, not because he was especially alert. During the broken bottle incident, seeing Achille swooping toward him like a frigate bird had spurred in Léon a jolt of adrenaline he misinterpreted as excess sobriety, a condition he quickly corrected. Like a leaky boat which reaches port only to sink at the dock, Léon played his fiddle flawlessly until the last note of *Home Sweet Home* ended the dancing. He convinced his wife Da-Dool that he needed no help, "no, no help at all," to find his way home and even managed not to slur when delivering to the bride the felicitations he'd rehearsed: "I offer sincerest condolences for your marrying such a slippery eel."

Her reaction was even better than he'd hoped — she actually spit out some sassafras tea she'd been drinking — so off he hurried, over the threshold, across the porch, down the steps: too fast. Achille's house, like most in southern Louisiana, sat on piers a couple of feet above the termite-infested soil. Léon's momentum sent him plummeting into the gatepost. Like a billiard ball, he banked off it and, tumbling, rolled under the house. His fiddle suffered not a scratch.

Begrudging the effort to crawl out, Léon convinced himself that staying put would be a kindness to Da-Dool, allowing her for a while to think he took a wrong turn and drowned in the sea, her oft-stated wish. Thus, under Achille's house Léon slept, never hearing townsfolk leave as the party ended. Never hearing the hubbub as those who stayed to tidy up improvised rain covers against the weather blowing in from the Gulf. Once the newlyweds had privacy, Léon snored through the bed-board creaking that heralded the bride's lost maidenhead and its first follow-up session a short while later.

When Léon finally woke, he thought he'd pissed himself — wouldn't be the first time — but that wasn't it. He was lying in seawater. Had Da-Dool gotten her wish? No again. From his dubious vantage point under Achille's house, by dim first light Léon could see that the Gulf of Mexico had covered Chenière. The only places dry were the peninsula's two "ridges," strips of slightly greater elevation where oak trees grew and the oldest houses clustered, but those were scarcely a few feet above normal high tide and nothing was normal about this one. Wind-blown drizzle and water past his ankles greeted Léon as he crawled out. What to do?

Léon wasn't only the best musician in Chenière, he was also its best boat-builder. Yet when Achille Cheramie had wanted that old hull he'd paid too much for made ready for water, had he come to Léon? Even asked Léon's advice? No. So why should Léon wake the newlyweds so Achille could secure the boat that he hadn't hired Léon to rebuild?

Hell with that.

Using his body to shield his fiddle, Léon sloshed across Achille's chicken yard, heading home to Da-Dool whose temper, he knew, would be as foul as the weather.

~

Through the night, as gusty squalls passed over, the handyman, Touloulou, had cursed Achille and grieved his own lost fortune, but when first light revealed the extreme tide he latched onto it as a good omen. High water drove rabbits to high ground, which was scarce in Chenière. Hunting this morning would be like fishing in a barrel. It being Sunday, hardly a soul in the village wouldn't splurge to buy a fresh-killed rabbit for family dinner.

Touloulou caught the scent of gun oil as he took his shotgun from the chifferobe. He lifted his covered bucket, frowned at its light weight, and remembered: he'd held off restocking ammunition because he'd been almost ready to leave Chenière.

He put the gun back. A fast boy could run down a rabbit. A thirty-five-year-old cripple couldn't. Regardless, Touloulou would have to hunt with a stick.

~

The rabbit heard him over the wind ruffling the wax myrtles. Must be the world's worst hunter, thought the rabbit, if that's the quietest he creeps. Well, whoever you are, you don't want me. I'm too skinny.

The rabbit was indeed thin. It worried him. He'd heard of malignancies that ate you away till one fine day you dropped dead. No symptoms except wasting thinness and chronic pain. Well, the rabbit was thin, no doubt about that. And pain? What's a rabbit's life if not pain?

Of course, it could be gut-worms keeping him skinny. Not that worms were a romp in the lettuce either.

As the noise grew louder, the hunter closer, the rabbit realized the racket was intentional. He's not stalking, he's driving. Clever. With this high tide there aren't many places to go. But driving only works if we panic and I'm one rabbit that never panics. Calm as a sea snail, steady as an oyster.

He spotted the hunter. The rabbit had assumed it was youths braving this weather. Instead, here was his old nemesis, the man people called Touloulou. The rabbit swore that if he was to die, it'd not be at the hands of this crippled Filipino. (Sadly, rabbits share all the prejudices of humans, plus a few special to rabbits; for instance, they consider turtles beneath contempt.)

The rabbit was well hidden, he reassured himself. All he need do is keep still.

Very, very still.

Absolutely still.

The rabbit bolted, dashing out between Touloulou's mismatched legs. The handyman brought down his club. The rabbit veered, the maneuver unconscious, unplanned, just random panic. *CRONK,* Touloulou's stick hit damp ground. The rabbit didn't slow down.

It's documented animals possess a sixth sense that warns of approaching danger. A musk ox can foresee an avalanche, a tiger can predict an earthquake, an elephant a tsunami. This particular rabbit, however, was clueless. It didn't realize Touloulou would've given it a kinder death than it would endure anyway a few hours later. Indeed, a kinder death than might await Touloulou himself.

~

At the exact moment Touloulou's staff was missing the rabbit, Achille's was hitting the bulls-eye inside his passionate, new wife for the third and final time. After packing me on my way and giving Mother her very first sexual climax, Achille — a little hung-over, a lot tired, and deep into post-coital bliss — drifted into sleep again, a rest ill-advised if not undeserved. Alone with her thoughts, buoyed by her afterglow, Mother almost forgot she'd had a premonition. The gusting wind outside pleased her. A storm would discourage visitors, giving her and Achille excuse to stay in bed, to do again what they'd just done. Again, again, again.

Swimming up her birth canal, I was feeling considerably less sanguine. The X-chromosomed sperm I'd previously found so attractive had just rammed me. Let's call her Calypso, after the murderous sea nymph who waylaid Ulysses and nearly cost him wife and kingdom. As pain shot through my cell, I tried the maneuver I'd gone for before becoming infatuated. Then, it would've worked. Now, she turned the tables, *BOOM,* delivering another blow worthy of Jack Johnson in the boxing ring. Stunned, I—

Wait. It's not my misfortunes I'm here to relate. Let's get back to our chronicle.

~

"Mommee will be mad," said little Tellia Dantin.

"She won't," Béatrice said, acting smart because she was one year older. But Mommee would be mad. Tellia's brothers had gotten tools from Poppee's boatyard and were drilling holes in the floor, cranking, cranking, hole after hole.

"Faster!" Mommee hollered, sounding mad but not about the holes. "You two—" She pointed at Tellia and Beatrice. "Chase the chickens out of the coop." Tellia wanted to know why but didn't dare ask with Mommee so mad so she followed Béatrice.

Outside was scary. Around the porch flowed water where water had no business being. Béatrice waded in, toward the chicken coop. Tellia stayed behind and started to cry.

Poppee came out of the house. Crouching beside her, he passed his bow across his fiddle. His fiddle started crying! Just like her! It surprised her so much her sobs stopped. Poppee stopped bowing. She saw him waiting. No need to cry if they could play a game.

"Meow, meow," she said and the fiddle answered, sounding like her mama-cat.

"Arf, arf" barked Tellia. "Arf, arf," went the fiddle.

"Caw, caw," said Tellia. "Caw, caw," the fiddle came back. Then she heard "caw, caw," a third time. That's when she noticed the birds. On Poppee's shed, on Mommee's clothesline, in the china ball tree. Gulls and pelicans and kingfishers and frigates, birds perching together that usually didn't. That was scary enough. Then Tellia saw at their gate, in water to his knees, the *rougarou!* She hurried behind Poppee.

"Looks like a bad one," the *rougarou* said. "You and Da-Dool need help battening up?"

"Move on, Jerome," Poppee hollered.

The *rougarou* left, but his shirt flapped in the wind, making him look scarier. Mommee came out. "Damn it, Léon, put that fiddle up and start being useful."

"I *am* useful," Poppee fussed back. He winked at Tellia. "I'm keeping *rougarous* away."

~

Just offering help, Jerome told himself. He wouldn't expect to spend the storm with them. Unless they'd insisted. Jerome wondered if Victorine needed assistance. Touloulou did her odd jobs, but he might be securing his own shack. A widow shouldn't have to fend for herself.

He found her moving stock to higher shelves. "Can I help?" he asked.

Victorine stepped around the counter and stood next to him. Most people didn't do that. "Monsieur Chabert, we live in an awful village full of awful people who spread awful rumors. Sometimes rumors are true, though, aren't they?"

"I'm not an animal," he said but knew it came out too fervently.

She appraised him a long moment before speaking. "You're a handsome man, Monsieur Chabert. If something unpardonable happened, I'm sure the fault would be mine."

It'd been awhile since Jerome had spent time in the company of women. It took him a minute to realize he'd been dismissed. The bell on the door jangled as he left.

~

Victorine counted items that wouldn't survive wetting. Maybe she should've let Jerome help. And if he transformed into a beast, with them alone, the winds raging? She shivered but knew it wasn't entirely fear. Victorine found her reflection in a candy jar. The glass mirrored olive skin with a thin nose, nothing African-looking about it. Framed by curly, not frizzy, hair. She was proud of her hair. Decades would pass before she'd have to start saving coffee dregs to dye out any gray. How terrible to pass those decades alone.

Forcing the door hurt her shoulder, so fierce the wind against it. Outside, to hold herself steady she gripped a porch post. Every breath tasted of salt. "Monsieur Chabert," she called, but he was already too far along the bayfront, hunched against the tempest, in water to his thighs. "Jerome!" Victorine tried again. He didn't hear.

Then she noticed two figures, one tall, one short, sloshing up from the other direction.

~

It sounded like an accusation. Zeph looked for who'd hollered: Madame Victorine, on the porch of her store. "Where are you going?" she repeated.

Zeph heard his brother mutter "uppity *négresse*" so he thought he better answer himself. "Getting my uncle's family," he called. "To pass the weather with us. Our house is stronger."

"And mine stronger than yours. Send your uncle here. Your family, too. Achille Cheramie and his wife. Anyone else you see."

"Anyone?"

"My door's open. Whoever helps get stock off the lower shelves will eat free."

Storms, Zeph knew, made creatures behave oddly, but Madame Victorine giving away groceries was the oddest event he could imagine.

"Round up the cousins," said Philo. "I'll tell Achille, but first I got another stop." He sloshed back in the direction they'd come.

~

The wind had awakened Clo and she couldn't get back to sleep. How strange, for the first time in her life, to have a room and bed to herself. She thought of her sister, a half-mile away, imagining things her sister and Achille had surely done, in a bed much like this one, last night after the wedding.

Clo let her hand inch across her thigh. She felt goosebumps rise under her nightdress. Through the cloth her finger found the delicate bud.

Massaging her secret spot — tickling herself Clo called it — was something she'd perfected a few months past. She did it whenever she could, even invented a lie to explain the bruise on her arm, the place she'd bite in the throes of the finish so as not to wake her sister sleeping next to her. Now she had all the privacy she could wish. Her fifteen-year-old fingers shuttled fabric across her sex.

Older sisters married first. That was the way of Chenière. It kept the world in order. But how unfair that when Clo's time came, Achille Cheramie, handsomest man in town, would already be taken. Of course, that wasn't necessarily permanent. Childbirth might go wrong, an outbreak of fever. Even always-lucky big sister, God keep her, could get snuffed like a candle. Then where would Achille turn, for solace, for affection, and after proper mourning, for a new wife? To his late wife's sister; that was also the way of Chenière.

Clo was starting to tingle down there. She bunched up her gown so she could touch herself directly and traded her fingers for the heel of her hand.

And if Sister turned out long-lived? Well, conjures could be bought. Charmed dust on a pillow or a cat bone under a step. Clo didn't know who sold such *gris-gris* but surely she could find a source if need be. What'd be the harm? Her sister was practically a saint, sure to go to Heaven. About her own eternal prospects, Clo felt much less certain. The tingling grew, the bud starting to bloom. She was getting close, very close.

SLAM! SLAM! SLAM!

~

Philo banged on the batten again, *SLAM, SLAM!* "Wake up!" he hollered.

A shutter flew open. Clémence Gaspard's head popped out, the breeze whipping his hair. "Damn it, boy, don't you—" Gaspard gaped at the expanse of water that had been his garden.

A second shutter opened — Philo had indeed knocked at the correct window. Clo leaned out, her face flushed and beautiful. Philo wanted to pay her a compliment but could think of nothing witty so he fell back on what he'd come to say. "Madame Victorine invites everybody to pass the hurricane at her store."

"Hurricane?" said Clo, as awed by the weather as her stepfather was.

"Let's go," said Clo's stepmother, joining her husband.

"Now. Right now."

Philo thought the woman unreasonable — a few minutes wouldn't hurt — but her impatience bestowed on him a miraculous gift. "Can you carry me?" Clo asked. Without waiting for an answer, she climbed out her window into his arms wearing nothing but her nightdress. Philo had to remind himself to breathe.

~

When Mother felt wetness creeping up her thighs, she assumed it was spillage from Achille's seed. He still lay atop her, pinning her to the bed so that through the veil of mosquito netting she could see little but the ceiling and nothing of the floor. His stubble of beard pleasantly scratched her shoulder.

As the dampness spread, wicking up the cotton nightgown bunched around her waist, she realized something was wrong. Eyes squeezed shut, panicked with a fear even less sensible than the awful reality, blood is what she felt, she decided. He'd speared her too deeply with his manhood, punctured her womb; now she'd bleed to death, dying for love, literally.

This starry-eyed nonsense was cut short when Achille shouted, "What the hell!" The now-limp part of him still inside her withdrew unceremoniously. He tangled then untangled himself from the mosquito netting and splashed to the floor.

Splashed?

Mother sat up. Water coursed inches deep in their bedroom. Embroidered linens from her trousseau floated on the ripples as Achille plucked shoes out of the flood.

"Hurry!" he screamed.

Mother climbed out of bed, threw open the shutters.

Breakers foamed against houses. Wind whipped whitecaps over what had been pasture. The bride saw a neighbor, waist deep in water, towing an oyster skiff crowded with terrified children.

Under her feet there rose creaking loud enough to be Hell's door opening. The world shifted. The bride fell. Though only twenty-six, Achille had already spent too many years at sea not to keep his footing when the house moved. He knew what it meant: the building had been fitted snug against winter drafts, thus nearly water-tight. Had Father been awake, he might've drilled the floor, letting the ocean enter, weighting the house to keep it in place. But he'd not been awake, so now, like a boat, their house was rising on the tide.

Achille pulled his bride to her feet. "We'll find better shelter before it gets too deep."

Out the window, past the shutter banging open then closed, across the expanse of invading sea, Mother saw no obvious refuge. She tried to match the nightmare before her with the images from her spell.

"I love you," Achille interrupted, "and not even the devil will make me give you up. No matter what happens, I'll keep you safe." Nude, towering out of the water, uncowed by the storm, he resembled a sea god.

He was doomed. While Mother, as awash in denial as she was in seawater, would never have then admitted it, my heroic, nude, godlike (if somewhat semen-depleted) father was a dead man, though his heart hadn't yet stopped beating. A dead man, because he'd slept late, because in creating me he'd let down his guard.

~

Gaspard wrung out his shirt tail. He felt bad leaving his wife and Clo on the porch, in the wind, wearing soaked nightclothes, but he wanted to hear the invitation from Victorine herself before bringing them in.

A swarm of nine- and ten-year-olds was pillaging the store. Guidry's General Mercantile didn't stock "cradles to coffins" like plantation stores up the bayou — Chenière locals were too self-sufficient to buy things they could make — but anything else that couldn't be grown or gathered or killed or caught on or near their low, seaside peninsula, or anything beyond fashioning from driftwood by tools a fisherman kept on hand, those items crowded these shelves, marked high enough for profits to cram Victorine's strongbox but not so dear that customers would raise their sails to shop on Grand Isle, where vying merchants kept prices down.

A pig-tailed girl held up a packet of needles. "These?"

A boy older than the rest nodded. When he noticed Gaspard's quizzical look, Zeph whispered, "In case somebody gets hurt." He pantomimed sewing stitches into his arm, then handed the penny peppermint jar to a boy who took it as reverently as a chalice. "Candy to keep the kids quiet," Zeph explained, though hardly more than a kid himself.

Achille, whatever his faults, had chosen a levelheaded deckhand, Gaspard decided. "You see the newlyweds?"

"Philo went get them," Zeph said.

"No, Philo's with us."

~

Clo wasn't scared until Zeph, coming onto the porch, went slack-jawed at how far the tide has risen. He handed her a blanket, a second one to her stepmother.

"I'm wet, too," said Philo, huddled on the top step.

"You have to go get Achille," said Zeph.

"Not me. I'm done." Philo nodded at Clo. "She's heavier than she looks."

Clo would've kicked him if she'd been wearing shoes. She turned to Zeph. "*You* won't let my sister drown, will you?" She watched him consider the expanse of water.

"Pock, pock, pock," mocked Philo. Zeph splashed down the steps. "We'll never see you again," Philo predicted.

"I better go with him," said Gaspard. "Y'all go inside."

~

Whirling on the flood, a hat box carried a mewling tabby that Mother recognized as little Tellia's cat. Offered one of its kittens, Mother had decided she'd settle into her new home before adopting a pet. Later she was sorry: finding no takers, Léon had drowned the litter.

Water was thigh-deep over the road but reached Achille's chest when he lost the path. He had set Mother onto the same door that during the wedding party served as table for

Victorine's custard tarts. It floated well enough, but against the wind Father had to fight for each step.

Through the rain Mother saw Sheep-head Bocage, the wind behind him, being pushed toward them at a churning run. When he got close Sheep-head anchored himself to the roadside fence. "Heard about Placide?" he hollered. "Hit by lightning, dead as biscuits, him and his horse."

Gripping Mother's doorknob, Father steered her to the fence. Mother felt they shouldn't dawdle but held her tongue.

"Why was the fool riding a horse in this weather?" Father asked.

"Trying to catch his cow."

"The one-eyed one that gouged him that time?"

Sheep-head shrugged. "She gives lots of milk."

Mother remembered the cow in her look-ahead spell. She didn't want to seem bossy, but the storm was getting worse. "Achille, we've got to get to Papa's."

"Clémence Gaspard's?" Sheep-head squeegeed rainwater out of his hair. "Nobody there."

Mother fought panic. Achille will figure it out, she assured herself. He'll find my parents. We'll be safe.

"I'm headed to Léon Dantin," Sheep-head continued. "Pass the storm in his hen house."

"Da-Dool would take us in," Father told Mother. The idea caught her off-guard. Several Chenière residents had done what Léon had, reinforcing as storm shelter a chicken coop or corn crib. Small buildings were easier to build high above hurricane floods and took less wood to cross-brace. Léon's hen house was as sturdy as anywhere they might reach, but she didn't want to go there. Léon had a beef with Achille, but that wasn't it. She'd rather pass the storm with her parents and sister, but that wasn't all of it either. The hen house kindled memories of her premonition. Images of swimming chickens. Danger to the man beside her. But she couldn't explain that so Father would understand, not in front of his poker friend, not here in this banshee wind, so when he said, "Let's go with Sheep-head," she did not protest.

With the gale now at their backs, they made good time. Hugging fence palings for their meager shelter, Father pulled Mother's door as Sheep-head pushed it, but Father being first in line meant that when Placide Guilbeau's one-eyed cow charged through the fence, it was Achille Cheramie, my dad, who was gored.

To Consider

Every spring, a thousand miles north, winter's snow melts into a flood. Swollen rivers feed the Mississippi which, over the eons, tore from its banks huge bottomland cypresses, giant trees impervious to rot, propelling them downstream.

Where the Mississippi meets the sea, coastal currents drove these goliaths west onto the Louisiana shore. Storms off the tropics, like careful engineers, lifted and shifted these logs into a magnificent interlocking tangle that lined the beaches of Chenière, and Grand Isle, and Grand Terre east of that. By broken roots and stubs of branches each tree clutched the ones beside it, an embrace as eternal as that of mythic lovers.

This chain of logs was already older than time when Indians whose names no one remembers wintered here to live off waterfowl and seafood. It lay there when the first Old World resident arrived, a runaway slave who claimed to be a Gypsy; from the ridge of logs he'd scan the surf for turtles he could sell as soup to the pirates across the pass. The logs were there when Europeans settled, with their lug-rigged sailboats and horned livestock. And by October 1st, 1893, alongside these logs lived the people you've just met and their neighbors, hundreds of souls each now facing the oncoming tempest. Let's recapitulate some errors they already made this critical day.

Touloulou's mistake was to believe an extreme tide offered more opportunity than danger. Victorine waited too long to accept Jerome's help, and Jerome didn't linger long enough to hear that she'd accept it. Zeph waded into turbulent waters out of pride, showing off for a girl. Gaspard followed out of altruism, which while not typically considered a sin, probably ought to be. Philo — well, Philo's such a mess I don't know where to begin, but you get the idea.

Mother and Father, however, made the most common error: following bad advice, turning left when one should turn right. Some with their lives, some less dearly, each of these people would pay for their mistakes. Perhaps that's as it should be.

But each would also pay for actions of their parents and grandparents and great-grandparents who, generation after generation, from the great driftwood raft harvested branches for firewood and sawed beams for boat keels and split palings for fences — fences like the one that didn't hold back Placide's wrathful cow — thus bit by bit making the interlocking tangle less impregnable than God had left it, so that on this day, buoyed by unimaginably high tide and pried by unbelievably strong wind, with a roaring no one stood near enough to hear, the huge logs began to wrench themselves out of the sand with all the evil humor of angry giants waking.

Lesson VI

RELIGIOUS TEACHINGS
(and their inherent limits)

Christian doctrine distinguishes moral evil (inflicted by man) from natural evil (of non-human cause). Do you think, to Mother, that distinction mattered one whit when she saw her bridegroom lifted high on the bloody horn of a one-eyed cow?

"Help him!" she shouted, though to do that Sheep-head had to let go her door. When he did, the wind seized it. Mother considered climbing off but doubted she could stand against the current. Her door skated over the water into Opil Angelleto's yard. She tried to catch Angelleto's lemon tree. Missed. Tried again, arm stretched full. Found a branch. Screamed! She'd driven a lemon spine a full three-quarter inch into the palm of her hand, almost through to the other side.

Mother forced herself to not let go. Pulled her door to the tree, every second excruciating, till she found a safer grip with her right hand and drew off the left. Lord, it hurt. Yet it was nothing. She turned to check on Achille.

Sheep-head was wading away. "Going get help," he yelled, but she knew he'd not be back. Forty feet across the lane, Father was a turbulent ocean away. Water to its withers, the cow had trouble keeping its muzzle out of the flood with Father impaled on its horn. It bellowed and tried to shake him off. Father bellowed too, in agony.

Then Mother saw something which amazed her: Father's arm crept up the cow's blind side, creeping, creeping, until he stuck his finger up the cow's nose. The cow thrashed. Father jammed his thumb up the other nostril and squeezed. Immediately the creature grew quiet. Not happy, not nearly happy, but calm. Father slid himself off the horn.

Where had her husband learned to immobilize a cow, Mother wondered. He was of the sea, not the fields. How many unexpected things might he reveal in a lifetime together? How many surprises would he offer her, week by month by year — if she could keep him alive?

~

Father fought through the water to join Mother at the lemon tree. "How bad?" she asked when finally he leaned on her raft.

"Not too," he lied, once he'd drawn enough breath to speak. "Might've cracked a rib. I'm going to make Placide dehorn that damn cow."

When he saw his words alarmed her, he remembered: Placide was already dead. Steady, Father warned himself. No time for confusion.

In the troughs between waves Mother examined the puncture. Wide, deep, ugly, it had somehow missed anything vital. "If we fashion a bandage," she shouted, "it'll slow the bleeding." Then he might not die from it, he thought. At least not today. He nodded, agreeing to her plan, but couldn't for the life of him think what the next step should be.

"Take off your shirt," she instructed. He did, though it hurt like Hell. As he held her door, with the shirt she tied his wound, a process slow and awkward in the wind and rain and pain and surf and surging current. Please, Sweet Jesus, Achille prayed, let me think straight long enough to get this woman someplace safe.

~

Blood bloomed in the cloth over the puncture, but soon slowed to a seep. Mother wondered what should come next. He was the man, she the wife; it wasn't her place to take charge. But he was moving slowly, time was short, the weather getting worse. "We'll put you on the door," Mother hollered. "I'll climb down and push. I'm strong enough."

Father shook his head. "Strong enough, not tall enough."

Mother looked anew at how high the water came on Father's body. Measured it against her memory of where she reached when they danced together. Where her eyes fell when they made love, once, twice, three times, what seemed a thousand years ago.

She wasn't tall enough. He knew best, after all. So she let him push her raft and pretend his arms didn't ache, his legs weren't numb, his side wasn't shooting agony with every step. "We're not going to die," he promised, shouting over the pouring, windblown rain.

No, not *we*, she thought, staring into his glazed eyes and remembering her premonition.

~

Léon and Da-Dool's empty house swayed in the wind. Twenty yards farther their formidable chicken coop did not budge. Father watched hens trying to roost in its leeward crannies, clucking with the bitterness of the displaced. Through a hatch pried partway open he could see people crowded inside. Léon and Da-Dool. Their kids. Sheep-head Bocage, waving him over.

"We have to get out of the water," Father said yet again.

"Not in there," Mother repeated. "Not there, no matter what."

His bride wasn't the sort to put her foot down. During their courtship, she almost always deferred to him, even when he didn't care much either way. So why make a stand now, so close to refuge? With his wound scalding him. He wondered if he'd have to force her, if he had the strength to do it. It hurt her to disagree with him, he saw that, so why did she? Achille knew she possessed powers not his to understand. But maybe she was just scared. A time like this, fear could get you killed.

"Let's rest with them awhile," Father said. "When there's a lull, we'll travel on, I promise. Find your mama and papa—"

"No!" Mother pointed to a trellis woven with muscadine vine, still in fruit but exposed to the wind, weak and insubstantial. "There. I can help you climb up."

Father hurt too much to argue. Maybe after he caught his breath he could talk sense into her.

~

Getting him atop the arbor was harder than she thought it'd be. It caused him such pain he couldn't help much. The woody vine scraped her skin and ripped her clothes. From the chicken coop, folks continued hollering, urging Achille and her to join them, a worse distraction because she knew that's what Achille wanted to do.

Finally secure upon the trellis, her husband collapsed into his hurt, but soon the wind rose with a terrible gust, picking up sheds, uprooting trees. The palings of Léon's fence began flying off like missiles. A galvanized pail hurtled into Mother's shoulder, the arm that held her door against the trellis. In the surge of pain she let go, but as her door swept away Father pulled her off it. With strength beyond mortal limits, he hauled her onto the muscadine arbor beside him.

"I've got you," Achille screamed, nose to nose yet hollering so Mother could hear. Mother felt the knot of cloth where she'd tied it over his wound and saw in his eyes the giant black pupils that told her he was in shock. She wondered what they'd done to deserve this.

~

With a groan, part of the arbor collapsed and Father thought, here it is, now my wife and I will wail among the lost. But the rest of the structure held.

New noises augmented the din as shutters tore off Léon's house, letting the wind enter, jacking its roof, collapsing each wall atop the last like someone folding paper. The chicken coop with Léon, Sheep-head, and the others barely wavered.

~

Into Mother's mind crept doubt. With refuge so close, why had she stopped Achille from taking them there? Who was she, a girl of seventeen, to know God's intentions?

When Léon's house was completely down, the wind lifted its broken walls. Each became a wooden sail which flew across Léon's flooded yard like a gambler's fancy card shuffle. When one slammed into chicken coop, the cries of those within were as loud as the impact, but the building stood. A second section, *boom!* A third, *bam!* The henhouse held.

~

Studying the skeletons of boats to rebuild his own, Father had learned about stresses and flaws, so as the walls of the house slammed into the henhouse, he guessed which brace would fail even before the coop's truss crumpled, the building ripped apart, and the people inside, some living, some already dead, were cast into the flood.

He understood why his young wife hadn't let him take her there. She'd foreseen this. She had powers he'd never guessed, like a witch or *diablesse,* so probably nothing he'd ever done or would do could be secret from her. Even in the midst of the storm, *that* thought terrified him.

~

Amongst screeching, swimming chickens floated lumps clothed in patterns and colors Mother refused to recognize as the Sunday outfits of children she loved. She fought back thoughts of people she would lose today, things she hadn't thought to do or thought of yet not done, goodbyes unsaid before anyone knew it was goodbye. She considered praying but feared it wouldn't help, because each tendril of vine proved divine capriciousness, as God's mighty wind shred leathery leaves yet perversely spared delicate late-season fruit.

She plucked a grape and squished it between Achille's lips. Pretended as she did that honey flowed from the moon to bathe the Earth instead of this foul water. Pretended they still lay in bed with Achille's heart beating, beating, beating strong against her breasts, and his bird soaring and diving and fluttering inside her. Pretended terror was joy and awful was good, pretending, pretending.

The trellis gave way.

~

It'd been strange to be in the chicken coop, especially in this weather, but now was stranger still. Tellia was floating in water but didn't know how she got outside. A big noise, everybody hollering, then *ka-plooosh*, in the waves.

Where was Mommee? Tellia needed Mommee so she wouldn't have to be scared anymore. She saw Mommee. Floating on waves like she was. Béatrice floated too. Strange, because Béatrice was trying to hug Mommee, but Mommee kept pushing her away.

Mommee wouldn't push Tellia away. Never.

Tellia swam toward Mommee, swam with her arms and legs like Poppee had taught her. When she got close, Mommee pushed her away too, like she kept pushing Béatrice.

Tellia tried to hug Mommee again, but Mommee pushed her again. Then waves were taking her too far. She was tired and scared and didn't know how much more she could swim. She had to hug Mommee, but Mommee didn't want. Though older than Tellia, Béatrice was crying like a baby. Tellia wondered if she should cry too.

An arm came around her. She was scared until she saw it was Poppee. "Take Bea!" Poppee shouted.

"I can't," Mommee yelled back. "I'm barely afloat as it is."

"Go with your mama." Poppee hollered at Béatrice.

Béatrice tried, but Mommee pushed her away like before. "Save yourself, Léon," Mommee yelled. "That's all we can do."

"They're your children, all that's left," Poppee yelled back. What did it mean? Poppee swam toward Béatrice, but it wasn't easy because he already held Tellia, so he could only use one arm, and the waves were mean, so he wasn't going fast. Now, he stopped swimming at all because in the way was a log, a *big* log like the logs on the beach. After it floated by, Béatrice wasn't there anymore. Neither was Mommee, neither one, not anywhere Tellia could see. Tellia wondered where everybody had gone. If it was someplace dry she wanted to go too.

~

Jerome had thought to beat the storm by sailing to abandoned Fort Livingston, just past Grand Isle. Its masonry walls, built to survive canon, stood stronger than any wind and higher than any flood. With luck, islanders taking refuge there wouldn't recognize him as the infamous Chenière *rougarou.* His plan might've worked had he not tarried to help his neighbors secure their boats. Now most of those boats had sunk anyway.

As Jerome tried to navigate around Achille Cheramie's capsized lugger, the same gust that flattened Léon's chicken coop swept Jerome's boat. He felt himself tip sideways, saw water rush to meet him. The bracing chill almost stopped his heart. When a shroud of sail hammered down upon him, Jerome flailed at the wet canvas but found no way out. Saltwater stung his eyes and burned his lungs. He couldn't tell up from down.

Fear gave way to panic, panic to tranquility. Jerome realized his time had come. Whatever waited when breath stopped, even if dark nothingness, at least he'd leave behind the fear of transformation, the day-by-day battle against the beast that, he finally admitted, hid within him.

You may decry Jerome's surrender and declare life too precious to give it up without a fight, even for the cursed. Yet had Jerome struggled, the tangled canvas wouldn't have settled long enough to trap a pocket of air. Had he fought, he'd have used that air too quickly, before he could get his bearings. Had stress led to transformation, the paws of a dog couldn't have slid the jackknife from his pocket and slit open a route to escape.

~

Mother's stepfather, Clémence Gaspard, waded behind young Zeph, toward Achille's house, not knowing it was empty. Death had been no stranger in Gaspard's life, but these last dozen years, joyful and serene, had let him forget how abruptly it could come.

On the day their first child was born, Gaspard and his wife had given the baby a name, Constant. They bathed him, bundled him, and blessed him best they could with no priest at hand. They infused in him their dreams, their hopes, their reasons to be on Earth. An hour before sunset, the child stopped breathing. They never knew why.

A second child, Laure, lived a year. They'd thought nothing could be worse than losing their first. They were wrong.

After that, though still welcome when he slid to Eune's side of the bed, Gaspard knew she used a potion, an herb or *gris-gris* she put inside herself to kill his seed. Gaspard began to visit other women. There was a widow who made him welcome, but he stopped seeing her when whispers grew. Once, two blocks off Basin Street in New Orleans, he spent so much at a fancy brothel that when he came home he had to lie that his load of oysters had spoiled before he could sell them.

When Gaspard's sister-in-law and younger brother died within a day of each other during the Fever of '78, it seemed just another tragedy to add to his numbing list. His brother owned no tomb. Gaspard, however, owned a brick double crypt and the children filling its vaults had been dead sufficiently long, so Gaspard unbolted the face plate and brushed the remains of two tiny skeletons into the catch-chamber, making room for new additions.

At the funeral he watched his brother's girls, ages one and two, looking confused and terrified. He was childless, wasn't he? With a good house and sound boat. When Gaspard announced he and Eune would take both sisters, no one argued. The girls moved into the house facing the bay, were bathed in love, and before long barely remembered their true parents.

After that, for Gaspard life grew better in all respects. He even seemed to catch bigger shrimp and raise saltier oysters. Often as not, now it was Eune who'd slide to his side of the mattress, and they'd shake out its moss stuffing like they were twenty, and he no longer looked at other women.

Now the girls were grown. One, last night's bride; the other no doubt soon a bride herself. But Gaspard understood he'd not be around to see it. Looming toward him on the inrushing tide was a massive log that until today had lined the beach. Chained by water chest-deep on him, neck-deep on young Zeph, neither left nor right could Gaspard escape and he knew it. Maybe, at least, he could save the boy.

~

Zeph felt himself shoved under a wave. Gagging on seawater, when his knees hit ground he fought his way back, sputtering when he found air, his temper firing to holler at Gaspard to be more careful. He saw the log that had swept harmlessly over him hit Gaspard with a *thump* like boats colliding. Gaspard's head exploded into spurting blood and flying viscera. The log cruised on like a ship of war. In its wake, Zeph saw another coming.

"Martyred St. Zephirin, intercede for me," the boy cried, but he doubted his patron saint could hear him over the howling wind and his own thundering heart.

~

Mother had also turned to prayer. Unfortunately, she'd grown up such a fervent Catholic that prayers unfurled without having to think much about them, thus leaving her mind free to ruminate on the burning in her lungs. Did Achille hurt as unbearably?

She felt him tug her hand. Time for the perilous journey three feet to the surface, where death waited if they mis-timed it. After the quiet underneath, the noise above was deafening. Mother's hair whipped like a flag. Every raindrop stung her skin. As she rose and fell with each wave, Mother saw huge logs streaming westward. Achille had timed it right. A killer had just passed, another was coming, but they had twenty seconds, enough to take in air, air, precious air. Time to glimpse Achille's face, to suckle encouragement there, but no time for words because the log was looming. Achille was tugging. Down they went.

With her left hand in Achille's, she groped with her right for something to grab so the job of holding them under wouldn't fall only on him. Last time she'd found a shrub; this time she wasn't so lucky. She clutched a fence, in her urgency not probing first. A wire barb lanced the flesh of her right palm with a fatter, shallower, more painful wound than the lemon thorn had pierced into her left. Much as it hurt, she dared not let go. She thought of the statue of Jesus that Father Premeaux carried on his boat; if she survived she'd bear similar stigmata.

Achille must be a fish, she thought. If he felt distress, it did not communicate through his hand. Is that how martyrs behaved? To distract herself, she began counting saints. St. Antoine, St. Marie, St. Joseph. St. Lucie, who forked out her eyes to avoid a bad marriage. St. Jerome, roasted on a brush pile by the Nipponese. St. Agathe, her breasts chopped off. Agathe would laugh at holding her breath, at shallow punctures in her hands.

Achille tugged. Mother released the wire. Breaking surface, she tasted the rush of air, its salty tang a joy. The fleet of logs was thinning. Through the downpour Mother thought she saw, far out of reach, lights in attic windows of a few still-standing houses. Next to her, her beloved Achille floated face down.

To Consider

Weighing the theologian's distinction of natural evil vs. moral evil, is bovine impalement natural or, since every cow has a cowherd, man-made?

If, as in this case, the cowherd dies before the deed, does that change the equation?

What role does intent play? Was Sheep-head Bocage's abandoning of Father wicked if we believe Sheep-head was going for help? Or at least believe that he believed he was going for help? Could Sheep-head's demise in the chicken coop have been divine reprisal for deserting a friend in need? Seems pretty quick. "Vengeance is mine sayeth the Lord," but Lord knows

He usually takes His sweet time.

And what about contrition? Do you believe God smote Clémence Gaspard with the giant log because Gaspard violated His commandment on adultery? Though Gaspard had long since reformed into model husband and father?

Far be it from me to question anyone's religious beliefs; nonetheless I have difficulty picturing God Almighty as some criminal court judge with too large a caseload. If not careful, we venture onto Greek Olympus or the Nine Worlds of the Norse, where loutish gods and demi-gods relieve their boredom by swaying the fates of mortals. When Léon Dantin watched most of his family drown, was the Egyptian cat goddess, Bastet, paying him back for that litter of kittens Léon drowned three days earlier? Was Jerome Chabert, buried in sailcloth, saved by St. Roch, patron of dogs? Or St. Guinefort, who *was* a dog?

Fine, say it's so. What did Mother do to deserve going through life with hands bearing scars like God's martyred son? And my father, Achille Cheramie? Apart from siring one wicked child, there were no sins blackening his soul grievous enough to call down a terrible death.

Were there?

Lesson VII

PITTING GOOD AGAINST BAD

Achille had come up for air a second before her, a second too soon, and had been hit by a log. Now, keeping his head above water meant going under herself, so Mother was once more forced to time her breaths. Getting only glimpses to assess his state. Listening for a heartbeat, impossible in that noise. Looking for the rise and fall of his chest, laughable in that downpour. Seeking light in his eyes and seeing none but knowing he wasn't dead. He couldn't be dead.

On his head, the gash was a terrible thing. Bits of pickled driftwood lay embedded in the wound. Blood washed away as fast as it flowed. Yet flow it did. Which meant his heart beat. Which meant he was alive. For now. Did she, could she, was it possible to love him enough to change his fate?

"Take me," she whispered to the heavens, but it wasn't her Heaven wanted.

~

Touloulou hugged the iron crucifix atop the tomb. He thought it was the Gaspards' crypt, one of the few double-deckers in the cemetery. The perch had saved him from the fleet of logs but wouldn't keep him alive if the flood grew much deeper.

Irrationally, Touloulou blamed Achille Cheramie for his

predicament. Hadn't the cripple spent years saving every penny toward passage to levee-shielded New Orleans and starting-out money once there, plus a little for a shrine to the Virgin if she would succor him through the forty-mile maze of bayous that led to the city? There he intended to apprentice as mason — bricks seem so solid — and would one day help build churches. His plans had been complete, his funds finally sufficient to board the very next packet boat that appeared unlikely to sink. True, even ignoring the disastrous card game, this storm intruded before his escape could've occurred. Still, he was certain his fate would've been less grim had Achille not stripped away his wealth. Apart from Victorine, Touloulou didn't know any rich people, but he was nonetheless of the firm opinion that misfortune befell them considerably less often than it did the poor.

With his short left leg he could barely swim. A tall hackberry tree stood forty yards away. Maybe he could make it that far.

Discarding his five fresh-killed rabbits, their ten dead eyes seemed to mock him. He ripped his game sack into strips which he braided into rope so he could tie in if he made it to the tree. Though he'd already promised eighteen months' service to the Blessed Virgin to reach this tomb, Touloulou saw no alternative than to up the ante.

"Holy Mother, conceived without sin, get me to that hackberry and I'll devote you an entire extra year." He formalized the offer with a sign of the cross.

The waves did not slack. A flock of cypress shingles spiraled by; Touloulou ducked behind the cross. "Blessed Mary, Mother of every soul, make it two years."

Used to negotiating rates for odd jobs, Touloulou raised no eyebrow when suddenly the wind lulled. He belted his sackcloth rope around his waist and scooched to the edge of the tomb. The water felt cold as he lowered his short leg into it.

~

Zeph knew there were things to do before giving up the ghost — prayers, confessions, whatnot — but that must be for dying in bed like his grandmother did, not when fighting all this shit. Logs had broken up houses, sheds, fences, puking debris into the water. As yet Zeph had suffered only bruises, but he knew, sooner or later, something would get him.

Maybe here it was. Big, moving fast, coming right at him. A rowing skiff! As it ripped past, a hand grabbed Zeph and draped him onto the gunwale. The boy hauled himself in, collapsed between two thwarts. Lapped like a dog at the bilge, sweet with rainwater.

Someone had jury-rigged an oar upright and fitted to it a sail reefed so snugly that barely two feet of canvas showed. In that wind, it was enough. Who did it? Who saved his life this time?

"Bail," shouted Jerome Chabert. "Bail before the rain sinks us!"

Jerome! Zeph scurried as far back as the skiff allowed; but while Jerome might be a *rougarou*, he was certainly master of the vessel, someone who must be obeyed. Zeph looked for a bucket, anything, to bail with, but no luck, so he kneeled into the bilge and cupped his hands, keeping one eye on Jerome.

SHRUUU-RAK, the sail ripped loose! Its sudden release cracked the oar serving as mast. The oar swung on a thread of splinters, missed Zeph only because he was stooped to bail, but caught Jerome in the chest, knocking him out of the boat. Zeph dove to the gunwale thinking, if he snaps at me I'll let him drown, but Jerome had already disappeared.

The skiff began to spin. Zeph realized why Jerome had rigged the sail: it let him run before the wind. Otherwise, swinging broadside, the boat would capsize. A sea anchor might help, but nothing aboard would serve. Nor was there anything to rig as trysail, except one thing: himself. If he stood up into the storm as a human sail, it might allow rough control over the boat.

Tails of rope hitched to the oarlocks, leftovers from Jerome's jury-rig, Zeph wrapped around each hand. He closed his eyes, called again on St. Zephirin, and rose into the wind. Immediately he regretted it. Bullets of rain stung. Small debris

— bugs, splinters — stabbed and jabbed.

Then, abruptly, the barrage stopped. The wind, the hail of projectiles, the profound noise, all finished with the finality of a hatchet swing. So this was death. Not that bad, Zeph thought. He felt warm light bathe his closed eyelids. The celestial glow of Paradise? Or the bonfires of Hell? He decided it must be the latter, because he heard many plaintive cries of lost souls. In Heaven, who'd have nerve to complain?

~

Mother watched the fortress of cloud retreat as fast as a horse could gallop. She'd never been in the eye of a hurricane, but she'd heard stories and listened closer than most children. Around this sunlit circle of calm the storm swirled. Maybe in five minutes, maybe fifty, the winds would come back as strong or stronger — now west to east, completing the circle. Water and debris, bodies and logs pushed into the bay would hammer Chenière again, this time sweeping everything out to sea.

"*Help! Help!*" Mother recognized the voice of Frederick Collins. His place was two down from Achille's house. Her house too, now. If it was still there.

"*Hilfe! Hilfe!*" Leopold Rebstock had lived in America thirty years. He spoke passable English and excellent French, but consciously or not, he'd reverted to his native German.

"*Pomo'c! Pomo'c!*" Taliancich, the Croatian. They say he introduced the big rake-like tongs to Chenière, which replaced oystering by hand and made everybody prosperous.

"*Aiutate! Aiutate!*" Marco Alario, whose brother was a *descadero* on the New Orleans docks, which was Marco's secret for getting the best price for his seafood.

And in her arms, making no sound, unconscious, bleeding Achille. Born in Chenière, he'd visited New Orleans nineteen times, never gone farther. Powerful as her love was, she wasn't sure how long she could hold him up. Now, during the eye, they had to get someplace safe. "*Au secours!*" she cried. "*Icitte! Au secours!*"

~

During this break in the weather, perhaps it's germane to recount my own travails at the time. Two inches up Mother's uterus, we wove through ranks of sperm, me and Calypso, that vamp upon whom I'd become fixated. She'd likewise become obsessed, determined to take me down. I supposed she sensed that of all the millions swimming, I, like she, was one of the few sperm with a serious shot at penetrating Mother's egg.

Calypso sidled up to a hapless, undersized sperm — he must've thought it was his lucky day until she swung that tail of hers and swatted him right at me. I saw the gamete coming, tried to dodge, but she'd chosen her moment well. Hemmed in by other sperm, no alley to escape, I was smacked full force. *Ow!* The runt was killed. I went careening into a dullard dog-paddling as if it was Sunday at the beach. *Ow*, again!

How dare I complain, you ask, when in the outside world, unbridled hell had broken loose? Well, a swimming sperm no more senses his mother's woe than a galloping thoroughbred perceives the Earth's rotation. Aren't we all, at the end of the day, self-absorbed?

Searching the chaos, I spotted Calypso. Putting on speed, I pushed past sperm I didn't recognize. Most came from Mother and Father's middle-of-the-night second lovemaking, but I was even overtaking veterans of their first coitus, that legendary assault on Mother's hymen. Those who embarked when I did during the early-morning third ejaculation, I had left far behind.

Romantics claim love can overcome any obstacle. Cynics say that's hooey. Well, in Mother's belly, without my love/hate/obsession for Calypso to goad me, would I have still advanced so far so fast? Or would I have instead lost the race, never been born, meaning that you, to your detriment, would've never had the advantage of my advice? Think about it.

~

"It's all right," the boy whispered and Tellia believed him. She let him pry her out of Poppee's arms. He set her on the bench next to people wet like her who weren't talking much.

"Monsieur Léon, it's me, Zeph Leboeuf," the boy said.

"Come, there's others waiting." He helped Poppee into the boat, but Poppee missed the bench, how silly, and sat in the bilge, *Plop!* It must've hurt because Poppee started crying again, *really* crying, while he said the prayer to the Virgin she'd just learned herself except Poppee put in his prayer the names of her brothers and sisters. Not her name, not "Tellia." She wondered why she was left out. Tellia decided to sit next to the boy. "Do you know about the cat who wore shoes?" she asked.

At first the boy seemed surprised, but then he smiled. As he began to paddle again, he said, "Once there lived a young man who inherited a cat…"

~

At the part where Puss in Boots began bargaining on his master's behalf, Zeph paused because he spotted a pail floating. Spearing its loop with his oar blade, he lifted the dripping bucket into the lap of one of his passengers. "Bail." His order was followed without question. Though only twelve years old, with Jerome gone Zeph was captain of the skiff.

Figuring the boat could hold another five, maybe six, people, Zeph tried not to stew over who to rescue next. He knew most everybody, and those he didn't bring aboard would probably drown. He didn't want to play favorites. Then he saw, thirty yards off, Achille and his bride. Zeph paddled as fast as his broken oar and overloaded boat allowed.

When he got close, the woman offered her husband to waiting arms before hoisting herself up. "You saved us," she said. Zeph wasn't sure. Achille looked dead until the jostle of being pulled aboard revived him.

"Is my family's okay?" the bride asked.

The image of her stepfather's head being torn off made Zeph's throat dry. If she saw prophecies like everybody said, how come she had to ask?

"Ma'am, this sunshine won't last. We got to pick up what people we can."

"Of course. Sorry. Let me know when I can help."

He hadn't lied, Zeph told himself. Merely withheld what she

didn't need to hear yet. Tellia tugged his sleeve. "Finish about the cat with shoes," she commanded.

~

Sun shining, air calm, but rolling swells confirmed that a few miles in every direction the storm raged. First things first. Get out of the water.

A spring Jerome spent lumbering in the swamps near Hahnville had taught him how to climb onto a floating log; nevertheless, his first two attempts only brought fresh bruises. His third put him aboard. When he stood to get his bearings, Jerome saw he was not alone on the giant driftwood log. His chest tightened.

~

The thin rabbit had never felt so weary. After all that swimming, nothing could force him back into the water, not even this man at the other end of the log who—

The human began writhing in anguish, apparently having some sort of attack. He dropped to hands and knees. Fur sprouted on his arms, crept from his collar. It shrouded his growing ears. My God, thought the rabbit, I hope his sickness doesn't pass between species. I have maladies enough of my own, thank you.

Hands and feet became paws. A tail snaked out of shredded pants. The rabbit racked his pecan-sized brain for tales heard as a nestling. Brother Cottontail outwitting Br'er Dog and Br'er Human. Or both combined into one? Fully a dog now, the creature was inching past the agony of transformation. The rabbit had to admit it had an exquisite coat. Reddish-brown, long and shiny. Why, with fur that sleek, the rabbit could have any doe he—

With a banshee howl, the man-dog leapt.

~

Everything was blurry. Achille felt like throwing up. The storm was blowing again, louder than a steamboat, but he felt neither wind nor rain. Must be indoors. Somebody's attic. How long had he been unconscious? A cut leaked blood down his face. He tried to wipe his vision clear, but a hand caught his. Damp cloth bathed his eyes. He could see again. Her enchanting face. Wait. It was Clo. He hadn't married Clo, he'd married her sister. Hadn't he? Hard to think straight. "Where's my wife?"

"Hush," said Clo. His head rested in her lap. When she bent to kiss it, her breasts felt soft against his skull. As she rose back into his line of sight, her smile fell away.

"You smeared his blood on you," his bride said, crouching to join them.

Clo dabbed at the scarlet staining her bosom. "How's Mama?"

"Crying about Papa," Mother answered.

Father wanted to reassure her, tell her things would be all right, though he wasn't sure they would. Before he could find the words, consciousness left him.

To Consider

So in which cases above did affection, compassion, mercy, etc., beat back wickedness? Do kind acts and gentler emotions indeed have a role to play, whether against evil sent by God or inflicted by man? If love can heal all wounds, might true, pure love keep you from hurt in the first place?

Well, whether or not love can outweigh evil, it can certainly provide its source. Think about it. When we perpetrate wickedness, isn't our victim often the person we love most? Proximity makes them convenient. Intimacy makes them vulnerable. Inflicting pain upon someone who cares for us is as easy as hunting rabbits during high water.

When Achille passed out again, for a terrible moment both Mother and Clo assumed he'd succumbed. When they found he still breathed, relief was tempered by exhaustion, terror, numbness, and grief. Always the less restrained, Clo wanted to lash out at the universe. The universe too broad a target, she walloped her sister instead. Not pausing to consider the hurt her words might cause, she let them fly like a pigeon crossing the park: "If he'd married me like he should've, like he wanted to, I'd have kept him safe. Told him about the storm in time. Sure, he courted you, but then he fell for me. He wouldn't break your heart so he broke mine. Now he's dying, and it's your fault. All your fault!"

Lesson VIII

DOING BAD TO DO GOOD

"Will this building stand?" Victorine resembled a queen addressing her admirals, even here, crouched in a corner of her attic.

"Achille's in no shape—" Mother began.

"I'm not asking him."

Asking me what, Father wondered. How long had he been out this time?

"They say you see things," Victorine continued. "What do you see now?"

"I see my husband needing his wounds re-dressed."

"It's nothing," protested Father, but Victorine lifted her skirt and ripped her petticoat, discarding the soiled hem, leaning close as she handed Mother the clean white fabric.

"Do you see this store? Will it be here tomorrow?"

His wife began changing his bandages. "How can you expect me to—"

"If the building goes…" Victorine lowered her voice, forcing Father to strain to hear. "Isn't it better to save who we can, not waste effort on those you already know will die?"

"I don't know anything. I'm just a simple fisherman's wife."

"I know you're a fisherman's wife," Victorine hissed. "I watched you jump the broom. I see that ill-fitting ring Achille made you." Father saw Mother study her ring. He'd planned to tell her it was homemade but not like this. He hoped she wouldn't be disappointed.

Victorine's voice sharpened. "I'm sure, last night, you gave Achille a gift you believed was as special as his ring. But you have other gifts too, don't you? Gifts another day I wouldn't care about. Today, however, your second sight might save lives."

"Most people don't think my spells mean anything."

"Most people are fools. What do you see?"

Father would've liked to keep his wife from hurting, but he doubted he could rein in Victorine, not if she was on a tear, not in the shape he was in. Besides, he also wanted to know what glimpse of the future his wife had seen.

"I can't call it up," Mother said, ripping the fabric from Victorine's petticoat into smaller strips. "Usually I try not to see. Bad stuff foretells. Never good."

"What 'bad stuff' have you seen?"

"Nothing that would help. What I saw made no sense at all."

Victorine gripped Mother's elbow. "You're holding something back."

"You're hurting me." Mother tried to pull free. "You're being cruel."

"You've no idea how cruel I can be." Victorine let Mother go. "Having second thoughts about my godmothering your first-born?"

Father saw Mother's tears well up. "I lost *my* godmother today," Mother whispered. "Théodulia Dantin. We call her Da-Dool. *Called* her Da-Dool. In my spell I didn't see your store. What I saw was that I'd lose somebody close and I did. She wasn't sweet, Da-Dool, but she was my godmother." Mother caressed Father's cheek again, then continued. "I lost my father too — he *was* sweet. I hope he knew I thought so."

"I understood he was your stepfather," Victorine said.

"What difference now?"

"It might mean you have someone closer to lose."

Father felt Mother's touch on his temple, soothing his wound as she brushed an errant lock of hair. "If I lost anyone closer, I couldn't survive it."

Her words stung Father. She was his wife. He must protect her. Who was she talking about? Must be Clo. He'd have to see that Clo made it through the storm. His wife's survival depended on it.

~

The attic was no longer square, Philo noticed. More diamond-shaped, with rafters pulling loose from the joists. When a bad gust came, the edge of the roof lifted, showering everybody with windblown rain. That wasn't bad because the attic was hot as Hell with so many people and so much lamentation, but how long could a roof hold like that? And if it tore off, would they just sit here in the rain?

Think about something else, Philo told himself. Like humping Clo, that would be a good thing to think about. Humping Clo, hammering her good. Philo imagined himself as pirate captain Jean Lafitte and Clo his whimpering captive wearing some old-timey bodice he could tear off her; yet all the ways he might hump Clo kept getting replaced in his mind by ways the roof might fly away. Slowly prying off. Picked apart shingle by shingle. All in one quick whoop. So imagine Philo's surprise when, with an earsplitting groan, the roof did not fly away at all but instead crashed down upon them.

~

The ax bit wood. Splinters flew, caught by the wind, carried off to Hell. Zeph swung again. His ax was too heavy, but the pouring rain made such noise and the wind kept trying to knock him down, so he couldn't explain that he wanted to trade for the lighter ax. Besides, who was he to complain if his shoulders hurt? All around him, the wounded wailed. Little Artemise Blanchard was bleeding to death, her neck punctured when the peppermint jar exploded under a falling rafter.

Zeph didn't want to think about that so he chopped with the tool he had, using it like Achille taught him: lift it high, aim it straight, let its weight do the work.

A hand on his arm interrupted him. Madame Victorine nodded to follow. It was she who'd put him and the others chopping in the first place, cutting loose a section of collapsed roof to make a raft. Zeph wondered how Philo escaped getting shanghaied into helping. Victorine put her arm around Zeph's shoulder, a surprising intimacy. It allowed her to pull him close so she could holler into his ear, but there also seemed something comforting in the gesture. That's what made him nervous.

"Without the roof to keep it square, the building won't stand much longer," the store mistress began. Zeph knew that; that's why they were fixing a raft. "When it goes," she continued, "those will drop." She pointed out a row of heavy rafters, shorn of lathe and shingles, wagging in the wind but still improbably poking toward the sky. As his eyes followed the path they'd fall, Zeph was startled to see Philo sitting on the debris-strewn attic floor. His first thought was, how stupid could his brother be lounging under those timbers? Then he saw: Philo's arm was pinned under a crisscross of heavy beams. Madame Victorine hollered into his ear again. "You must chop it off."

"Which piece?" Zeph asked. Hard to know, with the roof truss in such shambles.

With the blade of her right hand, Victorine drew a line across her left forearm. "Here, halfway to his elbow, cleanly as you can."

What? She couldn't be serious. "No. No, I'll chop through the beam."

"We've not the time."

"We'll lift it."

"We've not the manpower. His wrist is crushed. If you don't cut it now and he somehow survives, they'll amputate anyway."

"Where's my daddy?" the twelve-year-old demanded.

"Gone."

"Gone? Gone where?"

"Gone," Victorine repeated. "Your mother too. I'm sorry."

It sank in. He knew several died when the roof caved but hadn't stopped to wonder who. "Where's Achille?"

Victorine nodded toward where Mother cradled her again-unconscious husband, then turned to Philo, writhing, desperate to free himself. "Best close your eyes so you don't flinch when the ax falls," she said.

"Get away from me, you half-nigra bitch!" Philo yelled. Victorine acted like she didn't hear him. "You, too, you runty turd!" Philo hollered at Zeph.

Zeph watched the whipping wind loose Victorine's hair from its ragged bun. Her braids writhed like snakes. "Or you can let him die when the house goes," she told Zeph. "Maybe that's better. But decide. We need the ax to finish the raft."

Zeph hefted the heavy ax and tried to ignore Philo's cursing. Lift it high, he reminded himself. Aim it straight. Let its weight do the work.

~

As their slowly sinking raft neared a copse of oaks, Victorine pointed out a tree with massive, gnarled branches. Young Zeph nodded and bent to his improvised tiller. The boy had proved himself quite capable, she thought. She would send him up first.

Victorine knew she couldn't get everyone into the tree. Among those strong enough, it'd take two to hold the raft in place and one to boost people up. When those three were the last able-bodied aboard, the system would break down. Those remaining would likely be swept away. That wasn't her fault.

Euphrasine Chouest, who first spread the gossip about Victorine's possible Negro blood, she would send into the tree; the woman was strong enough to save herself but not enough to hold the raft steady.

Boudou Pizani, who'd always been kind to Victorine, was fat and had broken his leg; endangering others to lift him couldn't be justified.

Zeph's brother Philo, eighteen and strong, had endured his amputation well. If he could get into the tree, he might be able to hang on with his good arm. If he drowned, it would upset

Zeph, whom she needed, so up Philo would go.

Victorine assigned Léon Dantin to help boost people into the tree, meaning afterward he'd be stuck on the sinking raft. The group faced enough challenges without nursing a drunk who would soon be desperately craving alcohol.

As for Léon's daughter, tomorrow, before relief arrived, survival could depend on morale. Responsibility for an orphan might distract adults from their own tragedies. Saving little Tellia was a priority, Victorine decided.

Thus the store mistress chose for every person a task or place in line, and thus, though most never realized it, for each a likelihood of life or death. On and on, head by head, adults and children, Victorine passed sentence without passing judgment. She came to the Gaspard girls, one a hopeless flirt, the other a new bride, both young and strong. They'd lost their stepmother in the roof collapse and their stepfather earlier, but if they died as well, it'd not be by Victorine's doing. Into the tree with them.

The older girl's husband, Achille Cheramie. Achille, with those broad shoulders and achingly handsome face. The smile that always brightened the room as he looked up from the bouillabaisse Victorine often served him, a virile lord at her kitchen table, which had now been crushed to splinters. Achille's rib puncture would likely heal and his head wound wasn't fatal, though it'd forever mar his perfect looks. But it left him dopey, slow to react, too weak to hold himself in a tree in this wind several more hours. Too impaired to survive. Even his bride sensed it. Victorine sighed. Let Achille help hold the raft to the tree. He could manage that. Achille, Achille. Achille she must let die.

To Consider

Whether ends justify means is an old conundrum. As we see with young Zeph chopping off his brother's forearm, sometimes horrendous violence is intended for good purpose. Even Philo's lascivious fantasies about Clo were arguably benign, an attempt to relax in a tense situation.

Then there's Victorine, sacrificing a few to save many. How do you feel about what she did? Would you have helped or interfered? And would your moral compass have changed direction if *you'd* been assigned as last on the raft? See? Cleaving good from evil isn't simple, and self-interest compounds the difficulty. Let me provide one more example.

Swimming up the womb, I found my path blocked by a y-chromosomed brute twice as big as me and stupid as a fat cell. If *he* pierced the egg, Mother would birth an oaf. I never doubted my duty. If my stopping him gave the race to Calypso, so be it. I flicked my flagellum, but butting him only riled the monster. He swung his bulk back at me. I ducked. He missed me by a molecule, saw his error but couldn't stop. I followed in his slipstream as he crashed through sperm, killing six, wounding twelve, before drifting into the path of my lovely rival.

He saw Calypso and forgot me. Whether competition or lust he felt, I'll never know. Whichever, it was fatal.

Calypso had the same idea — take him out — but her sally would've failed as mine had if I hadn't supported her with another attack of my own. Our pincer movement compressed his sides, driving up his intracellular pressure. Every bully has a weak spot; his burst. As cell fluid billowed, he spiraled away like a balloon cut loose. Calypso smiled at me, as much as a sperm can smile. Echoing the Great Powers of Europe, we'd been enemies, then allies, now enemies again. Her tail snapped. She shot past me...

Almost. I shifted, levering her into Mother's uterine wall. The force applied was negligible, but as she bounced back from the curtain of maternal flesh, her tail was creased with a new, barely visible wrinkle. It was sufficient. She could swim, just no longer fast enough. If I'd retired from the race, left the field to her and our remaining siblings, still she couldn't win and she knew it. Thus an almost imperceptible flaw can mean the difference between riding as head of the parade or pushing a broom at fallen confetti behind it.

Calypso regarded me with admirable resignation. I knew if I wanted to share her final hours I would not be unwelcome, but I had a lifetime of things to do and thus an egg I needed to claim. I swam away and didn't look back.

Lesson IX

CHOICES & CONSEQUENCES

There'd not been rope for everyone, so Mother had refused it. Thus, when the great gust came, nothing tied her to the branch except the waning strength of her two arms. The wind blew its strongest, an ultimate test. Make it through this, they'd survive. All of them. At least that's what Mother told herself.

The transfer from raft to tree had succeeded better than expected, leaving Mother impressed, not for the first time that day, by the leadership skills of Victorine Guidry. Achille had been last into the tree, and that because, when the raft broke loose and it seemed too late, Victorine put her own life at risk to pull him up. The remaining few aboard had been swept away. Boudou Pizani fell in and didn't surface. Zeph said he saw Léon Dantin save himself in a tree farther on. Maybe so; the boy had good eyes. Or maybe he lied for the sake of little Tellia.

Mother peeked over her shoulder to where Father stood upright on the fat branch, rope tethering him to the oak's trunk. When he saw Mother looking he tried to smile, but the wind twisted his grin into something macabre.

The rogue gust plucked its first victim. There hadn't been rope for Clo to tie in either, and now she blew off the upper branch where she'd sought refuge. As her baby sister windmilled past, Mother felt her own heart stutter. In the worst moments of their lives, Mother had always held Clo's hand. Why, today, had she let her climb alone onto the higher limb?

Of all the people adorning the tree like overripe peaches, only one had the position and quickness to reach for Clo: Zeph. His hand shot out. He hooked the passing fingers of the girl who during a single dance the night before had become his first boyhood crush, but at age twelve Zeph had not the bulk to stop her fall. He tumbled out himself, down, down, just behind Clo. A hand extended, too late for her, intended for him. Without looking whose it was he grabbed it. Tellia. His weight would've pulled her from the tree too, except that she was tied in. He'd done it himself, double-checking every knot.

Afraid he was hurting her but more afraid to die, Zeph pulled himself up by Tellia's arm and used the wind to swing onto the limb. Lying flat, he faced his savior. The three-year-old stretched forward and kissed him on the nose. "You're my prince," she said.

Splash! Clo hit the crest of a wave, slid into its trough, kept going under. She shut her mouth and pinched her nose. Salt stung her eyes. When she came up sputtering, the current was already stealing her away. "Help me, somebody!"

When Victorine had decided to abandon Father on the raft, she never guessed that she would be the one to ignore her careful plan and save him. Yet if the woman was often incapable of predicting her own whims, with other people she could usually foresee their choices several steps ahead. Thus, when Clo fell, Victorine knew a sure-to-fail attempt at rescue was coming. When Mother tried to dive in after Clo, Victorine threw her body atop her rival's, pinning Mother against the branch. If Victorine hadn't, Mother would've dove in, probably drowned, and Victorine could've married Achille as had been her heart's desire. So why'd she do it? I don't know. I've made you privy to the deliberations of many people that fateful day, but Victorine's mind is a murkier place where I'd rather not intrude too deeply.

Watching Clo struggle, Mother tried to get loose but sensed

the only way would be to take the other woman with her. She was ready to risk her own life but wasn't sure she should risk Victorine's. If Victorine drowned, how many others would die for lack of her cold logic?

Mother watched her sister grow indistinct behind the rain. Clo wasn't a strong swimmer. Without help, she wouldn't survive. Then, blown in by the evil wind, another thought impinged. Feeling guilty the moment it surfaced, Mother pushed it from her mind, but it burrowed back. This vile, intrusive notion was that she'd misunderstood her premonition. Her precious bridegroom wasn't doomed after all. What the look-ahead had foreseen was that Clo would die. Achille was safe behind her on the branch. There he'd remain till the water went down. His wounds would heal. They'd grow old together. Not a day of her future happiness would go by unmarred because of missing her sister, but in recompense she'd have Achille.

Then she heard, "I'll save her!" Mother craned her neck to see over Victorine's shoulder. Victorine looked too. Father had untied himself. Standing free on the branch, after giving Mother a look that she supposed he thought was encouraging, he dove into the froth. "No!" Mother hollered. Victorine hollered with her. It was too late.

To Mother, it felt like a rib had been sliced out of her body. Did Clo have it right earlier? Did he love her sister more than he loved her? Again Victorine felt the woman under her try to squirm away. Again she prevented it. Again I don't know why.

After having been pelted in the tree with every wind-hurtled leaf and raindrop, Achille liked being in the water again. It cleared his head, which had been foggy ever since that log thumped his noggin. At least the head wound had made him fret less his punctured side; that injury flared with renewed fire the moment he attempted to swim. He tried shorter strokes; it hurt only slightly less. He rolled onto his back, let his legs do the work, but they didn't propel him fast enough. He had to catch Clo. Had to save her. He'd heard what his wife said earlier, back in the attic. If she lost Clo, she herself wouldn't survive.

Clo hadn't seen Achille dive in. By this point she'd given up on being rescued, even on saving herself. Maybe better, she rationalized, having your candle snuffed out clean when you were young and attractive instead of guttering through old age. Clo imagined tardy rescuers, finding her corpse, wailing at their failure to save such a beauty; how with reverence they'd dress her in garments finer than any she'd ever worn. The thought of pretty clothes offered comfort as seawater filled her lungs.

Achille reached the spot where Clo had been, but the lovely, lively girl was already in Neptune's embrace. "Clo!" he hollered over the howling wind. Treading water, he waited till a wave's crest lifted him but he still didn't see her. He was afraid to glance toward Mother, afraid she'd know he'd failed. After two more looks round, Father admitted Clo was gone and that he himself was in trouble. His abdominal wound seared, his cracked head bled again. He needed flotation, else he would die. He spotted something, swam for it. Someone's wooden bed, somehow intact. Hoisting aboard, he found himself facing Touloulou, who the evening before had attacked him with an oyster hatchet, and who now appeared as surprised as if pirates had just boarded his vessel.

"I'll get you your money back, every penny," Father blurted, thoughtlessly creating an obligation that might outlive him.

Touloulou had claimed this drifting bed only after the third tree he climbed fell into the storm like the first two. Getting into each had cost him further pledges to the Blessed Virgin, as had keeping this water-logged bedstead afloat. He now considered Achille's rash promise as vindication of his fealty to Holy Mary.

Mother didn't know that it was Touloulou's eighty-six dollars and twelve cents that paid for her wedding. All she knew was that her husband had found safety. If he found it in someone else's bed, the irony was lost on her. He was alive. Maybe he'd loved Clo more, but Clo was gone. They would pick up the pieces, have a life.

Or maybe not: Mother saw the bed heading toward a china ball tree, misshapen from being robbed too often for kindling. "Achille, watch out!" she cried, but the wind blew away her warning.

SMACK, the bed hit the tree and disintegrated. Back in swirling water, Achille now had Touloulou clinging to him, pulling him down. "Let go, Touloulou! You'll drown us both!" The cripple held him tighter. Anyone else Achille might've shoved away, but already feeling guilty about Touloulou's money, he let the man hang on.

Mother held her breath as Father swam toward a camphor tree. Still atop Mother, Victorine ached with anxiety, too. Father caught a branch with his fingertips. Mother let herself hope. To Hell with premonitions. Damn all second sight. Whatever her mind's eye had seen, Father had defeated it. He'd reached a tree. God would preserve him.

Of course, Father still had to get *into* the tree. Touloulou first. Hugging the trunk with one arm, with the other Father boosted the cripple up. Touloulou had endured a lot of practice climbing trees that day. Short leg notwithstanding, he lost no time finding a secure perch where the camphor's trunk blocked some of the wind.

Immediately, he almost passed out.

A couple of camphor leaves crushed into a spoonful of lard makes a decent chest inhaler for a head cold. A tree full of hurricane-shredded camphor leaves is overwhelming. Touloulou stuck his nose into the rain and out of the eddy of intoxicating odor. He took several deep breaths. His sinuses had never felt so clear. Drunk on camphor, Touloulou could offer little help to his former nemesis and recent savior Achille. Father tried shimmying on his own, but a floating spar from some lost lugger whacked him back into the flood. "Touloulou!"

His senses returning, Touloulou saw Achille's predicament. With both arms and his right leg wrapped around the trunk, all he could offer in a hurry was his left leg, the one three inches shorter. He stretched. Father reached. Missed by two inches. Touloulou repositioned. Too late. The raging tide carried Father away.

At this point, a lesser man would've been swept out to sea. A wiser man might've let the current carry him toward something else to climb. Father was a man in love. He'd married Mother convinced she was the woman for him and nothing in their brief but eventful marriage had indicated otherwise. Despite pain and exhaustion clouding his thoughts, there were certain things of which he was sure.

He didn't love Clo; he loved his wife.

He didn't love Victorine; he loved his *chère petite diablesse.* He couldn't wait to tease her with that name, ideally while lying in bed.

He was unwilling to leave her, even for a few hours, even for the storm of the century. Achille Cheramie had always been a strong swimmer. How strong would now be tested as he began to swim toward his bride, *AGAINST* the raging current.

"No! The tide's too strong," Mother pleaded.

"Grab hold of something, Captain," hollered Zeph.

"Go back, you fool," shouted Victorine.

"You're gonna drown for sure," mocked Philo.

Father didn't turn back. Most gave him up for lost. If you've read Homer (if you haven't, you should), didn't Ulysses' cronies assume he'd never see home, courting his wife and conspiring for his kingdom? No doubt biblical David's best pals put their money on Goliath. Thus it was for Father but only for a while. As quick as humans denigrate another's ambition and call it folly, if one among us does achieve (at the expense of someone besides ourselves), then we're as quick to claim that brave soul as our champion.

Thus as spectators realized that Father was making progress, naysaying faded. By the time he swam a third of the course, not seeming to tire, head wound forgotten, his side not restraining him, cries of "Go back!" became cheers of encouragement. Even the wind slacked, as if in awe of this heroic aquanaut.

By the time Father reached halfway, he'd become banner-carrier for all. Their knight-errant against unmerciful Fate. Amid Mother's worry sprouted a measure of pride. Victorine slid off her so both could watch.

Two thirds of the way, swimming strongly. In the oak, those tied in were straining against their ropes to see this hero, this Achille, vanquish the sea and wind.

Three quarters done. Almost there. *Huzzah, Achille, Huzzah!*

That's when the thin rabbit noticed him.

Rabbits have long served as symbol of fertility. Small wonder, when the creatures are so fecund the doe can conceive her next litter while pregnant with the last. Even this particular rabbit, disliked by most females because of his chronic whining, had fathered several dozen robust kittens. Thus I suppose we must appreciate the irony that, eighteen hours after Father's wedding, six hours after he begat his only son, and at the instant I was knocking on Mother's ovum to claim the prize of conception, this traditional symbol of new life became the direct instrument of Father's death. You see, my father didn't drown, as so many did, in the Great Hurricane of 1893. Instead, in the midst of that flood, he was in fact smothered under a piece of wet rabbit fur that, as it happened, was still attached to a living rabbit.

The thin rabbit, fear of drowning overwhelming its fear of man, treated the face that won Mother's heart like it was any random flotsam. Having barely escaped a *rougarou's* pounce and now desperately tired from swimming, once it latched on, belly pressed against Father's mouth and nose, the bunny would not let go. Father attempted to pry the creature off, an effort as desperate as the rabbit's urge to hold on, but exhausted himself and impeded by the necessity to tread water, Father was at great disadvantage.

Imagine Mother watching her new husband, who'd battled a one-eyed cow, dodged massive logs, and survived a collapsing general store, now succumb to a mere rabbit, a skinny one at that. Father was close to the tree. Victorine no longer held her down. If Mother could reach him, she might pull the rabbit off. With the impulsiveness of youth and the recklessness of the romantic, Mother dove into the churning flood.

What happened next? I happened.

I'd long since left the uterus for the left fallopian tube. We were bunched up, a few dozen leaders, swimming hard. None of us bothered trying to sabotage the others anymore; we were each wary veterans, wise to every strike and feint.

We turned a corner. There she was: the ovum. What a beauty! Fifty thousand times bigger than us and offering the promise of life.

We rushed her, all of us at once, picking our spots, snuggling into her jelly coat, each offering a bit of protein like a boy presenting a corsage to his cotillion date. Hoping to find a receptive receptor, I nudged, nuzzled, pushed, and shoved. I felt myself dissolving and didn't care. Burrowing blind, I didn't know I was in until I felt my nucleus lifted away to be co-joined as royal consort with the egg's. What rapture!

Mother felt it too. I know you laugh, but she's a woman of great sensitivity. It's the only explanation for what threw off her dive. Well, true, the forward tuck Mother decided would land her close to Father *was* a complicated maneuver — a precise geometric equation, not to mention a demanding physical feat for an exhausted, unschooled, not particularly athletic girl who had no time to practice and just seconds to plan. And yes, the blinding rain hid hazards in the water while the deafening wind took the intended simple dive and added two and a half somersaults. But mostly what skewed her aim was me ill-choosing my moment and, heedless of consequences, distracting Mother with the prospect of motherhood when she needed all her concentration for wifely heroics.

Mother actually landed fairly close to Father, but as her body hit water, her head hit debris which knocked her unconscious. Father would have no rescue. His rasping gasps drew the rabbit's pelt ever tighter against his face. With his last breath, all he managed to inhale were a number of unhappy fleas.

To Consider

I know what you're thinking. If Jerome Chabert or Touloulou, either one, had been a hair quicker, that damned rabbit wouldn't escaped them to smother Father.

If Clo had tied herself to the tree, Father would've never had to jump in to rescue her. If, that morning, Gaspard hadn't marched into the flood, later he might've been alive to make sure Clo tied in; and if Zeph hadn't marched off first, Gaspard wouldn't have followed; and if Philo hadn't goaded him, Zeph might not have marched at all. Guilt spins in circles.

In the tree, if Tellia hadn't reached out to keep Zeph from falling, he might have rescued Clo before Father ever jumped. He might've even rescued Father. Where was the little girl's own father to prevent such reckless behavior? Drunk. You could say drinking killed my father because, in a way, Léon's drinking contributed.

Or imagine if Victorine had actually poisoned the tarts the way she wanted to and almost did. Mother would've been up all night retching, with Father tending her but also seeing the weather worsen, taking precautions. Mother might've suffered a very bad bellyache but enjoyed a happier life thereafter with her loving husband beside her.

If, if, if. If *ifs* were skiffs, we'd all be poling down a sunlit bayou, wouldn't we? Should we fault Victorine for *NOT* attempting mass murder? Fault others for things they couldn't help? For actions whose consequences they could not guess? You decide.

Myself, I've examined it a thousand ways. Pulled apart every stitch. If Father overslept on a critical morning, it was the exertion of creating me that kept him in bed. If Mother mis-executed the plunge that could've saved him, my ill-timed burrowing into her egg disrupted her dive. I'm the reason my father is dead. I'm the reason I would never look into his eyes, nor hear his voice, nor recognize his scent, nor know how he parted his hair or held a spoon or told a story, except from the unreliable recollections of others or the pretense of my own imagination. He would never toss me into the air and catch me or show me off to his friends. He would never teach me how to catch a fish, or tell a joke, or lift high an ax that might cut away my shame.

It was my fault.

I'd like to say I did better the next time, but as you'll learn, I did not.

Appendix

HOW VICTIMS COPE

The debris that thwacked Mother was a door, the very bedroom door from her and Achille's now-demolished house. Her weight drove it underwater. When it bobbed up, she was atop it, sputtering enough to expel the seawater from her lungs but not enough to revive herself. Thus Mother remained blessedly unaware as the door rammed the clothesline pole which had snagged the corpse of Achille Cheramie. The jolt knocked loose the oversized gold wedding band from Mother's finger; it slipped under the waves, never to be seen again but never to be forgotten either.

The skinny rabbit would cling like a veil to Father's face until the next day when Touloulou cracked it over the head, roasted it, and served it at the impromptu wake as Father was buried by Zeph Leboeuf.

Mother, meanwhile, unconscious but alive, rode out to sea on the unhinged portal to her bridal chamber.

~

Once word of the disaster spread, the village drew swarms of rescuers, reporters, and looters. Though he had no interest in cutting jewels from swollen fingers, Judge August Randolph Pike also saw opportunity in the tragedy. Years before, Judge Pike had arrived from parts unknown to the sugarcane country along upper Bayou Lafourche, seventy miles southwest of New

Orleans and a like distance northwest of Chenière. Infiltrating plantation society via a judgeship in Thibodaux, through diligent effort and discreet graft, by 1893 he'd amassed a fortune sufficient to live comfortably, dress impeccably, and create all manner of mischief.

The day after the hurricane, Judge Pike called at Athena, Louisiana's wealthiest sugar plantation, which belonged to his dearest friend. Louis Bonreve had been born into Creole aristocracy. A bachelor though nearly forty, eccentric if not quite odd, his inclination toward passing obsessions was tempered by a deep-felt sense of his place in Southern history. He was someone people turned to for advice, as they'd turned to his father, grandfather, and great-grandfather, on the simple theory that anyone that rich must know things the rest of us don't.

Thus, while Judge Pike's keen mind could line up long, intricate rows of dominos, Louis Bonreve possessed enough wandering interest and spare cash to start those dominos tipping. Yet as this (honorary) Colonel of Militia liked to tell people, he was no fool, so he knew as the Judge rode up that his friend had come to ask some inconvenient favor.

"Yes, it's a terrible tragedy," said Bonreve once he'd heard the request. "But grinding season's our busiest time. If I'm not here the cane crop—"

"—will be harvested under the capable administration of your overseer. You're an important man, Louis. Do you think it fitting," the Judge asked, aiming his blade for tender flesh, "to stand back when the deserving but less fortunate need your help?"

Bonreve scratched the muzzle of the horse he'd been about to mount. "I suppose it's our duty."

"Of course, it is."

Bonreve left his overseer a detailed (and unnecessary) list of things to do and the order in which to do them. Telegrams were sent. A small side-wheeler, the *Laura*, was chartered. As Pike and Bonreve awaited the afternoon train to New Orleans to meet their hired steamboat, Bonreve saw coming onto the platform a certain Monsieur Gueydan who owned a modest plantation downstream from his own. Trailed by a porter burdened under too much luggage, Gueydan clearly considered himself a member of their party and seemed surprised to be expected to buy his own train ticket. As Gueydan shuffled off to book his fare, Bonreve raised an eyebrow at the Judge.

Judge Pike lit a cigar, puffing till he had it burning just so. "I thought coming along might give Gueydan a chance to demonstrate his unbridled bravery and deep-seated compassion. He's a candidate for sheriff, you know."

Bonreve sighed. Pike was always sponsoring some up-and-coming politician. Often several. Occasionally rivals for the same office. Even so, this choice seemed odd. "You're running *that* fellow against Sheriff Bourgeois, a proven war hero?"

"Sheriff Bourgeois has become too independent. A little competition might reacquaint him with the concept of loyalty. Besides, losing an arm in battle doesn't prove you're a hero. It may simply mean you're unlucky."

"You expect *me* to stand as witness to Gueydan's purported bravery?"

"No, I'll recruit journalists to do that. You're along to pay for the expedition." Judge Pike smirked, knowing full well that his friend would never consider anything so undignified as backing out at this late stage.

In New Orleans Pike discovered that any reporter willing to endure the hardships necessary to cover the tragedy had already left for the coastal hamlet. An unimpeachable witness would have to serve after all. Serendipitously, while the *Laura* was coaling up, a merchantman out of Bremen was towed to the adjacent Mandeville Street wharf. From it stumbled Hans Groetsch, a freshly ordained priest from Bavaria. With his concave chest and pimply face, few would've guessed he had substantial musical talent honed by years of instruction. Liturgy and pastoral teachings held no interest for him. He'd been contracted to serve as cathedral organist — his sole motive for taking vows.

Judge Pike, who knew a smattering of German as well as several other languages, convinced the young priest that the *Laura* would take him to the archbishop. Later, recognizing St. Louis Cathedral from a picture postcard he'd been sent, Father Groetsch grew alarmed when he saw himself steaming past it. As its trio of spires fell away behind them, Judge Pike explained there'd be a slight but necessary side trip before the priest could tickle keys at the cathedral.

From the Mississippi River the expedition entered the Westwego Canal, then Lake Salvador, then Bayou Perot. Each turn revealed worse destruction. With Caminada Bay too debris-filled to safely approach, Captain Richardson made for the pass near the old fort on Grand Terre before cutting west to reach the decimated village via the Gulf of Mexico.

Finding himself at sea alerted Father Groetsch to the extent to which he'd been hoodwinked. He complained, but no one aboard understood German except Judge Pike. Pike worried more about his protégé Gueydan, who sat repetitively inhaling the salty air to battle a queasiness the now dead-calm sea hardly justified. A weak stomach doesn't win votes.

What did make Judge Pike smile was watching Louis Bonreve pace the foredeck. Though the planter hadn't wanted to come, at each upcharge along the journey — for taking on the priest, for going the long way round — Bonreve waved that he'd cover the extra cost. Now, like a knight seeking the Grail, he itched to get ashore to do his noble duty. Pike congratulated himself that the deepest-pocketed person he knew remained so exquisitely predictable.

~

The door kept Mother afloat, but without shade, nothing spared her from blistering under the relentless sun nor prevented fickle currents from exiling her far into the Gulf of Mexico. Days passed before, through eyes barely open, she saw a plume of black smoke disfiguring the northern sky and deduced it marked a steamboat.

She tried to sit up. To wave. To catch the eye of someone who'd turn the helm, pull her from the sea, bring sweet water to her lips — Merciful Mary, she was thirsty! "I'm dying," she croaked. Her first words in days reverberated through her womb, but were nowhere near loud enough to be heard by the distant vessel. The *Laura* steamed on. I wondered how soon Mother's body would exercise cruel triage and slough me out as an unessential drain on resources.

~

The *Laura* anchored beyond the farthest sand bar. Its passengers were rowed ashore. Gueydan dry-heaved the whole way.

At Chenière, after a couple of looters had been shot, their brethren departed, finding in any case that the poor village offered slim pickings. As reporters roamed the wreckage filling newspaper columns, everyone else worked at evacuating the injured and burying the dead. Traveling Father Premeaux had run aground in Bay Adams. Young Father Groetsch had never conducted a funeral before, but any fool, including him, could smell what was required as victims' bodies ripened in the unseasonable October heat. Intoning Latin rites for seventy-two hours straight, he interred six hundred and nine villagers. Judge Pike dubbed him the "Fearless Funeral Friar." In print, the nickname shed the Judge's sarcasm and turned the young priest into a diocesan legend. Louis Bonreve sent word offering his friend the archbishop a pot of money to build a church near his plantation if Groetsch might be its pastor. Thus poor Groetsch, though he'd pledged himself to celibacy for the privilege, didn't spend a single day as cathedral organist.

On burial detail, moneyed Louis Bonreve sweated alongside destitute Touloulou Barthelme. Touloulou would finally escape Chenière but only as far as New Orleans, there to begin a pledged eighteen years, three months service to the Blessed Virgin.

Helping dig graves was a large, chestnut-brown, strangely-obsessed dog which no local would admit recognizing. "Did you ever see such an obliging beast?" asked the captain of the *Laura*. "If no one claims him, I may bring the cur home. He'd offer comfort to my wife and children when voyages take me away."

Locals exchanged looks, but none spoke up. Jerome Chabert — rechristened "Hurricane" — would move to a big back yard on Chartres Street in New Orleans. As time passed and his anticipated re-transformation into human form did not occur, he came to consider his new existence permanent. He never troubled chickens again, though not a day passed he wasn't tempted.

Keeping up with the adults, if not the dog, young Zeph Leboeuf did all his grave-digging with a three-year-old riding his back, her tiny arms encircling his neck. Her father, Léon Dantin, had saved himself after Victorine declared him expendable, but while interring his seven other children, he had to be prevented from crawling into the grave with them. After that, he mostly wept, suffered delirium tremens, and wasn't much use. His wife's body wasn't found.

Zeph's amputee brother, Philo, searched for the corpse of Clo Gaspard — he was anxious to defile it — but neither he nor anyone else found her either.

Many survivors, including Zeph, Philo, and Léon with his daughter, Tellia, decided to move to Leeville, ten miles inland on Bayou Lafourche. Less exposed than Chenière, Leeville was still close enough to the sea for a fisherman to earn his living.

Others chose to seek opportunity in New Orleans. As a boat bound there got up steam and Touloulou knelt in the sand praying for safe passage, Judge Pike volunteered to search for a passenger who'd wandered off. As with any offer the Judge made, altruism played no part in it. The missing woman was a tall beauty in her late twenties, with jet black hair and olive skin. Less in shock than other survivors, she exhibited a quickness of mind he could not help but admire.

Judge Pike found Victorine atop a mountain of broken boards. "It's dangerous to walk there, Madame."

She eyed the destruction around her. "Seems the worst danger's past."

"There may be snakes in the rubble."

"I expect to encounter many serpents in the days ahead. Why have you found me, sir?"

"Your boat's leaving. I know it must be difficult to say goodbye to a place you loved—"

Her laughter interrupted him. She saw his startled reaction. "Don't think me hysterical."

He stepped closer. Wood creaked under him. "It'd be forgivable of a widow who's lost everything. I have friends in New Orleans. Business interests. I could help—"

"Don't think me hysterical," Victorine repeated, "nor certainly don't think me naïve." She walked away across the debris. The Judge hurried to follow. The footing was treacherous.

"I see you've no patience for nonsense so let's speak plainly. A woman alone faces grim prospects if she has no protector, no money."

Victorine knelt, pried up a board, and drew out a strongbox, already starting to rust but its lock intact. "'No money,' you were saying?"

As boats left for Leeville and New Orleans, Judge Pike, hoping to salvage his original mission, convinced Bonreve to fund a few more days to comb the open Gulf for survivors. He induced a couple of reporters to tag along to document Gueydan's heroism. Unfortunately, as the *Laura* weighed anchor, Pike's protégé became violently seasick and stayed that way no matter how angry Judge Pike got. When the Judge insisted he help recover the first body — the late Da-Dool Dantin, it turned out — Gueydan threw up on her much the way her husband Léon had occasionally done. The Judge felt ready to terminate the expedition, but by then Bonreve had taken up the cause.

Neither Judge Pike, nor the crew, nor the reporters relished the many corpses bobbing on the sea. Bonreve, however, preferred the fish-gnawed dead to the occasional survivor found clutching some bit of flotsam. The dead did not embarrass you with their gratitude. The dead never deliriously mistook you for some recently lost loved one, an error accompanied by blubbering embraces that only the firmest hand could pry loose.

~

Another night, blessed relief from the sun, but with dawn Mother grew worse. I tried to generate the rosy glow of motherhood, but morning sickness was all I managed. "Hold on," I longed to say. "Survive this ordeal and I'll stay beside you forever, shield you from hurt, accord you the part of Achille that survives in me," but I as yet had no voice.

The day grew hot. Mother became delirious. Frankly, so did I. When I heard voices I imagined vicious mermaids: shiny scales, flowing tresses, sharp teeth. As Mother flailed, we were lifted into a row boat, from there hoisted onto the *Laura*'s deck, where Father Groetsch took two steps back and shouted, "*Geh!*"

Struggling with her rescuers had started Mother's stigmata bleeding, prompting signs of crosses and gasps of astonishment and a kissed medallion or two. With strength no one guessed she possessed, Mother rose, staggered, tore free when Bonreve caught her, and threw herself against the rail. Hollers went up. Jerome Chabert barked. Mother thrust out her arm, pointing toward the coast. "I'm leaving my heart behind," she cried. "How will I live without a heart?"

"It's not nearly so difficult as you suppose," replied Judge Pike.

Book II

The Corruption of Innocence

Surprisingly rarely can we blame lost virtue on some smooth talking rogue with pomaded hair. More often, the contest against evil itself corrupts. Each arrow we unsheathe to fight for goodness stains our hands and dilutes our purity.

To illustrate, I offer from my childhood sixty-nine occasions when I first violated, or witnessed the violation of, well-known Biblical directives. (For broadmindedness, I've also included shattered commandments of Mohammedans, Jews, Buddhists, what have you.)

When one of these moral turpitudes rings a bell from your own youth, mark the passage. Later, as homework, pen a short composition revisiting the moment when you yourself first whiffed the brimstone of that particular wickedness. Explain why, exactly, did you do what you did. How did you justify it at the time? Do you still consider those actions defensible?

Only by understanding how we acquired our flaws of character can we put those flaws to productive use. You can despair that you find yourself drowning in a moral gutter — or you can let me teach you how to swim.

Turpitude # 1

"Do not wrong a guest."
Exodus 22:21

Terse telegrams, General Delivery letters, and advertisements in far-flung newspapers eventually reunited Chenière rescued with kin — all except Mother, who had no one left. Until someone deduced what to do with her, Colonel Bonreve agreed to take her in.

The eighty miles the *Laura* steamed up Bayou Lafourche was the longest Mother had ever voyaged, but she was too weak to enjoy passing scenery. Once carried up the steps built into the tall bayouside levee, she beheld Athena Plantation's "Big House." Yes, it was huge. More surprising was how it contrasted with its master. Two decades older than she, Bonreve dressed like a prosperous undertaker. Yet down a long lane bordered with fern and liriope and canopied by giant, moss-draped oaks, his enormous house was as colorful as a butterfly.

Worried a carriage ride might set back Mother's convalescence, Bonreve had black porters tote her stretcher down the oak alley as if she was some rajah's maharanee. The mansion appeared to grow even bigger as Mother approached. A palatial staircase rose to a main floor perched nine feet in the air. An encircling verandah offered shady spots for musing any time of day, with tall jalousie windows inviting breezes into bedrooms and parlors and a dining room which sat thirty and the largest private library between New Orleans and Galveston. Gabled windows cut into the roof marked a huge, third floor ballroom where the plantation's current master had never once hosted a party.

Mother was installed in the garçonnière, connected to the Big House by covered breezeway. Bonreve dove into overseeing every swing of blade and turn of wheel as his vast acreage of cane was cut, ground, squeezed, cooked, and crystalized into sweet brown sugar. Judge Pike returned to his own plantation, Southern Crown, and his Thibodaux courtroom, promising to track down relatives for Mother. Monsieur Gueydan lost his election but garnered enough votes to remind incumbent Sheriff Bourgeois that Judge Pike should not be antagonized.

Once Mother emerged from her sickbed, all she could do was gawk. Every object shined. Every meal was a feast. Servants anticipated her whims. Not a single chore was asked of her. Though Bonreve hardly spared her a passing nod, he provided more clothes than she'd ever owned, all in black but otherwise of a fashionableness that would've made poor Clo scream with envy. As Mother donned these mourning dresses and explored this magical world, she discovered herself to be just one of several human oddments filling Athena's surplus rooms. These included a half-blind traveling portrait painter, Bonreve's doughty old maid Tante Elmire, and an elderly couple invited over eighteen months before to play "Around the World with Nellie Bly." Bonreve's fascination with the board game quickly waned, but he'd never asked the couple to leave, so they hadn't.

You'd think a man commanding an army of field hands, let alone three hundred plow mules, could handle a seventeen-year-old girl, but as Mother emerged from her sick room and later from her grief, the charm and vivacity that made her the darling of everyone else rendered Colonel Bonreve as jumpy as a thoroughbred. He wanted her out.

"How's the harvest going?" Mother would invite conversation.

"Fine," Bonreve would reply. "Has Judge Pike located your relatives?"

Or…

"Lunch's crème brulée was the most delicate thing."

"Yes, our cook is skillful. Have you given thought to your future plans?"

She began to avoid him, afraid he would use a chance encounter to tell her it was time to leave. Not that Mother had become spoiled to paintings on every wall or menageries of silverware lined up beside her dinner plate or sleeping on a feather bed with carved posts and cushiony mattress springs, though of course she liked those things.

Her problem was more elemental: the poor girl had no clue where she might go nor how she might make a living once there.

In a tub lined with porcelain, in a bath scented with oils, Mother wished she'd had the chance to be naked like this for Achille. She touched her belly and felt Achille's child quickening inside it but suspected her pregnancy presented a complication Colonel Bonreve would not appreciate.

As I said, Judge Pike had promised to make inquiries on her behalf. One chilly afternoon before Christmas he sat her down in the rose parlor to deliver his report. Days were growing short, so a fire had been lit, its flickering light sucked into the dark mahogany swirls of the furniture overfilling the room.

"I've concluded you have no living relatives."

"I told you that from the beginning," Mother smiled.

"It was important to be certain before exploring alternatives. Surely you don't expect to stay here permanently?"

"Did Colonel Bonreve ask you to talk to me about this?"

"Louis Bonreve breathes more rarified air than us. He's given to whims and might any moment show you the exit. Think how rocky your path will be then were I not available to make introductions."

"Introductions to who?" she asked.

"To *whom*. Certain women who might offer you lodging."

"Out of the goodness of their heart? I have nothing."

"Don't undervalue yourself. You're a lovely creature." He took her hand, an audacious intimacy. "With polish, you could rise quite high," he cooed, manicured fingers slithering up her wrist, "called on only by the finest gentleman."

Turpitude # 2

"Wrath."

5th of the Seven Deadly Sins

I wanted to tear Pike up. Beat him down. Rip him apart. As a ten week-old fetus, none of that was possible. Nor, it turned out, necessary. Mother yanked free, exposing the scars on her palms. "These don't mean I'm a martyr. If any serpent thinks to bite me, it better realize I'll bite back. That includes you, Judge." She curtsied and left. I wish I could've seen his expression.

My presence began to make itself known. Maids remarked how Mother's new clothes no longer fit. Yvonne, the cook, joked that Mother also had something baking in the oven. Someone told the Colonel.

"This will never do!" he said, squinting at Mother's belly.

"It's done, sir. My late husband's child. There's no dishonor."

"I never suggested there was, but it means you must stay here till the baby comes."

"You want me to stay?"

"What I want is beside the point. It wouldn't be honorable to abandon a woman in your condition." Overcome with gratitude, Mother dashed forward and hugged him. Bonreve reacted as a Congo River explorer might if attacked by a lowland gorilla.

Mother retreated. "Monsieur, you've given me so much. Like I woke up in a storybook." That too seemed to make him uncomfortable, so Mother added: "Not that I ever read storybooks."

He frowned. "Why not?"

"Never learned to read."

The next afternoon, Two-Tone Willie, the houseboy with a skin condition, pulled up in the carriage to unload our newest lodger. "Madame," the fussy, balding young man said once he tracked Mother down on the rear gallery, "I've been engaged as your tutor."

"How sweet of Colonel Bonreve," Mother said, more gracious than I, who suspected it embarrassed the great man to have illiteracy infest his guest rooms.

Soon, no dusting of spilled salt, nor fogged window pane, nor — my favorite — the ticklish skin of her belly as Mother enjoyed the baths she'd come to love, remained safe from her index finger drawing letters on it; within weeks, words; within months, full, correct sentences. As I listened from her womb, she'd read them back to me. Sucking my thumb, offering the occasional kick of encouragement, I contemplated the ways she sheltered me, fed me, the debt I'd owe her the rest of my life.

I knew I'd also had a father, but our only contact had been along that short corridor between scrotum and foreskin. What did I owe him for that brief journey? As an innocent unborn with yet no teeth to bite Life's apple, I understood little of causation and less of guilt. The only thing clear as leaded glass was that the death of the man called Achille Cheramie had left in Mother a great void, and that even after departing her womb it would be my mission to fill that emptiness, to become a hero like Achille, as strong and brave and true, not for my sake, but for Mother's.

The 4th of July, 1894, I emerged into daylight, was swatted, swabbed, and swaddled, then handed to Colonel Bonreve so he could present me to Mother. Even as a newborn I recognized the fineness of Bonreve's frock coat, though I soon realized what he never did: for daywear it was hopelessly out of fashion.

Mother took me. Her green eyes inventoried my various appendages. Her beaming smile testified that she found me satisfactory and her kiss confirmed it. Though my vision hadn't yet steadied, I tried to memorize every detail of her. Flawless skin flushed from having just given birth. Breasts plump to nurture her child. A face perfect, impossible to turn away from. A month shy of her eighteenth birthday, her eyes already promised wisdom while her smile teased with eternal mystery.

Bonreve cleared his throat. Mother's gaze left me for him, like a cloud covering the sun. "Madame…" he began. "Dearest girl…" he revised. "Your son deserves a living father."

I feared — probably Mother did too — that this was preamble to an eviction notice, but instead Bonreve surprised us both by dropping to one knee and crying out, "Woman, will you marry me?"

I realize Louis Bonreve typically answered only to God and his New York bankers, and I don't mean to sound old-fashioned, but as Mother's closest male relative shouldn't I have been consulted about this proposal beforehand? I thought so, so I flushed my face, filled my lungs, and howled.

Mother's deliberations were unseemly brief. "Of course, I'll marry you," she shouted over my wailing. Where was her vaunted clairvoyance? How could she not recognize this union as a huge mistake? Even with his black wavy hair and piercing blue eyes, after Achille Cheramie how could she find Louis Bonreve attractive? I howled louder.

"We'll marry on Saturday," Bonreve shouted above my din.

"I'm in mourning," Mother pointed out.

"Yes, of course, we mustn't forget your first husband."

"I haven't," she assured him.

"A year's bereavement *is* proper. I can wait another three months. But not one day more."

I expected her to stall, but she yelled, "Whatever you wish, dear. Now go, so I can nurse our hungry little man here."

"A planter's wife doesn't suckle her own babes," he informed her, growing hoarse from the shouting. "I've arranged a wet nurse."

I waited for Mother to declare that I'd nuzzle no nipple but hers. Instead she repeated, "Whatever you wish, dear." I cried louder.

Bonreve left to fetch the nurse. Because of my bawling, Mother and I at first didn't hear the scuffle outside, not until the Colonel hollered, "How dare you say she's beneath me?"

Mother edged across the bed to peer out the window. I quieted so we could listen. "Do you not perceive that your fortune prompted her quick acceptance?" asked Bonreve's adversary, whom I deduced must be Judge Pike. Interesting to put a face with the treacherous voice. A head taller than Bonreve, his sandy brown hair and Van Dyke beard were perfectly groomed.

"I'd come to believe romance was for other men," responded Bonreve, "until Providence sent me this exquisite young woman."

"*And* her child."

"I can deal with the child," Bonreve said. What, I wondered, did he mean by that?

Turpitude # 3

"Let the rich not boast of their riches."

Jeremiah 9:23

The Colonel loathed crowds but understood a grand wedding was expected of a prominent planter. Mother loved parties but had no one left to invite. Compounding these conundrums was how to decorate a house already gaudy as a showboat. Bonreve ordered buildings repainted, gardens replanted, gazebos rebuilt. Tante Elmire, a blood relation, stayed, but other lodgers received one-way tickets elsewhere so their rooms could be offered to prominent wedding guests. For lesser attendees, Bonreve booked as floating hotel a passenger steamboat so large a canal had to be widened before it could reach Athena. Young Father Groetsch, installed nearby at newly-built St. Catherine's Church, practiced hymns that might sound pleasing on the boat's calliope. Archbishop Janssens agreed to personally perform the ceremony. Debutantes from nine states, though strangers to Mother, jockeyed to be maids of honor. To give away the bride, Bonreve said Mother could choose anyone she wished. With a sly smile, she chose Judge Pike.

Meanwhile, I learned to hold up my head, grasp her thumb, and bend my face into a smile when I thought the situation warranted it. One such occasion came when Judge Pike, finding himself alone with us, told Mother, "Madame, I will never underestimate you again." It was also that day we first heard about the spiders from French Indochina. Had I mentioned those?

The Golden Orb Spider, *Nephila maculata*, spins the world's largest web. Bonreve spent a fortune importing one hundred specimens from Hanoi, complete with Tongkingese handler. Loosed in Athena's oak alley, the Asian spiders confirmed their reputation as magnificent web-spinners.

One might ask why Bonreve couldn't make do with the only slightly smaller webs of the Golden Orb's local cousin, the Banana Spider, *Nephila clavipes*, but importing spiders was actually the *less* outlandish part of his plan. He revealed the rest a few days before the wedding as we enjoyed the balcony's evening shade. "See those oaks now laced with web,' he cooed to Mother as Judge Pike and I listened. "Wedding morn young Negroes will scale their branches to shake out gold dust so that the giant webs will glitter above you as you march to the altar.

Actual gold dust. It's already been delivered."

Bonreve seemed to be waiting for a "thank you," but Mother couldn't even manage to close her mouth, so he settled for the delight of having surprised her. "I knew you'd love it!"

It fell to Judge Pike to respond. "Louis, the nation's reeling from last year's Panic. Fifteen thousand companies bankrupt. Five hundred banks shuttered. The Pullman porters' strike—"

"My little sprinkle of gold will hardly collapse America's economy."

"Maybe not, but it *will* paint a target on you *and* your new family for every anarchist, unionist, or angry Negro—"

"August, stop it! You're frightening my fiancée."

I'd never knowingly met an anarchist or unionist, but I had witnessed how angry my Negro wet nurse became when I clamped too hard on her nipple. Mother, however, contradicted him. "If I were afraid," she said, "I'd hardly be fit to wed you, Colonel."

Bonreve puffed with pride. He didn't realize Mother hadn't finished speaking.

Turpitude # 4

"Wives, submit to your husbands."
Ephesians 5:22

Before Athena, the only gold Mother ever possessed was a ring drilled from a $5 coin, and that briefly. Sprinkling the metal from trees struck her as vulgar. While she'd spent her girlhood being taught to obey the men around her, and she understood that if she let Bonreve make all their decisions (as he clearly expected to) that he'd do his best to spare her life's unpleasantnesses. Such a plush, powerless pedestal didn't sit right for her, however.

"So I'm not afraid, *not for myself,*" Mother clarified, "but if it puts our son in danger, well, I won't miss the glitter because the webs will be pretty already and shouldn't people be looking at the bride and groom anyway? So we're probably better off without gold dust, that is, of course, if you agree, Colonel."

The Colonel scowled. "Whatever you wish, dear. I only suggested it because I thought you'd like it."

Mother was surprised she'd won the argument, more surprised how easy it'd been.

Sulking at relinquishing his gilded folly, Colonel Bonreve never guessed he'd also just forfeited his entire concept of an obedient wife. Pike, meanwhile, began wheedling to have the now-surplus gold dust contributed to a "good cause" naturally requiring "plentiful funds" which, as usual, didn't include the Judge's own.

The big day arrived. Skies were blue, the bride angelic, decorations magnificent. Governor Foster was best man. A senator, two congressmen, and a U.S. Supreme Court justice stood as groomsmen, with Mayor Fitzpatrick of New Orleans downgraded to usher because he'd recently been impeached. When guests too fond of rum punch became entangled in spider webs, their shrieks were drowned by the calliope. Who could suspect a marriage begun with such pomp would spawn so many catastrophes? Well, I could, but no one listened.

Turpitude # 5

"Too much study wearies the flesh."
Ecclesiastes 12:12

Over the next few years, Mother reshaped herself into fitting consort for an eminent man. As I learned to walk, she learned to walk like a lady. As I learned to talk, she learned English and refined her native French. "I don't natter like a fishwife anymore, do I?" she asked as she bounced me on her knee one morning when I was three. "My elocution won't appall his associates, will it? Not that that perturbs him anyway as long as I light his fire every afternoon."

Actually, Two-Tone Willie lit the fires — the house had eighteen hearths. Afternoon was when Mother and the Colonel shooed me out and took their daily nap. Mother often spoke in riddles; it rarely succeeded to ask her to explain them. Neither did she ever mention her "look-ahead spells" though now and then I could tell she'd suffered one.

If Mother saw self-improvement as obligation, I loved knowledge for itself. In Athena's magnificent library awaited every topic to interest a gentleman planter: Shakespeare to Sophocles, metallurgy to metaphysics, the governors of Louisiana to the grub diseases of corn. Over 6,000 volumes in English, another 2,000 in French; I eventually read most of them.

When not buried in a book, I observed nature. Annoyed the cook, Yvonne, by performing chemistry experiments in her kitchen. Studied mathematics under the tutelage of the plantation accountant. "Adding's easy," he'd say, "but only subtract when no one's looking." I cried when Sheriff Bourgeois arrested him.

Negroes fascinated me the way poverty can only fascinate those who harbor no fear of joining its ranks. I hounded the maids and pestered the yard men. Most with gray in their hair could remember being slaves. All, old and young, still called Bonreve "Master."

Light-skinned blacks — octoroons, quadroons, a few genetically lucky mulattoes — enjoyed better clothes and lighter duties around the Big House, while the more African-looking worked the fields. Bonreve theorized darker skin stood up better to the summer sun, but I suspect it was also an aesthetic choice.

One exception was Nat Toussaint. Nat was a *griffe*, three-quarters black, the opposite of a pale-skinned quadroon. In his forties, about the same age as Bonreve, Nat had been a field hand since old enough to walk behind a cane wagon and toss back any stalks that fell.

One day, as Bonreve checked the crop for mosaic disease while his dark-skinned ranks lolled on the head-rows scooping fingers into lunch pails, Nat used his precious free time to gather wildflowers. He braved the hooves of Bonreve's nervous thoroughbred and broke the cardinal rule to never speak unless spoken to, offering up his bouquet, "For the missus."

After a moment's hesitation, Bonreve took it. The swirl of color was impressive but perplexing. "You spend your few uncounted moments cutting flowers for a woman you've barely seen, never spoken to, and who'll not give a thought to which Negro picked them?"

"Guess so, Master. But she might cast a fond thought your way if you give 'em to her."

The Colonel fingered the petals of a pink and yellow firewheel. "Back to work, boy."

"Yes, Master." Nat retrieved his cane knife. Negroes snickered. But at dusk, as Colonel Bonreve rode back to the Big House bouquet in hand, Nat jogged alongside and Athena had a new flower gardener.

Turpitude # 6

"Servant, obey thy master."
Ephesians 6:5

How Nat escaped cane field drudgery became legend. Soon every ditch bank from Lockport to Donaldsonville was stripped of wildflowers. No planter could exit his house without field hands offering floral arrangements like courtiers waving petitions at their king. Nat was special, however. He couldn't write his name, but he orchestrated color like a Parisian painter.

The spring I was four going on five, after the camellias dropped their blossoms Nat was pruning them. Bonreve strode onto the balcony, rising from his and Mother's nap. Leaning on the rail, he spotted Nat. "Fine day, isn't it?"

"Yes, Master. Fine day." Nat made sure to tip his hat.

Bonreve thumped his chest with his open palms. "I never waste a fine day. When I smell a flower that is sweet, I pluck it. Do you ever pluck a sweet flower, Nat?"

Nat seemed nervous about the direction of the conversation. "Pluck 'em when you ask me to, Master."

"I wait for no one to ask *me*, Nat. Here I stand, in middling years, and took to wife a girl of just eighteen. A lesser man wouldn't know what to do with such a nymph, but not me. Tell me, Nat. Tell the truth. Am I not in my prime?"

Thin ice. You could see it in Nat's face. "Yes, Master," Nat called from his camellia bush. "That you are. In your prime."

Satisfied that even the gardener recognized his majesty, Bonreve strolled back inside. Only then, Nat muttered, "But how loud will you crow when she hits *her* prime?"

Though I only half-understood his implication, that half made me giggle. Nat flinched, realizing he wasn't alone, calibrating the danger. His face changed. Intellect faded, replaced by a countenance as placid as a yoked ox. The transition was so abrupt it made me shiver. I wanted those bright, intelligent eyes back. I needed a friend.

"I was thinking the same thing," I lied, tiptoeing over.

Nat remained guarded. "Don't mean you ought repeat it."

"I'll never tattle," I said, "not to Colonel Bonreve, not to anyone, not ever, I promise." I offered my hand.

"Master's son don't shake hands with yard nigras," Nat admonished, but then he gave me a wink. While I so much wanted to inquire whether the mismatched primes of Mother and the Colonel might pose her danger, I feared jeopardizing our fragile new friendship. I decided to ask the priest instead.

Though he lived at his rectory, Father Groetsch took many meals at Athena, I suspect haunting our halls less for the *bisque d'écrévisse* than for our Bluthner grand piano. At Mother's insistence, every evening I spent an hour at the bench with him. Although he ignored my questions regarding adults' primes, under his tutelage I did become something of a musical prodigy. By age five, I could whip out Mozart. The New Year's Eve when 1899 surrendered to 1900, performing Beethoven's "Appasionata" I bobbled not one note.

It was also that evening, as midnight chimed in the new Century of Progress, that I acquired my first mortal enemy.

Turpitude # 7

"Gluttony."

2nd of the Seven Deadly Sins

The morning began at the orchard. Boys from the Negro

Quarters whacked branches with bamboo staves. Late-season pecans dropped. I searched the grass like an Easter egg hunt and passed each nut I found to Nat. He'd squeeze them two at a time, *TOCK*, cracking their shells.

I climbed into the buggy with Mother. Giddyap! As we rode, I picked pecan meat and cached it in my handkerchief. Our destination: the sugarhouse, a sticky, noisy place full of large machinery and inbred cats tolerated to keep vermin in check. Since I'd nearly fallen into the crushers the year before, I was banned from the milling plant, but preferred the cavernous boiling room anyway with its whirring clarifiers and overpowering odor of molasses. There, cooked-down syrup was "struck" into raw brown sugar under the eyes of a chemist who reminded me of King Arthur's Merlin. Or maybe I just flattered him saying that so his hot molasses samples could join my morsels of pecan to cool into pralines.

Riding back, the two of us with our still-warm candy, Mother and I snuggled against the crisp breeze. In the fields, Negroes cutting sugarcane sang as they always did, their French a dense, barely understandable Creole. "Listen to them, Mother," I said. "Singing in the new century."

She smiled, at twenty-three even more fetching than she'd been when I was born. "Hear them?" I asked. "Think they're as happy as you and I?"

Her smile grew rueful. "They sing because they're forced to, the overseer makes them, because if they're singing they can't chew cane, raw cane, cane that's hard and fills your mouth with gritty pulp and is nowhere near as tasty as those pralines stuffed in your handkerchief, but cane is still the sweetest thing most of them ever taste, even the kids, kids like you, except they're not rich and don't have a handkerchief full of pralines like you and never will." My gaping mouth revealed half-chewed candy. "Not your fault so you might as well swallow," Mother went on, "though not eat too many more unless you want a bellyache to ruin tonight's party. Still, maybe you should think sometimes how those pickaninny kids have it rotten and you don't and how your mama offers up her pom-pom on a daily basis to see that you don't so cut her slack now and then, okay?"

We rode another two hundred yards before I had the nerve to finish chewing.

Awkward in groups, Colonel Bonreve rarely attended parties and, his wedding excepted, never threw them, but Mother convinced him that for something as momentous as a new century's beginning, it was his duty to host a celebration for neighboring planters, Thibodaux merchants, and any white employee he paid enough to afford a starched collar. With Judge Pike wedging onto the guest list his coterie of political aspirants, Athena grew crowded. A colored band from Donaldsonville set up on the balcony. People danced. When the band took a break, I ascended the piano. No one danced, but they were all impressed.

At the stroke of twelve, ignoring the expensive fireworks, everyone glued their lips to their escort's. Couples too old for such foolishness. Couples yet unmarried. Couples no one knew were couples! Children who'd dodged their bedtimes began aping the adults. I outran the nearsighted daughter of the Colonel's tailor, but Tante Elmire ambushed me with a hug reeking of rum and grenadine. I fought free and continued my mission. To inaugurate the new century, I wanted to kiss Mother, kiss her to seal our pact, that it was us, together, forever, no matter what the world threw at us. Hacking through creased trousers and ankle-length skirts I reached a clearing where a nightmare vision stopped me in my tracks.

Turpitude # 8

"The arrogant shall be punished."
Proverbs 16:5

The Colonel bludgeoned Mother's lips with his cruel mouth. Husband or not, century's end or not, as a substitute, a placeholder, oughtn't he have shown more restraint?

Fingers gripped my shoulder. "Your intentions?" asked Judge Pike.

"Knock off his head."

"My. Are you sure a headless spouse is what she wants?"

Was I? Mother put up no fight, but I knew why: she was singing in the sugarcane.

Like a lingering cough, the kiss persisted. After younger couples pulled apart, after older couples found seats, past any minimal decency. A drunken guest piped, "Here, here!" Other inebriants took it up.

The Judge tightened his grip. "Bending others to our will succeeds more readily when not undertaken in public."

"What's it to you?" I demanded. He didn't answer. The Colonel continued his vile assault. Escaping the Judge, I exploded forward, striking like a battering ram, crying, "Let my mama go, you poo-poo head!" (Remember I was only five-and-a-half.)

Host and hostess sprang apart, startled but undamaged. That might've ended it, except for all the planter's punch the crowd had swilled. Chuckles here, titters there, a trill by the mantle, a guffaw from the dessert table, hilarity engulfed the ballroom. Even servants laughed, everyone did, *except* me and the Colonel.

His face went crimson. Mother looked back and forth between us. Her smile faded.

"It seems one young man has enjoyed far too much excitement tonight," she announced, hustling me away before the Colonel could do me harm. At the door she handed me off to Antoinette, our chubbiest maid. "Get him to bed. If he tries to sneak back, you have my permission to spank him."

It felt like betrayal, but I understood it to be further proof of the pressure Mother was under. Changing into my nightshirt, from my bedroom window I watched buggy lamps wink as guests departed over the bumpy bayou road. In Mother's parable about singing in the sugarcane, Colonel Bonreve clearly represented the gritty pulp. The praline she could not have? Easy: my true father. What was I? The leaves of the cane, to be burned off at harvest-time? Or was Mother summoning Achille's son to mold himself more into a man like Achille?

How could I? I'd never met my father. Didn't know his ways. Mother was reluctant to speak of him, especially when the Colonel was nearby.

Bonreve had probably long detested me as a living reminder that he'd never be the man Achille Cheramie had been. Now I'd embarrassed him further, called him poo-poo head in front of everyone. A shamed ogre never forgives. Was I ready for lethal combat?

I decided to thereafter sleep with one eye open. It isn't easy to do.

Turpitude # 9

"Do not condemn the blameless."

Matthew 12:7

Shrove Tuesday, 1900, found me set upon by thugs I at first

believed were masked assassins. Watching from the balcony, the Colonel laughed. To my dismay, so did Mother. The two laughed together less with each passing week, so it was startling, particularly in such circumstances.

Turned out the assassins were actually youths from neighboring plantations. Bells bedecked their garish Mardi Gras costumes. Beating the ground with sticks — *tap tap, tap tap, tap tap* — they made me kneel to pray, issuing warnings of dire punishment if I missed a single word. I recited my prayers without flaw; declaimed the Gospel of Luke, abridged; and was well into Pope Pius IX's Canon of Papal Infallibility when the teens left to seek a less worthy adversary.

The Winds of Lent blustered through our forty days of penance. To throw off Bonreve, I maintained the rituals of childhood — playing games, begging toys, staging tantrums. Meanwhile, in the Big House library, Shakespeare provided a comprehensive primer on familial foul play. Since the bard's tragedies end, well, tragically, studying them increased my anxiety. Lilies bloomed; I couldn't see their beauty. Blackberries grew ripe yet held no sweetness. May came, then June. I felt no closer to being the reincarnation of Achille Cheramie. July 4th, 1900, I turned six. After months of constant vigilance, I felt sixty.

"Thank the Colonel," Mother prompted. She'd given me a dashing bowler hat. Now the Colonel presented his own birthday gift, a three-inch tall Napoleon Bonaparte to command my army of toy soldiers.

"Thank you, sir," I told him.

"Thank you, *Father*," he corrected. Technically, he was right. I'd been officially adopted. Judge Pike himself filed the papers.

"Thank you, *sir*," I repeated.

The two shared a look. "Say 'Father,'" Mother growled. I pressed my lips together to make it clear I'd utter nothing further. Not a battlefield Napoleon might've chosen, but how could I venerate Achille Cheramie if I let this usurper have his title?

The Colonel pried Napoleon from my fingers, dropped it in his pocket, and left the room. I expected Mother to share my outrage, but she seemed angry with *me*. "Do you know how hard it was to convince him to buy that for you?"

"How much could a three-inch general cost?"

"Ever heard of the Louisiana Purchase?" she asked.

"Everybody has." Then I saw maybe Mother hadn't, at least not until recently.

"Know who sold Louisiana? Napoleon. Your stepfather's ancestors lived here at the time. The family's still angry about it. The Colonel wanted to give you a King Louis number fourteen. It's whom he was named after."

"Louis the XIVth was no general. He just danced around Versailles."

Mother blew up. "What's it matter to either of you? The reason they're little chunks of lead is because they're long dead. There's a whole living world out there and I want the Colonel to show it to us. Why make that harder?" Her voice lowered to a hiss. "Am I asking such sacrifice, next to the sacrifices *I* make to see you wear fine clothes and get little French generals? If I do *my* duty day after day after day, is it too much for you to call the blowhard 'Father'?" She threw her arms wide, displaying her bloodless stigmata, mementoes of the day she conceived me.

After that I referred to Bonreve as "Father" whenever addressing him, admittedly seldom as possible. I never got Napoleon back. Whenever I broached with Mother what burdens the Colonel imposed on her that I might lighten them, she'd prattle about "the silliness of a woman's heart" and how I was "worth everything, even the worse parts that haven't happened yet." Knowing of Mother's second sight, I'd inquire what those "worse parts" were. She'd never say.

Turpitude # 10

"Be not amazed at this fatal gift
nor marvel at the horse's size;
hurl back this deceit, this suspect offering,
and beware of Greeks bearing gifts."
The Aeneid, Book II

Virgil's verses aren't usually considered religious instruction, but with Romans worshipping multitudinous gods, who can be sure? Certainly I should've heeded the warning.

That fall I broke an arm falling from a hayloft while conducting a scientific experiment, prompting Mother to decree my education would henceforth be supervised by professionals. The Colonel had carpenters erect a one-room schoolhouse behind the plantation store. I was its only student. Teachers never lasted long.

In 1901, Colonel Bonreve announced that on my 7th birthday he would give me a pony. Mother fretted I was too young and — remembering last autumn's broken arm — too fragile. The Colonel assured her he was riding, jumping, even shooting from horseback at my age, and that such manly activities "would make the boy more healthy and whole."

Contrary to pattern, I took his side. I would prove my mettle, master horsemanship, and teach the Colonel just how capable an opponent he was facing. Under the combined determination of both men in her life, Mother assented. I would have a pony.

Richard Bourque was a Cajun who grew up on a houseboat in the swamps behind the plantation. Through some fluke of endocrinology, among a family of eleven children, all robust six-footers, including the girls, "*Petit Richard*" topped out at a slender four foot ten, so at age seventeen he was plucked from the swamp and obscurity to become Athena's jockey. During a career illustrious but short, Bourque took to an adequate food supply as readily as he took to horses. Growing nearly as wide as he was tall, he showed such knack for training the thoroughbreds he could no longer profitably ride that he was appointed master of Athena's racing stable.

Bourque led my gift from the barn. A birthday indulgence, Nat assisted him instead of some swaggering groom. I gasped. The roan-colored coil of muscle was no "pony" at all but instead a spirited young thoroughbred. Danger oozed from his flanks. Evil glinted in his eye.

"His name is Marauder's Revenge," Bonreve announced.

"What a perfect name for a child's pet," I observed.

Mother's look was transparent: show your gratitude, show it profusely. I clung to her skirts. She nudged me away. I clung tighter. She crouched wearing a smile big enough for the Colonel, losing patience near the horse, to see, but her eyes were serious. "I tried to get you out of this," she whispered, "but you *had* to have a pony."

"That living, breathing tyranosaur is *NOT* a pony," I protested, my voice low as hers.

"Doesn't matter, because you wouldn't let me stop it, so now you have to go through with it because if my fears had kept you off the horse the Colonel would've been indulging a silly woman but if *your* fears keep you off it means his adopted son is a coward and that idea is poison to your future."

"*If* I have a future."

The son of Achille Cheramie was *not* a coward, however, so I finally let Bourque offer me up to the snorting beast. My butt found the saddle. With an encouraging nod, Nat handed me the reins. I waited for bat-like wings to unfold from Marauder's flanks or flames to billow from his nostrils.

"Start out walking him," Bonreve urged. I realized this was all a clever plot to kill me and make it look like an accident. Nevertheless I was unprepared when, a half-second later, without forewarning or preamble, Marauder bolted. Perhaps the Colonel goaded him with some sharp object. Maybe the horse in his long, bony head decided this was his last chance to avoid the humiliation of being a rich kiddie's pet. Either way, off he sprinted with me barely hanging on.

With the agility of a man half his age and a quarter his waistline, Bourque swung onto another horse stationed nearby. Unfortunately, hot pursuit convinced Marauder this was a race. He galloped faster. And faster. And faster! So fast he might've overheated if not for the cooling urine streaming down my legs. Somehow Bourque maneuvered ahead of us, reining in, blocking our path. Marauder's forward momentum stopped.

Mine did not. I sailed over Marauder's neck, over Bourque, over Bourque's mount, then over ditches and trees and acres of paddock, circling on updrafts like a turkey buzzard. I waved at Mother, far below. Landing I don't remember — perhaps that's best.

Turpitude # 11

"God does nothing without revealing his plans to his prophets."
Amos 3:7

Bonreve himself carried me to the Big House. A doctor was summoned. The quack poked, prodded, and forbade me sleep for hours, netting a considerable fee. He also prescribed an infusion to calm Mother which I saw her quietly dump into a potted canna lily.

By fall, Marauder — still officially my pony, though I refused to go anywhere near him — was deemed ready for competition.

His first start occurred at Raceland, a shaggy mile-long oval near the Bowie Sawmill. Neither Mother nor I wanted to go. She'd been headachy all morning. I feared I'd be substituted for the jockey. But Bonreve insisted.

As the horses lined up, Mother suffered a sinking spell. At first the Colonel thought she'd swooned because — dare he hope — she was with child, an event he deemed long overdue. It wasn't that.

"Something's wrong about Marauder," insisted flushed and sweaty Mother.

"Our son's horse? The horse I wagered on?"

"Change your bet, Louis. Marauder won't do well. He might even die."

"Good woman, you think yourself a better judge of horseflesh that Richard Bourque and I together?" He turned to me. "Is that what she thinks?"

"I know what I know," Mother said before I could rush to her defense. Colonel Bonreve had married Mother without knowing about her occasional clairvoyance and — perhaps *because* she could see the future — she never brought it up, nor did she explain it now.

"When we first married, you indulged my every whim," she pointed out.

"When we first married, I didn't realize you were quite so whimsical."

Hiding under the silk flowers of her hat, Mother said nothing more. The bet stood.

Turpitude # 12

"Husbands, treat your wives with understanding since they are more delicate than you."
1 Peter 3:7

An eighth-mile in, Marauder jammed a hoof into a muskrat hole. Horse and rider tumbled. Each broke a leg, interrupting the jockey's career while definitively ending Marauder's, who was put down with the starter's pistol. Barely had the shot gone off before the Colonel began plaguing Mother with questions that saw no surcease in the hired carriage back to Bowie Depot, during which Mother meticulously studied a loose thread in her sleeve. Nor on the smoky train to Schriever Station, while Mother picked at the errant thread until cloth began to unravel. Nor in the Colonel's grand two-horse landau, in which before it reached Athena, Mother dismantled her entire cuff. I pretended to sleep.

The Colonel viewed Mother's gift as a resource to exploit, like a salt lick or stand of timber, but her second sight didn't perform on command, let alone his command. As time passed, when she couldn't predict fluctuations in sugar prices, the sucrose percentage of any given field, or the onset of the next financial panic, he deemed her foresight useless, loudly.

Mother deemed *him* useless, more loudly.

He expounded that mystical visions were the domain of superstitious European peasants.

She expounded that she could hardly know that since he'd never taken her to Paris and Vienna as he'd promised numerous times.

He opined she was an hysterical woman.

She opined he was a close-minded blockhead.

He announced he'd heard enough from her on the subject.

She announced she'd heard enough from him on *any* subject and boycotted their naps. Forgetting she ever learned English, her French reacquired the backwater accent of her youth, stretching vowels till they lay flat, letting *j*'s become *h*'s like they do along the coast. House servants grew even better at receding into the wallpaper. After the Colonel asked Father Groetsch if he'd ever performed an exorcism, the priest found excuses to skip my piano lessons.

This open warfare was not only making her miserable, I feared it also put her in danger. In his every idle moment the Colonel plotted against me. That was well established. If this bickering kept up though, sooner or later he'd plot against Mother too. Thus I embarked on a perilous strategy to offer myself as sacrificial lamb. To deflect his wrath from Mother, I would intentionally prod the dragon to draw his fury upon myself.

Turpitude # 13

"The eye that mocks the father
shall be plucked by ravens
and eaten by vultures."

Proverbs 30:17

Considering the man hated me, getting under his skin proved surprisingly difficult. When I rearranged his desk, a piece of furniture I was forbidden to approach, he simply put each inkwell and letter-spike back in place. When I left toys in his path, another grave sin, he silently stepped around them.

When I repeated every word he'd say, sentence after sentence, he'd ignore me until I grew too bored to keep it up.

I traded "Father" for "Mister," even "Master" uttered with a sneer. Master hardly noticed. When Judge Pike's laughter alerted my nemesis that I'd pinned to his backside a note reading, "Forgive my flatulence," it earned only a mildly ominous "I'll deal with you later."

Whether because of my efforts or in spite of them, the Colonel's posture toward Mother eventually softened. Mother remained insolent. Sleeping on the balcony. Taking lunch before he rode in from the fields. At Sunday mass, handing Father Groetsch "a box for the poor" full of trinkets Bonreve had bought her.

One morning, the Colonel off grafting citrus, I found Mother inventorying crepe flowers and silver bijous. She dangled a fanciful Christmas stocking. "Shall we hang this one come the holidays?" Her attempt at cheeriness failed so dismally I was too stunned to answer. Her finger traced the stocking's Alpine mountains. "I thought a husband like him would be your key to the world," she said, "but have you seen any Seven Wonders? Have we been to London and Vienna? It takes a crowbar to get him off the plantation, and when he does travel, he'd never dream of taking us along."

Having her complain of him to me was something new, new and worrisome. "What happened to singing in the sugarcane?" I asked.

"A woman tires of the same old song."

Turpitude # 14

"Put not thy hand with the wicked man's."

Exodus 23:1

The Colonel grew more miserable. I wouldn't have minded except Mother did too. One afternoon as I hid from the acrimony under the front steps, he came down to mount his horse. Thinking himself alone, he laid his forehead against the creature's neck and just stood there. He looked so forlorn that, though he hated me, I pitied him.

I reasoned that if I could patch things between them, Mother might be happier — certainly safer. We might travel the way she so desperately wanted. On such an excursion Bonreve might well toss me off a moving train, but the priority had to be Mother's well-being, not mine.

"She likes pretty dresses," I called out.

Startled, the Colonel spotted me, but his eyes drifted away before he spoke. "She does, doesn't she?"

Thus it was, Christmas '01, Colonel Bonreve presented Mother the latest gown from Paris, daringly form-fitting with high waist and low neckline. Mother looked lovely in the embroidered violet tulle, but as soon as he admired her reflection in the cheval mirror, she declared the outfit too cumbersome to get into.

To eliminate that inconvenience, the Colonel budgeted an additional maid to help Mother dress. To the girl — a fair-skinned octoroon named Melpa, fifteen years old and quite pretty despite a chipped front tooth — Mother gave the just-bought Paris gown. Afraid to be the black pawn in a white dispute, Melpa squirmed when Mother had her try it on. When the Colonel walked in, he looked like a boiler popping its rivets.

"It was my idea!" I lied.

"Out," he shouted. I was determined to stand up to him, I was, but when Melpa scooted I found myself following. The door slammed behind us. I felt like a coward.

"He won't hurt her," Melpa assured me. "A man crazy in love never hurts the girl tickling his heart." She almost convinced me and at the time probably believed it herself. Melpa slapped my shoulder. "Tag, you're it!" I gave chase down the back steps, *thump, thump, thump*, till I hit the walk where Melpa had already stopped.

From his horse Judge Pike froze me with a raised eyebrow. "I need to talk to the boy." Melpa dipped a curtsey and bolted. "That dusky nymph is whom your stepfather hired?" asked the Judge as the Paris gown disappeared into the cookhouse.

"Mother chose her," I said. "The Colonel complained Melpa lacked decorum." Which was true, but I liked Melpa anyway.

"A maid that pretty is rarely the mistress' choice," said the Judge. "I suppose your Mother has her reasons."

"Mother always has her reasons."

"Mm. Tell me, young man, what favor could Colonel Bonreve do *for you*?"

"Me?"

"Something big, big enough to make you burst with joy."

I weighed my answer, knowing the Judge usually wheedled anything he wanted out of Colonel Bonreve. "For him to go away and leave Athena to Mother and me."

The Judge erupted with laughter. "Your ambition's impressive, but be gracious if he offers a bauble a bit less grand."

It took weeks to unravel the conspiracy I'd just joined. Since an estranged spouse meant an unhappy, tight-fisted Bonreve, the Judge also sought to reconcile Mother and the Colonel. His scheme to do so would wind and circle and double back from that afternoon's brief conversation until it led to the precipitous events climaxing on my 8th birthday.

Turpitude # 15

"A man wearing women's clothing is an abomination."

Deuteronomy 22:5

One day the Colonel and the Judge rode by as I reenacted the Battle of the *Monitor* and *Merrimac* in a puddle near the herb garden. A magnolia leaf represented the Confederate ironclad, while a laurel twig served as the Union ship. *Boom*, *boom*, I imitated canon. Since I had an audience, I added the shrieks of dying sailors.

The Judge said, "If you had someone carve proper replicas, with detailed paint and moving parts, the gift would warm the boy's heart and thus perhaps melt his mother's."

At the time the Colonel only grunted, but that evening he wildly outdid the Judge's suggestion by announcing he was ordering me a full-size pirogue. Remembering the Judge's admonition to be grateful, I cried, "You mean it, Father?" and hugged him, laying it on thick, surprising Mother and flustering Bonreve.

Several part-time pirogue-makers lived in the area, but the Colonel sent all the way to Leeville for the boatwright, Léon Dantin, survivor of Chenière. I suspect the choice was another ploy to earn Mother's favor. When she walked to the bayou to greet Léon, she found his hair white and body wizened. Apart from him confiding that nowadays he seldom picked up his fiddle and even more rarely the bottle, they didn't say much. Their worlds were different now, and their shared past too painful to talk about.

Léon's daughter, Tellia, shared none of her father's melancholy. Deeming me a great improvement on the cypress-root dolls Léon carved her, Tellia undertook to dress me in his clothes, her clothes, Mother's clothes. I didn't object. To a boy not quite eight, a girl of eleven seems infinitely wise. Besides, Tellia told stories, grand stories. Sweeping her arms and flouncing her hair, she'd speak in whispers and roars and sing-song about the dog-man Jerome Chabert and the secretly-Negro miser-woman Victorine. Best were her stories about the famous storm that blew apart chicken coops; and its hero, valiant Zeph, a Sinbad with a Cajun accent.

One day as Tellia buttoned me into the infamous Paris gown, I coaxed her into talking about my father. "Your daddy wasn't no chickenshit, but he wasn't brave as Zeph. Far as I know, he didn't save nobody. Except he did help a man named Touloulou climb a tree."

I welcomed Mother's interruption, embarrassing though it was with me wearing a skirt. When I asked her to deny Tellia's slanders, Mother began to sniffle. Tellia slipped from the room. "You're sad because you remember how heroic he was," I said.

"Probably," Mother agreed unpersuasively. "Tricks of mind, I don't know. I worry about you because you're so, well, like you are."

Unsettled by her ambiguity, I clutched her legs, wrinkling the ribbed silk skirts we both wore. "You mean, how I'm like Achille?" My lip quivered and though I tried to hide it, Mother noticed. She pulled me closer.

"Your mama's what I am every morning, what I am every night. What's it to either of us what sort of man your papa was? You're you, he's gone, you'll never stand side by side. Measuring today against yesterday never makes anybody happy. Memory grinds the edges off yesterday till it shines like a jewel, though it wasn't a jewel, maybe not even shiny. If I weren't a foolish woman, maybe the ghosts would let me find contentment and the living not bedevil me."

Turpitude # 16

"Envy makes bones rot."

Proverbs 14:30

I watched Léon Dantin whack his adze, hollowing the log, shaping the pirogue. I imagined myself that rich boy turned fishermen in the Kipling serial I'd read in *McClure's*; a Captain Courageous, just like my father. As befits a brave sailor, I showed increasing impatience with Tellia draping me in pleated skirts. When my first baby teeth fell, I took it as sign I was leaving childhood behind and resolved to fight evil, do good, and only buy grown-up things with the money the tooth mouse left under my pillow.

The eve of my birthday, two men arrived. Philo Leboeuf's right arm ended at the elbow, while his buck teeth seemed to mock the recent gap in my own. His handsome brother, in his early twenties, introduced himself as Zeph, the same Zeph who, per Tellia, represented the true hero of the Chenière hurricane. My playmate leapt into his arms to recount her adventures since she'd seen him last, tales in which I felt owed a more dramatic role. Of all the founts of envy — wealth in other hands, power you do not share, etc. — the most insidious is beauty directed toward another. Though no Helen of Troy, Tellia was impishly cute and the first girl near my age to pay me any sustained attention.

On their skiff, the Leboeuf brothers had brought several bushels of live blue crabs. To boil them, the Colonel gave leave to rob the cordwood stacked on the levee for sale to passing steamboats. With easy authority, Zeph bid me help his brother haul some. It marked the first time this stepchild of privilege had been asked to do a manual chore. I jumped at the chance, though it meant working alongside the surly amputee.

Philo loaded my arms. "Watch for coral snakes hiding on the logs," he said. "They bite you dead." I eyeballed every chunk of wood. Philo moved onto other perils. "This seems territory for a *rougarou.* They eat little boys: breakfast, dinner, supper." I loathed him for trying to scare me, loathed myself for being scared. "Course, near to water, watch closest for that sea-witch what followed us here. You see her, run." With my burden of cordwood, no way could I run, and Philo knew it.

"Not a witch, a *sirène*, a mermaid," Zeph explained after I tattled on Philo. "Every oysterman down the bayou sees her now and again. She doesn't eat anybody."

"I wasn't afraid," I lied.

Zeph clapped me on the back. "That's 'cause you got the blood of Achille Cheramie."

"Tellia said he wasn't a hero like you."

"Shame on her! Achille Cheramie was the biggest hero there ever was. Help me cook these crabs and I'll tell you 'bout some great big things he did, things I saw with my own eyes."

As I helped carry cistern water, I heard how my father had a back so strong he could out-pull an ox, arms so strong he could out-swim a tarpon, a bite so strong he could out-snap a snapping turtle. When logs needed splitting, Zeph taught me how to use the ax: "Lift it high, aim it straight, let its weight do the work. That's how your daddy showed me."

Apparently mermaids fell for Father all the time, but he'd spurn them because he loved Mother. I learned how my papa could convince shrimp to leap out of the water right into his bushel, just by smooth-talking. "And sing? Ho! A voice so sweet mockingbirds would hang their little heads, saying, 'Prize is yours, Achille. We can't beat that.'"

"I'm musical myself," I said.

"See? In the blood." As we dropped blue-green crabs into the bubbling cauldron they turned orange, and I heard how one winter, with everyone starving, Achille shot the last bullet in all the village so accurately it went through a deer's left ear, killed it painlessly, continued out the right ear, and brought down three Canada geese flying by.

Wonderful to know one's father was a hero, but terrible too. As Zeph told these stories, dancing with the firelight across the blackness of his pupils I saw Achille, a yardstick against which to measure myself. I wasn't as strong or as brave. Wasn't as tall, nor showing signs I'd grow to Achille's stature. Not as quick, nor agile, nor as generous of spirit. And Mother knew it.

Turpitude # 17

"Women should dress modestly."

1 Timothy 2:9

Judge Pike arrived from Thibodaux, Father Groetsch from St. Catherine's. A few privileged servants settled themselves on a blanket off to the side, the closest thing to a meal shared with Master I'd ever seen. Melpa joined them, red, white, and blue ribbons tied in her hair, which Nat shyly admired. I guess Melpa saw the question in my face because she offered, "Your mama said she'd dress herself."

"We'll wait," the Colonel announced.

He and the Judge discussed politics. Father Groetsch arranged a bib to protect his cassock. Servants gossiped. Tellia and I helped Zeph scoop the first batch of crabs, then the second. Still we waited for Mother.

Gasps from the Negroes announced her arrival. Colonel Bonreve couldn't have appeared more startled if the *sirène* had crawled ashore. Mother wore the same worn-out shift that hung on Melpa the day the girl arrived. Without the pigeon-breasted, hourglass shape a corset gives a figure, Mother looked like a different woman. Less civilized. Almost wanton. A *sirène* herself.

Turpitude # 18

"Whoever knows the thing to do and does not do it, sins."
James 4:17

"This is a lot like what I wore last time I enjoyed a crab boil," Mother said.

The Colonel oozed disapproval. The Judge looked away. Yet, as we feasted, everyone relaxed. With laughter, those born on the coast taught those reared in plantation country how to eat a crab without being covered in its juices. Mother's old clothes proved judicious; Groetsch's bib, insufficient. Nat cracked claws for Melpa.

Our bellies full, Tellia fetched her father's fiddle. After raucous encouragement he accepted the instrument and eyed the one person who'd not cheered him on.

"What song, Madame?"

"You know," Mother answered.

Léon began *The Waltz of Unending Love.* Mother hummed along, quietly at first, then louder and louder until everyone watched her. As she rose to dance, I walked over to join in. She ignored me. Next the Colonel tried to take her in his arms. She brushed him aside too, swirling in her threadbare beauty, dancing with the ghost only she could see. With the music of her old life filling the air, her first husband haunting the glimmer and her second frowning from the shadows, how could she not compare them? How could Bonreve, for all his wealth, not be found lacking? And what about me?

When the melody surrendered to the last crackles of the cookfire, Mother appeared surprised to find her arms empty. Without even a nod, she left the shrinking ring of firelight for the darkness of the oaks.

Colonel Bonreve looked around the circle. Only Judge Pike would meet his eye. "Perhaps *I* could help her see past whatever troubles her," said the Judge.

"Good luck," replied the Colonel.

I knew Pike would never make that offer without some secret agenda. Mother was in a strange mood; maybe, as Nat once predicted, she'd reached *her* prime. She should have a chaperone, but Tante Elmire lay asleep in bed, the Colonel sat nursing his pique, and no servant would dream of navigating such treacherous waters. It was up to me. Yet if the Judge said we were allies, fighting on the same side to reconcile the couple and thus insure Mother's safety, wouldn't I be a fool to complicate his efforts?

Easy to believe what you want to even when your gut squeaks, "No, no, don't swallow that horse-do." Inside I knew the Judge to be a scoundrel and Mother unhappy thus fragile, rendering their murky rendezvous so perilous it made sea-witches seem like cocahoe minnows.

But I didn't budge. Fortunes would fall and people would die because of it.

After ten minutes, Mother returned. To the Colonel's surprise she sat next to him. His perch an anvil the plantation blacksmith had loaned to Léon, the Colonel had to scoot onto its horn to give Mother room. She wove her arm through his, found his hand, entwined his fingers. Though the Colonel tried to maintain the decorum he so prized, he couldn't hide his grin.

I wondered what the Judge had said to cause this change in Mother. When he returned moments later, he stood beside the dying embers though the night was warm. His somber gaze avoided the reunited couple. Pretending to watch Léon play, Judge Pike tap-tap-tapped his finger against his lips, keeping time to his own secret rhythm.

That night, Mother didn't sleep on the balcony.

The next morning, my birthday, Tellia was anxious to set off so they could stop at the big 4th of July Fireman's Picnic in Thibodaux. Along the tow path Philo yanked the bridle of the mule hired to pull their boat. Zeph maneuvered a pole to prevent them snagging the bank. Léon bowed his fiddle, fingering no melody, merely whining ripostes to the mockingbirds carping from the overhanging trees. Tellia waved goodbye but shed no tears. I hid mine.

Neither Mother nor the Colonel rose early. After lunch, over birthday cake, Colonel Bonreve announced that he'd himself teach me mastery of the pirogue, although I'd never seen him in any small craft not rowed by someone else. He addressed Mother with mock seriousness. "You, Madame, shall not attend. The boy has suffered too many feminine influences. Time he becomes a man, or at least, dresses like one." I thought that meant a spy had informed him about my dress-up games with Tellia but perhaps not because he then presented me with one last gift: a pair of ankle-length trousers. Eight is young, some would say, to give up the knee-pants of childhood. I hurried to put them on before he could change his mind.

As we walked to the bayou, I felt a knot growing in my stomach. If the pirogue capsized, swimming would be harder in trousers than knee-pants. Colonel Bonreve may have reconciled with Mother, but why should I think he hated *me* less? My chest began to heave, but my worry was misplaced. The Colonel did *not* plan to drown me. He meant to see me eaten alive.

Turpitude # 19

"To battle the beast,
be like the beast."

Revelation 13:4

Sitting on the grass, the Colonel demonstrated paddling technique. I prolonged the exercise as long as I could, misunderstanding the simplest instructions, a tactic I'd seen Negroes employ when assigned an unpleasant chore. The Colonel's evil designs lent him infinite patience. Eventually we launched. I set out like brave Ulysses, dipping paddle as Bonreve had explained. The pirogue shot across the bayou like a water bug. Not bad!

I tried another maneuver, twisting my wrist like he'd shown. The pirogue spun a tight circle. "Well done!" the Colonel exclaimed.

Succumbing to his flattery, for just a moment I felt capable. Competent. In control.

Then came a bump. Water sloshed into the pirogue. Already-scant freeboard shrank by an inch. Another bump. More water. I looked for what was knocking my boat.

On Louisiana's bayous by 1902, after a century of trade in their hides, alligators had grown rare. Rarity offers slim solace, however, when one confronts a large, energetic specimen. The greatest 'gators grow to eighteen feet. This fellow only came to thirteen and a half, about as long as my pirogue, which he then bumped a third time. *Kerplosh*, I fell into the water.

"Don't be afraid," the Colonel hollered as I stared into yellow teeth each big as my thumb. I jabbed my paddle at the monster. The 'gator snapped it like a toothpick. I tried to scream. Bayou water poured down my gullet. The Colonel didn't shout, nor produce a weapon, nor heroically dive in to save me. Instead, he held out a feeble branch. "Catch hold, I'll pull you ashore," he said. "Catch hold or you'll be eaten, but no one should hold me responsible." Well, perhaps those weren't his *exact* words. Truth is, I might've risked doing what he advised, but the 'gator, *CRUNCH*, snapped the Colonel's branch as easily as it had my paddle.

What, I wondered, would Achille Cheramie do in such a situation?

Having read that an alligator's powerful jaws are entirely designed toward closing, not opening, I changed my tactics and swam *toward* the beast. Throwing my arms around his snout, I hugged it as fervently as I'd previously only hugged Mother. The 'gator swung his head to throw me off. My eight-year-old body flew loose, landing on his back astride him. It was difficult to determine who was most surprised. Me? The alligator? The Colonel? Or Nat, who having heard the commotion had come running.

Alligators don't present much by way of ears, but larger ones tend toward jowly, so to hold on I pinched the creature's fat cheeks. Forget carnival rides at Spanish Fort in New Orleans. Forget the Chicago World's Fair. For sheer thrill nothing beats trick-riding a gigantic reptile as he spins round and round like a sideways top, as desperate to throw you as you are to hang on.

The bayou being shallow there, the 'gator couldn't go deep. At the highest point of our arc my face would splash above water just long enough to inhale precious air. During one such breath I noticed my pirogue coming toward me. From its stern paddled Nat. In the bow, flourishing the stub of that silly branch, Colonel Bonreve.

Rotating underwater again, my head swiped the bottom. Greasy clay shampooed my hair and temporarily blinded me. Thus I didn't notice a catfish approaching to see what the ruckus was. Opening my mouth to be ready to direct my rescuers when I broke surface, to my astonishment (no doubt the catfish's as well) I caught him in my teeth. Leaving water for air, I could holler no instructions with a wiggling fish in my mouth. Then I was again underwater.

When I next came up, I slammed into the Bonreve's branch. My jaw clamped shut, else the catfish would've gone flying. The Colonel and Nat whisked me aboard the pirogue. My weight added to theirs sank it, leaving us each exposed to attack but I the most bite-sized.

Turpitude # 20

"God warned the serpent,
'I will put rancor betwixt
thee and the woman.'"

Genesis 3:14-15

At this precipitous moment there arrived a sizable garfish, a nude, buxom teen-age girl, or some combination of the two. She walloped the alligator's jaw, stopping him cold. Nat, the Colonel, and I made for the bank with all due haste.

"Did you see what blocked the 'gator?" I asked once ashore.

"No," the Colonel said too quickly.

"Not me," echoed Nat. He wouldn't meet my eye.

Their fear of sounding foolish notwithstanding, we'd been saved by a mermaid, no doubt the same *sirène* that followed the Leboeuf brothers inland. Why had she helped me? My hypothesis — I realize, in retrospect, this may sound farfetched — was that the mermaid was none other than dear old Calypso, my lovely rival sperm in the race up the birth canal. After I'd creased her tail conception day, she must've hobbled out of Mother's womb by the same portal we entered it and, once in the sea, by some devious manner transformed herself into a mermaid. (She'd always been clever.) Now she'd returned to show there were no hard feelings.

I kept this theory to myself.

Soaked to the skin, we trudged home. I gave Nat my catfish as thanks for saving my life. "Wasn't nothing," he mumbled, but I knew he appreciated such a fine fish for his July 4th dinner. I saw the Colonel waiting to be thanked as well. He could wait till the oceans froze.

At the Big House, Colonel Bonreve told the tale. It chafed not to contradict his many self-serving embellishments and fabrications. When he went to change, I said, "Mother, may I tell you what really happened?"

Turpitude # 21

"Woe to lawyers who saddle folk with grievous burdens."

Luke 11:46

"There *was* a 'gator?"

"Which the fiend you married tried to feed me to."

"You mean the same goof who just dripped all over this rug?"

"He wanted to murder me. Like before."

"Before?"

"I've detected a pattern."

"If you mean getting thrown by that poor horse your last birthday—"

"Not just that. Remember that Christmas at the mill, when he tried to grind me up with a wagonload of cane."

"You fell onto the crushers because you were loopsy-doopsy," she accused, "because you'd eaten half the candied bourbon balls Judge Pike gave Tante Elmire for Christmas."

"So why'd the Colonel take a drunk four-year-old to a sugar mill?"

"Merciful Lord, how have I offended Thee?" Mother muttered as she started upstairs.

I caught her skirt. "My broken arm."

She pulled my long-healed arm loose from her silk taffeta. "Here's what I remember: each mealtime for a month, you chattered how every mechanic in the country was trying to build a flying machine and wouldn't it be wonderful if it happened at Athena first; then one day you claimed to have invented the perfect design."

"I wanted the Colonel to pay for it, not take over. Give his money then stand back, like he does with Judge Pike."

"Judge Pike's ventures never let the Colonel boast he's advancing science while strapping on silly wings and leaping out of a hayloft. He jumped several times before he let you. He could've missed the pile of straw as easily as you did."

"But he didn't, did he?"

"Don't repeat these accusations, not to anyone, you hear? *Do you hear?*" I withered before her reprimand. "I should see if he feels like a nap. If there was an alligator, he must be rewarded, else next time he might not save your little butt." She disappeared upstairs. Clearly the time was not right to mention the mermaid.

Putting on dry clothes, I went outside just as Judge Pike rode up, not as usual from the levee road but instead through the fields.

"I thought you and your stepfather would be at the bayou trying your birthday present," he said.

"Then why didn't you go there?"

Turpitude # 22

"Thou shalt not covet thy neighbor's wife."

The 9th Commandment

...because he was calling on Mother, not the Colonel. Judge Pike had ridden the back way to avoid being seen. Lately I'd discovered certain novels shelved so high it took the library ladder to reach them. Flaubert. Zola. Some Russians. Page after page of affairs and assignations. Their stories seldom ended happily.

The Judge's quarterhorse swished its tail, awaiting instructions. "They're napping," I said. Pike's gaze drifted to the balcony where through shuttered jalousie windows, in an heirloom walnut four-poster, lay the couple he'd reunited. We both heard a prolonged moan that could have only come from Mother.

"A nightmare," I explained.

"Indeed." Clicking his spurs, he turned his horse. This time he took the levee road.

The next day we heard Judge Pike had been called to New Orleans on urgent business and might be gone indefinitely. Mother took the news with a smile as indecipherable as Mona Lisa's.

After what came to be called "the birthday incident," the Colonel sallied out every afternoon to kill the rogue 'gator, or so he claimed. Realizing he actually meant to become the first planter in the South with a taxidermied mermaid on his wall, I often climbed the levee to warn the *sirène* who'd saved me, but never found her. Neither did Bonreve. His final safari ended with a parade of field hands lugging back a huge, reptilian carcass, the very alligator I had fought. Its hide was tanned then fashioned into a pistol case for the Colonel, a jewelry box for Mother, a belt for me. I also received a pair of its huge teeth, intended as mockery, no doubt, of my own then-missing incisors. If the Colonel could slay giant alligators, what chance did a toothless child have?

Turpitude # 23

"Praise not thyself
while disparaging others."

7th of the Ten Essential
Precepts of Buddhism

With my demise imminent, using my penknife I began etching into a live oak a testament fingering Bonreve, warning Mother, and bequeathing my playthings. Carving letters into tree bark is not as easy as novels make it sound. I'd managed only "Dear Mo" when I sensed someone behind me. Nat frowned at my mutilation of the ancient tree.

Embarrassed, I folded up the knife. Tears were close. "Nobody cares if I live or die."

"Ain't true."

"You, too. You'd like it if I was murdered. You'd get to cut flowers for my funeral." My tears began falling as hard as an April downpour.

In sight of the Big House, Nat took great risk kneeling and spreading his arms to let me enter their shelter. As I wept, nuzzling my cheek against the comforting bristle of his chest hair, my nose encountered a small, smelly pouch. "What's this, Nat?"

"Nothing."
"Then why are you wearing it?"
"No reason."
"Where'd you get it?"
"Nowhere a white boy ought go."

Turpitude # 24

"Let even angels who preach heresy be cursed."
Galatians 1:8

The red flannel pouch bore no Christian icon. I'd read about Buddhism and Zoroastrianism and various other isms, but this rang no bell there either. "Does it protect you like a St. Joseph scapular would?"

I guess I sounded pretty plaintive. Nat looked left then right, making sure we were unobserved. Lifting off the talisman, he draped it around my neck, tucking it inside my shirt. "*Gris-gris* be powerful protection, 'less any soul see you got it, which case you get a whipping. If Cap'n hear I give it, I get a worse whipping, so hide it good."

"What'll *you* do for protection?"

"A colored man learns to get by."

Grateful as I was, I noticed the obvious protuberance on the front of my shirt. "I'm not sure how well I can hide it."

Nat frowned. "Try down your pants."

I tucked it into the front of my trousers. "Sticks out there, too."

"But folks be less likely to mention it."

Days passed. I perceived no new murder attempts. The only

one to acknowledge the lump created by my *gris-gris* was Melpa. Since helping Mother dress took only a portion of her day, Melpa performed additional duties, always with cheerful industry. Ever a student of science, I'd lately grown interested in anatomy. Particularly fascinating were the gluteal muscles as they flexed and constricted in the course of human locomotion. Sweeping feather duster over mantel and chair, lithe Melpa had magnificent gluteals.

"Can't say I'm not flattered," she said, shifting her gaze to the bulge of the mojo in my pants, "especially you such a young fellow. But Jack and Jill ain't going up that hill. Humpty Dumpty won't trip that fall. For sure lose any notions of the weasel going pop."

Though familiar with all the relevant rhymes I had no idea what she'd just refused me, but if she referenced Mother Goose, so could I. "Melpa, as regards hickory, dickory, and dock, what'd be the harm if the mouse ran up the clock?"

Her hand flew to her mouth, hiding the chipped front tooth that alone marred her perfect looks. "Wicked boy!" she cackled with no hint of disapproval. New to this pond, I'd hooked a trout my first cast.

"So," I said, "will hi, ho, the derry-o, the farmer take a wife?"

Another guffaw, so loud I worried someone might investigate. As her laughter subsided she once more shook her head. "Won't happen."

"Why not?" I demanded, though I still had no clue what would or wouldn't occur.

"Won't happen," she repeated. "You know why."

Whatever the subject of our conversation, we'd referred to it via nursery rhymes. Nursery rhymes associate with childhood. Ergo… "I'm too young?"

She glanced at my crotch again. "Truly don't seem *too* young. What you be is too white." Scarcely a shade lighter than her, but I knew she meant white in the racial sense. A giant barrier existed between us. "When brown takes to straw with white," she said, her smile gone, "brown suffers, every time."

"Takes to straw?" I asked.

"Won't happen," she intoned yet again as if reciting some poem by Edgar Allen Poe. Then she left with the parlor half-dusted, left with her flawless seventeen-year-old, café-au-lait skin; her oddly attractive chipped tooth; and her sculpted gluteal musculature.

A couple of weeks later, Nat mentioned I might as well throw the mojo into the bayou since its potency would've faded by then. He claimed to have no idea where to find a fresh one. I once more stood undefended.

Turpitude # 25

"Deviousness entangles the wicked in his own sin."
Proverbs 5:22

Plotting my demise was but one of many tasks occupying the Colonel's days. He had a plantation to run. Labor problems were chronic, which most planters boiled down as "darkies forgetting their place." Tumultuous debt markets perversely contradicted the Colonel's "reasonable, absolutely reasonable" but nonetheless substantial credit needs. And even grand Athena endured the troubles assailing every farmer since the first Sumerian sowed barley to brew beer: not enough rain, rain at the wrong time, too much rain.

In '03, as winter ended, too-much-rain aggravated a heavy snow melt up north. The Weather Service predicted flooding throughout the Mississippi Valley, including Bayou Lafourche. Levees were inspected, weak spots shored, sandbags stockpiled. By February, armed guards materialized. Ostensibly their job was to look for "boils" where water bubbling from a crawfish tunnel or muskrat den demanded immediate action. One doesn't shoot a crawfish with a rifle, however, nor load heavy deershot to kill a three-pound muskrat. If these mercenaries fired, they'd be shooting at people. The threat no one spoke of but everyone feared was sabotage.

Any levee break would flood plantations for miles up and downstream, but only on the side of the bayou where the break occurred. By releasing surplus water, a crevasse would relieve the pressure on the opposite bank's levee. Thus, if the left bank levee broke first, the right bank would be spared, and vice versa. When you couple these principles of hydrology to the frailties of human nature, and consider it took surprisingly little effort to start a crevasse, it's easy to understand why in times of flood a bullet might await anyone spotted with a shovel where he had no business being.

That year, Mardi Gras fell on February 24th. As a former "King Sucrose," Colonel Bonreve rode as marshal in the Thibodaux parade. Mother and I joined the crowd along Second Street to watch the torch-lit procession. Despite the lovely costumes, everyone mostly talked about the rising water.

We watched an Oriental-themed float go by. The horses pulling it were painted like zebras, drawing scattered applause. A stranger stepped up beside Mother, standing close, looking at her boldly. She stared at him as if something were familiar, but in the darkness she didn't recognize him and neither did I.

"Has it been that long?" he asked.

Judge Pike! It'd been nearly nine months actually. Stylish in a blue blazer and cuffed trousers, his face was different, his beard gone, his mustache curled at the ends. "You've grown lovelier," he told Mother.

"Well, you're still not handsome," she teased, "despite waxing your mustache. But your clothes are nice. Fashion suits you."

"You're making fun of me."

"I bet New Orleans society has been throwing their

daughters at you." A band marched by. To hear over the trombones, Mother and the Judge took turns putting their lips to the other's ear. On their faces I watched the come and go of smiles and wistfulness. The band passed, its music receding. When the dancing torches of a troop of Negro flambeaux-carriers took the couple out of shadow, Mother and the Judge stepped apart. Her hand found my shoulder. "You read books. What should our friend do to win some debutante's heart?"

"In novels, it's usually something grand and romantic," I said.

Mother fixed him with a look. "There you go. I spy Mrs. White. I should say hello. Nice to see you again, August."

Pike's eyes followed her until she disappeared into the crowd. I hurried to follow her.

Turpitude # 26

"Fountains broke and Heaven's floodgates opened."

Genesis 7:11

While not a turpitude per se, that verse was so oft-quoted during those anxious days I felt I ought to count it among the sixty-nine.

The bayou kept rising. One day I found Mother in the low-ceilinged, ground-level storage area. A herringbone pattern of orange bricks stretched empty wall to wall, no crocks, no crates, no barrels. Hooks hung bare that usually held hams in muslin sheaths, brown from the smokehouse. Mother's eyes combed as if some clothes-wringer or butter churn might suddenly reappear. "What are you doing?" I asked.

"Wondering what I forgot that Victorine Guidry would've thought of."

Tellia had mentioned this Victorine person. Like much about her Chenière life, Mother never had. Before I could encourage further reminisces, she left to organize the evacuation of crocked meats from the cookhouse.

In the wee hours Sunday, March 22nd, frightened voices woke me. Stumbling onto the balcony, I heard a steady roar in the distance and saw the Colonel galloping toward the bayou. If the levee had broken, upstairs in the Big House was the safest place to be, yet in nothing but my nightshirt I hurried down the back stairs and up the alley of oaks. I kept expecting my bare feet to find mud, splash water. Would a bayou Niagara dump alligators into our yard? A mermaid?

At the levee crest, astride his prancing thoroughbred, Colonel Bonreve looked like some mythological creature himself. The noise was louder here, but I saw no raging torrent. Crouching low, I stole over the slope to hide myself in the canebrake beside the stream.

Across the bayou, water sluiced onto Waverly Plantation through the top of the opposite bank's levee. Men tried to fill the crack, the white planter sweating beside field hands, but no sooner did a shovelful of soil fall than it washed away. Sandbags became like stones in a brook as current swirled around them. Shouting men had to step backward again and again to retreat from the widening cascade. A tall mulatto, too slow or too dedicated, tumbled in and was swept down the far side as the levee break grew thirty feet across.

Instead of horror, I felt relief. It was happening to them, not us.

Hearing a noise, I turned, expecting to find some furry creature, the sort whose burrow causes crevasses. In my mind I was slaying it and it would be the animal that caused the disaster and I would be a hero like Achille.

It wasn't an animal. No plausible justification could I discern for this man to be in a pirogue among these reeds across from the area's worst crevasse in a generation. He held a shovel with a muddy blade, enough to get a man lynched. I knew what he'd perpetrated, yet I couldn't prevent my lips from asking: "What are you doing here, Judge Pike?"

Turpitude # 27

"Take no part in works of darkness, instead expose them."

Ephesians 5:11

"Help me ashore," the Judge instructed. He braced himself on my shoulder. His weight drove my bare feet into the blue clay. "Hide this somewhere," he said, handing me the shovel. I took it. I suppose I was caught up in his air of authority, but while the Judge excelled at strategic, long-term schemes, improvising was not his strong suit. "We'll send this downstream before someone spots it," he said, shoving the pirogue from the bank. Unfortunately, the crevasse drew water so fast the bayou had started flowing backward toward the suction. The pirogue headed the same way. Of course, it was spotted. Of course, the spotters looked for whence it came. Of course, a dozen accusing fingers soon pointed our way. And when I turned to ask the Judge what we should do, of course he was no longer there.

A bullet ripped through the shovel blade, the tearing metal striking a high C sharp. Mud spattered me with incriminating evidence as the shovel flew from my hand.

A second shot whizzed by. Though a wider miss, it proved the first was no fluke. I was now a wanted fugitive. Object of a manhunt. The turkey in a turkey shoot.

I sprinted up the levee then down the landward slope. More shots rang out. My heart pounded louder than the C sharp ringing in my ears, but there arose a louder pounding: hooves. The Colonel was riding me down. I stumbled, tumbled, hit ground, *ooph!* Picking myself up, running again, behind me the thunderous hoof beats ceased abruptly as the thoroughbred put a foreleg into the same hole I had. Down he went, the Colonel with him.

The horse whinnied protest but wasn't injured. The Colonel didn't even drop his rifle. He could've shot me as I fled. Could've run after me and with his longer legs caught up. Could've sent his minions to warm my trail as Sheriff Bourgeois was called and bloodhounds loosed and all manner of awful things set in motion. He did none of that, because at his feet water gurgled from the fissure which had tripped his horse.

A boil.

Bubbling from a rabbit hole.

Turpitude # 28

"When you do caring works, don't sound trumpets as hypocrites do."
Matthew 6:2

"Let him go," the Colonel called back his henchmen. "Help stanch this seep before it turns into a torrent to match the other side."

His caution bought me a temporary reprieve, but getting cleaned up and back into bed wouldn't be easy with the house in uproar. Had Bonreve recognized me? If so, why hadn't he called my name? Was there a worse fate he was planning for me? Would he stopper the boil? If he couldn't and Athena was ruined, what would happen to Mother and me? Then, the question most perplexing, why had the Judge done what he'd done?

A voice startled me. I plunged behind a ligustrum. "How bad is it?" Mother asked, but who was she talking to?

"It broke through the west bank," answered Judge Pike. "There was also a boil on this side but they stoppered it. You and yours are safe."

"I heard gunshots."

"Panic's to be expected."

I shifted so I could see them. The Judge offered his arm. Mother ignored it. "Those poor people," she said.

"The bayou was too high. It had to give somewhere."

Mother gave him a long, strange look. "I better prepare for refugees."

She walked away. The Judge seemed uncertain whether to follow. I was loading up my own words for him when he blurted, "*I* breached the levee."

His confession froze her. Slowly she turned around. "Why?"

"You know why."

I knew. Greed. His plantation was on this side too. He'd sacrificed the right bank to spare his own property. Evidently Mother thought along the same lines. "Are you that selfish?"

Her accusation wounded him. "Madame, I keep Southern Crown only because a gentleman is expected to own a plantation. My interests in New Orleans dwarf my holdings here. A left bank flood might destroy your husband. It would hardly wrinkle my brow."

"You did it for Louis?"

"I did it for you." Mother flinched. "Impetuous I know, impetuous being the thing I'm usually not," he continued. "See what you drive me to? I couldn't sleep for the thought of you being impoverished. We have a bond, you and I."

She said nothing.

"Madame, you kissed me."

Kissed him? When, I wondered. Mother held her tongue. As I knew well and the Colonel knew better, the woman could wield silence like a whip.

"You kissed me. The night of the crab boil," he reminded her, his voice rising. *That's* what they'd been doing?

"And you kissed me back," Mother answered with utter calm. "Held me close."

"To comfort you," he protested. "If for a moment I fell victim to your allure—"

"It was my fault?"

"I didn't mean that," he blurted. "You bewitched me. You always have, no matter how I fought it. When I tried to sabotage your engagement, you outwitted me every turn. Raised in ignorance, you reshaped yourself into a queen. I've never met another woman so…"

"Devious?"

"Capable. And physically desirable. I can't deny that."

"That night, you pushed me away. Said I should put things right with my husband."

"Wasn't that proper?"

"More proper than bankrupting half your neighbors over a schoolboy crush?"

"Don't be cruel."

"Cruel? People could be drowning as we chat among the jasmine. So we kissed, and now months later you return and do this terrible thing, and you say it's on my account? What are you after?"

"I ask nothing."

Ha! I was about to jump out and quash this nonsense when Mother began walking toward him. Passing in and out of moonlight, never had she looked more magnificent.

"My son loves tales of gallant knights. I've learned not to believe them."

I didn't like being mentioned, liked less what happened next.

"If I needed solace now as I did that night," Mother continued, "and if you took me in your arms again, to comfort me as you tell yourself you were doing then; and if I had the nerve to kiss you again, how would it end this time? Would you send me back to my husband? Or push me to the ground, there, behind the ligustrum."

What?

"Hike my skirts and rip my bloomers and take what you can't even admit you want." The Judge tried to reply, managed only a squeak. I was in no better shape. Then Mother said, "Because I'm not sure I'd stop you."

Turpitude # 29

"Avoid sexual immorality."

1 Thessalonians 4:3

"You cause this terrible flood and say you did it for me," Mother continued. "I'm not surprised by the cruelty; I knew you were cruel. What I am is sickened. And flattered. And curious. If you did this… this 'grand, romantic gesture'…"

My God! Had *I* given Judge Pike the idea with my idle comment back at the parade?

"I find myself wondering what else might you be willing to do. Take us away from here, my son and me?"

There I was, mentioned again! Seeing Judge Pike at a loss for words made Mother smile. She leaned close and kissed him. Kissed him! Mother had gone as mad as the Judge! The Colonel might ride up any moment, rifle in hand.

When Mother broke the kiss, she had to push with both hands to escape the Judge's embrace. Might he actually throw her down next to me to do things I could barely imagine and would not allow? He looked like a starving man at a banquet, but when he took that next, fatal step toward her, she stopped him with a single raised finger.

"Assemble your best offer," she said, "but I make no promises because I don't know my own heart. I'm twenty-six which is old enough for any sensible woman to realize thrill is brief, happiness tricky, and even the handsomest man rarely ends up a prize. On the other hand, twenty-six leaves years stretching ahead if I don't die of fever or something and unless I make a move they'll linger with me trapped on this plantation beside a man who brings me little joy and who for some reason I can't understand causes terror in my son—"

She was doing this because of me?

"—which as long as we're talking about him you mustn't for a moment forget I'd never leave my son behind so where I go my boy goes that is if I go anywhere with you—"

Blessed Mother! While I hated being party to tawdry duplicity, I'd have liked it less to be left out.

"—or go anywhere with anyone besides you, August, except there is no one else at least no one willing to flood their neighbors for me as stark raving mad as that is so again, take your time, wind up your pitch, and we'll talk another day, okay?"

The Judge watched her disappear down the path. Crickets droned.

"I heard everything," I told him.

Judge Pike looked over. There wasn't enough surprise left in him to be startled by my sudden appearance. "Then repeat it back," he whined, "because I'm not sure I absorbed it all the first go-through."

But I was already barreling through the darkness, hoping to sneak into my room to hide and think and weigh and plan, to unravel if I could the fraying threads of good and evil. Yet fast as I flew, I couldn't outrun the Judge's heinous crime and Mother's response to it. Maybe she wasn't a saint. She was still my mother. My duty was to protect her, even from herself.

Turpitude # 30

"Don't even mention sexual immorality."
Ephesians 5:3

It took weeks to repair the crevasse, months to drain the flooded acreage, months more to render inundated plantations habitable. Refugee Negroes camped atop the right bank levee, sharing it with livestock, until that ribbon of land grew as squalid as a Calcutta slum. White hirelings found beds of hay in left bank barns. Despite efforts to segregate maidens from bachelors, love affairs sprouted like yams.

A couple of planters stubbornly remained in the dry upper floors of their flooded houses, but such mildewy accommodations suited few, so most of the right bank planter class accepted offers of board at Big Houses on the left bank. No rent was asked; it would've been ungentlemanly. On the other hand, refugees could hardly haggle when hosts set exorbitant rates to feed their levee-bound mules or offered low-ball prices to buy now-surplus equipment.

Mother, however, asked nothing in return as she coaxed the servants to provide every comfort for her sometimes demanding lodgers. She found additional desks so that my one-room schoolhouse finally had a complement of pupils. One would never have suspected that the whole time she was contemplating the sort of indiscretions one reads about in French novels.

If the Colonel identified me on the levee that night, he gave no indication. With so many witnesses about, his attacks ceased: a good thing, because I needed the respite to devise a course of action regarding Mother. I knew from books that women who dallied ended up swallowing arsenic or leaping in front of trains, but even all that reading left me unsure how to prevent it.

Planters often disparaged their Negro Quarters as hotbeds of adultery. If so, Nat must possess at least hearsay acquaintance with infidelity. Furthermore, Nat would keep mum about whatever I asked him, just as I'd never mentioned his (as it turned out, astute) comment that the Colonel might face difficulties when Mother entered her prime.

I found him planting salvias along the walkway to the cookhouse. I'd have preferred a less public forum, but I dared not wait. "Nat, I need your advice, but it's a delicate subject. Our conversation will require discretion."

He said nothing, didn't look up, but his dirt-caked finger painted a cross over his heart.

"I'd like a thorough explanation of attraction between males and females."

At that, he did look up. "Wondered if them red curls caught your eye." I knew to whom he referred. Among the refugees lodging with us was one of Judge Pike's former, and less successful, political protégés. He and his wife had a daughter a couple of months younger than me. Aralee Gueydan had hair the color of a burning barn. "Go talk to her," Nat advised before I could set him straight on the true nature of our conversation.

"What I want to know, Aralee couldn't tell me," I said. "I'd like explained how two males may pursue the same female, the why of it and the mechanics of its deceptions and, mostly, how to put a stop to it."

Nat fought back a smile. "So it's the other fellow got your nose twitching?"

If Aralee and her parents sought refuge from a flooded plantation a mile down the bayou, we also took in a prominent family from a mansion upstream. This second clan, the Whites, had a platoon of sons; no one was sure how many, probably not even them. Among this multitudinous brood existed a cruel bastard (I speak figuratively; I had no reason to doubt his parentage) named Pierce Douglas White, my age but three inches taller. This malevolent incubus tortured cats and sabotaged clotheslines and considered Aralee promised to him, with wedlock to ensue in a decade. Besides his ability to shimmy up trees or hit baseballs into the clouds, Pierce had a great-grandfather who'd been a delegate to the Continental Congress. His grandfather was once Governor of Louisiana. His Uncle Ed lived in Washington, D.C., where he sat on the Supreme Court even though he'd fought for the Confederacy.

I was just a kid the Colonel adopted to get the wife he wanted.

Nat's hands set blue flowers into soil mulled with manure, but his eyes saw into my soul. "Ain't always the sturdier fellow who turns a girl's head. Be lots of ways to win that derby."

"I want the complete list."

Nat couldn't help laughing. "Don't need no list from me, young master. Jump right in. The plays come natural."

Eureka! Though in front of me the whole time, it took the naïve genius of Nat Toussaint to show me I had a perfect case study ready at hand. Aralee could represent Mother. Pierce White would stand for equally reprehensible Colonel Bonreve. I would play Judge Pike, thereby learning the motivations, methods, and manipulations of "the other man" and so becoming knowledgeable enough to keep Mother from ending up like Emma Bovary or Anna Karenina. If my plan ignored the feelings of Aralee or Pierce, well, that's how it had to be, evil in service to good.

As I walked away Nat called after me, "Just remember, sparking romance ain't like sowing corn. It don't always sprout in straight rows."

Turpitude # 31

"The heart is deceitful, wicked, corrupt, and incurable."

Jeremiah 17:9

I found Aralee enjoying the tree swing. "Mademoiselle, we have a bond, you and I," I said, employing words the Judge used crevasse night. I believed it a pretty good opening.

"You're funny," Aralee said as she swung by.

"Is funny desirable?"

Her feet kicked up dust as she stopped the swing. "Funny's all right. Dull's what you should never be."

Useful information already. I wished I'd thought to bring my notebook. "Shall we stroll?"

She frowned. "My governess might not like that."

Her governess, Caledonia, an ancient octoroon, was likely off stealing a nap. "Perhaps I could help her see past whatever troubles her," I offered, though not precisely in the same context the Judge said it crab boil night. Good enough for Aralee, though. We strolled.

I had no way of knowing how closely our chat resembled crab boil night's fatal conversation, but to spark Mother's interest the Judge must've said something heroic, so I announced, "A sea-witch was spotted near here. If you like, I'll climb the levee and dare her to attack me."

"Why would you do that?"

"Because it's a grand, romantic gesture."

A mischievous smile spread across Aralee's face. "Did you lure me here to steal a kiss?"

Finally getting somewhere! Since a kiss apparently occurred

crab boil night, and again crevasse night, here was an avenue to follow. Aralee's head tilted back, ruby lips pouting. Ringlets of auburn hair danced across her cheek. As I tried to memorize each detail…

Kaboom, I was hit by a cannonball.

Turpitude # 32

"Bless them who persecute you."

Matthew 5:44

Well, it felt like a cannonball. The cannoneer: Pierce White. His missile: a day-lily bulb. A whole ammunition locker rolled into the tail of his shirt, Pierce had undone a half-day's planting by Nat just so he'd have projectiles to batter me. He threw another, thumping my forehead. I flinched but didn't run, partly to deny him satisfaction but mostly because his arrival completed the triangle I wanted to replicate, fueling hope I'd learn something to help Mother. Also, there remained the admittedly diminishing possibility of Aralee and me kissing.

"I've fallen victim to your allure," I told her, offering my arm. She seemed uncertain whether to take it, especially after my head jerked sideways from another day-lily rhizome pelting my ear.

"Maybe I could walk with you a little ways apart," she said.

"Perhaps best," I granted.

As Pierce took pot shots at me, he also lobbed denunciations: my daddy acted soft toward nigras; he wasn't really my daddy; I was a squirt. I kept my dignity, but it was fragile. At first Aralee seemed frightened by this feud between her suitors. Eventually she began to giggle. After he ran out of bulbs, Pierce performed handstands and somersaults, then played his trump card, offering to treat Aralee to a chocolate float. I was suspicious. I knew of no plans to make ice cream and the manufacture of sweets in Athena's kitchen was something I monitored closely. Not just ice cream but a float, a *chocolate* float. My mouth watered wondering how Pierce would manage it. Hollering at us to follow, he dashed off. Aralee ran after him. Blindly, so did I.

Turpitude # 33

"Love your enemies."

Ibid., yet no easier.

I heard the shriek. Behind the cookhouse, past the herb garden, we found Pierce laughing and pointing, saying here it was, the chocolate float, a "hot fudge Monday," the day indeed being Monday, washday. He'd grabbed Melpa's feet and dumped her into a tub of sudsy, scalding washwater. A moment before she'd been contentedly laundering. Now, upended, her legs waved in the air, then she popped up with a great splash, wailing like a mink in the teeth of a trap.

Aralee was as shocked as I — points for her — but was unwilling to get involved — points taken way. Maybe she thought Pierce might dunk her too. She ran for the house. Pierce cackled and chased her. Melpa scrambled out of the washtub, pulling down her skirt, sliding up her sleeve to check her reddened skin. I hurried over. "You all right?"

She slapped me. A Negro striking a white could get lynched for it, but Melpa was too upset for caution. Then she looked again and realized it was me, not Pierce, who stood before her.

She threw her arms around me. Great heaving sobs escaped her, each one pressing her seventeen-year-old breasts against my not-quite-nine-year-old chest. For a moment I forgot Aralee and my experiment. I hunted for words to apologize for Pierce and my own too-passive response, apologize for all the white boys who'd ever done her wrong or would. I hadn't words for all that so I said, "Let me get the soap out of your eyes."

With a finger I mopped the bubbles that mingled with her tears. She forced a chipped-tooth smile. "Go chase your redhead. We all rooting for you."

Turpitude # 34

"Condemn not, that ye be not condemned."

Luke 6:37

My reports on Pierce's cruelty drew embarrassed looks but no justice. Even Mother muttered excuses. When I grew so desperate I approached Colonel Bonreve, he acted as if I was to blame. "Seems it hardly matters how carefully we rear our children," was all he said.

Most assumed Melpa had provoked Pierce. Didn't surprise me the Whites and Gueydans thought that. It did shock me that many colored servants agreed. "I like Melpa, don't get me wrong," said Two-Tone Willie, a frown on his brown and pink face, "but high-yellow gals like her can get haughty. Better dunked in a washtub now than scourged worse later if she forgets her place."

On the balcony one squally afternoon, Aralee hosted a tea party for her dollies. Pierce formed up ranks of lead soldiers (including a General Napoleon that had once briefly been mine). I kept an eye on Aralee. Her fiery hair was tastefully dressed. Her skin shone fresh as morning cream. She shielded both curls and complexion half-hidden under an extravagant bonnet, so that every glance was a gift bestowed, every other moment torture.

When without a sound she mouthed the words, "I like you better," my heart skipped three beats. A second later she gazed at Pierce. Telling him what? Uncertainty drove me mad. And if a girl could so torment a boy, perhaps under the right circumstances a boy could do it to a girl. Might Judge Pike turn the tables and torment Mother? Could even Colonel Bonreve? Maybe Mother *was* in her prime, but for how long? One of Richard Bourque's thoroughbreds, if well-tended, might live till thirty, but its racing career ended by nine or ten. Then what?

Epiphany hit. The answer I needed. It was all I could manage to await the appropriate moment to explain to Mother what she must do.

Normally the *garçonnière*, "boy's quarters," served as guest house, but these days it lived up to its name. I shared it with a troop of young, male refugees, even obliged to cede half my mattress to my nemesis, the cad Pierce White, who farted in his sleep and routinely stole covers.

An hour past bedtime, I threaded my way through the cots, tiptoed across the breezeway, and crept upstairs. A finger of yellow light glowed under Mother's door. I knocked, knowing the Colonel had sojourned overnight to New Orleans. Brushing out her hair, Mother seemed curious but not displeased by my interruption. "I've found the solution to romance," I announced.

She smiled. "I'm all ears."

Highlights gleamed in her silky hair. I would miss it, but that couldn't be helped. "First, we shave your head."

"Pardon?"

"So the hood will fit."

"Hood?"

"Don't worry: with holes for your nose and eyes. The eye-holes will have blinders like Richard Bourque puts on racehorses so they—" I saw her face in the mirror. "What?"

"You think I'm so troublesome that—"

"Not you! The men around you. You're beautiful, Mother. Men fall in love with you and despite what poets claim, love is bleak, dangerous, not worth the trouble."

"I disagree. Forget the Colonel a moment. With your father, love was like sunshine, sunshine you could carry around inside you. Who wouldn't want that?"

"Achille Cheramie was a special case."

"For me he was. He set me afire. Sure, love can be bleak, stormy, miserable even, but to go without love, that's miserable too, so feeling awful now and then is just one of those things people have to put up with, like mosquitoes, but on any given day no thrill in this world beats the crashing waves of man to woman love or, I suspect, man to man love or woman to woman love though I haven't personally tried either, but I do remember the joys and trials of boy to girl love as I suspect you have an inkling or you wouldn't be thinking about this so much and what was your question exactly?"

I hadn't come with a question, but if she was in an answering mood I thought I might as well pose one. "Does Judge Pike set you afire?"

"He'd like to think so."

"I suspect the Colonel doesn't kindle blazes either."

"No danger of burning the house down," she said. "It's true, some girls only care that a fellow triggers sparks. My sister Clo was like that. Other girls rather a quiet guy who'll sit and listen to their troubles. Then, all certain girls want is a bub to hold a job and be a good daddy because the girl has babies on her mind though I hope that's not the case with Aralee, at least not yet."

I wasn't there to discuss Aralee, but knowledge is never wasted. "Mind if I take notes?"

"Be my guest." She started brushing her hair again. I took a pencil from my pocket and a leaf of stationery from her dresser.

"Every girl wants to be loved, so if you care you have to show you do and that's how sweets and flowers serve, not just because she wants those things but because she wants to know you were thinking of her, considered what she'd like, and troubled yourself to get it, so she can see you love her enough not to be lazy about it."

"Do not be lazy," I wrote.

"Other times, you have to try the opposite, pretend you don't care when you do, force the girl to go after you, but that's a risky play because—"

"Wait. Which one's the correct approach?"

"That's what I'm saying, it depends. Polite and respectful's often perfect. Other times a woman wants a fellow bold, ignoring the supposed-to's as long as he doesn't go too far."

"Avoid excessive liberties," I scribbled, realizing I'd need more paper if she meant to fully cover the topic.

"And while a girl may tumble with her heart, you have to get past her head, too. For a worrier, offer strength. If she's a mothering sort, looking for a fellow with cracks to patch and hinges to oil, then you do better appearing something of a mess, which in your case, no offense, might be best since it'd come pretty natural to you."

"Which approach works best on you, Mother?"

"None that involve a hood."

I'd jumped the gun, presenting my hood idea before I perfected a design. Decrypting Mother-Colonel-Judge dynamics required additional research. I resolved to test Mother's theories on Aralee.

What you no doubt realize, what Mother saw, and what Nat knew from the get-go, took me a while to admit: for the first time in my life, I'd fallen in love. I vowed never to let that prickly web of confusing emotions interfere with protecting Mother from the Judge or myself from the Colonel.

It would be a busy summer.

Turpitude # 35

"Not by might shall a man prevail."
1 Samuel 2:9

As he resettled into his nearby plantation and local judgeship, Judge Pike's excuses for visiting Athena grew thin. How many times did he ride in only to have narrowly missed the Colonel? No doubt he'd been spying from the levee, biding time till the Colonel left. "Who can help it?" he'd say as he dismounted to wait, all day if necessary, as if back in Thibodaux no miscreants needed sentencing.

With the dexterity of a prima ballerina, Mother eluded his every attempt to ensnare her into a moment alone. It drove him mad, which was fine by me. He could only cause her grief, and besides, I'd hardly forgiven him for handing me his shovel the night of the crevasse.

One day, seeing eventual conversation was unavoidable, Mother agreed to coffee but made him cool his heels till she could get free. Since I couldn't prevent this meeting, I decided to sabotage it. With the Judge pacing in earshot, I observed to Madame Gueydan how Athena's flowers were showing their finest spring blooms, which always put Mother in a delightful mood whenever she received a bouquet our gardener Nat prepared. I was afraid I'd laid it on too thick, but no, because moments later I heard the Judge bark, "Cut me some flowers, boy."

"Flowers for who?" asked Nat.

The Judge blushed. "Flowers for *whom*. Flowers for whom, *sir*. What business is it of a yard nigger to whom I give flowers? Are you being uppity, boy?"

I saw panic in Nat's eyes. "No, sir. Not me, sir."

"You know curiosity killed the cat, don't you?"

"Yes, sir. Killed that cat dead, sir."

"Nat meant no harm," I intruded. "It's just he knows what flowers everyone likes."

Nat flashed gratitude as he assumed the dumbest "dumb darkie" persona in his repertoire, looking as brainless as his wheelbarrow. "Yes sir, know what all 'dem ladies likes," then, catching himself, adding, "that is, in the way of flowers, sir. Colonel's aunt, Mizz Elmire, like carnations. Monsieur Gueydan's wife—"

"I want a bouquet for the lady of the house," the Judge snapped, "as is proper for a guest to offer."

"Master's wife?" said Nat, "Master's wife like—"

"Roses," I sprung my trap. As Nat knew, but the Judge didn't, Mother had hated roses since before I was born. Was revolted by their scent. Said they reminded her of dashed hopes and impermanence. Even had Nat transplant them away from the house.

"Yes," said the Judge. "Prepare a large arrangement of red roses."

"Yes, sir, Mister Judge, sir," mumbled Nat as he threw me a dirty look.

I didn't see Judge Pike present the roses, but later he rode away unsmiling and I saw them in the trash. A good day.

That same afternoon, I had Nat prepare another bouquet for Aralee. As he did, noticing his eyes weren't on the flowers, I followed his gaze to where Melpa was swinging a carpet beater. Apparently Nat also admired Melpa's gluteals. "Call her over," I said.

He looked as if I'd suggested he fly to the moon.

"Make another bouquet, call her over, give it to her."

"I'm nothing but a yard man."

"You're master flower gardener at the grandest plantation on Bayou Lafourche. If she's looking for a colored man — I happen to know she doesn't want a white one — she could aim no higher than you, Nat."

"Master'd string me up if I picked his flowers for a colored woman."

"Say the bouquet is for whatever parlor she's tidying. Say I ordered it. Tell her you made it especially pretty because you think she's especially pretty."

He considered. "Might work."

"She won't be beating that rug all morning."

His hands became a blur of sheers and floral hues. A joy to spend even a moment in the presence of such an artist.

Melpa looked up as Nat approached. I couldn't hear his words but saw her chipped tooth gleam. A good day had gotten better, but I saved the best news of all: Pierce White had caught mumps. So had most other children. Our one-room school, closed by the epidemic. Thus I was threatened by neither rival nor distractions when I found Aralee dangling her legs from the bayouside dock.

"For me?" she asked, nodding at my flowers.

"Actually, I had my gardener pick them because I enjoy beauty for its own sake."

"Sometimes you're poetic," she marveled, "and sometimes such a rascal. Like two different people in the same body."

"Which do you prefer?"

"Whichever one lets me have a blossom. I'd be so grateful I might give him a kiss."

My breath stopped. I glanced around to make sure Pierce had not escaped quarantine. On a bench, Aralee's governess, old Caledonia, had head careened and mouth agape, dead sleep.

I offered a yellow flower. I'd envisioned a kiss mouth to mouth, but so intoxicating was the touch of Aralee's sweet lips to my cheek, I cannot say I was disappointed. Especially once I realized our game was just beginning.

"Pretty, but it's pink I wanted. May I have it, too?"

"Would my reward be another kiss?" I stammered.

"Seems fair."

I counted the flowers in my hand. Might I expect eleven kisses? Before Caledonia woke? Before Aralee hurried to the

Big House fearing a storm because she thought she heard thunder which would actually be my pounding heart?

The fourth to last flower, when I thought I might die of anticipation, her lips finally met mine. My first real kiss. Though I'd begun courting Aralee only as a way to study Mother's quandary, that kiss pushed from my mind everything but the nine year-old temptress beside me.

That evening I played Debussy's "Clair de Lune" with Aralee beside me on the bench. The dozen perfect blossoms filled a vase atop the piano. Since Aralee's usual sleeping quarters now lodged mumps-ridden girls, the garçonnière was boys' ward, and — like everywhere else since the flood — the balcony buzzed with mosquitoes, it was deemed harmless if Aralee and I slept side-by-side on a palette in the parlor. As her mother snuffed the lamp, Aralee gave me one more kiss. "Now we'll recognize each other's lips," she whispered, "even in the dark, forever and ever."

Next morning, Madame Gueydan roused the whole house with her yelping after she found Aralee and me sleeping entwined like lovers.

Turpitude # 36

"Show hospitality to strangers."

Hebrews 13:2

Banished to bunking on the mosquito-ridden balcony until the mumps epidemic ran its course, my first morning back in the garçonnière I woke to find the mattress beside me empty. Pierce already up! I dreaded how he might use the head start.

Dashing out, I bumped into a field hand. Thirty or so, thin

as July cane, he said, "Must be nice sleeping late whenever you want."

I'd never heard a Negro speak so insolently to a white, even a white child. "Out of my way!" I said, imitating Judge Pike's imperiousness.

"That how it be? When I come offer a mighty charm for forty cent? Hoof! Now the price be sixty."

"You're the one who gave Nat the protection *gris-gris*," I deduced.

"*Gave*?" He snickered. This fellow was trouble.

"I don't need a witch doctor's protection, thank you." I tried to step around him.

"This don't bespoke protection. This trick bag draw *love*."

Curiosity bit me. "What love charm could be worth thirty cents?" I asked, reframing negotiations in case I liked what I saw.

"A extra potent bag of Come-To-Me foot magic worth every penny of seventy-five."

"Foot magic?"

"Sprinkle it where she walk. She cross, next fellow she look at she be his. You can use that, I know. For that sorrel-haired gal who go be delighting that other fellow 'less you put this mojo working."

If this scallywag knew of my secret love, I realized my infatuation must be apparent to the whole plantation. Was it ethical to use magic to woo a good Catholic like Aralee Gueydan? I would've never considered it had I faced a lesser rival than Pierce Douglas White, with his governor grandfather and Supreme Court uncle and baseball prowess. "I'll give you two bits."

"For this trick?" He dangled a rust-colored flannel pouch that smelled of decay. "Red for extra power. Might take sixty."

"You said you'd take forty," I reminded him.

"Before you sassed me."

"Thirty. Not a penny more."

He shrugged. "Maybe the other white boy give me sixty."

"Pierce would consider it witchcraft. Report it to his father, who'd inform the Master, who'd throw you off the plantation." I had no idea whether any of those mentioned would do any such things, but neither did this lout.

"Okay, forty," he backtracked.

Exactly forty cents sat in my pocket, but I smelled blood. "Twenty-five," I said. "I might've paid forty, but you sassed *me*."

He eyed me a moment, then without another word thumped away. I'd overplayed my hand. I should've patched it up, given him the forty, but at that point I possessed a measure of pride that the rest of the morning would knock out of me. Somewhere on Athena's acres waited Aralee Gueydan. With, I feared, Pierce beside her.

Girls like sweets — Mother had said so — and the Colonel had ordered a ginger cake to go with lunch. I'd invested considerable study in how such a verbal request is rendered, hours later, into a slice of heaven on a saucer. Thus I knew that hired cooks routinely err at measurement. Whether dough for bread or batter for cake, they invariably prepare more than fits the pan. Once mixed, the extra might as well be baked. Since one would hardly serve these "mistakes" to the master and his family, they logically get divvied among the kitchen staff.

If cooks are sly, so are boys. I knew that next to the off-limits ginger cake cooling in the pantry would be a few ginger cookies. If taken by me to give to Aralee, the cookies would be missed only by servants who couldn't complain since that would imply the tidbits were an intentional act of pilferage, instead of innocent (albeit suspiciously chronic) mixing bowl miscalculation.

Yvonne and her helpers were off letting the cookhouse cool from the morning's baking. Envisioning Aralee daintily chewing, my finger dusting a crumb from her Cupid's bow lips, I walked through the pantry door and into a scene of horror.

Turpitude # 37

"To even approach adultery is sin."

Surah Al-Isra 17:32,
the Noble Quran

My first notion was that Judge Pike must've been famished. He was pressing himself against Mother and in turn pushing her against the copper screen of the pie safe, as if trying to get at the sweet cake within. "Not now," Mother was saying. Of course not now. The cake was for lunch. Unless she meant the cookies, but those I needed for Aralee.

"I can't wait any longer," the Judge cried, and that's when I realized it wasn't cake he wanted! (Well, maybe it was but not the sort I knew.)

"Then you know what you have to do," Mother said.

"What does he have to do?" I asked.

Mother and the Judge flew apart. Jars rattled on a bumped shelf. "I'm not sure how much you overheard," the Judge stuttered, "but hearing only part of a conversation it's easy to misapprehend." His attempt at sober demeanor was undercut by rouged lips, an even sillier affectation than his mustache wax.

Wait! He hadn't rouged his lips! He'd kissed her! Had Mother lost all sense? I despised the Colonel but couldn't imagine calling this loose cannon "father."

"Here's what happened," Mother began, but I didn't hear the rest because I ran. Ran like a skinny rabbit in pure blind panic. Heard them cry "Stop!" but didn't. Then wished I had because, barreling from the cookhouse, I slammed into Colonel Bonreve.

Turpitude # 38

"Avoid lustful misconduct."
3rd of the Five Precepts
of Buddhism

Usually too subtle for brute physicality, Bonreve batted me aside. I dashed after him, back into the pantry to save Mother, but it was Mother who pushed me out again. "Go! You mustn't be part of this!"

"But—"

Bending, her whisper harsh: "If he links you to this it'll ruin your future." Her hand found my bottom, gave me a shove. The pantry door slammed. Alone in the kitchen, I heard bumping, then thumping. "Stop, stop!" Mother pleaded but the two men kept knocking around until a deafening crash marked a collapsing shelf of preserves. Light syrup and morsels of fig lapped out under the door. That ended the roughhousing but started all three voices hollering at once. I wanted to listen but was afraid what I might hear. I'd never felt so small, so insignificant, like the farthest star in the galaxy blinking into darkness. Mother didn't want my help and I wasn't sure what I could do if she asked for it. I fled into the sunshine. No one around, servants evaporated, houseguests all remembering urgent business in their rooms.

Maybe I couldn't save Mother, not from the Judge nor the Colonel nor herself. Rescuing Aralee from Pierce would prove I wasn't a complete failure. The cookies were inaccessible, but flowers had succeeded on a previous occasion. It's a very human impulse, when we can't control the consequential, to grab at any straws we can bend. They let us deny our impotence, albeit unconvincingly. Nat, however, though he held a dozen hydrangeas, refused to hand them over.

"Was you started it," he said. "Me giving Melpa flowers every day. Greet her empty-handed now, she go take it for a slight." I grabbed for the bouquet. Nat raised it out of reach. "No! You get your way too much. You spoiled rotten, be God's truth!"

Never had Nat spoken to me like that. He showed no sign of apology, nor any move to cede the bouquet. Melpa exited the house, flashing her chipped-tooth smile, worthy, I admit, of any blossoms a man might pick. But also in danger. Pretending to be a yard man, the conjurer I'd met earlier poked a hoe at dandelions, but his gaze focused on the girl. Did Nat see the threat? No, a fool in love, with Melpa sixty paces off he was already offering his bouquet.

The juju man, twirling the hoe on his shoulder, crossed in front of Melpa. His dangling left hand held a small red pouch. I couldn't see the Come-To-Me dust I'd refused to buy but knew he was sifting it over her path. I dashed forward, drawing the conjurer's evil eye. As Melpa stepped across the hot-foot dust, he whinnied like a stallion, drawing her gaze. The trick was set.

I reached her, grabbed her arms, shook her. "Nat loves you, Melpa. Nat cuts flowers for you, every day. This brute will only use you." She brushed past me like someone dying of thirst brushes past reeds to reach a riverbank, sashaying to the cad who'd hexed her.

Failed Mother, failed Melpa. Made an enemy of a powerful sorcerer, and in some dark nook Pierce was probably getting much too friendly with Aralee.

I'd also let down Nat. As I walked back over, he tossed the hydrangeas into his wheelbarrow. "Melpa better off without me anyway," he said. "Foretold I got a bad end coming."

I ascribed his gloom to the hurt he felt. It shames me I grabbed his discarded flowers. Had I been in less rush, I might've noticed that behind one blue petal lurked a disgruntled honeybee.

Turpitude # 39

"Lust."

1st among the Five Evils of the Sikhs

Aralee was still howling from the bee sting when I delivered her to her parents. Shooed out, I ambled down the hall to Mother's bedroom. Empty, except for the intoxicating scent of her lavender toiletries; so intoxicating, in fact, that when the Colonel approached, rather than step out and say, "Excuse me, I was looking for Mother," I instead panicked and hid in her armoire.

The Colonel wasn't alone. Mother reminded him to lock the door. Topmost thing I must never do was go near this room during their naps. It wasn't naptime. The Colonel had, at least before their altercation, planned to accompany Judge Pike to Thibodaux. Catch the Southern Pacific to New Orleans. Mother and I would enjoy two whole days without him. Apparently the Colonel desired a nap before getting on the road, what with his exertions in the pantry. Little could I do except get comfortable, hope no one opened the armoire, and wait till they fell asleep to sneak out.

No doubt you think I was impossibly naïve, even for a nine-year-old. Those were simpler times. We lived far from the wicked city to which the Colonel never took us. During my last encounter with coitus I'd been a sperm, too youthfully preoccupied to wonder what exertions by others led to my own adventures.

"You'll pop my buttons," Mother admonished.

"Haven't I given you servants to sew them back?" The Colonel's voice was oddly husky.

With the armoire door cracked a quarter-inch, I put my eye

to the sliver of light. The Colonel was unlacing Mother's corset. I'd seen Melpa unlace Mother; the Colonel accomplished it in half the time. He was even faster peeling off his jacket, which that normally fastidious man tossed onto a chair. Suspenders fell. Shirt tails swept out of britches. It appeared the Colonel was himself hiding a mojo down his pants.

With surprising gentleness, he slipped off Mother's camisole. I'd been an infant when I last saw Mother naked. The years had little changed her pleasing form. As the Colonel kissed her, she bumped into the armoire, batting closed its door. Somewhere in there the key turned and I was locked in.

"We should talk first," I heard Mother say.

Evidently the Colonel disagreed because I heard nothing else intelligible for some time. Footfalls, creaking springs, and for a while, silence. The silence didn't last.

In darkness, growing woozy on aromatic cedar and vetiver sachets, I heard sighs, then moans, eventually groaning, grunting, and grinding of bed boards. Even the raciest novels left the actual lovemaking to the imagination. None mentioned the noise. Would that I had still been an earless sperm instead of an armoire-prisoner forced to listen to their racket. I thought I'd go mad. Maybe I did. It would explain much that happened later.

Turpitude # 40

"Lust" again.

1st among Christianity's
Seven Deadly Sins

"Shall I lace you?" I heard him ask.

"No need. When you get downstairs, send Melpa."

"All right." He sounded disappointed. "I know you're blameless."

"No woman's completely blameless," Mother responded.

"Even if you weren't, it wouldn't matter." Then he added, "But I won't be anyone's fool."

Listening to his footsteps recede, I imagined his progress out the jalousies onto the balcony, descending the steps toward his saddled horse and pressing duties in New Orleans. Eventually the armoire opened. Mother was wearing her summer robe. "You've had a busy day," she said, "and it isn't yet noon."

My first thought was she'd had a busy day too, but I thought it impolite to say so. "What just happened?"

Mother pulled the coverlet to hide the wrinkled sheets. She did it one-handed, the other balled into a fist. I saw her consider then discard a number of possible replies. "The physical part of love." Her fist opened. A crumpled handkerchief unfurled Judge Pike's monogram. Laying it on her knee, she tried to rub flat its wrinkles.

"In the pantry, what did you mean when you said the Judge knows what he has to do?"

Mother studied me a long moment before kissing my forehead, tactile comfort I sorely needed. "Colonel Bonreve will be away two days, Judge Pike probably longer, giving us plenty chances to talk, so take your time and pick your questions because I'm sure you have lots though I warn you I won't answer them all, but I do want you to know, know for certain, that I love you as much as any mother ever loved any son and if sometimes, actually often, I don't begin to understand you, well, I push that from my mind and love you all the same." She blew her nose with Judge Pike's handkerchief. "When you get downstairs, send Melpa up. The Colonel usually forgets."

Two days later, Colonel Bonreve returned from his business trip with a black eye never satisfactorily explained. The Judge didn't return at all, not for months.

Mother never revealed what she'd asked of the Judge in the

pantry, much less what incited her naptime moaning with the Colonel. Nat likewise refused to discuss the physical mysteries of love. When I coaxed Melpa into elaborating on how and why couples "take to straw," her fondness for metaphor only further befuddled me. Hidden among out-of-date seed catalogs in the library, some well-thumbed Parisian photogravures depicted copulation but shed little light on its particulars. When finally I received a detailed elucidation of sex, it came from an unlikely source.

Turpitude # 41

Need I cite the repercussions when Eve offered Adam the fruit of forbidden knowledge?

Genesis, and mankind's
sorry history ever since

She looked uncertain whether to stay or swim away. "Sorry about your alligator friend," I said to keep her talking.

The *sirène* scowled. "Him? Hell with him. He acted beastly."

"He was, after all, a beast."

"You're saying I should've known better?" she spat.

I'd come to the bayou looking for Aralee, but encountering a mermaid presents a rare opportunity and I owed this one a debt. "Better than what?"

Under her defiance I saw hurt. "Better than to run off to his 'gator hole so quick. The way I always do. Better than to let him use me till he had enough, saying I was like a trotline entangling him instead of the last, best chance at love a stinky brute like him would ever get."

"I'm ill-equipped to offer love advice," I admitted.

"Well, I've stomached every last thing wrong with it. What do you want to know?"

Literature often depicts mermaids as duplicitous so I determined to take what she said with a grain of salt; but if she had answers, I had questions. I took a long moment to arrange my queries in proper order. Finally, I began.

"In engineering the triangle is stable," I said. "Each side supports the other two. In romance, however, the triangle seems always ready to come crashing down, true no matter whether it's most accurately diagrammed as equilateral, isosceles, or obtuse, the latter I must say seeming most aptly named."

She stared at me, looking utterly confused. Not a good start.

"Okay," I said. "Instead, let's begin with the traditional romantic grouping, the pair. The couple. If you assemble a couple of any other object, watermelons, cannonballs, what have you, they find balance, the heavier below, the lighter above, there they stay. With people, the couple shifts up and down like a see-saw. When one wants to sit, the other feels like dancing. When—"

"You think a lot, don't you?"

"Mother says, too much."

"Never spent time with a fellow who thinks. That is, about more than the obvious." The mermaid's plump breasts rose like lotuses in the water. I noticed her drifting toward the bank, which the slow-moving current couldn't explain. Was this how *sirènes* lure sailors?

"Let's save romance for another day. What can you tell me about sexual intercourse?"

She snickered. I thought that meant I'd get no answer; boy, was I wrong. Relaxing against a cypress knee, the *sirène* proceeded to explain with intimate detail and frank enthusiasm traits a woman (or at least a mermaid) finds attractive; patterns of flirtation; stages of arousal; conscious, sub-conscious, and purely visceral triggers that decide whether one will consummate the act; how to know when foreplay has completed its job; the relative merits of myriad coital positionings — who knew there were so many — and, lastly, the finer points of post-orgasmic etiquette. If listed separately, the things I learned that day would by themselves constitute sixty-nine turpitudes, and indeed, "sixty-nine" is what she called one of the techniques described. By the end she was breathless. So was I, though I'd hardly uttered a word. "Come here," she said.

"Why?"

"After all that, I have to say?" She glided closer. I felt sensations I didn't understand.

"You realize I'm only nine."

"I'm half fish. You get it where you can."

"You don't even know my name," I objected.

"And you don't know mine. Sometimes it's best that way." She arranged her hair to accentuate her breasts. I recognized several clues of interest she'd just inventoried.

"I think I do know your name," I said. "Calypso."

"Calypso? No, it's Clothilde, but guys call me Clo."

"My mother had a sister named Clo. She drowned in '93."

That got a reaction. "What's your Mother's name?"

I told her. Clo swept hair over the breasts she'd just uncovered. "Who's your daddy?"

"Achille Cheramie."

She wailed. "No wonder you look… Never mind. Even I have limits." Her great tail swished, brown water sprayed me, and that was the last I ever saw, yes, my Tante Clo, in the bayou. Didn't matter. Her encyclopedic sexual knowledge had been imparted. One can't un-bite the apple.

I decided to keep the encounter to myself. Mother had enough on her plate. Anyone else wouldn't believe me, or if they did, might ask what the mermaid and I talked about.

Turpitude # 42

"Safeguard your fellow man."

Epistle 33, the Rasa'il
al-Hikmas of the Druze

Looking for Aralee is why I'd gone to the bayou in the first place. The mermaid's recital gave my hunt inexplicable urgency. I searched the balcony, the ground floor work area, around the yard swing. Woke the pigeons in the pigeonnière, the doves in the dovecote. No Aralee. I'd about given up when whim steered me toward the stables. Richard Bourque was away at auction and whichever grooms he left were off shirking, so no one was around. After the harsh sunlight, the stables felt dark. Hanging bridles smelled of oil soap.

The first stall lay open. I remembered how the Colonel once brought me there, back when he was pretending he'd turn me into a horseman. Images from that day bubbled up. A yearling colt, legs bound. A couple of grooms, proud when their filthy jokes made the master laugh. Richard Bourque scraping blade across whetstone, *shoop, shoop, shoop*.

Give Bourque this: he was quick about his carnage. A spurt of blood, a douse of blue disinfectant, done. The colt writhed. "Show the boy," instructed the Colonel. Bourque shoved his bloody hand toward my face. Atop his splayed fingers lay the severed testicles. I felt my breakfast rise in my throat.

"We do it so they'll be less troublesome," the Colonel's said, "and to protect the bloodline. Inferior offspring mar Athena's reputation."

Later, Mother said he didn't mean anything by it, but how could he have not recognized the metaphor? Not known how it made me feel?

From the stall, I heard a noise, not quite recognizable. I shut my eyes, waited to hear it again. Horses rustled in their boxes. Mud daubers buzzed in the rafters. A mouse scuttled through hay. Then there it was again, a girl, a cry that might've been "No!"

"Aralee," I called. Muffled response escaped the far end of the stables. I started toward it but found my way blocked by a horse, saddled and ready. Had somebody walked it in while I was in the empty stall?

I recognized the creature. One of Athena's most successful racehorses, now retired to stud, he'd sired Marauder along with many others. Why was such a valuable horse unattended? Who would dare saddle him with Richard Bourque away? His bridle was hitched midway down the row. It left a narrow passage next to his swishing tail. To get to Aralee, Aralee who might be in trouble, I had to go past him.

He stared at me with a huge eye, pulling at his tether. I tried to go around. He kicked. I dodged it but only by retreating. I tried again, he kicked again, closer. Hoof hit wood, echoing like a mallet. Other horses began pawing in their stalls. Somewhere a mare neighed. The stallion answered. I saw his penis growing longer. I heard Aralee crying, "Stop!"

Pierce!

I dashed. With a flash of steel, the deadly hoof struck. *Slam!* The horseshoe hit the wooden wall, but I was past.

In the last stall, Aralee lay sprawled in the hay with Pierce atop her. His hand groped under her skirt places a boy mustn't visit. His other hand rasped the flatness of her chest where breasts would one day rise. She battled to buck him off. We were nine years old, all three of us, all curious. An hour earlier I'd heard countless mysteries revealed by a talkative mermaid. Pierce chose to solve those riddles in a manner more blunt. Aralee might've followed him here, might've offered him kisses like she sometimes offered me, but now she said no. Pierce might've been bigger and stronger than me, but I was the son of Achille Cheramie.

"Let her go!" Grabbing Pierce's shoulders, I pulled him off.

Pierce punched me in the gut. I fell against the boards that framed the stall. My mouth opened, but breath wouldn't come. I saw Aralee try to run. Quick as a snake Pierce slapped his arms around her thighs, drawing her back, pulling her down into the hay.

With a gasp my breath returned. Even before my head cleared I was on hands and knees crawling toward them. I grabbed Pierce from behind, pinning his arms. Aralee punched his chest, hard, wild blows. One missed, flew past his shoulder, hit me in the eye. I thought I'd been blinded but didn't let go of Pierce. "Run, Aralee!" I hollered and she did. Pierce and I wrestled in the hay. I held him tight to give her a head start and because I knew that, once loose, Pierce would beat me up. As we rolled around, my head must've hit the side of the stall. I blacked out.

Turpitude # 43

"Flee youthful passions."

2 Timothy 2:22

My nose bled. Pierce was gone. The eye Aralee hit was blurry. The stallion, unsaddled and in his usual stall, nickered as I walked by.

Finger and thumb pinching my nose, approaching the Big House I encountered Caledonia. She displayed more temper than I'd realized the crone possessed. "You should be 'shamed!" she hollered as if spiriting her charge onto a hay bale had been my doing. "Boys will be boys and when they do they should get whipped!" Servants usually didn't speak so frankly, but after seventy years of service, I suppose Caledonia felt she had the right.

"Where is she?" I asked.

"Don't dare go up there!" I interpreted to mean my former bedroom. It'd been ruthlessly colonized by Monsieur and Madame Gueydan, but when I got there I witnessed its evacuation: valises open, hat boxes stacked, Aralee folding the dress she wore the day we traded flowers for kisses.

"I looked for you." She said it like an accusation. Looked for me but found Pierce.

"Out!" snarled Monsieur Gueydan, pointing at my bleeding nose. "I don't want my family blamed for staining Colonel Bonreve's rug."

Mother's door was locked, which other than naptime was unusual. Downstairs I found only servants. I must've been passed out in the stables awhile because it seemed the Whites had already left, their whole clan loaded into bateaux and rowed to their by-now-dry plantation.

Mother and the Colonel reappeared to see out the Gueydans. Goodbyes showed little warmth. Last aboard the Colonel's landau, Aralee leaned from its step. "You'll have a black eye."

"Not your fault," I told her.

"That's what Daddy says." Fingers emerged from the coach to clamp her shoulder. "I'll never forget you," she promised as her father yanked her into the carriage.

My shiner turned purple then green, but no one teased me because the school again housed only me and the teacher. My bed moved back into the Big House. No one, not Mother, not Melpa, not even Nat, wanted to hear the truth of what happened in the stables, so I told Tante Elmire. "Poor, dear child," was all she'd say.

Old routines returned. Stolen joy in Mother's company. Playing piano with or without Father Groetsch. Pestering Nat as he worked his flowers. And of course, the Colonel plotting to murder me.

As stepson of the master, each morning I enjoyed the perquisite of depositing my bodily refuse, indoors and in private, into a blue enamel chamber pot which servants carried away. Worrying that such a regular schedule might leave me vulnerable to ambush, I began varying the circumstances of my defecation. One morning in the outhouse near the horse barn, I hadn't been seated long when I heard, "not 'round here, not this morning," and recognized the Cajun accent of Richard Bourque.

"Nor in his bed," replied the Colonel. "I'm off to look for that bear the logging crew spotted. Thought the boy might want to come."

The boy. Me. As their voices faded, I shat with glee. If I'd done my morning duty on the pot in my room, I'd have been a literally-sitting duck and no doubt used for bait in his bear misadventure. Emerging from the crapper, I crept back to the Big House where I found Mother sitting on my yard swing, her face pale. "Has the Colonel gone?" I whispered.

"Toward the swamp," she murmured. "Rifle across his saddle." She caught my arm. Gazed at me with a look I dreaded.

"A spell?" I asked. Whenever she suffered a spell, I always inquired what she'd seen. She rarely said, but this time was different.

"The Colonel has a case full of guns," she intoned as some Greek oracle might. "Someday he'll take one out like he did this morning only you'll be there and the gun will go off and there'll be pots of blood and I won't be able to stop it."

Need I say I was nonplussed? "What should I do?"

She scratched at her stigmata. "I've no idea," she answered with more honesty than tact. "If one of you has to die I hope it's him, but how's that likely since — and I say this with love — there aren't many manly things you're good at and I don't expect shooting will ever be one."

So much for my being in her eyes the reincarnation of Achille Cheramie. Didn't matter. Evidently I'd soon be dead.

Turpitude # 44

"Do not desire her beauty."
Proverbs 6:25

Tormented by Mother's premonition (let alone her assessment of my manliness) that night I suffered nightmares. Woken by a tap on my door, I feared it might be the armed-and-ready Colonel. Instead, Melpa entered carrying a glass of milk I hadn't requested. Mother predicted the Colonel would shoot me; poisoning me first might make for an easier shot.

"Where'd the milk come from, Melpa?"

"A cow, silly."

"You milk her yourself?"

She set the glass on my bedside table. "I've been a good maid to your mama, never stole a flea, slipped away only when she didn't need me."

"Who gave you the milk, Melpa?"

"Shut up." Melpa leaned over and kissed me. Laws (admittedly not always obeyed) forbade breaking this cross-racial taboo, but Melpa's lips were too soft and yielding for me to turn away. "Grow up in one piece," she whispered, then she slipped out.

Next morning, servants were abuzz that Melpa had "got herself in trouble" and was gone.

"She could've stayed," lamented Nat as he mulched sasanquas. "Master was nice 'bout it. All he said, 'Let Father Groetsch marry you to the baby's pa.' But Melpa too bright to marry a man sowing heartbreak like the ju-ju man. Worse, one whose coming days carry such sorrow as me. So she left."

I should've offered compassion. Instead…

Turpitude # 45

"Do not seek after wizards."

Leviticus 19:31

"I know where you got the protection charm," I said. "Who else but that rascal who razmatazzed Melpa? Where do I find him?"

Nat gathered his tools, avoiding my gaze.

"It's a matter of life and death," I emphasized.

"You go get me in trouble."

"I won't," I pledged with hand raised.

"Easy talk. What you know about this lowdown world?"

"I read voraciously."

Nat stared at me the way a man with cancer contemplates a graveyard. Finally he whispered, "His name be Conquering John the Doctor."

Each year after the cane was cut, I could see the Negro Quarters in the distance, but visiting was forbidden. Like Marco Polo, or Columbus, or any other explorer we honor despite them being Italian, I prepared for my expedition. Unsure what held value in such a foreign place, I assembled a variety of trade goods: a pair of socks, an arrowhead dug up on the plantation, a stick of peppermint candy. I hid my allowance in my shoe. Noon meal done, Mother and the Colonel retired to their nap (and all that I now knew went with it). I stole away.

The Quarters consisted of several rows of unpainted cabins built among a copse of stunted oaks. Garden plots were fenced with scraps and branches. Outside of them, no blade of grass dared show itself to the roaming flock of scrawny chickens. Dogs lay about, ribs protruding, eyes crusty, bellies distended with worms.

I saw no one lazing around, stealing hens, dancing the Snake Hips, nor any of those other malfeasances of which planters habitually accuse blacks. That didn't surprise me. Like most plantations, Athena's regimen was "Can to Can't." Workers toiled from when dawn let them barely see the end of their hoe until well past sunset when they couldn't see at all. Six days a week, seven in grinding season, babes slung on mothers and toddlers, well, as they say, "If you can walk, you can work."

For their labors, the Negroes got these shacks and a small wage paid in tokens redeemable only at Athena Plantation Store. If you ran out of tokens, the storekeeper offered credit: by law, no worker could quit a plantation where he owed debt. It wasn't slavery, not quite, but it was close. I'd like to say I was sickened by the poverty that supported my affluence. Instead I simply counted shacks till I identified the one Nat warned I shouldn't visit. I didn't want to go in, but I couldn't protect Mother if I was dead.

I climbed the steps, crossed the small porch, looked in the open door. Beyond the hanging herbs and open crocks and drying animal skeletons the man I'd come to see lay sprawled in a hammock. I knocked on the door jamb. One eye opened, measured me, and decided I justified the effort to open the other eye. He sat up and scratched himself. Leaned left and farted. Got up to pour cold coffee from a chipped enamel pot, offering me none.

"So you got a worried mind 'cause Master wants to kill you and you be hunting a trick to protect yourself." It wasn't a question.

"Who told you?"

He shot me a look of contempt. "He-cats always plot 'gainst the last tom's kittens. You just itty-bitty or you stupid too?"

"I'm small for my age. That's not a crime."

He sipped his coffee, decided it was stale, spat it out the door past me. "Person grow out of itty-bitty. Stupid lasts a lifetime."

"I can read, write, calculate, and I'm a prodigy on the piano."

"Ain't you something!" he exclaimed, sarcasm lurking

behind his leathery smile. "I can uncross the hexed, draw you love or luck or money, make the blind man see his shadow. Ain't that a notch more than scribbling and playing piano?"

"Some people would think so," I allowed without admitting I believed him.

"So how come you live in the Big House and I slap skeeters here?" he asked, waving his bony arms at the shadowy corners of the tumbledown cabin.

"Because Mother takes good care of me," I said.

"Oh, assured your mama be a fine woman. Past that, what be the reason white folk got what you got and I got nothing but what you see?" Apart from the staples of his trade, little on view held value. Some food items, a few knick-knacks. For a man who claimed he could draw money, there was little sign he had any — the result, I supposed, of an impoverished clientele.

"The world isn't fair," I told him.

The smile that'd been lurking came out full. "Guess you not stupid at that," he chuckled.

Turpitude # 46

"They sinned by listening to him who astonished with sorcery."

Acts 8:11

"Empty your pockets. That junk you brought. The money in your shoe." How could he know? "But next time you need a trick bag it go cost twice that."

"Next time?"

"'Less you mean to kill the master outright."

"I don't want to kill anybody."

"Good, 'cause seems you can't near afford it."

Conquering John the Doctor was what country folk call a "two-headed person." One head, like yours, houses normal faculties. The second, invisible head exists in a world of magic and spells, *gris-gris* and *wangas*, rootwork and hexes. He called what he did "hoodoo," distinct from the religion "Voodoo" with its *orishas* and crossroads god Legba. Conquering John was less priest than spiritual mechanic, his unwashed but nimble hands confecting charms, spells, and tricks using elaborate ritual and bits of desiccated miscellany.

After several presumptuous questions Conquering John prescribed a "hand," sometimes called a "mojo." With feigned regret he confessed it was the most expensive protective spell. Its key ingredient was High-John-the-Conqueror root, which later investigation determined is a relative of the sweet potato. Conquering John claimed this turd-looking but potent tuber was named after him. No doubt the contrary is true. He added other items: metal shavings off a magnet, a bone from some tiny rodent, common table salt, dirt from St. Catherine cemetery. He sewed the mish-mash into red flannel, held it over my head, and chanted a fast, bored mumble. It took a few times through before I caught every word.

Help him, Lord, for he be stuck in mud and neck deep in water.
His throat be parched for he lament more troubles than he got hairs top his head.
Call out from the grave all the mighty horsemen to ride and run off his enemies.
Protect him and save him, Oh Lord, whether he be worth your blisters or not.

As he repeated it nine times, he threaded the pouch onto twine and looped it around my neck. "This go keep Master's malice off you while you save up to come see me some more."

I resolved never to patronize Conquering John again.

Three weeks later I was back. How could I keep away, when

each day the potency of my protection spell diminished? Hadn't Mother confirmed my stepfather meant to murder me? "Pots of blood," she'd said, rendering every idle glance from the Colonel into a plot hatching. How was I to know whether any given bellyache was due to lethal poisoning or merely excess praline candy, a vice which in my anxiety I often indulged?

I'd wait till my absence wouldn't be noticed and scurry to the Quarters. Conquering John would sell me a whittled candle, or anoint me with a sour-smelling concoction he called Powerful Indian Juice, or he'd "smoke me." That last I rather liked: nothing to carry, nothing to bury, and the herbs he burned smelled nice. Once I suffered nine days with nine twigs in each of my shoes; he called them Devil's Shoestrings. Another time he gave me a second-hand bottle filled with bright red liquid. After the house went to sleep I bent to my knees like the lowliest maid to scrub my bedroom with his "Keep-Away Floor Wash."

Meanwhile, his prices underwent steady inflation. When I complained, he'd add on more for "giving him guff." I learned to keep my mouth shut. Besides every penny I saved, one by one cherished treasures left my possession for his: a penknife, one of my two alligator teeth, a newspaper clipping chronicling the Wright Brother's flight which he took though he couldn't read.

Christmas '04, Mother and the Colonel (who'd despaired of me ever mounting another horse) bought me a bicycle, but I dared not ride it to the Quarters for fear its tracks would give me away. That January, with the cane cut, for lack of other cover I ran bent over through the ditches to avoid being spotted crossing the fields. Then winter downpours filled the ditches. Nothing colder than February rainwater, nothing harder to remove than Louisiana clay. Spring brought out snakes. Twice I felt stony terror as water moccasins rose, opened their cotton-mouths, and struck. The first one nearly stopped my heart as it missed my hand by inches. The second, a snake fatter than my arm, went for my ankle. Foiled by my high-top shoe, its fangs left two shallow punctures in the burgundy leather.

Both times I backed away, went around, continued my journey. I couldn't do otherwise. In relations with Conquering John I was like an opium smoker to whom the matron of the den is liberator and oppressor, both at once.

Eventually he ran through all possible protection charms and launched me on the offensive. Confusion spells. Lock-Up-With-No-Key name papers. Crosses or jinxes were not only (of course) more expensive, they were riskier. Before Conquering John could conjure a Make-The-Fool-Go-Away, I had to steal one of the Colonel's socks. (In fairness, the charm did send Bonreve overnight to Baton Rouge.)

One evening Conquering John insisted on selling me "Urge-to-Wander" foot track magic. "This be a powerful charm," he said, "but risky too. Gotta be just so 'bout how you place it."

"Then maybe I could buy something simpler, and less pricey." He ignored me. I'd seen him use foot track magic on Melpa, so I knew its power. The intended victim must pass directly over it. Once he does and absorbs its spell the powder is rendered inert, but until then the trap will "hotfoot" the first person crossing it whether he or she is whom you want to hex or not.

That night I dreamed Urge-To-Wander put the Colonel aboard the Limited, off to confer with his bankers in New York, blessing Mother and me with two untroubled weeks. Next morning, I hurried to dress, scooted downstairs. Crawling under the front steps, I waited until boots clomped on the gallery above, then opened the flannel pouch and sifted a line of *gris-gris.* Grand Athena had broad front steps, but Bonreve was a creature of habit. He always walked the left side, his hand slicing the air precisely two inches above the rail, as if planning for a day in old age when he'd slip and need to catch his fall.

A heel hit the top step, its mate the next, the third, the fourth. Then, unlike any occasion before, the Colonel's footfalls stopped partway down, well shy of the magic dust which he must cross to be sent wandering. As I mentioned, the Colonel was a creature of habit. This was most extraordinary. I held my breath.

"Come here, young man," he said, "and bring whatever that is in your hand."

Turpitude # 47

"Do not judge, lest you be judged yourself."
Matthew 7:1

To avoid hotfooting myself, I approached via an elliptical path.

"No. Walk straight toward me. Here along the railing."

"I can't."

"Why not?" Colonel Bonreve sat upon the steps like God on Judgment Day. What could I answer that wouldn't incriminate me?

I marched over the track I'd sprinkled. Inside me something tingled, like a movement of gas that doesn't quite escape as a fart. "Sit beside me," the Colonel said, "and give me what you're holding." I did. He poured leftover brown goofer dust into his palm. "What's this?"

"Dirt." The truth, if not the whole truth. My every fiber felt like dashing away. I wasn't sure if it was fear or Urge-To-Wander.

"How have you been spending your allowance?"

I mumbled something, I'm not sure what.

"Speak up. I give you a fixed amount each Saturday. On what do you spend it?"

"This and that."

"This and that," he repeated as if he didn't know with complete certainty that it was evasion, a condemned prisoner bargaining for extra breath.

"Mr. Percle, who manages our mercantile store, said you used to purchase notions for Mr. Gueydan's daughter, but lately you haven't bought anything. Not even candy. If you're saving your money, that would indicate prudent financial stewardship, a quality men admire. I could open an account for you at Merchants & Planters Bank in Thibodaux. Will that be necessary?"

"No," I said so softly he probably couldn't hear. Hotfooting crept up my legs.

"Stop fidgeting," he said. I tried. "If you're not spending your money, and not saving it, where does it go?"

"Pierce White steals it." Except at Sunday mass, I hadn't seen Pierce in months — but all I could think was how I wanted to run away. My blaming Pierce made the Colonel sad. He poked the Urge-To-Wander powder and licked his finger. Was goofer dust poisonous?

"Since you cannot account for your allowance, we'll assume you lost it. Why give you an allowance if you're going to lose it?"

Wasn't it time for Mother to leave her room? Might she not join us and change the subject? She never came this way first thing, but mightn't this morning be different? But even the servants had disappeared.

"So we agree, no more allowance. I'll inform your mother." He upended the flannel bag. Residual hoodoo sifted away on the morning breeze.

"May I go now?" I asked.

"Hardly."

Turpitude # 48

"Anger."

2nd of the Five Inner
Evils of the Sikhs

Squeezed onto the saddle behind him, I'm sure he felt me trembling, but he didn't speak until we reached St. Catherine's Church and he lifted me down from the horse. "Later, as you walk home, consider how your behavior hurts your mother."

My behavior? What about what yours? Those so-called naps? How you gawp at her son when you think I'm not looking? Dreaming you'll snuff me out.

This I wanted to say but didn't. He clicked his stirrups. His horse started home. The church door awaited me like a portal to damnation.

Turpitude # 49

"Confess your sins that your soul may be healed."

James 5:16

In the annual auction of pews, Bonreve of course outbid all to sit his family furthest front. Thus on Sundays I'd only see the congregation as they shuffled to communion. Yet even out-of-sight and reverent a crowd proclaims itself as bodies stir and rustle. Empty, a church lies quiet as death. It smells of candle smoke and mildew instead of what a hundred parishioners had for breakfast. Most of all, an empty church stirs questions of redemption which I wasn't eager to consider. Shifting knee to knee, every muscle screamed at me to move. I wondered where Groetsch had gone, how soon he would come back, and why he had so overreacted to my confession. Hoodoo (which he'd labeled witchcraft) seemed to me a reasonable response to the Colonel's designs on my life and I'd told Groetsch so.

The priest returned. "Stand." I did, gratefully: my knees were giving out. He opened his fist. Hard raw rice sleeted to the floor. "Kneel."

"But—"

"Kneel!" he thundered.

I'd had enough. Reaching up, I grabbed him by his clerical collar. "Repeat a word of my confession to the Colonel and you'll be in big trouble."

"You're threatening me?" Father Groetsch had never been the sharpest hoe in the toolshed. Of course I was threatening him, though with what I'm not sure.

"Big trouble," I repeated. His Adam's apple bobbed. Something about me scared him. I gathered up my sins and left.

Urge-To-Wander kept me three nights traipsing woods and fields, unable to compel myself home. When I returned, muddy, famished, full of apologies, punishment came not from the Colonel but from Mother. I'm not sure if he ever told her why he took me to church. I'm pretty certain Groetsch didn't tell either of them why he no longer had time for piano lessons, but by then, though no one said it, everyone realized I would not live up to my early musical promise. Sure, I'd always be able to enliven a dull party, but I'd never be invited across the globe to play at a major cathedral. Of course, that hadn't quite worked out for Groetsch either.

With the cessation of my allowance, like any prudent merchant Conquering John cut off my credit. "Magic and charms now be cash and carry," he said, pointing at me with the pestle with which he'd been pulverizing snakeroot. "And goodness sake, you do find scratch to buy something, don't get caught with it."

I'd grown used to his protection, wasn't sure I could survive without it. Yet as he once admitted, I wasn't stupid. "You shouldn't be grinding that yourself."

He eyed me.

"Does Colonel Bonreve cut his own cane? Archbishop Chapelle sweep churches? You're a maestro, Conquering John. Why perform chores that are beneath you?"

He snorted.

"You wouldn't have to pay me. Just provide a trick now and then."

I didn't think I'd sold him until, without looking up, he said, "Fetch me a dipper of water." I did. Later: "Boy, run that dog off my porch." I did that too. Soon I was stemming dried herbs and rendering them into powder. I became his errand boy, his pack mule, and most of all, his scavenger, gathering ingredients not only for charms he made me but also those he sold to others, as Conquering John enjoyed the unfamiliar pleasure of ordering about a white person.

When I hounded him with questions — What if he put cat urine instead of dog urine in a Love-Me-Forever? Used red thread instead of black to stitch a five-spot? — usually he enjoyed lording his knowledge over me, but sometimes he'd complain, "Root doctoring be the only good job the white man don't take. Fuck your milky ass if you think to learn my ways, steal my trade, leave me cutting cane like a common nigger. That happen, last thing I do is lay a mean hex on him that wronged me, and I know some powerful mean hexes." Of that I had no doubt.

One humid afternoon, mid-June, 1905, the Colonel and Mother sipped coffee from demitasses as lightning rent the sky. Farther along the balcony, I played with my toy soldiers. I'd requested a tubful of *bagasse*, the squeezed-dry pulp of sugarcane, and from it had fashioned a San Juan Hill which my troops were attacking. Mother was first to notice the solitary rider. The Colonel rose, leaning on the bannisters like a knight defending his castle. "I wondered whether it was fool or demon riding horseback through a lightning storm."

"Without doubt, fool," replied Judge Pike from his horse. "However, a fool who knows he's been one. I bring terrible news, I'm afraid." Terrible, yet he smiled.

"One might wonder if you visit when bad things happen," said the Colonel, "or whether bad things happen when you visit."

Turpitude # 50

"Let my people go or
suffer grievous pestilence."

Exodus 9:1

Bronze john, black vomit, yellow jack; frightening names for the occasional plague that killed tens of thousands from Boston to Galveston over the past century. A few years earlier, Major Reed of the U.S. Army discovered the *Aedes* mosquito transmitted yellow fever. Occupied Havana was cleared of the pest, but the South's largest city, New Orleans, enjoyed no such eradication. As pouring rain overflowed gutters, Judge Pike explained the situation. "A hundred cases. Twenty dead. It'll get worse and won't stay contained to the city. Thursday the mayor will declare a State of Emergency." No one bothered asking how the Judge received advance notice.

"You brought disease into our home?" the Colonel accused.

"You think I'd come if I carried sickness? I wanted to warn you but dared not put it in a telegram. Besides, I wondered if my friends had forgiven my bad behavior."

Neither the Colonel nor Mother took that bait.

The rain stopped. Steam rose from every leaf. The portable *cave à liqueur* was rolled out and brandy poured. After his litany of doom, Judge Pike regaled us with stories of his first-class travels and noble honors and important friends, pretending they mattered little to him. The seeds he'd planted in society and politics a decade before had borne plump fruit. No door was closed to him, his assistance often sought, and he'd become nearly as rich as the Colonel. He often glanced toward Mother to include her in the conversation but his gaze never lingered. When he looked at me, an invitation to complicity sparkled in his eyes. Before leaving, he presented me a folder crammed with sheet music: Tin Pan Alley, Ragtime, tunes adults claimed were ruining the younger generation. I didn't like the Judge, but I couldn't hide how much I loved his gift.

"Best play these only when your stepfather is out. He's not as modern as you or I."

As the Judge predicted, the epidemic spread. "Fever in Houma." "Cases in Leeville." "It's reached Thibodaux." To his ill-disguised chagrin, Father Groetsch once again became the "Fearless Funeral Friar." Armed guards who in spring defended the levees spent summer patrolling the dirt road beside it, setting up ad hoc quarantines. Judge Pike arranged legal immunity in case they had to shoot anyone.

As stubble grew into tall, green stands of cane, Athena settled down to weather the siege. Bayou Road no longer heard the cries of Levantine peddlers hawking clothes from trunks carried on their shoulders; no more ready-to-bargain Cajuns with fresh-plucked night herons hanging from their saddles; no more Sicilians, full of song, pushing wheelbarrows full of bananas and coconuts. My new schoolteacher never showed up. The piano tuner skipped his annual visit.

Colonel Bonreve commanded us like Robert E. Lee. Bridges were dismantled, turning drainage canals into moats. Cisterns, water barrels, puddles — anyplace mosquitoes might breed —

were dosed with kerosene which, lighter than water, filmed the surface and poisoned larva.

Tiptoeing to the Quarters became impossible, so my work for Conquering John ceased and with it my source of hexes. With the priest no longer coming round and the Colonel busy, I could play the New Music they abhorred. One day, despite Tante Elmire's warning that my "devil's symphony" invited disease, I was hammering the keys with the new *jass* music filtering out of New Orleans. When I saw Mother listening from the doorway, I added extra syncopation to my rousing finale.

"Could the spells you buy ward off yellow jack?" Her question caught me off-guard; I'd expected applause.

"Spells?"

"Hoodoo. Root-work. Whatever you call it."

"Mother, I—" Her expression told me denial would be neither credible nor necessary. "Don't see why not."

She revealed an embroidered coin purse. It looked heavy. "Protection for you and me."

"Can I buy one for Nat?"

"If there's enough money."

"The Colonel?"

A brief pause. "Your stepfather doesn't believe in magic."

"What if he catches fever and dies?"

"You'll become very rich," she said, further muddling my feelings toward the man.

Turpitude # 51

"Those who practice sorcery shall burn in fire and brimstone."
Revelation 21:8

The bullet sliced the sugarcane. A quarter-second later came the report of the rifle. The night was dark, the cane thick, the sniper far. It'd take incredibly bad luck for him to hit me, but my luck hadn't been running good. This was the third night I sneaked out trying to visit Conquering John. Again I'd been spotted by the quarantine guards. I wondered how many eleven-year-olds had been shot at as often as I. Would the Colonel pay a bounty if they blasted me?

I heard the patrol moving to flank me. Among the Colonel's hired gunmen were some who'd fought in Cuba in '98. Though seldom sober they understood tactics. A moment before, I'd thought I'd run the worst of the gauntlet; now I knew graver danger lay ahead. Mother would be furious if she suspected the risks I was taking. I decided to retreat before I was recognized. Thus ended my third attempt to reach Conquering John.

Next morning at breakfast, Father Groetsch brought news that in New Orleans, Archbishop Chapelle had died of jack. If high clerics were falling, no one was safe. Mother was counting on me. Nat too, even if he didn't know it.

I caught the tail of some story the Colonel was telling about a midwife halted by the quarantine, forcing a common parlor maid to step in and deliver her mistress' baby. It hit me: hadn't I mingled ingredients and sewn mojos and occasionally composed incantations? Perhaps the apprentice was ready to strike out on his own.

Camphor leaves and mule hoof trimmings, a cobweb and

three silver dimes, I scavenged fresh. Other items I retrieved from worn-out charms I'd secreted into my cast iron bedpost. Conquering John often recycled ingredients, especially when it was raining or he had a waiting assignation. That left one critical component.

With Sunday masses suspended, a trip to St. Catherine's for graveyard dirt was out of the question, but the Colonel had once given me two teeth from the 'gator he'd killed. One I traded to Conquering John and later saw him grind it up as substitute for cemetery dust. I still had the other.

Pulverizing an alligator tooth isn't as easy as Conquering John made it look. Banging with one's shoe only damages the shoe. Sneaking into the cookhouse, I broke Yvonne's nutmeg grinder, ruined her coffee mill, and dulled several cleavers before discovering that a mechanical pecan cracker does an admirable job.

I sought the privacy of the *pigeonnière* to assemble the tricks. As pale gray birds milled around me, I found I didn't have enough ground 'gator incisor to complete three charms. Two and a half, maybe, so one would be only half-strength.

Inserting ingredients one at a time into the three red pouches, twenty-seven times in total I recited…

Deliver her or him or me who wears this hand, Lord, for thy tender mercy's sake.
Keep us from languishing and shove away all sickness but especially yellow jack.
The mosquito in its pride doth bite us and its poison is like the poison of a snake.
Call up the spirits and saints, Oh, Lord, and tell them to smash that skeeter flat.

My mind was not as focused on the ritual as it should've been. I sweated who would get the half-strength mojo. Not Mother. That left Nat or me. I devised a long list of thin justifications for me needing, deserving, by all rights ought-ing to have the stronger charm. Pigeons cooed agreement with every excuse I invented, but pigeons are seldom lauded for independent thought. In the end, I took the half-potency trick for myself.

After presenting Mother her charm and explaining how she must hide it from the Colonel, especially during "naps," she gave me a big kiss. I brought Nat his mojo, though there it took coaxing. While he readily believed a flannel pouch could ward off fatal disease, he doubted my skill to craft one and, unlike Mother, immediately recognized it as a home-made job. Weathering his truculence, I started to regret not keeping the stronger charm myself, but finally he looped it around his neck. I marched to the Big House feeling grown up. Even Achille Cheramie, as far as I knew, had never mastered hoodoo.

But like flies to a crawfish boil, doubt flew in. Who was I to cast spells? On matters of life and death? I was a boy, a know-nothing, a poser! If something happened to Mother! Each evening, worry brought the same nightmare: *Urk, urk, urk*, the Colonel unscrews a Mason jar. Out buzz mosquitoes dripping pestilence. They swarm toward — depending on the night — Mother or Nat or me. Friday it was me…

I woke sweating. My skin prickled. Just another dream.

Yet one prickle persisted…

Turpitude # 52

"Animal killers, in their next life,
shall be eaten by creatures
they murdered in this one."

Srimad Bhagavatam 11:5:14
of the Hindus

Jabbing me like a needle, the Colonel's assassin, a mosquito, measured me with her compound eyes, not quite gorged but, like Don Juan interrupted by a husband, prudently pulling out. *Whap!* I smashed her.

Four days later, symptoms set in.

Turpitude # 53

"Sin brings death."

James 1:15

I cooked with fever, shivered with chills, suffered head pains and back aches, nausea and sweats. I jaundiced yellower than the Lady Banks roses Nat tended in a corner of the garden.

Achille Cheramie died diving into a hurricane to save his bride's beloved sister, succumbing only to the combined malevolence of wind, flood, massive logs, bovine cyclops, and devilish hare. I would die from a mosquito bite.

When I began spewing vomit black with blood, traditional sign of a fatal case approaching resolution, the priest was called. Much as he dreaded the disease, the Fearless Funeral Friar relished performing *my* Last Rites, that is until I began gagging up a giant hairball, an enormous mass like a soul escaping Hell, that choked me an hour before past my lips came a quintet of wiggling fingers. *That* stopped the friar's jabbering.

I retched a cufflinked wrist, a sleeved arm. Mother wept. The Colonel decried my lack of decorum. Passing that first shoulder was excruciating but no worse than my dismay once I dislocated my jaw vomiting out the head of Pierce Douglas White and realizing the rest of his body was still to come. You think I'm making this up but I'm not. The memory is as clear and painful as my broken arm a few years prior. How Pierce got inside me, I've no idea. Hiding from justice, no doubt.

The entire rest of the night I endured his nattering complaints as bit by bit he slithered out. With my mouth so stretched, I couldn't respond when he taunted me by asking if I'd noticed how Aralee's pair of kumquats were ripening into tangy lemons. Mother ignored his blather. Father Groetsch sealed his ears with candlewax.

What happened to Pierce after I upchucked him, I'm not sure. When next I saw him, at Sunday mass after the quarantine had been lifted, he appeared undamaged. Five hundred souls died of yellow fever that summer. Thanks to Mother's solicitude and my homemade hoodoo, I wasn't one of them. When I felt well enough to stroll the garden, Nat offered further endorsement. "Never heard of a hoodoo doctor white boy," he confessed, "but your mojo kept the jack away even when I got swarmed by skeeters." Thus, after recovery, I didn't call on Conquering John, seeing no reason to pay for Evil-Go-Aways when I could conjure my own.

One evening like any other, climbing into bed, something tickled my ear. I jumped, supposing it one of those extravagantly large flying cockroaches that somehow creep in under any closed door. It wasn't. Palmetto bugs may be disgusting but present no actual danger. What I was looking at might be lethal. Someone had filled one of my socks with cemetery dirt. Buried in this goofer dust were thirteen nails dressed with conjure oil, a spell to eliminate a vexing problem. If this lay under my pillow, somebody considered *me* the problem.

Turpitude # 54

"He who curses his father shall be put to death."

N°. 582 of the 613
Mitzvot of the Jews

"No juju outside of business hours," he hollered.

"Come out *now*, Conquering John!"

I heard curses, his hammock creaked, and a female voice grumbled. Life stirred in other cabins, but no one lit a candle. Conquering John strut onto his porch. A precisely held woman's straw hat covered his privates, but he was otherwise naked.

"I know the hex under my pillow came from you," I said.

"So ask yourself, what man 'round here who hate your ass can 'ford the best?"

"*Colonel Bonreve* hexed me? And you admit you sold it to him?"

Conquering John threaded the bony fingers of his free hand into my nightshirt's collar and lifted me into the air. Eye to eye, nose to nose, his lady friend's hat tickling my shins, he lowered his voice. "Know what I admit? Admit I got a missy inside who crave entertaining. Admit we 'joyed a good start 'fore you come a-hollering. Admit if we can't finish 'fore her husband get back from shooting craps, I go be riled with you some big." He tossed me to the ground. Laughter seeped from several cabins. Even the wormy dogs chuckled.

Into the woods to gather bloodroot. To the kitchen house for chimney soot and sulfur match heads. From the maid Antoinette's sewing box I took nine pins, careful to point them toward where the Colonel slept as I crept back to my room.

The wicked travailed to do me wrong; now let his evil hex fall upon his own head.
He dug a pit to trap me, but Holy Ghost I beg, shove his damn self into that abyss.

Since I neither hanged myself nor slit my throat nor experienced urges to jump into the bayou and drown, my impromptu hex-removal must've worked, but I suffered no delusion this would end it. Going head to head with Conquering John, sooner or later, probably sooner, his tricks would outconjure mine. If he sold countervailing *gris-gris* to my stepfather and me, never could I match the buying power of the state's wealthiest man. I no longer even received an allowance. I needed help, but it was too risky to draw Mother in deeper. Nat lacked power because of his Negroism. Groetsch would have me chanting novenas. Aralee was but a girl and, off on her parents' plantation, possibly not rock solid in her affections for me. Only one person could I think of.

Pedaling three miles to Thibodaux, I primped at a public fountain before going into the courthouse. My heels clicked over the marble floor. The building possessed an electrical generator, not just for lights but also to turn ceiling fans. As swirling blades created a cooling breeze, I regretted that the Colonel was too tradition-bound to install a similar system at Athena. Though maybe I underestimated him: he'd embraced hoodoo, hadn't he?

Painted onto a door's frosted glass was the name of the man

I'd come to see. His clerk showed me into a courtroom. Though empty, it was easy to imagine it crowded with pleading defendants, lying witnesses, pitiless jurors. Judge Pike swept in, black robes flowing. "Should I administer you the oath before we discuss whatever's on your mind?"

Turpitude # 55

"From him that would borrow, turn not away."

Matthew 5:42

"I need money."

"Why come to me?" asked Judge Pike.

"You're rich."

He smiled down from his bench, having sat me in the witness box. "I mean why not ask your stepfather, who's wealthier than I."

"It's to thwart him I need the money."

"You believe he's trying to harm you?"

"I'm sure of it, your honor. And he's employing the dark arts to do so."

"Well, this is a grave development. You plan to use these funds to flee? Timbuktu, Ulan Bator, some other exotic hideaway?"

I ignored the twinkle in his eye. "Counter-hexes are expensive. I'll pay you back someday."

"'Someday' constitutes a troublingly vague repayment schedule." His wisp of a smile infuriated me. "I won't loan you money, especially not to purchase sorcery, which is pure bunk, incidentally."

I hadn't expected him to, not without coercion, but I had to try. My next card was risky: "What if I told the world who caused the Waverly Crevasse?"

He paused before answering. "There you encounter the Statute of Limitations. After a prescribed calendar duration, a given crime becomes no longer actionable."

"Your reputation will still be ruined."

"I suspect not."

"I'll stand as witness to your sabotage."

"If you don't mind prosecution for slander."

"It's only slander if it's not true."

"Correct. Truth, however, is whatever notion the better class of people can be induced to believe. I'm a respected judge. How easy to sow whispers. 'A spoiled, unstable child.' 'Uncertain parentage.' 'Dabbles in the occult.' Shattering your credibility wouldn't raise a sweat."

He was right. Like the potency of a mojo or the flavor of a marmalade, leverage over another deteriorates with time. I started to climb from the witness box. "Stay where you are," he commanded. "I never said I wouldn't help you. I said I wouldn't give you money to buy voodoo."

"Not voodoo, hoodoo."

"Don't quibble. In return for my help there's something you must do for me."

Turpitude # 56

"Accept no bribe, for bribes corrupt the innocent."

Exodus 23:8

The Judge toyed with his gavel. "I wish to speak to your Mother."

"You speak to her all the time."

"Not in private. You must arrange a meeting, a secret meeting, a rendezvous."

So that's where this was heading. "I'm not sure she'd be willing."

"Neither am I, which is why you may need to transcend methods you consider ethical."

"In your world, is there a line between right and wrong?"

"Of course. It falls wherever I draw it. What are you now, twelve? Too old for naiveté. Right and wrong and rules and laws are flexible concepts. Codified in high-priced darkness. Passed in bold hypocrisy. Adjudicated by men like me. There's a line all right. If you're smart you stay on my side of it."

"The world can't be that corrupt."

"I guarantee it is." He banged his gavel. "Guilty!" *Slam*, again. "Innocent!" *Slam!* "Guilty, innocent, guilty! Life or death, years in prison, fortunes forfeited, all to the convenience of those who hold power. Against that, what's a little quiet infidelity?"

I rose in the witness box. "You admit that's what you want?"

"Sit down. Hasn't time come to speak plainly? The question is what does *she* want? I'd never use force, not if she pushed me away and meant it. I don't think she would. Not if we had a chance to chat and touch and not be interrupted. Which, again, is where you come in."

My gut roiled with images of the Judge and Mother and the sweat-soaked goings-on Tante Clo described. You see, I wasn't sure she'd turn him down. During the half-decade their on-again, off-again, unconsummated passion had fouled the air, I'd come to realize that adultery didn't always lead to suicide or public scandal. Sometimes secrets were kept, and who better to keep them than my enigmatic mother and this devious judge? Who was I to say it shouldn't happen?

"If I do this, you'll protect me from the Colonel? Now and forever?"

He nodded. *Quid pro quo*s were the Judge's stock-in-trade. The vile bargain he'd proposed was to him a routine transaction.

"I'll need a lock of your hair," I said.

"Whatever for?"

"It's basic to any Come-To-Me charm."

Turpitude # 57

"The go-between should remind the woman about the weaknesses of her husband, his jealousy, his roguery, his dullness, and all his other faults."

Kama Sutra, Chapter 6,
Duties of a Go-Between

I found Mother at the milking barn surrounded by two

dozen Negro children. Previously, dairy surplus had been sold to passing steamboats. Mother stopped that, instead letting the milk clabber and straining the whey, portioning the delicious result to children from the Quarters. It was one of many procedural changes she enacted that Bonreve was tolerant of but bewildered by.

"You're wearing that look," Mother said.

"We need to discuss love's complications and consequences."

"That's the look I meant." She dolloped cream cheese into a girl's tin pail. The girl flashed a smile then ran off with her breakfast. Mother continued serving the line of children. "If you're talking about a mother's love for her son, you shouldn't worry about that."

Might she feel the same if she knew about my conversation with the Judge? I lowered my voice. "I'm here about man-woman love."

"A subject that never gets tired. When you bicycled off yesterday, I wondered where you were bound. Gueydan Plantation, to see your Aralee?"

I liked the sound of "my Aralee" but dodged the question. "What if a woman loves a man who's unworthy?" I ignored that each kiddie peered at me.

"You're as worthy as anyone," Mother said.

"We're speaking hypothetically."

Plop, cream cheese hit galvanized metal. "Unworthy doesn't necessarily kill the deal. Sometimes a girl, Aralee included I suppose, sparks to a guy who sweeps her someplace dark."

"Is darkness what a woman like you wants?"

Mother served the last child in line, scraping the sides of her basin. "Most women, myself included, are creatures of mood who change what they want hour by hour and minute by minute or worst yet to a fellow like you she doesn't change her mind at all but invites a completely contrary notion into her head and heart at the same time and dares the poor bastard to satisfy both contradictory desires at once, like he was a magician, which in almost all cases, he isn't." She walked to the cistern to rinse her utensils.

"Is Judge Pike a magician?"

"He won't put Mr. Houdini out of business."

"Am I?" I couldn't resist asking though it was off-topic.

"Some days I see magic in you, some days something else. Whichever side you fall, or even if you insist on wearing both hats in turn, I'll be there to champion you, no matter what."

As she shook her ladle dry, I understood which sort of *gris-gris* I needed to create.

In the woods that night, I found Judge Pike's horse tied to a holly. With no moon, I could barely make out the Judge, waiting for Mother in the shadows right where he told me he'd be. I took the *gris-gris* from my pocket, wedged it under the pommel of his saddle, and crept away. The Judge didn't see me come, didn't see me go, nor did he know I never mentioned this supposed rendezvous to Mother. I wonder how long he waited before he gave up.

My trick worked exactly as conjured, and because of that extra long-lasting Keep-Away charm Judge Pike would not return to Athena for a long time, though not quite long enough for him to forgive me.

Turpitude # 58

"Harm not the boy in any way."

Genesis 22:12

The cat stunk. Cats are normally fastidious groomers, but this one was dead so its stench was hardly its fault. By the height of the moon I guessed that four bug-bitten hours had passed since I'd stripped out of my clothes amidst a copse of reed then swam the bayou in constant terror of being eaten by ferocious alligator, ravished by incestuous mermaid, or both.

As 1905 became 1906, I'd found myself back under the thumb of Conquering John, buying his mojos whenever I could scrape together enough money and sweetening the deal with my labor. Nearly twelve, I enjoyed more freedom to roam. It became nothing to bicycle the bumpy road to St. Catherine's to gather him cemetery dirt. Naturally I'd collect a pinch for myself as well. Sneaking out at night was trickier but not impossible. Thus, here I was, assigned to exhume a neighbor's black cat that Conquering John had heard died.

Wandering nude through gardens and fields, I found the grave. It was all I could do not to puke breast-stroking back across the bayou holding the putrid carcass with my mouth. Once I'd dressed and trudged to his cabin, Conquering John had me debone the cat — I believe its name had been Sambo — the way I'd seen our cook debone Muscovy ducks.

A black cat bone enhances any mojo. Since the only thing Conquering John carefully counted was money, I felt safe pilfering several vertebrae from Sambo's tail, but those bits of backbone seemed small potatoes next to the rest of the skeleton, some of which would go into hexes on me Conquering John would sell to the Colonel.

That was the problem. With cyclical regularity I had to either buy a fresh trick or fix one myself. I couldn't stop because the Colonel wouldn't. If I fell behind, I'd run across a bottle spell or suspicious sachet and realize I was feeling its effects. Dizziness. Dyspepsia. Confusion. Oh, what confusion! Even as Colonel Bonreve hectored me to go shooting with him, or horse-riding, or any number of other dangerous activities.

1906 became 1907. On the 4th of July, I turned thirteen. Slow to mature, I looked ten; Pierce White by this time sported fuzz above his lip.

That year President Teddy Roosevelt visited Louisiana for a bear hunt. Finding a cub in his sights and (unlike the Colonel) being a man of compassion, he spared it. American factories had spewed out upholstered "teddy bears" ever since.

In September, the papers reported how Queen of Temperance Carrie Nation frothed, aghast, while touring New Orleans' "Storyville" district with its saloons on every corner and brothels in-between.

October arrived but summer wouldn't let go. People remained loathe to eat oysters, fearful of the heat. Thursday, the 24th, Antoinette announced that the Colonel wanted me in the library, the summons rendered strange by her expression. Antoinette appeared frightened.

Turpitude # 59

"The fifth most heinous sin is to destroy the inheritance of an adopted son."

Menog-i Khrad 36:8,
Sacred Book of
the Zarathustrans

"Lock the door," the Colonel said, "and bring me the key."

I did, though hardly eager to surrender control of the exit.

Papers lay scattered on his desk, unusual for a man so tidy. Telegrams, account books, letters inked by typewriter thus not bespeaking friendly correspondence. A handwritten list of a half-dozen items: he was prepared for this meeting. I wasn't.

"Do you think yourself mature enough to discuss unpleasant matters in a manner that is, shall I say, man to man?"

"I think so," I said, wondering what I'd done this time.

"Man enough to assist me in taking a, well, manly solution to the problem?"

Again I said, "I think so," though by that point I wasn't sure.

"I'll get right to it then. Have you been following the copper market?"

This was his idea of getting right to it? I shook my head.

"Suffice to say an attempt to corner the stock of United Copper failed, a good thing in general I suppose, but when that house of cards fell, it brought down Knickerbocker Trust in New York. That started runs on other banks, which in turn issued demand letters on outstanding paper, which unfortunately included sizable loans backed by the assets of Athena Plantation incorporated, Athena Lumber incorporated, Athena Moss Gin incorporated, and so on and so forth. Do you understand?"

"Not entirely."

"I failed to exercise prudent financial stewardship."

Anxiety burned a hole in my gut. "Meaning?"

"We're broke. Bankrupt. No pot to piss in. This plantation's been in my family since 1792 and I've gone and lost it."

I didn't know what to say.

"Though your mother's no doubt grown accustomed to comfort, I'm sure she possesses sufficient strength of character to accommodate reduced circumstances. For myself, frankly, a simpler life would be relief. If it allowed me to share her company more hours every day, I'd happily forego these trappings." He waved vaguely around the room. I began inventorying the books I'd hate to lose, speculating where I might hide them.

"So your mother and I would be fine. The problem, I'm afraid, is you." I didn't know where this was leading but could think of no direction I'd even remotely enjoy. Nor was I encouraged when he rambled to his gun case. "You've never been much for chores but neither have many chores been asked of you, so it's conceivable even you might adjust to deprivation. The problem is, each time your Mother saw you she'd be reminded of the education you weren't getting, the grand start in life that was almost yours."

A key emerged from his pocket then disappeared into the gun case lock. Beveled glass framed in mahogany swung open, liberating enough armaments for a small war. Recalling a long-ago premonition of Mother's, something about a gun from this case and pots of blood, I broke into a sweat.

The library door was locked. I'd done it myself. On the opposite wall, jalousie windows led to the balcony. Do I pause to unlatch them, considering that humidity might make them hard to open? Or leap through, calculating that shattering glass would cause less injury than the lead shot sure to be chasing me?

The Colonel checked the cylinder of a nickel-plated .32 Smith and Wesson. If I was going to flee, it had to be now. Then the Colonel did the most extraordinary thing.

Turpitude # 60

"Thou shalt not kill."

The 5th Commandment

Bonreve offered me the gun. "Take it," he said.

He wanted me to kill myself. What a fool. With the perfect aim of Achille Cheramie, I'd shoot *him* and be done with a dozen years of battle. I reached for the .32, certain he'd snatch it back. He didn't.

"Do you have the strength to pull the trigger?" he asked. "I don't mean physical strength. A hair trigger, it takes the slightest touch. What I mean is the strength of conviction to act so decisively. To shoot knowing with irrevocable finality that death will ensue?"

"I can pull the trigger," I said.

Clearly, bankruptcy had driven the Colonel mad as a March hare. "When you do it, I'll be looking away." At least he wasn't so cold as to want to watch. "Like this." He struck a pose, reaching for a book. "What do you think?" What did I care seemed more the point. If he expected me to fire a .32 slug into my brain, why should I give a flying flute what he'd be up to? He contorted an arm behind his back, as if trying to scratch an unreachable itch. "Come as close to this spot as possible. So the bullet will pierce my heart."

What?

"I'd prefer death be instantaneous, but if it takes a while, you shouldn't think you let me down or any such nonsense."

He didn't want me to kill myself. He wanted me to kill *him*. Yet the man had been plotting to murder me since New Year, 1900, and had just explained I was the only thing preventing his and Mother's happiness.

"I don't care to seem dense," I said, "but are you saying I should shoot you?"

"How else will your mother remarry a man more financially prudent?" He returned to his desk, checking off an item on his handwritten list. "Promise to tell her, not soon but someday, that at the end I regretted never showing you two Rome and Vienna the way she always dreamed of. I was too afraid that if we traveled she'd find a man she liked better."

The weapon grew heavy in my hand. Looking in the case, I realized it was the smallest he owned. He'd chosen it for my comfort. I recognized a Damascus rifle I'd seen many times slung across his saddle. "Did you ever kill that black bear?" I asked.

"No," he said. "I saw it three times. Once I had a clean shot for a good forty seconds but couldn't bring myself to fire. I suppose that's not something a planter should admit."

In that sentence I learned a truth that had been in front of me my entire life but which I'd never before perceived. Louis

Bonreve, lord of Athena Plantation, honorary colonel in the Louisiana militia, and generous patron of many worthy causes, lived in as much subjugation as any field hand inhabiting the Quarters, because Colonel Louis Bonreve was a life-sentenced prisoner of his upbringing, his social class, and his own expectations.

He consulted his list again. "This is important," he declared, not appearing to notice the lethal weapon I held. "I'm aware I ask an onerous favor. I don't request it lightly. No one else do I trust who wouldn't risk grave consequences. If I took my own life, well, with suicide comes scandal and I'd as soon spare your mother that indignity. Also, a suicide wouldn't be permitted burial in the churchyard. After the money I've poured into St. Catherine's, that would seem a particular shame. So, again, I know I ask a great deal but nothing beyond a fellow who rides wild alligators, consorts with witch doctors, and runs like the wind before blazing bullets as levees fail."

A day for surprises. "At the crevasse, you recognized me?"

"You forgot I bought you that nightshirt on one of my trips to New Orleans?"

"So you knew it was me you were shooting at?"

"No. I never shot at you, though others may have. In the heat of anger I shot — not very straight — at Judge Pike, who's often been an unworthy friend to both of us."

Colonel Bonreve was mad all right, but what generous, benevolent madness. Hopeless to appeal to self-preservation; he'd made up his mind to die and was a stubborn man. Generously, benevolently stubborn, but stubborn nonetheless. I had to convince him his death would render those left behind worse off. "If I do what you ask, I'll go to jail."

"On the contrary. A few years hence, once you became a truculent adolescent, it might be different. Now, the world will rush to console you for quite natural feelings of guilt over your role in the terrible accident. Which brings up the next point, which is probably obvious. Tell *everyone* it was an accident. Say I planned to give you the gun on your birthday and let you examine it, not realizing it was loaded. Sound reasonable?"

"Reasonable as any lie," I threw back, "but lying is a sin. Killing you, a worse sin."

"You refer to the Ten Commandments?"

"'Thou shalt not kill,' is rather explicit."

"Did you know many Baptists phrase that one differently? In their Bibles it's written, 'Thou shalt not murder.' Since I'm asking you to do it, our business here hardly constitutes murder."

"Forgive me if I don't entrust my immortal soul to the dubious doctrines of a Protestant sect."

He smiled. "You're an odd duck. I suppose I am too. Perhaps that's why I always felt such affinity for you."

If he was sincere, and in his despondency I couldn't imagine him otherwise, then for the last dozen years I'd seriously misjudged the man. Now with my eyes opened, surely it wasn't too late to put things right, to unravel this turn of misfortune and use it to fashion something good, to retrace all my crooked steps and this time take a straighter path. Between us, he and I together, maybe we could at last fill the hole Achille had pierced in Mother's heart.

"You can't leave Mother defenseless," I said as gently as I could.

His smile flew away. "Did you hear what I said? I'm bankrupt. I held wealth most men only dream of but in my arrogance didn't squirrel away a single cent. If I'd saved just the money I spent on those damn wedding spiders! Buried it where lawyers could never find it so we'd have it now to live on, the three of us. Modestly to be sure, but who needs servants? Who needs racehorses? You don't even like horses."

Even in his turmoil, he checked his list one last time, begging the question how a fellow so methodical could've misplaced such a large fortune. I didn't think I'd like being poor, but I doubted his death would make it more palatable. He folded his list and fed it to the candle. I threw my arms around him. "I don't want you to die. Mother needs you. *I* need you, Papa." I wasn't pretending.

He hugged me back till finally, gently, he pushed me away. "Now I'm going to walk to the bookcase."

"I won't shoot you!" I tossed the revolver onto his desk. Together, father and son, we'd find some solution. I believed that with my whole heart.

He didn't. "Then I'll do it myself after all. Spend eternity buried in a barnyard like any common suicide." The Colonel picked up the pistol. I tried to grab it back. There came a *snap* like a fragile branch broken by an evil wind.

Turpitude # 61

"Give no opportunity to the devil."

Ephesians 4:27

Judge Pike pried the gun from my hand. Where had he come from? Mother stood there too, her expression unreadable. Hadn't the door been locked? I'd done it myself. Given the key to... What should I call him now? For years I maligned the man. Now I'd killed him. Patricide seemed to be turning into something of a habit.

Murmuring at the door. Broken open, its cypress frame so cracked it'd have to be replaced. Filling the doorway, faces: Yvonne, Antoinette, Two-Tone Willie whose powerful shoulder was likely the one that defeated the lock. They were looking at the Colonel sitting dead in his chair. Blood seeped down his shirt, dripped from his leg, puddled at his feet.

The Judge side-stepped to block their view. "Don't let your imaginations scamper. You heard a noise, came running, saw the master dead. If anyone, even the Sheriff, asks, you can't recall more than that. Understand?" Black faces nodded, not about to buck a white man in these newly uncertain times. "Willie, find Mr. Bourque. Have him ride to get Sheriff Bourgeois. The rest of you, downstairs."

The Judge closed what was left of the door and brought a chair for Mother. "Sit, Madame." Mother sat. "You were asleep," he told me. "You fell asleep reading." From the shelf he grabbed a book at random then smiled when he saw its title: *The Greek Tragedies, Volume VI, Oedipus the Tyrant.* He put the book in my hand.

"You were awakened by the gunshot, but you'd been dreaming, so it took a moment — no, several moments — to understand what happened. Then you picked the gun off the floor." He looked around, choosing a spot. "Here. You understand?"

I looked at Mother for guidance. "Your son's innocent," he told her. "I see no reason to cloud that with facts which could be misconstrued. Our sheriff is a simple man. The death of someone so prominent might inspire many theories and much mischief. Do you agree?"

Mother nodded. When the Judge again asked me, "Do you understand what you're to say?" he and Mother presented a unified, irresistible force.

"I was asleep." My lie earned the Judge's smile. He knew exactly what I'd done. Why was he concealing my guilt?

"How'd you know?" Mother asked him. I blanched.

"How?" the Judge repeated. "How did I know Louis was about to... I didn't. I'd come to tell him a telegram arrived from New York. J.P. Morgan stepped in to save the market. Louis wasn't ruined after all."

Turpitude # 62

"Let young widows remarry."

1 Timothy 5:14

"Wait downstairs," the Judge told me once I rehearsed his story. As I walked to the door, Mother caught my arm. She hardly had to tug for me to sit in her lap, something I hadn't done in years. I was too heavy, but she didn't complain. The Judge frowned.

"Madame, there are things we must discuss the boy perhaps ought not be privy to."

Mother made no move, nor would I leave the comfort of her arms unless forced. The Judge gave in. He began pacing the library like a lawyer addressing court. "I'll do my best to protect you from the dual scandals of a suicide husband and an at best careless, at worst murderous son." I didn't enjoy his description though I couldn't fault its accuracy. "While you wear the veil of mourning, I propose we conduct ourselves with scrupulous propriety. I understand if you're skeptical of my restraint, but I can be patient if I know that, in twelve short months, you'll permanently become mine." He paused, awaiting a response. The Colonel sat in judgmental silence. Mother scratched at the healed-over stigma in her palm, as if something was caught in the pockmark that she wanted to dig out.

Almost fourteen years before, when Mother was seventeen, pregnant, and then too, newly widowed, among the mahogany furniture of an adjacent parlor Judge Pike had offered promises of comfort in exchange for an arrangement vague but vile, unspecified but definitely immoral. Now he'd made a legitimate — albeit ill-timed — proposal of respectable marriage, yet his new proposition struck me as infinitely more contemptible. He wanted to replace my dead father. Both my dead fathers. Please, Mary, Jesus, Buddha, whoever, have her say "No." *Tick, tick, tick* went the grandfather clock.

"Madame, I just proposed."

I was as agitated as him to hear how Mother would respond. Or *if* she'd respond. *Tick, tick, tick*. Her fingernail scratched the other stigma.

"Madame, surely—"

"Four years ago you could've had me," she interrupted. "I was willing to run off with you as long as you made sure my boy got the best upbringing and care and education, but you were afraid of scandal and preferred something quiet and dirty although my poor husband, whatever his faults, never deserved to be treated that shabby, but I was slipping off the edge and almost ready to give you what you wanted, my virtue and all that went with it, and if you think that's easy to admit in front of my son then you're mad, but I thought if you needed me so badly then maybe just maybe you could give me back some of the fire my first husband gave me that one and only night we had, but no to that too, because when Louis walked in on us in the cookhouse you denied everything, denied it though he didn't believe you, because he wasn't a fool — except maybe today sitting dead like he is — but he wasn't a fool then and he ran you off even if you told yourself you left to be gentlemanly, but we both know you were being chickenshit cowardly, so now it's not at all flattering that you come around proposing with my husband not yet cold when it's just so convenient and can make you even richer than you already are—"

"Money has nothing—" the Judge tried to interject, but Mother plowed on.

"—so if you want an answer I'll give you one. It won't be 'no,' it'll be 'Hell, no' because I will never marry you. Never, never, never."

Silence filled the room. The clock even stopped for a moment.

"Madame, my feelings—"

"I don't give two cents for your feelings. Go away and let me mourn my husband."

The conversation was over. Barely controlling his hurt and fury, the Judge left. I basked in Mother's solace, delicious though undeserved. Thirty-one years old, yet thrust into a second widowhood. I'd protect her; I just wasn't sure how.

Turpitude # 63

"Obey the authorities."

Romans 13:5

Sheriff Bourgeois was a thoughtful man of sixty with an old-fashioned long beard and one arm, the other shot off by a Minié ball at Petersburg on his 18th birthday. He inspected the Colonel's wound, the .32, the book I'd been reading. I told the story as the Judge had instructed. The Sheriff had questions, none of which I could answer for having been asleep over my book, which seemed a more obvious lie every time I repeated it.

When the Sheriff finished, Judge Pike surprised me with his own query. "Young man, will it be necessary to have you set your hand on the Bible and swear before God that you told the truth?" I slapped him the harshest look I possessed. He returned a calibrated smile. "Because if you weren't telling the truth the Sheriff must haul you to prison, though you're a child, because lying to the Sheriff is that serious a crime. You understand?"

I whiffed duplicity but nodded anyway.

The Sheriff also had questions for Mother, to which she gave answers the servants would echo. She heard a noise. Came to investigate. Discovered the Colonel.

The Judge's rendition had one variation. He believed the library door had already been forced before he and the others arrived. That having Two-Tone Willie shoulder it open was required not by the lock but rather because the broken frame had jammed it shut. I wondered at his insertion of this detail. Had I known where he was leading the Sheriff's reasoning, I might've snatched up the murder weapon and shot the Judge then and there.

"Think your husband might've been affected by this latest financial panic enough to kill himself?" the Sheriff asked Mother as gently as he could.

"Yes!" I wanted to shout but didn't.

Mother shrugged. "Louis rarely shared business matters with me."

"I was his confidante in that arena," said Judge Pike. "Colonel Bonreve was not unduly troubled and in any case wasn't a man to take his life. I don't possess your experience, Sheriff Bourgeois, but I have tried a number of homicide cases. To my eye, that's what this was. Not suicide. Murder."

Turpitude # 64

"Cloak not the truth in falsehood."

Surah Al-Baqarah 2:42,
the Noble Quran

"I suspect the killer forced the door," the Judge said. "When the Colonel drew his pistol to defend himself, the villainous darkie snatched it away, shot poor Louis dead, and made his getaway before the boy could gather his wits." I was shocked by this elaboration on our agreed-upon story. Mother seemed less surprised but undoubtedly cautious.

"Why do you say a darkie?" asked Sheriff Bourgeois, a decorated Confederate veteran.

The judge walked to the desk. "Who but a darkie would traffic in this?" He reached under the Colonel's corpse and appeared to pull out a hoodoo charm, holding it for the Sheriff to see. "I spotted this earlier," the Judge explained, "but left it in place till you arrived so not to disturb evidence."

I recognized the mojo: the same Go-Away that a year-and-a-half earlier I'd planted under the pommel of Pike's saddle. Its potency would've long since waned, except now it might have the power to send someone to the gallows.

I didn't hear much of what followed. The gurgling of acid in my stomach drowned it out. When I realized the Judge and Sheriff were leaving, I hurried after them, but Mother caught my arm. "The water's too deep, the current too strong," she said. "Evil takes its course. You can't stop it, no more than you can turn a hurricane's wind."

She didn't understand. A Negro to be arrested. Incriminated by mojo. Many, white and black, would sleep more contentedly with Conquering John gone. As he climbed the gallows, he'd cast his last, greatest hex on the boy who caused his fall. Maybe the wind couldn't be bent, but I had to try because I was already in the storm, certain to drown in the ripples of Conquering John's vengeance if I didn't save him.

I broke loose. Ran out. Saw the Judge and Sheriff and just-arrived Father Groetsch conferring halfway down the staircase, a Renaissance painter's allegory: the devil corrupting church and state. "Conquering John the Doctor is innocent!" I hollered. The three turned, as did the nervous servants a dozen steps lower.

"A *doctor* murdered Colonel Bonreve?" asked Father Groetsch.

"No graduate of Heidelberg, Father—" and here the Judge's eyes bored into mine "—but the juju man isn't the killer. The nigra we want is the flower gardener."

Turpitude # 65

"Do not despise prophecies."
1 Thessalonians 5:20

I felt Mother's hand on my shoulder. She needed no clairvoyance to recognize my turmoil. Conquering John would've implicated me without a second thought, but Nat would never betray me. If I confessed now, I'd be charged with perjury, if not murder. Judge Pike had made sure I knew how serious it was to lie to the Sheriff. He'd lied too, but who'd believe that? Even with Mother on my side, how easy to discount her as a she-wolf defending her cub. And if I brought that fire on myself, did I really believe I could defeat the Judge if he'd decided to make Nat his scapegoat? Did I think I could stop the hurricane?

No, but sometimes you have to dive in anyway. Achille Cheramie understood that and now I did too. I dashed to the Sheriff. "I shot Colonel Bonreve," I proclaimed in the loud, clear voice I imagined such a confession called for.

"Not what you said upstairs," Sheriff Bourgeois pointed out.

I jabbed a finger at the Judge. "He made me lie!" Judge Pike burst into laughter. "It's true!" The Judge laughed harder. I looked to Mother. She might back me up that the Judge had induced false testimony, but she had no way of confirming whether I shot my stepfather, and if so whether it was mischance or murder. I was on my own.

The Judge wiped his eyes. "Sorry. Hardly occasion for mirth, but I suppose it broke the tension to hear the boy lie to protect his gardener. Your loyalty is commendable, young man, but misplaced. To perjure yourself because the scoundrel once plucked roses for your mother..." And with that I knew why the Judge, who never forgot a slight, chose Nat as his sacrificial lamb. Like much else that day, it was my fault.

"Shall we go," the Judge asked the Sheriff, "before the killer makes his getaway?"

I kicked with all my might. My shoe met the Judge's shin. His squeal promised me a head-start. I scooted past the Sheriff on the side where he had no arm. At the foot of the stairs I threaded an octopus of grasping black limbs, all pantomime, because no servant sincerely wanted to keep me from my mission.

Outside, darkness. Having lost sense of time since called into the library by the Colonel, I'd expected to find Nat close by, but nightfall meant he'd be in his shack. Several horses were hitched. I turned them loose, slapped their rumps to scatter them, and sprinted toward the Quarters, leaping ditches, hopping ruts, knowing that if the effort burst my heart that would be insufficient punishment for what I'd done.

At the Quarters, no candle burned anywhere. I stumbled over a dog. It nipped me before slinking under a house. Never before had a Negro's dog had the nerve to bite me, even such a modest warning peck. "The master's dead!" I hollered.

No response. They knew. Knew the moment it happened. Even if Yvonne and Antoinette hadn't left the house. Even if Two-Tone Willie went straight to the stables to wake Richard Bourque. A plantation owner didn't die, let alone by gunshot, without the Quarters knowing.

"They're going to blame a Negro!"

Likewise no reaction. What did I expect, surprise? When did anything bad happen and the white man *not* blame a Negro?

Conquering John's voice rang out. "Git back to the Big House, boy. Even I can't hobble the devil now."

It hit me that I didn't know which of these cabins was Nat's. Yet I'd called him friend. I spoke into Conquering John's closed door. "Where's Nat live?"

"Heaven, pretty soon. Though I 'spect they go make him pass by the back gate."

If he knew Nat was suspected, did Nat know? Then perhaps he'd fled. Found a pirogue and was halfway to Thibodaux where someone would sneak him to Schriever where he'd climb into a boxcar. Come morning, he'd be in New Orleans, then Memphis, Chicago. Get away clean. I believed that with all my heart, so why were my tears plummeting like Niagara onto the bare, beaten earth?

A door opened three cabins down. Nat waved me over.

Turpitude # 66

"Offer your body as sacrifice."
Romans 12:1

"You could get away."

"Not once they set the hounds loose."

"You'd have a chance."

"Ever seen a body chomped by hounds?"

"So unfair," I said.

"Ain't that the truth," he seconded. "Maybe it not be so bad. If I go peaceable, don't give no guff, be a chance they hang me proper 'stead of lynching me."

"It's my fault."

I hoped he'd deny that, but he only looked away. My legs itched to walk out, to abandon him. I loved Nat, but at that moment I yearned to not feel the weight of those big, sad eyes upon me. Maybe he'd prefer to be alone. Had prayers to say. A will to make. I looked around the cabin. It'd be a mighty slim legacy, even had he skill to put words to paper. But perhaps I wasn't so far off, because he mumbled, "One thing you might do."

Never in our long relationship had Nat ever asked me for a favor. "Anything," I promised.

"Miss Melpa got herself a baby," he said. "Itty-bitty, one-night chance the boy be mine." A son he'd never know! "If they let you keep this plantation," he went on, "once you get growed you go be a big man. Plenty money. 'Stead of handing it all to Conquering John, might you could have somebody hunt down Melpa, pass something to the little one now and again."

"I will, Nat. Of course I will," I said, grateful for any chance to atone. "I'll find your son. See that he and Melpa want for nothing. Make sure he's educated. Started in a profession."

He seemed embarrassed about accepting so much (purely hypothetical) largesse. "Well, that be good, I guess, if it not any trouble." He looked up, then I heard it too. Hooves. Hushed voices. The *click-clack* of weapons being checked. "Best you git," Nat said. "Do nobody good for you to watch them 'bout their business."

I had no fear left of whatever the Sheriff or Judge might do me — guilt and shame had crowded it out — but to respect Nat's wishes, or so I told myself, I slinked out the back door. It felt like the blood had drained from my body, all of it, leaving not enough to feed a mosquito.

When I got to the Big House, the Famous Funeral Friar was circling the dining room swinging an incensor of smoky perfume. The Colonel's corpse lay on the table. Mother sponged the tiny hole in its chest, swabbed the gaping exit wound in its back, rendering Louis Bonreve's body pristine the way she'd not been able to do for Achille Cheramie.

Judge Pike poked his head into the room. "Madame, when you're done I'll need you and your son in the library. I'm afraid something else has come up."

Turpitude # 67

"Be content with what you have."
Hebrews 13:5

"How much do you understand about inheritance law?" Pike posed the question as any sober attorney might. Standing next to Mother, I felt her body tense.

"I know that, since Louis already owned Athena before we were married, I don't inherit it." She put an arm across my shoulder. "Our son does."

The reminder of my inheritance hit me like a mis-thrown baseball. The legacy I'd promised Nat belonged, in my ill-formed thoughts, to some vague, far-off future. Here I would soon become the richest man in the state. If the Sheriff took Nat to await trial, there'd be time to hire lawyers, gather evidence, collect —

"*Normally* that would be the case," I heard Judge Pike say. "Under the Napoleonic Code, which shapes law here in Louisiana, *normally* the children inherit. *If* Louis Bonreve had children." I saw Nat's chances slipping away.

"He adopted the boy," Mother emphasized.

"There's a complication. Documents mis-filed. I begged Louis to let me handle it."

"You did handle it."

"I *would've*. Louis chose otherwise. If I *had*, this would've never happened."

"What would've never happened?" I asked, my voice an octave higher than normal.

"You would've never missed out on a grand inheritance, my boy." He had the nerve to tousle my hair. I almost bit his hand.

"With no children, the law decrees, secondarily, the estate

passes to the deceased's brothers and sisters."

"Louis was an only child," Mother pointed out.

"Third, to nieces and nephews."

"Never had any."

"Fourthly, to his parents."

"Long dead," Mother said, her bosom heaving.

The Judge smiled. "Fifthly, to his spouse."

Mother didn't answer that one so quickly. "I inherit?" she asked.

"*Normally* that would be the case," Judge Pike enjoyed repeating. "Another complication, I'm afraid." I knew the man set traps for a living, but I'd never before stood on the pan as the jaws sprang. His smile remained, but any kindness in it evaporated. "No death certificate was ever filed for your first husband, I'm afraid, so your wedding to Louis Bonreve, no matter how ostentatious, was not legal. That leaves you with the status of mistress." How dare he call Mother a mistress! "Naturally, a mistress," he continued, "holds no right of inheritance."

"Even you can't make these shenanigans legal," Mother said.

"When enough important people owe you favors, anything is possible."

"Who gets the plantation?" it fell to me to ask.

"Sixthly," beamed the Judge, "to the nearest collateral relative. In this case, Louis' aunt, Elmire."

"A kind, simple woman you believe you can control," Mother accused.

"I of course stand ready to offer her prudent counsel."

Maybe Tante Elmire wouldn't listen to him, I thought. She *was* a kind, simple woman. She liked me and liked flowers. Maybe I could talk her into helping Nat.

"The heiress to Athena will be a tempting target," Mother observed. "You better hope she doesn't find a cagey lawyer husband who'll throw your wise counsel out on your ear."

"Funny you mention that. It seems Elmire discovered love late and this very day accepted the proposal of Richard

Bourque."

No! The horse trainer would never buck the Judge. Nat would go to slaughter like a head of livestock.

"I'll fight you," Mother said. "Claw and nail. I know important people, too."

"I know their secrets."

"I know secrets about *you*," Mother threatened.

The Judge looked at me. "Best instruct your mother on the statute of limitations."

"You won't steal my son's future," she vowed.

"Precisely on account of your son you should fold your cards and slink off now, Madame, before Sheriff Bourgeois has time to reexamine the boy's role in tonight's foul play. Once we hang your gardener, he won't be around to deny this was actually a conspiracy, a tawdry, murderous plot, all about money. The boy did confess on the staircase, after all."

Mother held me tighter. "The Sheriff wouldn't swallow—"

"Not right away, maybe, but if you keep picking this scab, I will too. How long do you think this young miscreant will hold up under cross-examination?"

"As long as it takes," I interjected, but Mother didn't seem sure.

"Imagine your son in my court enduring question after question till he's in tears—"

"I won't cry!"

"—till he's no longer sure what his name is, till the interrogation cracks him apart and they drag away the pieces to languish in a hole somewhere until a judge who owes me a favor decrees him old enough to execute."

Silence fell. I imagined the scratch of hemp around my neck. Finally Mother said, "All right, August. I'll marry you."

The Judge smiled. "I'm afraid that offer has been withdrawn."

Mother opened her mouth, a bitter retort on her tongue, but in the end didn't speak. What would be the point? "What happens to us?"

"I once saw you plucked from the ocean. Now I'll watch you be thrown back." His hand rasped a document across the table. "Two passages on a paddlewheeler heading for New Orleans. It should dock at the landing any minute."

"I have to bury my husband first."

"Madame, he was never your husband. Your presence at the funeral would cause—"

"Scandal?" She didn't try to hide her contempt.

The Judge shrugged. "It gratifies me you appreciate your situation. The Sheriff expressed keen interest in settling this matter quickly. Shall his intercession be required?"

Mother picked up the tickets. "We'll need time to pack."

"Actually, you won't. While no one begrudges you the clothes you're wearing, nothing else here is yours. Except this..." He dropped a pair of coins onto the table. "From me, two cents, representing the value you so generously placed on my affections."

He waited for Mother to wallow in regret. Instead, she picked up the coins. "Thanks. From now on every penny will count." It put a chink in his smugness, and she had one last act of defiance left. "I'll not leave the house bareheaded. Neither will my son."

The Judge forced a laugh. "I cannot imagine Athena's new mistress would deny you each your favorite hat."

My nicest bowler hung downstairs. There I found Tante Elmire supervising the post-mortem stopping of clocks and covering of mirrors and trying to make sense of all that'd happened. "Tante," I said, "you have to help Nat. He's been falsely accused."

"Yes, so sad. The menfolk will clear it up. Judge Pike is very wise." Then she was off down the hall. "Antoinette! I need my salts."

The Judge made sure a hat was all Mother took. She came downstairs tying on an unflattering explosion of cabbage-like rosettes. I suppose fashion was not foremost on her mind. Past the servants' grave brown faces, we crossed Athena's threshold for the last time.

Pike had ordered a flag hung from the dock pole, symbol to request a stop, and had timed his discourse on inheritance law to conclude just as the steamboat *Audrey* pulled abreast. As he escorted us toward the levee, I let him and Mother walk ahead. With the Big House curtains drawn and the moon only a sliver, our path was darkly ominous.

Halfway down the oak alley, I turned for a last look. Before me stood Conquering John proffering a basketful of mojos. "I know you broke," he said. "I-O-U be good enough."

It hit me like a hammer. "*You* put that first hex under my pillow. Or had it done. And the others, to scare me so I'd buy from you. The Colonel never bought hoodoo."

Conquering John actually looked proud of me for having finally figured out his deception. "Not like I go be the last man, white or black, to snooker you."

I tried to be furious but didn't have it in me. "Which is your strongest protection trick?" I asked. He nodded toward a bottle spell. "Get it to Nat," I said.

He was, I think, impressed. "Don't count on it to save him," he said. "Even the most puissant *gris-gris* got a limit, 'specially in the white-man world."

Much later I would hear that the jury of white planters deliberated only one minute, forty-nine seconds before finding Nat guilty of murder. Judge Pike was even swifter passing sentence.

As the gallows was assembled from parts stored behind the sheriff's department stables, the jailer let Nat practice walking its steps so he wouldn't embarrass himself when his time came. Nat thanked the jailer for this generosity.

Turpitude # 68

"Lay aside malice."

Peter 2:1

We were booked into "Kentucky," but our stateroom was empty. I found Mother on the Texas deck observing the parade of plantations, saying "Good-bye," I suppose.

"It was me," I whispered. "I shot him."

"I know," she said. I tried not to weep but failed. "Don't cry," she said.

"I can't help it," I blubbered.

"Well, it's unnecessary, because I never loved him, not really."

I supposed she said it to comfort me, but it made me feel worse. In my last moments with Louis Bonreve, I'd decided he deserved more of our affection. "He loved us," I said.

"I don't doubt that, but love always mixes into other things. I was the youth he feared losing. Proof each afternoon of his manliness. You might've been the playmate he always wanted — if you'd cooperated — and the heir he'd been bred to believe he must have. He hoped you'd be just like him, king in a kingdom as small and closed as the village I once saw washed away, only, okay, much plusher. Servants are nice, I don't deny it."

"Is that why you married him?" I asked.

"For comfort? No, though that's what everyone believed. When I was about your age I began to envision my life ahead, to plan, to dream. There was only one thing I wanted: to be a wife. To be a wife with all the love and motherhood and happy home that went with it. The lumpy tag-alongs that came with my dream, the scrubbing floors and boiling diapers and worn out before my time, did not deter me in the least." She took a breath. "Be careful of dreams. They have sharp teeth."

"So you married the Colonel to be a wife again?"

"No. After I lost your father, the hole inside me was too big for any other man to fill, at least not so soon after. No, I married Louis Bonreve only because I thought that if you became his son it'd give you the world. I thought I owed you that. Never did I guess you'd fight me on it every step."

I considered leaping the rail and feeding myself to the alligators. Sharp teeth would've been as welcome then as they were abhorrent the day the Colonel tried... Except he hadn't tried to feed me to the alligator, had he? On that day Nat helped save me from the beast.

"Nat knew what was coming," I whispered as if his foreknowledge lessened my guilt.

"Of course, he did," replied Mother.

I thought she misunderstood. "Not just since the Sheriff came. For months now. He told me he was doomed to a bad end. He knew."

"Of course, he knew. I told him." What? "Told him he was doomed, wouldn't live out his days, would die badly." She paused, unsure she should go on. "Die badly and it'd be your fault."

"My fault?" Nat doomed and it was my fault?

"Not because you meant him harm, just because that's how it'd be, and I said if he had sense he'd give you a wide berth and at first he was offended because he thought I believed him a bad influence, so I explained it wasn't that, but I'd suffered a spell that let me glimpse the future, his future, and it wasn't a pleasant future, not one bit, and I wanted to apologize that my son would cause his downfall, because I thought he was perhaps the most decent man on the plantation, but that wasn't going to save him because after all Jesus Christ was a decent fellow, if we can believe half what priests tell us, but look what happened to poor Jesus, and for Nat it might be worse, him being Negro, and spending time with you would make his situation riskier, and he understood that, he did, but he said that you, at least some of the time, were a good child but without many friends and that you seemed to have chosen him to be your friend and if that was the case he wouldn't turn you down because that's the sort of man Nat is, or was, depending if they hanged him yet."

Had I been a candle that I might've sputtered into darkness.

Turpitude # 69

"Do not seek vengeance."
Leviticus 19:18

I watched the boat's great paddlewheel lift water and let it fall, an endless cycle like the suffering generations of a cursed clan. To avenge Judge Pike's injustices I would follow him into Hell — someday — "someday" of course being a troublingly vague repayment schedule.

Meantime I vowed to never let Mother again fall prey to any man so evil. Unfortunately, at age thirteen, I never guessed there were *women* just as bad as him.

BOOK III

Employing Bad Against Worse

Here we reach the crux of your curriculum. Before starting each of the tutorials which follow, first compose the requested essay. *Only then* compare your own shameful declaration with what I wrote.

Do your homework! Though confessing iniquity may make you uncomfortable, it hones skills necessary to re-purposing manageable portions of wickedness toward nobler purpose.

Tutorial I

DESPERATE MEASURES

Recount the most extreme act you ever committed; describe what triggered it; explain whether the good you sought outweighed the evil you accomplished.

Whistles screamed. Coal smoke scorched the air. Like ants after rain, lines of stevedores rolled barrels, trucked cotton bales, and toted coffee sacks. Dodging the foot-deep mud that moated the snaking plank walkway, Mother and I topped the levee, the Mississippi River and our old lives behind us. Before us stood New Orleans, twelfth largest city in the nation, biggest by far in the South. A manufacturing hub. One of the world's great ports. A cesspool of wickedness and corruption.

Setting out, we dodged automobiles and the horse-drawn vehicles that in those days outnumbered them. Someone sang from a window. Bells pealed, street vendors cried, and streetcar wires crackled. Crossing Canal Street, we entered the "French" Quarter, inhabited mostly by Sicilians. Laundry hung from every lacework balcony. Crispy loaves we couldn't afford beckoned from shops.

Past the cathedral where Father Groetsch never played organ, we found a teeming public market. Aproned men with gartered sleeves loaded the baskets of hard-bargaining women. Children darted, most working, a few playing, some picking pockets. Choctaw grandmothers scooped fresh gumbo filé. Negro mammies touted pralines I had no money to buy. A Palermo dandy with a brush mustache offered to slice the salamis hanging behind him. My belly was so empty I could've eaten one whole.

In all that great emporium, little to eat would two cents buy, so Mother revealed why she left Athena wearing her ugliest hat. For years she'd secreted into its lining any occasional bank note she could stash without the Colonel noticing. The horde accumulated to $29.

We purchased a humble meal — no pralines — and found a spot to eat and argue which of us would hold our money.

"I'm your mother."

"True, but as regards the city, your life's been as sheltered as mine and I, at least, have read Dickens."

We divided the cash and took lodgings that at dear, lost Athena would've been declared unfit for mules. Each morning, we picked bed bugs off each other and swore we'd spent our last night under a leaky roof. Each evening, still jobless, we'd find another hovel, usually worse.

Work was scarce, the unemployed abundant. When she could produce no references, most employers shut their doors in Mother's face. A few gave her long interviews, enjoying the chat with a stunning woman, before they turned her down, blaming the ongoing Banker's Panic. Some did offer money, but only to do things no decent woman would.

When we tramped up Esplanade or to the mansions of the Garden District to beg charity of people who in better times had visited Athena, we found gates barred and butlers surly. We didn't know what awful stories had been told about us but were pretty sure who told them.

To take pressure off Mother, I decided to secure employment as a newsboy. When I went to apply, however, I found half the urchins in the city already lined up. One threatened to garrote me with my suspenders if I got the job instead of him. I marched upstairs to the editorial offices to pitch myself as reporter; I nearly got pitched out the window. At Werlein's music store, they wouldn't let me near the piano to show what I could do. At a drayage barn, on a plasterer's crew, even with a humble grocer, they'd look at my soft hands and laugh me out.

When the money in her hat was spent, Mother sold the hat. The next day I sold mine. After brushing it up and bargaining hard, it bought a single fried mullet. Sitting bareheaded on the curb, we savored the fish. A brass band dirge so befitted our circumstance that at first we didn't notice it. By the time we did, green sashes and shiny trombones were in sight.

Licking her fingers, Mother wiped my face with them. "As the procession goes by, join in and find out who died and were they skinny or fat or bald, knowledge a friend would have, but find out like you already know and don't give me that look because I've seen how—"

"Mother!"

"Hush, listen, they're almost here. Say you're distant family, related through your daddy but he's dead too and—"

"I get it! After a funeral, people gather. Where people gather, often there's food."

She smiled. "I'm not going to let you drown."

The deceased was Irish. He'd been waked all night. Every last mourner was as pickled as the corpse. As long-lost cousins we were welcomed with open arms and whisky breath, but every hint about congregating met some version of "going home to sleep it off." There'd been food all right, food and copious drink, but we'd missed it.

In St. Louis Cemetery N°·1, after the mourners left we knelt beside a random tomb. Hungry, homeless, broke, I tried to be strong, but when Mother surrendered to despair, I did too. I cried for Nat whom I'd destroyed; for Colonel Bonreve whom I'd misjudged; for Mother whom I'd let down. And yes, for the books at Athena I'd never again open, for the hunger in my stomach that wouldn't relent, for the fool I'd been consorting with Conquering John the Doctor and Judge Pike the Monster.

The cemetery sexton limped over to investigate why tears were falling on a grave with no fresh flowers. When Mother saw him, she reacted so strangely that he halted in his tracks.

"Don't you recognize me?" Mother asked. "Surely you do. My late husband spoke his last words to you."

What new ruse was this? The Colonel spoke his last words to *me.*

Mother went on, her words in a rush. "You haven't forgotten Achille? Achille Cheramie?" The man's eyes flew wide. "See? You do recognize me, Touloulou." Mother nudged me forward. "And here's Achille's son."

The sexton got over the shock more quickly than I did. He eyed me. "Boy, you owe me eighty-six dollars and twelve cents."

~

After protracted negotiations, when Touloulou threw in temporary room and board, I agreed to start working off the debt I hadn't known I'd inherited from the father I'd never met. Since his cottage was tiny, Touloulou lodged us in the upper berth of a double-decker crypt. Somewhere in the city a certain Emile Charbonnet was knocking on death's door; until it opened, his future resting place was ours. Macabre nature aside, the tomb was cleaner, drier, and freer from vermin than any place we'd slept since arriving in the city, nor was it much more cramped. Certainly we were glad of it when, after Touloulou bid us good-night, rain began to pour.

Each day Mother roamed from sundries shop to ropewalk to hosiery factory hoping for an opening, but "Come back in a few months" was the best she got. Meanwhile, I pulled weeds and scrubbed crosses and moved piles of bricks. Each evening Mother massaged my sore muscles and kissed my blistered hands. When she thought I was asleep, she wept.

My efforts provided only stale bread for our sustenance but did allow me to learn how Touloulou had hoped to become a mason but arrived in the city too poor (thanks to a certain card game) to buy training, so he'd settled for this menial job, and that for beggar's wages because of some eighteen-year penance to the Blessed Virgin, also partly Father's fault.

"What was my papa like?"

"Too damn lucky. 'Cept about that rabbit."

"Who were his friends?"

"Gambling, whoring eels who counted themselves high and mighty 'cause they suffered no dread of the sea. Well, that bit their butts. Your pa was also pals with Victorine, a *négresse*, or at least an octoroon, who pretended she was white like me." (Touloulou's skin was brown as tobacco.)

As he sat in the shade watching me whitewash a long wall of brick burial ovens, he recounted how the hurricane-refugee village of Leeville weathered poorly the Fever of '05. Of six hundred residents, sixty died of jack, among them the pirogue maker Léon Dantin. To no one's surprise, Léon's daughter Tellia married Zeph Leboeuf the moment she turned sixteen. I wondered if she ever made him wear a dress.

Mr. Charbonnet, whom I never met but for whose health I prayed nightly, lingered a week before succumbing to his bad heart. The eve of his funeral, to cheer Mother I recounted the marriage of Tellia, inventing humorous details, making Leeville sound like fairyland. Mother laughed, but eventually grew quiet. "We'll starve if we stay in New Orleans," she said.

She'd always wanted me to see Vienna, yet I suspected Europe wouldn't be friendlier. "At least we're in the South. Winter's coming," I reminded her.

"Mm. Oyster season."

"Please don't talk about food." For supper, Touloulou had provided us each a half-pint of meatless bean soup thickened with sawdust.

"In a fishing village, no one starves," Mother said. Though her tone was wistful, her eyes were calculating. She was hatching a plan I feared I wouldn't like. A fishing hamlet? Despite that we were always hungry and soon to be homeless again, despite that the city reeked of chaos and bubbled with malevolence, I was falling in love with New Orleans. Here, neither planter nor businessman nor scamp nor scoundrel had a lock on possibility as they elbowed each other, sometimes brawled, to steal advantage or claim pleasure in a risqué opera sung each day in ninety-nine languages, a frenzied ballet to the new jazz music throbbing from every disreputable joint. Mother longed to see the wider world. Well, here it revealed its ugliness and splendor. Temporary setbacks mustn't keep us from tasting its fruits.

"You'll find a job," I promised.

Her eyes focused fifty miles away. "Browning onions, celery, peppers. Watching for the red sails. Waiting to see what they bring for the skillet."

"Chenière was destroyed, Mother."

"Leeville wouldn't be so different."

I sat up, bumping my head on the tomb's low ceiling. "Leeville? Where one in ten dies of jack?"

"The fever's passed. Your friend Tellia lives there."

"With her husband. I'm reaching an age where he might misunderstand my affections."

She smiled. "Or understand them too well? That'll work itself out. There'll be other girls who — how should I say it — who'll *appreciate* how special you are because after all if they're living in Leeville how picky can they afford to be?"

My misgivings fermented into panic. "Mother, New Orleans is the land of opportunity."

"Not if you're broke. Not if Judge Pike poisons every well."

"Screw Judge Pike! We'll scrape together pennies, build on that. Give me a few years, I'll deliver you this city on a platter."

She studied me a long moment. "Tomorrow, we hitch a ride to Leeville."

~

Monsieur Charbonnet enjoyed a lovely funeral. Afterward I admired several vacant tombs, but Touloulou ignored me.

Mother dragged me to Lugger Landing where planks ramped into the brown Mississippi and dark-eyed Sicilians unloaded sweet potatoes and oysters, but no Leeville boats were in, so we left. Though I had no idea where we'd sleep that night, I was relieved. Pinching a copy of the Picayune from the seat of an untended carriage, I meant for Mother to check job listings. Instead she scanned the shipping register. "'A packet leaving Wednesday' — today, right? — 'via Barataria and Leeville.' We'll beg mercy of its captain. You should look well-behaved but hungry."

"The latter, at least, will not be difficult. Mother, if we have no money to buy passage—"

Like a volley of cannon, her anger exploded. "Then what do you propose?" she shouted. The force of her rage set me shaking. She was trembling too. "I'm not seventeen anymore. Can't expect to find some silly millionaire who'll want me, or anyone who wants you, smart as you think you are, so I'm sorry, I know you feel I should've accepted Judge Pike's proposal—"

"Never!"

"—but when he offered it I didn't believe there could be anything worse. Now I see I lacked imagination. There's much worse. There's sickness. Starvation. As we'll find out if we stay here. Sorry if you don't fancy the life of a fisherman, sorry you'll never see the world. I won't either so stop carping so I can get on and do whatever needs be to get us through this."

My heart broke into a thousand pieces seeing how much she hurt. Embarrassed to have raised her voice, Mother once more buried her nose in the newspaper. She started walking, again counting on the tug of my hand for navigation, so what happened next was entirely my fault.

On Barracks Street, where an alley met the sidewalk, a couple of sailors loitered. They looked like characters out of Treasure Island, lacking only peg legs and parrots. While they exuded a certain menace, it wasn't enough to make me cross the street. As we reached them, the two pushed off from the wall, one to block our path, the other stepping down from the curb, cutting off the route around them.

I nudged Mother, but she was already looking up, aware before I that along with the two on the sidewalk, three more sailors lurked in the alley. One stepped behind us, boxing us in. Of the other two, one pissed against a wall as his mate, finished, was buttoning up. Now those two noticed the mother and son their comrades had corralled. Well, mostly they noticed the mother.

"What a fine little fellow," chirped the sailor in the street. He reached out to pinch my cheek. Still holding Mother, I stepped back to avoid his grubby hand, a tactical error, as it put us a half-step into the alley. The three closed in, a moving phalanx that forced us deeper into the passageway, farther from the safety of the street. Trying not to panic, I glanced behind us. The last two sailors inched toward us as well. The one who'd been pissing had not returned his member to his pants. It hung raw and reptilian. His finger tapped it right then left, like a cat toying with a lizard. "Lady see anything she likes?"

Mother recoiled. The three from the street drove us like cattle farther into the alley. The sailor who'd buttoned his fly began to unbutton it again. "I'll scream," Mother said.

"That could go hard on the boy," the tallest sailor warned. "Us five sail in a couple of hours. No port of call till Gibraltar. Can't board that tramp without one last game of scratch the itch." Two lizards were out now, both waking up. I wondered which sailor I should kick first, but Mother held me back.

"I see why you'd think I'm an easy mark," she said. "Clothes torn and dirty. So thin my ribs show. But I can shout to bring a patrolman, the whole time clawing your eyes. Be awful to lose an eye, wouldn't it?"

A side of Mother I'd never seen. I was about to see another. "Though, maybe, I *could* help you out. Provide a sweet memory for your sea voyage. Of course, y'all would have to help us, too." She took a breath. "With three dollars."

I couldn't possibly have heard correctly. The men exchanged looks. Lizards danced upright. While I knew the purpose of an erect phallus, no way could I imagine Mother congressing with these ruffians.

"I'm sure we got three bucks between us," the tallest man said.

Mother brushed back a wisp of hair in a most alluring gesture. "Three dollars *each*," she clarified.

"Each? We could visit a parlor house for that."

"If one lets you in smelling like you do, go, go with God. Go to Hell too if you think a respectable woman's virtue isn't worth three dollars apiece. But if you do recognize the bargain you lucked into, cough up the money and give it to the boy," at which point, without stopping for breath, she handed me the Picayune still open to the shipping register, "who'll take it to the Allen & C°· offices and book us passage to Leeville on the steamboat *Melanie*, straight ticket, no meals, no berth, and with part of what's leftover buy two cold lunches and wait for me where the *Melanie* docks so that after I help these men play their little game I'll join you and we'll picnic and never talk about this again though I know you'll plague me with questions about it but I won't answer them not ever so," turning to the sailors again, "if you fellows have fifteen dollars cash and the sense to spend it on a good woman instead of one already used up then we better get started before I change my mind because if you think this is easy for me or would be for any woman then you're just, well, just men I guess and like most men you don't understand a single thing about how a woman thinks and you never fucking will."

I was startled by Mother's use of profanity. The sailors, accustomed to salty language, were I think more surprised to find a woman whose train of thought made so few stops. The lizards had gone drowsy. "What'll it be? In or out? My son and I also have a boat to catch."

The tall sailor pulled a five-dollar gold piece from his pocket. "Anybody got change for a half-eagle?"

I wondered how to stop this. Five against two, we'd been outnumbered. With Mother giving in, I wasn't sure I was up to such odds. Then I saw her fear. It'd been there when the sailors accosted us, but she'd pushed it aside. Now it was back, along with regret, and worry, some of which no doubt was on my account. I had to prevent her desecration. Earlier, Mother had threatened to scream. Now I would holler. Loud enough to wake the dead. Police would come running. Militia with swords drawn. I opened my mouth, but the words that sounded weren't mine. "For the love of God, you can't do this here," someone barked. All seven of us turned. A burly man in a checkered suit wore a well-groomed ear-to-ear mustache.

"Our business is with the lady," the tallest sailor said. "Where we do our business is our business, not yours."

"Mine if it concerns sporting women," said the burly man. Mother bowed her head. In my innocent mind "sporting women" conjured images of that new fad, tennis, which many consider disreputable for ladies, explaining Mother's blush perhaps, except that Mother never exhibited any interest in the game. When it came to exercise Mother was as languid as a cat.

My childish attempt to disbelieve reality was interrupted when the tall sailor spoke, "Get out of this alley, bubb, or we'll toss you out."

"There again you're mistaken," the burly man replied. He handed me his hat to hold. It never occurred to me to refuse, such was his air of authority. He strolled up to the biggest sailor and with no fanfare hit him a hard right hook. *Thump* echoed as fist smashed jaw. The man went down, *thump* again. Two others, the ones who hadn't yet pulled out their lizards, pounced. One threw the next punch, but the burly man grabbed the fellow's mate, used him as shield to block the blow, and swung him hurtling against the brick wall, *poonk*. Turning back to the other, he let fly that right hook again. *Thump*, another man down. Not nine seconds had passed. Two sailors were on the ground, another against the wall seeing stars, and the last two hurrying to put away their lizards, which now hung limp as laundry.

"Pick up your mates and move along," the burly man instructed. He was so sure of being obeyed that he was reaching for his hat when the sailor who'd hit the wall spoke up.

"You can't best us," the sailor said, but he didn't sound sure.

The burly man's handlebar mustache bent into a smile. "Thought I had."

"Five of us. Muscled-up from reefing sail and shoveling coal. A couple of lucky punches don't mean you can best us."

The burly man shrugged as if conceding a point of no consequence. He stuck two fingers into his mouth and blew. His whistle was shrill, loud, and carried a short but distinct melody, *G, E flat, F sharp*. In no time at all, it drew out of nowhere a quartet of thugs sporting ugly scars and obscene tattoos. Sliding razors from sleeves and fitting brass knuckles onto fingers, they lined up beside this strange Pied Piper. How had he manifested such a troop, apparently out of thin air?

The sailors glanced around for a safe retreat, but the burly man had lost interest in fisticuffs. "Try 306 Liberty Street," he suggested. "Tell Miss Sadie I sent you."

The sailors mumbled thanks and left. The thugs likewise melted away, mumbling regret over the missed opportunity to maim someone.

Our savior studied Mother like a bookie peruses a racing form. "How old are you?"

"Thirty-one," Mother replied honestly.

"You look younger."

"I feel older."

"Woman like you shouldn't be on the street. Boy!" I jumped. He took his hat. "Gather your things. Taking your mum to a place more fitting."

"Thank you," I whispered, though we had no things and I worried what he might consider "fitting."

He turned to Mother. "You can thank me after we settle you in."

Tired and hungry, concerned yet grateful, we followed the man in the checkered suit. He introduced himself as Elliot Dixon. His hand found Mother's waist, a shade too intimately guiding her toward our unannounced destination. Cutting left on Dauphine and right on Bienville, I hoped we were heading someplace he would stake us a meal but, passing several hash houses, he did not pause.

We ended not far from Touloulou's cemetery. Lining several blocks across the street from a massive railroad station was a row of mansions, each four or five stories tall, gaudy with colorful awnings and domed turrets. Amongst them were saloons, most not yet open, though it was lunchtime. Dixon led us up the steps of a grand red brick house. Behind its dozen arched windows, curtains were drawn. A black doorman scrutinized Mother. His uniform was impeccable, but his face wore the scars of a former boxer. I gave him a smile he didn't return.

We entered a parlor with tasseled furniture and curlicued woodwork. The carpet was patterned with flowers and diamonds, the wallpaper flowers and stripes, the upholstery flowers and more flowers. Had pastel colors been lethal, we would've been dead already. "What is this place?" I asked, though I was afraid I knew.

"Whatever it is, it's plush," Mother offered when Dixon didn't answer.

"It's garish," I corrected, but before I could say more, Dixon thrust me onto an over-cushioned divan, gave a paneled door a knock, and led Mother in. "Got one," he told someone I couldn't see, "but she's carting her little boy with her."

"I'm not so little!" I hopped from the sofa, but the door closed behind them. I put my eye to the keyhole, but it was plugged. A young woman appeared. Eighteen at most, hair the color of straw, her barely-tied gown revealed that she wore nothing underneath. "No offense, but is this a house of ill repute?" I asked.

"Ain't you young for that dance?" she laughed as she put her ear against the door's mahogany veneer. I leaned to eavesdrop as well.

Inside a woman was speaking, her accent guttural like Father Groetsch's. "On the street, winter chills will consumpt your little *junge*. Summer, mosquitoes'll dose him with yellow jack."

"I had yellow jack. One can't catch it twice," I hollered through the door, startling the young woman in the skimpy gown.

The accented voice ignored me. "Here, you'll earn plenty to put him in boarding school or something. They'll teach him to read."

"I can already read!" I informed the mysterious speaker. The dressing gown girl put finger to lips to shush me, as if I was committing some outrage, as if I weren't the injured party for being kept out of the interview. "Mother, you don't need this," I shouted. "I'll take care of us!" Unfortunately my brave promise was undercut when my empty stomach gurgled loudly enough to be heard through the door.

Mother spoke gently, "My boy is… special. I'm not sure a regular school—"

"Then an orphanage," the unseen woman suggested.

I banged on the door. The girl beside me scooted, wanting no blame for my intrusion.

The door swung open. Imagine Tante Elmire dressed as a Prussian general and you have Baroness Brunhilda von Kempe. She gazed at me through her monocle, the huge goggle-eye no doubt intended to intimidate. Knowing I dare not show weakness, with as authoritative a tone as I could muster I said, "I should be party to these negotiations."

Baroness von Kempe widened her eye so that the monocle fell across her protruding mono-bosom, but made no move to eject me as she tramped back to her overflowing desk.

"Orphanages aren't bad," offered Dixon, his bulk testing a spindly chair. "Grew up in one myself."

"An orphanage is out of the question," I announced, afraid to look at Mother.

"I don't run a charity," the Baroness snapped.

"Understood," I said. "And while I might accept charity on Mother's behalf, I'd never ask it for myself. I intend to work for my keep."

"You're too young to be much use."

"He's thirteen," Mother chimed in, trying to help.

"Doesn't look it," Baroness von Kempe shot back.

"I'm small for my age," I explained.

"Then how much stove wood could you carry? How could you tote chamber pots down all those stairs without spilling piss?"

"Hardly the tasks I'd expect to do," I said.

"Look, young man," the matron snorted. "We don't engage in that sordid trade here." Today I understand what sordid trade might involve young boys. At thirteen, I had no clue. It showed. "Do you understand what kind of business I run?" she sputtered, unsure whether to laugh, become angry, or take me seriously. I had to coax her into that last option or Mother and I would return to the street hungry. Yet no way would I allow my mother to become a prostitute.

"I don't care what business you run," I said. "Who am I to tinker with such obviously successful operations?" Mother's eyes asked, where are you going with this? "Keeping your books is another matter," I continued. "Numbers are numbers. Receipts in, expenses out. Adding is easy; subtracting… Let's just say I'd exercise prudent financial stewardship."

"He is good at arithmetic," chipped in Mother.

Her endorsement lent me courage. "Likewise, as your secretary—"

The Baroness looked as amazed as Dixon.

"—I could insure that your letters had proper grammar and excellent penmanship, thus giving their recipients the impression of you as a woman of subtlety, sophistication, and substance, worthy of any accolade she deigns to accept."

Von Kempe turned to Dixon. "Where'd you find this pair?"

He shrugged. "Barracks Street."

"A humble way station," I couldn't help injecting, "on the path Destiny chose to lead Mother and me to your door."

"Can you count money?"

"Count, tabulate, credit, debit, reconcile, and forecast." (I'd learned the words in Athena's library; I was pretty sure I could eventually figure out what they meant.)

"Pocket one penny and I cut off a finger," she warned.

I raised both hands. "I arrive with ten. I expect to leave with an equal number."

This time she did laugh. "You sleep in the carriage house, work for board till we see how you do." She turned to Mother. "You, Room 9. Clothes and necessaries come out of your share."

"But she will not engage in prostitution," I announced. Mother gave me a look I couldn't read, or maybe didn't want to.

The Baroness was more transparent. She put her monocle back in. "Then your *mutti* better be damn good at something else men will empty wallets for."

I pulled Mother's hands onto the table. Her stigmata caught the dim electric light. "Marked by God."

"Which might put some men off," the Baroness said.

"A gift that lets her see the future," I continued.

"That true?" Dixon asked.

"Now and then," Mother confessed.

"Often enough to keep gentlemen coming back," I promised. "Coming back and spending money. Isn't that the point of your establishment?" I squeezed Mother's wrist, trying to convey that she must not contradict me.

"Be the only house in the District with a soothsayer," Dixon said. "Might keep 'em buying liquor after they get their pricks tickled."

The Baroness looked dubious. "Let's try you out. Tell my future."

I hadn't planned this far. If Mother'd had headaches recently, they'd come from hunger, not visions. Everybody waited. Mother sat there. The madame's patience was burning down its short fuse. Then Mother leaned across the desk, extending her arms, inviting the Baroness to lay her hands onto Mother's scarred palms.

The moment the Baroness touched her, Mother twitched. We all jumped. Mother's fingers closed around the other's hands like a spider cocooning a fly. Alarm flickered in Baroness von Kempe's eyes. Another spasm wracked Mother's body. Her eyes began to flutter, half open, half closed. Quite impressive.

"I puh… I per… I perceive," Mother rasped, "two figures in the mist. Have they come to do good, or do ill? I cannot see, I cannot see… Wait! One, the younger, sits counting a great pile of coins. The other—" Mother's eyes opened, her body stopped twitching, her voice returned to normal. She looked directly at the Baroness. "—the other keeps adding to the pile."

The Baroness cackled. "Let's see if your prediction comes true, because long as you earn as much as my other girls, I don't give a quivering quim how you do it."

Thus began Mother's career as a fortune teller. As for me, knowing next-to-nothing about double-entry bookkeeping meant I also didn't know how to skim. Within a month, the Baroness dismissed her outside accountant (who'd been cheating her blind) and promoted me, at age thirteen, to be in-house comptroller of one of New Orleans' most successful brothels and personal secretary to its deservedly notorious madame.

Tutorial II

BAD INFLUENCES

*Relate an encounter with ill-chosen company.
Explore what attracted you to such persons.
Explain how you avoided adopting
their wayward habits
(if, indeed, you did).*

I was as spoiled and fussed over, teased and badgered, as only a boy with a dozen "big sisters" can be. If my sisters spent each evening draining the lust and emptying the pockets of their many gentlemen callers, that came to seem the most normal thing in the world. I learned that Baroness Brunhilda von Kempe had been born Hildie Kemperer in the steerage of the steamer *Gudegast* midway between Hamburg and Galveston, in which latter city she grew up on the streets, learned her trade on the wharves, and fled "when it got too hot."

These were the glory days of prostitution in New Orleans, when from "the District" red lights shone as numerous as stars in the firmament. Back in 1897, the New Orleans City Council, prevented by state law from making prostitution legal, passed an ordinance making it *illegal* — everywhere *except* thirty-eight square blocks alongside the Southern Railroad terminal on

Basin Street. Folks started calling the area Storyville, to the dismay of Councilman Sydney Story, whose legal stroke of genius created it. If my field of study was to be wickedness, here among the *demi-monde* I found myself at Oxford, le Sorbonne, and Harvard, all on one sweaty, liquored-up campus.

Reformers called our industry "the Social Evil." We called it, "the Life." Throughout the District, in every boudoir, bedroom, bunk, closet, crib, or cabaret, men were paying for the fleshly deed my Tante Clo first described to me; except Clo, for all her seeming thoroughness, hadn't begun to cover the variations in method, motive, and mercantile arrangement for temporarily joining two bodies into one.

As with any society, there were strata. The lowest serviced clients in alleys or by-the-half-hour assignation hotels. A rung up was the bawd who leased a one-room crib, if she was lucky with a street-facing window to pitch passers-by. "Sweetest titty in the city, two ripe ones, right here." "Hey, handsome mister, I got lots of what you get so little of at home."

If the crib whore had no window, it meant sharing her earnings with a "cadet" who could pimp her a flow of customers or, dangerously, trolling the streets herself. There she'd rub shoulders with tenderloin regulars, the roughnecks and smart-boys and out-of-their-depth tourists drunk on nickel-a-bucket beer; macs shooting craps and kid tap dancers and the old riverboat captain who'd tell long, boring stories to anyone who paused to pet his ancient dog.

She'd sidestep darting twelve-year-old pharmacy runners delivering condoms or cocaine. She'd dodge the bass fiddles and banjos and brass horns of musicians, a thousand rushing musicians, late for their gigs blowing waves of sassy ragtime out of the saloons and wine dens, where they played with jasm at all hours. Out of the chop houses and gambling parlors, where they jousted with solos that got bluesy after midnight. Above all, out of the dancehalls where strutting the Belly Rub or Slow Drag or Ballin Jack were forms of foreplay; or the cabarets where along with the music, hootchie-coo dancers peeled or she-boys shimmied or stage comics told dirty jokes, while most any cabaret girl including the waitresses could be jazzed for coin in the curtained booths or upstairs rooms.

Any man seriously interested in clean sport ignored the cribs and meat markets to visit a proper brothel. There were myriad choices: good-time houses with white girls to service white men, Negro houses for Negro men, and more controversially to those pushing the new Jim Crow segregation laws, high class houses where white men coupled with octoroons, quadroons, mulattresses, even pure black harpies. There were "French" houses specializing in oral sex, "Italian" houses offering anal intercourse, "Japanese" houses staffed with faux geishas who did miraculous things with their hands. "Boudoirs" where she-men pleasured punks were less flagrant but nonetheless available.

Fifty-cent houses back up in the District served the working man. Three-dollar houses along Franklin and Customhouse Streets catered to the middle class. Along Basin Street itself, for the elite stood a row of five-dollar bagnios like Maison de la Victoire, and Lulu White's Mahogany Hall, and Josie Arlington's Palace, and Baroness von Kempe's.

Five-dollar houses, except no gentleman ever actually got his ashes hauled for just five dollars. First he had to tip the doorman just to get in. Then he'd find all inmates busy until he bought an overpriced drink in the parlor. Once he got a girl's attention, flirtation would ensue, *if* he bought another drink or two as well as expensive cocktails for the bawd. (It became one of my duties to refill champagne bottles with tinted seltzer and brew the tea that went into the special bottle of Raleigh Rye from which poured my sisters' drinks.)

Before the girl would go upstairs with the trick, she'd taunt him into leaving a big tip for the "Professor" who took requests on piano. Even after splitting their tips with the madame, Basin Street Professors were the best-paid colored men in the city.

Once upstairs, the trick would cough up his five dollars plus surcharges for anything beyond a straight jazz using basic positions; then he'd have his penis squeezed to check for the ooze of gonorrhea; then he'd be doused with potent blue disinfectant in the interest of general hygiene, unless he paid extra not to; then he'd have applied a previously-used but more or less well-washed condom, unless he again paid extra not to; after a little manual or oral stimulation to rekindle the mood, finally the act he came for would ensue. As little as four minutes later, the girl would be putting her kimono back on, all smiles and compliments, hinting that a largish gratuity would be appropriate. Back downstairs, in case he had any cash left, he'd be pressed for another tip for the return of his hat and walking stick.

Repeat that four or five or eight times a night, more often on weekends or during carnival or when a convention hit town. Now multiply that number by ten or twelve girls and recognize that the prostitute herself sees nothing from the liquor and gives madame half from the lay, and you realize that a high-class brothel like the Baroness' was a money-making machine.

When I started keeping her books, the Baroness was taking in $7,500 a month, or about 300 times the wages of the average working man. Unfortunately, she had expenses to match. Paying the non-screwing staff of maids and laundresses. Replacing worn-out furnishings and carpets. Supplying inmates with doctors and potions to keep them healthy and douches and sponges to keep them childless. Liquor, linens, laundry soap. Food for the pantry, coal for the grate. Advertising: in the Blue Book, the Mascot, and to the "street arabs" who worked the railroad stations. Commissions to cabbies who brought new customers and procurers who brought new girls.

And rent. No tenant on Earth pays higher rent than a madame. In a business of shadowy characters, none reigns more obscure than her landlord. Redheaded Sophie swore the mayor owned our building. "His Honor admitted it after he fucked me that time."

Gladys was convinced it was the Church. "Don't the Catholics own St. Louis Cemetery down the street? Mary

Magdalene and them?"

Even I, the bookkeeper, wasn't sure who our landlord was. All I knew is that each month I handed a fat envelope to Elliot Dixon which he passed to some worthy who didn't want his name attached to a bagnio.

Draining profits even faster than rent was bribery. I handled petty graft, such as each morning before bedtime putting a few coins on the stoop beside the milk bottles so that the patrolman going off shift knew we appreciated him. Big time corruption was again Dixon's domain. He'd haul gobs of money from the Baroness, from Minnie White's and Czarina Pavlova's and Edna Johnson's, even from Maison de la Victoire where he was the madame's fancy man. The loot, less his skim, would go to city hall, police headquarters, and the capitol in Baton Rouge. In return, no matter what headlines reformers might foment, no laws, no ordinances, no crackdowns — at least none with teeth — arose to inhibit District commerce.

Another method of taxing the demi-monde was actually popular with higher-end prostitutes. Every year on Mardi Gras night, Elliot Dixon, assumed to be fronting for various bigwigs, hosted his "Anonymous Gentlemen of the Scarlet Venus" masquerade ball. Bawds would spring for the pricey tickets and show up in fancy gowns, eager to hand their *cartes de visite* to rich potential customers. For if the women hailed from Basin Street, the men behind those masks came from mansions along Esplanade and Prytania. Legend had it (and no woman more eagerly believes fairy tales than a hooker) that every year a new Cinderella or two would be born at the Scarlet Ball, as one perfect waltz elevated a public whore to private mistress.

Our first February in the city, I was appalled when Mother wanted to attend. She was a fortune teller; if she went, men would assume she was a prostitute. When reason didn't work, I staged tantrums till she agreed to stay home. We spent Mardi Gras evening on the balcony outside Room 9 watching carousing skull-and-bone gangs and Negroes feathered up as wild Indians chanting their *Bombuché*. Despite the free show,

Mother exhibited no gratitude for how I'd saved her reputation.

Missing the Scarlet Ball wasn't the only reason for her melancholy. Her fortune-telling career had begun well. Men, once they'd sported, while waiting for friends to finish, happily bought readings. Working out of the green parlor, sometimes Mother would gather a crowd, for whatever her forecasts lacked in accuracy, she made up in drama and wit. If any recognized her from Athena, it wasn't spoken of, at least not where I could eavesdrop.

But as many a pretty whore has discovered to her dismay, carousing men prize novelty. Mother's clientele began to thin. Lowering her fee didn't help. By that point the Baroness was paying me a (very) small salary. I spent it buying Tarot cards, a Gypsy tea cup, a crystal ball. Each prop helped but only awhile. I resurrected Attract-New-Business tricks I'd learned from Conquering John, burning an old shoe, painting a five-spot with menstrual blood. Results were indifferent. The Baroness' wise cracks grew caustic. We'd now been at Basin Street three months; some nights Mother didn't get a single customer. The past week had been busy with carnival, but after Mardi Gras night the tourists would go home.

Around dawn, woken by the Baroness' carriage returning from the ball, I assume Mother also heard my sisters singing, off-key but joyously, "The Man Who Broke the Bank at Monte Carlo." A few hours later I knocked on her door so we could attend Ash Wednesday services. She wouldn't come out, complaining of a headache. Unlike every other resident of Basin Street that morning, Mother, I knew, suffered no hangover. When I returned from the cathedral, a cross smudged on my forehead, her headache had passed and she carried the worried look she usually wore after a spell. "What did you see?"

"You want to know the future, pay up like everyone else." Though I'm pretty sure she was kidding, she never did tell me what vision she'd suffered. That evening, our parlors so empty that most girls sat embroidering song lyrics onto sofa pillows, Mother conferred with the Baroness in her office. When they came out the Baroness announced that henceforth Mother would see clients in her room, privately.

Though I never credited Mother with a head for business, with this new setup, Room 9 soon swarmed with customers. Previously, gentlemen bought her fortune-telling as afterthought. Now they came specifically to see her and usually left directly after their reading. "What did she see in your future?" I'd ask, but all I'd get was, "She made me promise not to tell."

When I asked how she'd harnessed her unruly clairvoyance, Mother replied, "I saw the writing in the tea leaves," which you must admit sounds like something a mystic would say. She explained that spectators muddied her visions. "You in particular are a terrible distraction, so never, ever come near my room when I'm in there telling a fortune."

No doubt part of her popularity arose from being that rarity, an honest fortune teller, willing to divulge even what men didn't want to hear. I know this, because on occasions when I broke my promise and stood outside her door during her private sessions, I heard the men inside wail and moan, grunt and groan, lamenting no doubt the sour fate she'd foretold. Yet, proof of the curative powers of honesty, the gentlemen always left her room looking much refreshed.

Yes, I know what you're thinking, but I'm like everyone else: I can make myself believe anything when I cannot bear to believe its opposite. Day by day, pebble by pebble, we build towers of self-told lies, leaving us that much more vulnerable when the battering ram of truth brings them crashing down. But let me not jump ahead in my story. Mother was a fortune teller. Of that I had no doubt.

She suggested we use her rising income to enroll me in school, but the Baroness insisted my job was full-time. I wasn't wild about school anyway; I was learning so much already. Helping the Professor choose playlists and covering on piano when he took breaks. Organizing the erotic "circuses" and "Oriental dance revues" to entertain special customers. Across

Basin Street, working the massive Southern Railroad terminal, when a train clanged in I'd stuff handbills into men's palms even as I studied the faces of women, hoping to spy Melpa so I could keep my promise to Nat. I got to know the station's tap dancers and spasm bands. Pickpockets taught me secrets of their trade in exchange for dirty stories from mine.

Creating advertisements, I was so inventive that copycats became a problem. If I promoted a harlot as "alluring," each whore on Basin claimed herself alluring in the next edition of the Blue Book. If I touted a "seductress," soon every bagnio overflowed with seductresses. I burned through adjectives like Sherman burned through Georgia.

Likewise, whenever a new inmate required a fresh name, usually my nomination was acceded most likely to entice customers. Lulu became Lulu, Delilah, Delilah, and Sugarplum, Sugarplum because I dubbed them thus. Yet when I mentioned reward, not money but favors in kind, they'd laugh. Slow to mature, at age fourteen I looked nine or ten. To the girls upstairs I remained a little brother: cute, clever, asexual.

Mardi Gras 1909, nothing could dissuade Mother from attending the Scarlet Venus Ball. When I determined to go along to keep her out of trouble, Ell Dixon refused to sell me a ticket. "Lord, don't I have troubles enough?" he whined. So I studied Mother's ticket and counterfeited a copy. It was a masquerade ball. Once I got in, who'd know me?

Experience sewing mojo bags served me well making a Hermes costume from the discards of my sisters' wardrobes. What I failed to account for was that I stood four-foot-two, shorter than anyone there. The ticket-taker laughed as he booted me out of the queue. I might've given up — apart from the occasional fetishist, no one enjoys humiliation — had not a carriage caught my eye.

Most gentlemen arrived by automobile, Mardi Gras a night for showing off. Yet here came the horse-drawn landau of the late Colonel Bonreve. Stepping from it, masked but unmistakable, was that libeler and levee saboteur, Judge August

Randolph Pike.

I coiled to spring, to gouge out his heart if he had one, when I noticed the fellow accompanying him. Not only was I confronted with the man I hated most; with him was Pierce White, whom I never liked either. No doubt these scoundrels had come to troll for beauties, with Mother the most beautiful woman there. Yet I let precious seconds pass. Why? To consider strategy? To plan my attack? No. In a fit of pique because Pierce now stood a head taller than I. To his list of precocious accomplishments add an early growth spurt.

They bypassed the line, spurring grumbles, but the ticket-taker waved them in. Evidently the Judge possessed as much clout in the city as he did on Bayou Lafourche. I dashed after them, my plans vague but murderous. "Whoa!" roared the doorman but I was too quick.

Inside, on the stairs, a hand grabbed me. Elliot Dixon, the only person who wore no mask, said, "No means no, pipsqueak." To the raucous music of a Turkey Trot, I became part of an outbound parade that included Dixon, a couple of his thugs, and between them someone dressed as Shakespeare's Puck. The rosy-cheeked grin of Puck's enormous *papier maché* head was undercut by the whimpering escaping it. Outside, the line pretended not to see us go by.

One end of the building butted a restaurant. On the other lay a shadowy passageway which led to a courtyard fringed with lush greenery and rickety verandas. "Take off his head," said Dixon. I gasped, but the thugs only yanked off Puck's mask, revealing the terrified face of an occasional customer of the Baroness. Already balding at twenty-five, he'd had his fortune read by Mother once and on his way out flipped me a Liberty nickel.

"What'd he do?" I asked.

"He didn't listen." Neither had I.

"Let me show you how it's done," Ell said as he slid onto his fist a heavy brass bar with holes for four fingers. He wrapped the assemblage in his handkerchief.

"I'll pay anything if you just let me go," begged the young man.

Ell ignored him, giving the brass knuckles a couple of test punches into the palm of his other hand. "See? Protected. Even a paw like mine, knuckles are delicate." His fatherly tone reminded me of Nat showing me how to worm up a hook to catch perch.

I won't describe the beating. I'd prefer not remembering it at all. Puck collapsed halfway through, but Ell was counting his blows and hadn't reached what he considered the appropriate number. Propped against a windmill palm, the young man bled onto the costume head in his lap. Scarlet trickled down the caricature grinning cheeks.

When Ell decided he'd inflicted punishment sufficient to whatever the transgression had been, he again crouched beside me. Was I next? No, it didn't seem so, because now he offered me the shiny brass and bloody handkerchief. "Good chance to practice," he encouraged. "Like a whack or two at him yourself?"

Ell hummed patiently. He certainly brought workaday cheerfulness to his brutality. "Thank you, not at this time," I said. He shrugged, pocketed his lethal appliance, and tossed the gory handkerchief to his victim, who was far beyond moving fast enough to catch it.

"Go on home," Ell said as he walked me out of the courtyard. "Hate to catch you inside again and have to drag *you* here for the treatment." He left me outside the ballroom entrance. As costumed gentlemen and masked whores streamed in around me, I thought of what I'd just seen, and of Mother, and Judge Pike. What if she didn't recognize him in time? What if he made her some proposition? Would she be forced to accept? If she refused, as my heart said she would, would Mother be dragged out for the treatment?

Along with the piano inside, the horn section set up on the second-floor balcony played a Mooche which set the crowd hollering when it segued into a Funky-Butt. My gaze climbed to the rooftop, its row of brick chimneys. I no longer believed in Santa Claus, but might there be something to his fabled mode of entry? I made for the adjacent restaurant.

Cursing chefs and frenzied waiters catering the fete next door barely listened to my story of a lost kitten on their window ledge. Marching upstairs, I raised a sash and dropped three feet onto the roof of the building Dixon had rented for his soiree. Heading for the nearest chimney, through the soles of my shoes I could feel the rhythm of a Texas Tommy. I'd learned the Tommy one rainy afternoon from Lulu, who brought it and the clap with her from San Francisco.

Possibly it was vibration from all those couples a floor below. Perhaps I unconsciously assayed an injudicious step-hop-kick myself. Or maybe the roof hid rot, or termites, or some flaw of construction. In any case, with a sudden *KA-BA-WOOF* I crashed through the slate, fell through the attic, burst through a ceiling, and landed atop a pile of overcoats next to a fornicating couple. They'd not removed their masks, nor much of their costumes, and despite the cloud of plaster dust paid my arrival little attention except that the fellow hollered, "Wait your turn!" Living in a whorehouse, I'd espied the carnal act before. These two demonstrated nothing innovative so I brushed off my costume and left to look for Mother.

In the ballroom a line of impatient couples waited for the room I'd left. Scanning the dance floor, in the swirl of color I saw princes and princesses, damsels and demons, but not Mother, nor the Judge, nor Pierce. I did see Elliot Dixon, however, so I burrowed into the thickest part of the crowd, seeking a spot from which I might discreetly watch the room.

At the piano, an exquisite Kimball grand, its raised lid allowed maximum volume to match the soaring brass on the balcony. Running the horses was Too-Late Baquet, whom I'd heard of but never heard play. "I need to hide in your piano," I told Too-Late.

"Not damn likely," he muttered. We were curtained by the backs of people watching the dancers, but when the song ended, who knew who might look our way. I hopped onto his bench. "Down, little man," he said. I climbed into the piano. A squeeze even for a boy barely topping four feet, it took a contortionist's skill not to dampen any strings.

"Get out of there or I'll call Mr. Dixon," said Too-Late, orchestrating his threat with syncopated sixteenth-notes.

A recurring theme in our treatise is that sometimes it's necessary to do evil to prevent greater evil, even when you hate yourself for doing it. Over his sheet music, I looked the pianist in the eye. "Know what the Citizen's League would do to a quadroon Professor who keeps a white boy in his Kimball?"

"I didn't put you there," he whispered in panic.

"Says you," I intoned, lowering the piano lid, hiding my shame but leaving a crack through which I could watch the room. I found a position I thought I could sustain. It was cramped, but no worse than the knothole into which Dixon would stuff me if I was caught.

~

"Have you spoken?" I asked.

"Not sure what I'll say," Mother answered through the mask that hid her face.

"So you haven't talked to him? Not a word?" First good news all night! During a deafening forty minutes peeking from the piano and fighting off charley-horses, I'd spotted Mother. Spotted the Judge. Felt the ebb and flow of despair as their orbits retreated and approached. Keened my dismay in the highest octave when he asked her for a dance. Luckily, a Boston Dip; prancing higgly-wiggly does not promote conversation. When the Dip ended, he'd offered to get her punch — a sure sign of interest, I feared, so I'd risked sticking my finger through the crack to signal her over.

"Dare I wonder what you're doing in that piano?" she asked.

"I can't let Ell Dixon see me. You have to leave. Now."

"Why do I have to leave if it's you Ell's looking for?"

"Mother, don't be difficult."

"Then don't be demanding. I haven't been to a ball in nine

years, not since the New Year's Eve party I had to beg Louis to host, then after your bad manners and 'poo-poo head' outburst he never would do it again. Well, now I'm here, and I'm going to mingle and dance and flirt a little. Might even flirt with the Judge, or maybe kick him in the groin. Either way I'm not leaving."

I hated when she acted immaturely. "Are you going to force me to nag you into it?"

She laughed. "Nag all you like. You're stuck in that piano. For once, I can simply walk away." And she did.

Well, she hadn't spoken to him. That was something. Perhaps Judge Pike suspected who lurked behind her mask, but her voice hadn't yet confirmed it. Still time to engineer her escape though, as I was reminded when Dixon crossed the room, I had to do it without leaving my hiding place.

The Judge strolled back from the punch bowl with Pierce at his elbow. "...a most delicious creature, and something familiar about her," I heard Pike say as they passed.

Traipsing across the pinblock to the keyboard end of the piano, "Play a waltz!" I ordered.

"Not damn likely," replied Too-Late, evidently his favorite phrase.

I threw my voice into dramatic falsetto, "Help! Help! I've been enslaved in this piano by a ferocious Negro!" The poor Professor cursed, but I heard the one-two-three, one-two-three beat I needed. Grumbling came from the balcony as the brass section was forced to switch tempo.

As I'd hoped, the Judge, though almost to Mother, turned on his heel. Handing Pierce the two glasses of punch to hold, he started back toward Mother, but — as I'd also hoped — someone else had already asked her to dance. A waltz always flushed out men too intimidated to try a Chicago or a Fish-Tail. As the laggard trombone caught the new rhythm, every shapely woman, Mother included, was whisked onto the floor. Take that, Judge Pike!

But instead of waiting his turn, the Judge tapped Mother's

dance partner on the shoulder to cut in. The gentleman refused. Good for him. Then the Judge slid aside his mask to reveal his face. Immediately the fellow bowed and backed away. Damn! The Judge took Mother in his arms. She didn't struggle. One-two-three, one-two-three, they matched the other dancers in a gentle rhythm that would allow disastrous conversation. I saw the Judge speak, then await Mother's response. Her mouth opened. He'd hear her voice. The game would be up. I had to act.

I began plucking piano strings. One-two-three, one-two-three, became one — one and a half — three — four; one — two — two and a quarter — two and seven eighths — five. The cornetist cursed. "Stop whatever the hell you're doing," hissed Too-Late.

I didn't. The dance floor descended into chaos. A fistfight broke out. I heard a whistled *G, E flat, F sharp*, Ell Dixon's call to arms. I kept up my musical sacrilege until Judge Pike left Mother and marched to the piano. "You play like some Russian composer," the Judge carped at Too-Late.

I danced across the treble bridge to the far end of the piano. Reaching out, I tugged the sleeve of a buxom harlot, a beauty of about seventeen who'd just exited the cloak room. Above her mask danced mischievous eyebrows, sweaty but perfect skin, and an explosion of blonde curls. She saw my eyes in the gap between piano and lid. "Costs extra to screw in a piano," she said.

My finger pointed at Mother. "See that woman?"

"Noticed her all evening. I like the way she moves." The girl actually licked her lips. Lord, is nothing simple? Haranguing the Professor, the Judge was nine feet away. What if he noticed this young harlot was also lusting after Mother? What if he noticed she was talking to a piano? I had to hurry this along.

"Go tell her that her son, his fear for her fate producing apoplexy, rushed back to Baroness von Kempe's and she better go to him before he succumbs to his fever which has reached 112 degrees and—"

"Hundred and twelve? No fever goes that high. Give me something I can work with."

"All right, forget fever. Tell her..." What? It was hard to think with every muscle cramping. On the dance floor Mother waited for the music to recommence. The Professor had long since agreed to forego atonal stylings, but the Judge, who'd drunk too many Sazeracs, continued to berate him for the sheer pleasure of bullying a black man who could never strike back. I saw Ell Dixon sauntering downstairs. Behind him, his goons had headlocks on the two fellows who'd thrown punches after my mischief with the tempo had thrown them into each other. If they got the treatment, that'd be yet more sins on my soul, but it gave me an idea.

"Tell the woman Ell Dixon caught her son in the piano, gave him the treatment, and dumped his barely-breathing leftovers back at Baroness von Kempe's."

The blonde smiled. "*That* jimmies. How much will you pay me?"

True to her calling, I'll give her that, but having neglected to sew pockets into my costume, I carried no money. "Payment comes with Part Two of your assignment," I lied.

"Part Two?"

"Yes, Part Two." What the hell could Part Two be? Then I smiled for the first time all evening. "See that fellow?" I pointed at Pierce.

"Three bucks, I'll French him in the coat room," she offered.

"No, don't fellate him, *inebriate* him. So drunk he can't perform the carnal act which he no doubt hoped would cap his evening. When he's good and soused, reach into the secret pocket of his costume where in his wallet you will find sixty dollars. Take it all."

Over her mask, blonde eyebrows perked up. "All?"

"It's carnival." So why not be generous? Besides, I doubted Pierce carried sixty dollars. I was almost sure he had no secret pocket. "But first give the woman her message."

"Should I tell her there's bones broken, you might lose an

eye or something?"

"I trust your mendacious instincts."

The head-full of blonde curls bounced over to Mother. Even at distance, even masked, Mother's eyes read shock, pain, doubt. She glanced at the piano but couldn't see me and, as I'd hoped, didn't come to check for fear of being held up by the Judge. True to her maternal impulses, Mother left. I gave her a head-start, then enjoyed the Judge's astonishment when a diminutive Hermes climbed out of the piano. I'd saved Mother from the devil's craw and was feeling pretty good.

Back at the Baroness', was Mother angry over my deception? Well, she *sounded* angry, but I put that off to high relief at finding I wasn't actually hurt. Intending to return to the ball, she made it halfway to Rampart Street, quite a distance considering my crisscrossed arms hobbled her knees the whole way. Eventually she turned back, acknowledging that even if able to drag me there, she'd hardly manage to dance.

Next morning, Ash Wednesday, Mother wouldn't open her door for me. I walked to the cathedral alone. Afterward, a palm cinder crucifix on my forehead to evidence my penitence, I caught up on brothel correspondence. Spiking invoices to be paid but discarding pleas for charity (as per the Baroness' standing instructions), suddenly my breath caught. My fingers trembled. I picked up the ominous letter. Addressed to "Baroness Brunhilda von Kempe," privately-messengered that morning, it bore Judge Pike's handwriting.

~

Bad, but could've been worse. He was looking for Mother and gave a fair description of her, yet seemed unsure it had actually been her he'd danced with. I threw his note away and went back to work, but kept thinking about how persistent the Judge was. About how he'd probably sent similar notes to every high-class madame on Basin Street, and who might say what. About whether he sought to do Mother further harm, or gloat over her fallen station, or whether, slimily repentant, he might arrive sliding a glass slipper onto Mother's foot, then whisk her to God-knows-what private hell his demented idea of devotion might construct. It crossed my mind how coincidental it was, that awful night a year-and-a-half past, that the Judge showed up just moments after the Colonel was shot.

I dug out his letter to answer it. Three drafts later I was satisfied. There'd been a woman fitting the description, the Baroness wrote, back in the fall of '07. The unlucky creature contracted syphilis then boarded a boat for Havana to die as she'd been born near the seaside. Nothing had been heard from her since.

Close to perfect, I thought. Plausible; sad though not maudlin; and mentioning the pox ought to cool his boiler. Besides, American troops had that very month finally left Cuba. If the Judge put a snoop on her trail they'd be dealing with a government preoccupied with newfound independence. I forged my employer's signature, sealed the letter, and set it with the outgoing post, never expecting what would be its actual result.

A few months later, I read of the city council establishing a trade mission in Cuba. The Times-Democrat listed its worthies, mostly n'er-do-well sons of wealthy families given impressive titles and no doubt one-way tickets. The last paragraph mentioned that accompanying them would be he who conceived the mission: eminent Judge August Randolph Pike. I prayed he might die of some tropical disease.

~

July 4th, 1909, I turned fifteen. I celebrated at Marcet's shooting gallery firing at mechanical ducks too heavy for even a direct hit to topple unless the barker, needing a winner to flog traffic, flipped a hidden switch. He never flipped it for me, but I kept firing anyway, like a U.S. Marine shooting up Honduras to defend the banana trade. *Pow, pow,* brandishing a pop gun while once my father killed a deer and three geese with one shot. *Pow, pow,* remembering times I could've but didn't go shooting with the Colonel. *Pow, pow,* could've but didn't keep my promises to Nat. I should've then and there searched Back-o'town for Melpa and her child, but no, *pow, pow,* I kept firing impotent cork bullets. A terrible thing to look back with regret; when remorse is well-entrenched by age fifteen, a terrible thing indeed.

While the worst of Mother's pique over the Scarlet Ball passed, our relationship remained cool. Whenever I'd say something witty, or correct someone who misspoke, or simply ask to be left alone, Mother would apologize to the parlor for her "surly teener." Better than "surly child" I suppose, but still unfair. Though everyone refused to recognize it, and admittedly I didn't look it, I'd become a grown-up.

Not that I was paid like one. Limiting how hard I could bargain for my services, I had to think of Mother. Novelty had again worn off. To offset her income's slow decline, I doctored the books. Not stealing, just re-apportioning so Mother appeared a better earner. As far as seeking some other situation, well, honestly, leaving the Life never occurred to me.

As usual, August was slow — girls and customers alike often considered it too hot to fuck — but the politicians Ell Dixon represented still expected fat envelopes. If the Baroness, not always rational in her management, decided to trim inventory, there was risk she'd start with Mother, who at thirty-three was her oldest lodger. Having come up with an alternative cost-cutting plan, I wanted to see if it'd work before presenting it. I walked the few doors down Basin Street to the marble steps at Maison de la Victoire. Too early for the doorman, my second ring was answered by a nude, honey-colored Venus gnawing a biscuit.

"I'm bookkeeper for Baroness von Kempe. I wish to see your proprietress."

"Well, I declare," she said, slapping the half-eaten biscuit to her ample bosom.

The madame was an attractive but no-nonsense woman of about forty. Unlike her lodgers, she didn't seem to be Negro. "I've no interest in what techniques your girls offer nor how much they charge for specific services," I said.

"At your age, I hope not," she said with the beginning of a smile. I decided I liked her.

"I'm older than I look," I said, "but be that as it may." I held up a sheet of paper. "Here are our suppliers and the prices we pay for liquor, linens, disinfectant, et cetera; every item necessary to run a respectable brothel." She looked intrigued. "While you and the Baroness fiercely compete for the dollars of the city's better gentlemen — and I'd never suggest you do otherwise — I think it'd serve you both to share certain information."

"In other words," she said, "make suppliers vie for our business as vigorously as we vie with each other. Hildie's idea or yours?"

"While I act in her interest, I took this upon myself. Baroness von Kempe frets enough between the customers and her girls."

"Don't we all?" Her delicate hand extended toward my precious list.

"Your bookkeeper will supply me with like information?"

"I keep my own books. You'll get your figures. A job too, if Hildie ever forgets what a gem she's found." By that age I knew never to trust flattery from a prostitute. Nonetheless her compliment pleased me.

Baroness von Kempe screeched when she learned I'd formed "a cartel" with her rival. One reason she eventually approved the arrangement was that the two houses didn't compete for girls. Madame de la Victoire lodged octoroons; her inmates, while mostly fair-skinned, were colored. Baroness von Kempe's girls were white. That's why Elliot Dixon brought Mother to her instead of Madame de la Victoire with whom he had a closer relationship. The Baroness refused to let me share information with Madame Josette (who ran a "French house," though Josette herself was Belgian) nor Czarina Pavlova (neither Russian nor royalty — someone said she'd been a mail-order bride to a Croat oysterman from Pointe a la Hache). Madame de la Victoire did share with them however, so that interlocking treaties evolved, making Basin Street an even more complicated web than already rendered by the commerce of lust.

The rapprochement I engineered bore further fruit when Madame de la Victoire accepted an invitation to tea from Baroness von Kempe. I found the two chatting like the old friends they'd never been. The Baroness mentioned my mother roomed upstairs.

"She only reads fortunes," I pointed out.

Madame de la Victoire smiled. "I wonder what she'd say mine held."

For some reason Baroness von Kempe thought that the funniest thing. "Why don't we ask her? Go get your mama."

Mother's entrance provoked an extraordinary scene. "It's you!" she exclaimed.

"You know each other?" blurted von Kempe.

"No, I don't believe we do," said Madame de la Victoire.

She was lying. I saw it in her eyes and in Mother's confused retreat. "Forgive me," said Mother. "I thought you looked like someone else."

Madame de la Victoire smiled thinly. "We all make mistakes, don't we? Now I must prepare for the evening trade. Perhaps this delightful fortune teller can read my palm some afternoon. If the young man could see me out..."

In the foyer we found ourselves alone. As I started to open the door she put her hand on mine to stop me. "How old are you?"

I told her. I suppose she did calculations in her head, but the mathematics didn't tax her. This grand lady stooped so that we were eye to eye. She'd not yet tied her hat back on. Her hair, black as Creole coffee, woven fashionably atop her head, smelled of vanilla.

"I cherished your late father," she confessed.

"If Colonel Bonreve patronized—"

"Not Bonreve." Her hand found my shoulder, testing my musculature the way the Colonel used to inspect his colts. "If ever I look at you strangely… If ever you find me capricious or cruel, or if I reward you with kindness you haven't earned…" She let the thought linger then, without finishing it, walked out.

Though double-teamed by the Baroness and me, Mother insisted she'd been mistaken and had never met Madame de la Victoire before that day. Neither of us believed her. The Baroness forbade Mother to call at Maison de la Victoire, but that only lasted till September 21st, the date of the great 1909 Grand Isle hurricane. On the Mississippi, three hundred barges sank. On the bayous, three hundred corpses floated. As the storm eased we crowded the house's highest balcony to watch the bowl of backswamp behind the city fill with water, congratulating ourselves that with the eye passing to the west, we'd been spared the worst wind.

Afterward came the usual relief efforts. Storyville chipped in, with Madame de la Victoire and Mother leading the collection of clothing, food, and funds from the whores and pimps of the District. Mother cried each night. What conversations the two women had when they were alone, I don't know, but you've no doubt guessed what took me months to pester out of Mother. Madame de la Victoire was Victorine Guidry, the storekeeper from Chenière who'd almost been my godmother. She'd financed Father's boat, attended their wedding, witnessed his death. The mysterious rival to Mother whom Touloulou claimed was secretly part Negro.

Mother stressed it was not my place to bring up past events unless Victorine spoke first, and never to reveal any of it to the Baroness. "Who are we to strip her veil? Hardly a woman in the District hasn't hidden, spruced up, or invented her past, including me."

I promised discretion, but it hardly mattered: while I had a thousand questions I wanted to ask her about my father, Victorine was not a woman from whom one could pry secrets.

~

July 4th, 1910, I turned sixteen. The same day, Melville Fuller, Chief Justice of the U.S. Supreme Court, died. To replace him

President Taft elevated Edward Douglas White, uncle of my nemesis Pierce Douglas White. With all the grave melodrama that plagues sixteen-year-olds, I begrudged Pierce this additional celebrity and wondered after Aralee. To suffer peaking adolescence but appear only twelve (on a good day) would rankle under any circumstance. My extra burden was to live surrounded by women who would've had no scruples plucking my virginity if — if, if, if, that cruel word again — Mother, the Baroness, even Elliot Dixon, had not declared me off limits until I sprouted facial hair. (Hair pasted-on or painted-in failed muster; I tried both.)

In my three years in New Orleans, I'd avoided conjuring. Hoodoo rekindled too many memories, too sorrowful wondering whether I'd ever find Melpa and have the wherewithal to help her child. But the urges of a sixteen-year-old sent me visiting Touloulou (who hounded me over my debt) as a pretext to gather cemetery dust. I trailed Ell Dixon to a barber to collect razor stubble from the brawniest man I knew. To hasten sexual development, whore's piss seemed an obvious ingredient and, what's more, was readily available. I even jimmied the lock on the ornate valise of "stiffeners" the Baroness sold to elderly clients.

Word got out. My sisters boisterously rooted for my success. The Baroness docked my pay for the aphrodisiac trimmings. Mother gave me peculiar looks. I sprouted not one follicle.

The problem was not with my conjuring, it turned out. One evening Gladys, facing a customer who despite her wiliest wiles couldn't pop his cork, left the fellow hanging (in two senses of the word) to borrow my mojo. She later reported its effect on her limp trick was immediate and dramatic.

Soon I enjoyed a thriving side-business selling charms to the bawds. Any hint of venereal disease and I'd send them to a proper doctor, but for everything else — love, luck, money, Come-To-Me, Go-Away, Other-Woman-Grow-Ugly — I was their man, or, unfortunately, boy.

Late 1910, the holidays had been profitable but the girls

discontented. Inmates bitched the Baroness worked them too hard, kept too large a share, failed to screen out men who were uncouth, unclean, or unlikely to tip — common complaints at any time in any brothel, but holiday blues leavened grumpiness into near-mutiny. Eviction was a madame's ultimate sanction when a girl grew too fond of opium or liquor, skimmed more that could be forgiven, caught something nasty, or committed the gravest sin, outstaying the blush of youth. But when half the girls threatened to decamp together, the case that Christmas, leverage switched to their side.

To defuse tension, the Baroness declared we'd all take an outing at her expense, a sort of strumpets' picnic. I confess I chose the specific event. On the last day of the year, the aviator John Moisant intended to win the $4,000 Michelin Cup by breaking the record for distance flown. I hoped it'd please Mother, reminding her of how Colonel Bonreve and I once built a flying machine — a happy memory if one glossed over the ensuing broken arm, and my having later believed it a murder attempt, and the fact that our machine didn't actually fly.

Everyone exhibited good cheer when we boarded the St. Charles line, heading for an aerodrome set up at Little Farms west of the city, but at Carrollton we transferred to a farmer's open dray which I'd oversold as an "old timey hayride." The weather grew colder. As every chuck-hole jolted the wagon, fourteen women chorused "Ooph!" while the sudden uplift of feathered hats resembled a covey of quail flushed by a spaniel.

We finally reached the "aerodrome." An open pasture next to a slaughterhouse, it reeked of putrid offal and fresh cow shit. A candy apple vendor had set up, but he'd scorched his syrup, worsening the stench. Bleachers tacked from rough-cut lumber meant the slightest lateral movement drove splinters into one's ass. Whether by dress or demeanor, people recognized the Baroness' girls for the sort of girls they were. Men leered, kids ogled, wives rebuffed.

The race course was defined by two barely visible pylons a

couple of miles apart. Mr. Moisant would have to circle them ninety-one times to break the existing world record. Calculating how long that'd take, and how surly the freezing, snubbed, buttocks-punctured women pinching their noses around me would become, I prayed for engine trouble to end the exhibition early, a sacrilege that's haunted me since, for on only the second lap, Moisant's flying machine dropped out of the sky. The world's greatest aviator was dead.

On the grim ride home, as we departed Carrollton Station the electric railway rode smooth as a magic carpet after that God-awful wagon. In typical overreach, the Baroness tried to capitalize on our rallying spirits. "If any good comes from this tragedy," she announced, "perhaps it'll make y'all see the benefits of your present situation instead of leaving me to chase some rainbow which will sooner or later slam to Earth every bit as hard as any bit of aviation foolishness got slammed out of this silly boy's head."

Silly? I never seemed silly when saving her a fortune every month, as even she acknowledged. "On the contrary," I proclaimed, "I've decided to become an aviator myself."

I don't know why I said it. I didn't mean it. Aviation was clearly just a dangerous fad.

"Don't be foolish," said the Baroness. "Aero-planes cost money. What little you have—"

"—is what little you pay me, but I've keys to your cash box, don't I?" Reckless, reckless.

"You know what happens if you steal."

"You'll cut off my finger. Okay, take it." I offered an upraised finger: the middle one.

The Baroness frothed. "Might not be a finger I cut."

Girls tittered. I understood what body part she meant. "Much good that appendage has done me," I responded, aiming accusing looks at each of them, ending with Mother.

Back at Basin Street, that bleak New Year's Eve descended into woeful. When midnight began the year 1911, girls bestowed desultory kisses on tipsy clients. Baroness von

Kempe's smooch woke an elderly city councilman who'd dozed off on the divan. I expected to be left out. Instead, Mother took my face in her hands and kissed me on the lips.

"I never want to hear again about you becoming an aviator," she said as the kiss broke, "though your crazy ideas are maybe partly my fault because I've been keeping you a child, thinking of you like a child, but you're not a child anymore because face it I was married when just a little older than you are and those were simpler times in a simpler place especially compared to a bawdy house where temptation is all around even if you look too little to be tempted but that's because your body's small but your mind's big, big enough for two or three people at least, and temptation is in the mind so your great big brain must be chock-full of it so you know what that means?"

I had no clue.

"Means tomorrow you become a man."

Tutorial III

PERILOUS DESIRES

Recount when you were first led astray by sexual urges. (If you're too young to have had such urges, put this book away!)

New Year's Day, 1911, everyone slept late except me. It was noon before anyone came down, two before we lunched, three before New Year's gifts were exchanged, four before I was deflowered. Mother offered the house rate of $5 to any girl willing to render her colt into a stallion. With several willing takers, the Baroness set up a Dutch auction. Girls bid down the price they'd accept to bed me, four dollars, three, two-fifty. They also described techniques they'd employ. Never had my sisters acted so unsisterly.

When the price reached zero, it began rising again as girl after girl proposed to pay *me* for the privilege of ending my sixteen-year dry spell. When a new girl bid $10, the Baroness cried, "Sold!" and whispered as she handed me off, "I get my usual cut."

The girl was pretty, large-breasted with curly blonde hair. "What's your name?" I asked.

"New house, guess I need a new name."

"Around here, that's my job," I boasted. "From today on, you're…" What should I name her who would guide me through such a key rite of passage? "Calypso!"

"Good as any," shrugged Calypso as she led me into Room 3. "Just don't forget you owe me sixty bucks."

"Sixty? You only paid ten—"

"Not for that. That was to show the others I'm a good sport. You owe me sixty 'cause of the time at the Scarlet Ball when you had me tell your mother that cock and bull story about you being beaten, then lied there'd be sixty dollars in the pocket of some other young fool."

I recalled the incident, her carnival mask, her blonde curls. Mardi Gras night I hadn't seen her face, let alone everything else she now revealed as she undressed without the least shyness. I won't bore you detailing my first traipse into the secret garden. Suffice that I wanted to repeat the exercise, with Calypso and every girl there. Alas, I could no longer expect to be remunerated for it; soon, I couldn't even get a discount.

To earn money to buy sport, I became as avaricious as any of the bawds. Selling hoodoo charms helped, until I flooded the market. I took chores for extra cash, jobs no one wanted, emptying chamber pots or washing out condoms or going around with the red pasteboard box of poison to bait for mice.

Even paying full price, I was never flattered or cajoled like other clients. My big sisters felt no incentive to extend my pleasure, cater to my fantasies, or pretend they were enjoying the act if they weren't. For their own sexual gratification, at least half our inmates preferred dancing the horizontal ballet with fellow women, but those who did enjoy a well-maneuvered penis took shameless advantage of my eagerness to instruct me in what they liked and how they liked it, demanding of a randy sixteen-year-old services they wouldn't dream asking from a regular customer. It never occurred to me to complain. From these ad hoc lessons, within months I became an extremely proficient lover. Meanwhile, my voice dropped, hair sprouted, and I grew eight inches (in general height, though my phallus indeed beefed out as well), tall enough to be called on to intimidate unruly customers, though not as tall as 6'4" Achille.

Mother's reaction to these changes was baffling. After my boyhood was auctioned away, we rarely spoke of matters sexual. One day on the stairs, I coming down, she going up, I paused, stood straight, shoulders back. "Look at me, Mother. Not a kiddie anymore, am I?"

She said nothing. No woman on Earth forged a sharper sword from silence.

"Doesn't the man before you remind you of my father?" I demanded.

"You think all your higgly-piggly with Mr. Wiggly makes you the man your papa was? Achille Cheramie *died* trying to save my baby sister. I don't want you to get yourself killed, but when's the last time you sacrificed, gave the least thought, to rescue anyone or accomplish anything besides what you've been doing upstairs?"

"Mother, I make a hundred sacrifices every day just to make your life easier."

"Name them."

I stammered.

"Okay. Name even just three of these sacrifices," she said.

Who can recall sacrifices when put on the spot like that?

She spread her arms. "So here we are." Her stigmata caught the light, shadows on her soft hands.

~

July 4th, 1911, I turned seventeen. For three weeks I'd endured half-rations sex-wise to save cash toward buying Mother earrings, expensive so she'd know I sacrificed. I'd present them at that trendy new restaurant, Galatoire's, my treat. We'd nibble fancy dishes and sip exotic cocktails and bare our souls. My catalog of things to talk about included exactly one hundred ways I contributed to her well-being: nightly prayers, candles lit at the cathedral, cooking the books to ensure her earnings never declined, etc., etc. Down the list, some items were a stretch, but surely before we got that far Mother would acknowledge her son to be the living embodiment of Achille Cheramie.

On my way out to the jewelers, I nodded to Ell Dixon, who'd brought by a new girl. Though something was familiar about her, I paid little mind. If she lodged here, I'd enjoy her soon enough.

Halfway across Basin, it hit me. I hurried back. From the office voices rose, the Baroness bargaining hard over Dixon's latest find. In the parlor the girl sat tugging at her bodice as if the showy outfit was unfamiliar. "Tellia?" At first my childhood playmate didn't recognize me, then her eyes flew wide and her arms flew open to crush me against a ripe bosom of which there'd been no hint when I saw her last.

~

A rope broke, a spar fell, and her husband Zeph's shinbone shattered. The village of Leeville had no doctor, so they'd boated to the city. Some fellow loitering outside Charity Hospital, working on commission, had with dire warnings about publicly-funded medical care redirected her toward a private doctor who, unlike the hospital, charged whatever the market would bear. A pretty young woman desperate for money was sure to meet Elliot Dixon sooner or later. In Tellia's case it was sooner.

"Zeph had no objection to how you intend to pay his medical bills?" I asked as we galloped down the sidewalk.

"We never discussed it. Doc fed him laudanum." Faced with losing his leg to gangrene and his wife to prostitution on the very same day, Zeph might've well been better off dosed with that bitter tincture of opium, morphine, codeine, and alcohol. We paused to let an ice truck go by. She glanced back toward the Baroness'. "I thought the bumpety-bump happened on the premises," Tellia said. Evidently she didn't understand what I'd done, the sacrifice I'd made, the mortal danger I'd embraced by spiriting her out of the bagnio, thus defying my notorious employer and also notoriously unforgiving Ell Dixon. Like a pulp novel hero, I'd rescued her from whoredom. Now I would save her husband's leg. Mother would see it as heroic, akin to Achille diving into the flood. Only with a happier outcome. Wouldn't that give us something to chat about at Galatoire's!

As we wove through the Southern Railroad terminal, my giddiness evaporated. Above the clang of a cooling locomotive, above the hum of passengers and cries of touts and rattle of porters' carts, I heard *G, E flat, F sharp*, the whistle that said Elliot Dixon intended giving someone the treatment. A tremor shot through my body. That someone was me.

~

Zeph's brother Philo looked exactly as he had at Athena nine years before, same buck teeth, same truculence. Zeph, however, appeared far from the robust, affable young man I remembered. Doped and delirious, he was tied into bed to keep him from touching a leg even bluer, bloodier, and more swollen than Tellia had forewarned.

To save her husband's limb, she'd found the city's most respected surgeon. Unfortunately, Dr. Cazenac charged accordingly. Without a second thought, I coughed up the money I'd planned to spend on earrings for Mother and my birthday celebration at Galatoire's. Even so, my bankroll represented only half what the doctor required. Off to a previous engagement, he would return in two hours and perform surgery to save the leg — *if* we had the balance of his fee in hand. If not, he'd graciously amputate for half-price. Philo offered to saw off Zeph's leg, no charge. Tellia and the doctor pretended he hadn't spoken.

Dr. Cazenac left for his July 4th picnic. I left to "get the money somehow." Waylaying a lucky passer-by, I traded my smart coat and hat for his shabby ones, regrettable but necessary to delay the moment I'd be recognized by who-knows-who and have my whereabouts reported to Ell.

Attract-Money tricks never work fast nor, frankly, attract much. No, my readiest source of cash was the Baroness. I'd convince her the girl had been pox-ridden, which would mean

I'd actually done von Kempe a favor, so I could beg an advance on salary.

Of course if Ell was still there...

I entered on tiptoe. Saw no one. Remembered: the holiday! No doubt everyone was off to Spanish Fort or West End, nibbling hot dogs then puking them up on carnival rides.

In the Baroness' safe I found only nine dollars, not nearly enough. On the mantel clock a brass angel played the lyre, *tick, tick, tick*, eighty minutes left to get the money for Zeph's operation. Though barely worth testing the Baroness' promise to chop off my finger — or something more precious — if I stole from her, I took the nine. Mother complained I never sacrificed for others. Now I had.

Mother. Even with declining earnings, she probably had some money put-away. There was awkwardness to having *my* brave sacrifice require *her* to cough up cash — it was a Judge Pike sort of play — but I saw no alternative. I knocked at Room 9. No answer. Tried the knob: locked. Mother had despaired of our luncheon date, I deduced, and joined the others railroading to West End. As with the Baroness, I'd have to borrow now and ask later. I preferred not to think how that conversation would go.

Bless ever-careless Gladys in Room 5. Passing through her unlocked room onto the balcony, I crept toward Mother's open window but, poised to climb in, I saw Mother was there after all, lying on her bed. She didn't see me, but here's why: Mother was kissing Calypso, the buxom, blonde whore who'd taken my virginity and whom I'd enjoyed several times since.

Nor was this a kiss hello. Not the peck on each cheek Fifi the French girl bestowed. Mother and Calypso were sharing passion, kimonos open, eyes closed, hands exploring. The sight split me in two, one part of me with roiling emotions I couldn't face; the other calm, cogent, divorced from self. My rational half understood what I was watching to be a mundane occurrence on Basin Street. The Life drew lesbos like sugar draws ants. If a young lady was already condemned by her family as a woman-loving freak, a fish-kissing muffer, an unholy grass-eater, then the additional stigma of being a whore wasn't much extra burden, especially considering that lodging at a parlor house paid better than any other job available to a female and, in off hours, offered a convenient sorority of good-looking women where a girl didn't have to deny her crushes or hide her assignations.

So: all entirely customary. Routine as the nude female form, which I witnessed day in and day out. Only this was Mother. Thirty-four now but exquisite as ever. No sag to her breasts, no wrinkles in her pearl-white skin. No change at all, except, of course, gender preference.

Observing Calypso stroking Mother's sex, I found myself pondering questions of spirituality. If God made us in His image, did homosexuals exist as expression of His curiosity, His passion for variety, His devotion to love in as many forms as He could manifest it? If so, then might non-believers likewise mirror His own doubts? Hedonists reflect His wild streak? If that was indeed how the moral universe operated, then might even an abject sinner like me serve some higher purpose and be every bit as touched by the Divine as Mother was presently being touched by Calypso?

Those metaphysical musings occupied my mind. Neck down sang a different tune, one altogether more visceral. My gut clenched. *Mother!* My bowels churned. *Mama!* My heart didn't so much beat as clatter. *Mom!* Most alarming, I grew a magnificent erection. It stretched my drawers even as it stretched my previous limits of shame. Watching Mother and Calypso, I felt mortifying jealousy; mortifying because I wasn't sure of whom I was jealous, whose place I wanted to take in this coupling.

A strange birthday already, this was more than a Catholic boy could handle. When I found my hand, unbidden, rubbing the front of my pants like a housemaid polishing the silver, I knew I better go straight to church. The sound of Mother's passion camouflaged my exit. Chanting 'Hail Marys' occupied my mind. Not till I walked a mile and a half in the blazing sun then entered the cool, perfumed twilight of St. Louis Cathedral did I remember my mission to secure funds for Zeph's operation.

Though the church was almost empty, its grand organ echoed through the nave like seraphim singing. The altar beckoned with stunning murals, exquisite carvings, and golden candlesticks. Those last, I decided, would be easiest to fence.

Between trains, petty thieves at the railroad station often discussed technique. Look purposeful, they all agreed. Walk steadily but not so fast as to arouse suspicion. Above all, act like you belong there. Hopping the communion rail, I climbed the marble steps to the altar. Took a gold candlestick, heavier than I expected, and started back.

Oops…

Awaiting me was "le Suisse," a guard whose braided red uniform imitated those at the Vatican. Was the halberd he carried for show, I wondered, or was that eight-foot-long battle ax as sharp as the saw that would cut off Zeph's leg if I didn't get back in time?

'Act like you belong there,' I remembered. "You should be ashamed," I said.

"Ashamed?"

"Ashamed," I confirmed, brandishing the candlestick as I hopped the communion rail. "When's the last time you polished the gold?"

"Not my job—"

"Tell it to Archbishop Blenk."

I strode away, fighting the instinct to look back, but soon heard, "Stop!"

The rest of my lesson at the railroad station: "If acting like you belong there doesn't work, run like hell." I did, but a nontet of nuns clogged the aisle between me and the exit so, pointing at thin air high above the stained-glass windows, I shouted "*Regardez-vous!* The Blessed Virgin!" Sixteen eyes promised to the Lord looked, but the ninth nun (whether more pious or less gullible, I'll never know) genuflected, thrusting out the other knee as a black-clad hurdle I did not clear. My flight was briefer than Moisant's. My jaw hit the stone floor, the clatter of candlestick echoing through the cathedral. My nose skidded into a fine leather shoe.

"Is this who claims he saw the Virgin?" I heard a familiar accent ask. That's when I noticed the music had stopped.

Was it possible after all these years that Father Groetsch had finally been transferred to his original posting, a joke by God at my expense? Yes, there he stood, the Fearless Funeral Friar. He appeared as startled to see me as I was him. As I rose the oversized candlestick caught his eye. "Sinner!" he proclaimed, wrenching it away.

Though now empty-handed, I'd have happily abandoned the whole adventure, but Groetsch blocked my exit, the nuns my retreat, while *le Suisse* pushed through them toward me flourishing his halberd. Suffice to say I gave them a merry chase, up the aisles, between the pews, around the statuary of numerous unamused saints. Cornered at last, I fled up the stairs to the organ loft.

After his purgatory at St. Catherine's, Groetsch had found the musical paradise he sought. If redemption was possible for him, why not for me? Granted I'd hardly embraced celibacy as he had nor, actually, forgone any other pleasure I ran across and could afford, but doesn't the Gospel of Luke tell us there's more rejoicing over one repentant sinner than over ninety-nine persons already virtuously dull? I could repent. I was ready; and it seemed God was ready to have me because there in front of me the giant organ beckoned, its ornate keyboard an open invitation to praise the Lord in the way I best knew how.

I forgot I had an angry priest, a Swiss guard, and nine confused nuns in hot pursuit. A long lost playmate awaiting me, her husband awaiting surgery, his surgeon awaiting payment. An awkward conversation with Mother coming and Ell Dixon planning to give me the treatment. My butt found the seat, my feet the pedals, my fingers the keys.

A better musician might've essayed Bach; a holier man, some

beloved spiritual; but a sinner worships to the rhythms of the street. Where celestial angels sang a moment before, now jazz poured out of every *fond* and *anche* of the Grand-Choeur manual. Responsive even to my inadequate touch, the colossal Cavaillé-Coll pipe organ made me for that one moment a better musician than I'd ever been, perhaps a better man. Listen, God, listen! Mother, can you hear? (Even though you're a dozen blocks away and admittedly pre-occupied.) Do you acknowledge that your son has become a new and righteous person?

Groetsch arrived. He wrenched my arm. I shoved back. Who was he to interrupt my hot-swinging redemption? The Suisse raised his halberd to cut off my fingers the way Baroness von Kempe often threatened and might do yet. Fearless in my rapture, I kept playing. Defending his keyboard, Groetsch caught the weapon before it could fall. I riffed on, certain that God, listening, was ready to gather up the fragments of my soul and forgive my church-robbing, mother-lusting ways.

Yet bliss, even spiritual bliss, is fleeting, as I was reminded when Groetsch slammed the organ's fallboard on my fingers, *yowww!* The halberd swooped inches above my head. Time to go.

Nuns blocked the staircase. I leapt over them. In a steep dive, my outstretched arms swiped off six of nine wimples. Haste to restore their head coverings kept the sisters from falling on me like she-wolves when I crash-landed into a wooden pedestal. The "poor box" atop it lurched, leaned, wobbled, then, heavy with rattling coins, fell into my arms. Did that sudden advent of cash money signal that God had pardoned my numerous and ongoing transgressions? Or did it merely demonstrate that our Lord knows it's customary to tip the piano player? People often say, "time will tell," but it's not always true.

~

The doctor's parlor was stuffy. In the next room, thanks to the "poor box" money, Zeph was under the knife though not yet out of the woods. Meanwhile, like a snake hunting mice,

Philo paced behind Tellia, eyeballs glued to the bustle of her dress, the fancy one on loan from Elliot Dixon. Having only one complete arm added to Philo's viper-like quality.

The doctor entered, apron bloody as a butcher's. "I shudder at the outcome had you entrusted these fractures to a lesser surgeon." A prediction of full recovery, a reassuring peek at now-peacefully-sleeping Zeph, a promise he'd be released in the morning. Somehow all the malfeasances I'd perpetrated had reassembled themselves into something good.

Giving Philo the address of a cheap but clean brothel, I promised we'd meet him later. The brothel was real; about meeting him, I lied. Tellia and I walked to the river to siphon the bilge of Zeph's leaky lugger. Giddy on relief at her husband's prognosis, she blossomed into the girl I remembered, vibrant and chatty as I cranked the boat's hand pump while clouds painted a brilliant sunset.

The lugger's pair of hard bunks was too obvious a hide-out with Dixon hunting us, so we bought supper from a push-cart and found an out-of-the-way rooming house. It smelled like the dachshund the proprietor's daughter was washing in the lobby. I'd told myself we'd get separate rooms but remaining funds barely sufficed for one. Tellia expressed neither surprise nor disappointment, merely followed me upstairs.

The room smelled better than the lobby. Tellia unpinned her hat. I sat on the bed to pry off my shoes. I'd sleep on the floor and give her the lumpy mattress; at least, that's what I told myself, but I became distracted when she unbuttoned her dress. Under it, the corset gave her trouble. "Never wear these in Leeville," she said. "Mr. Dixon loaned it. Said looking like a lady would help me get hired at the whorehouse."

Looking like a lady? Maybe, though not sounding like one. Her English was barely passable, so we spoke French. Hers had the drawl of the coastal marshes, the accent I heard in Mother's speech when she was angry. Tellia backed up so I could unlace her. "What's it like living down the bayou?" I asked.

"Thinking of leaving New Orleans?"

"Wasn't before today."

"Helping us got you in trouble?"

"Nothing I can't handle," I lied. Despite my fumbling fingers, the corset slipped off. Her chemise, I'm sure, once possessed the normal weight and opacity of milled cotton, but I could imagine the cauldrons of wash water it'd endured, the thumps with a battoir, the caustic bars of lye soap, all of which had rendered it sheer as muslin, as insubstantial as my weakening resolve. The weight of her breasts played across the fabric as she walked to lay the corset on the dresser, the outline of her pubic hair appeared as she ambled back to the bed. I wanted this woman. Wanted her but knew I should refrain, not for her sake but for mine. I lived in an abyss of corruption, but on this my seventeenth birthday I'd chosen a new path, trudging the day's heavy toll of lies and thieving and sacrilege to reach a higher road where goodness would prevail over evil. Like St. Michael I would stomp the devil. Like Achille Cheramie I would face the hurricane. Mother, whatever her sexual preference, would be proud of how I'd changed.

"I need one more favor," Tellia said as she sat beside me and placed her callused but gentle hand across where my member lay hidden under my clothing. She began to stroke it. What she said next, if she said anything, I can't be sure. To keep my cork in its bottle, I ran the Baroness' payables in my mind. Due August 1st to Consolidated Liquors, $756.19. Due August 5th to Canal Street Printing, $62.08.

Through the discipline of accounting the crisis passed, but my phallus remained erect and her hand was still moving. "You mentioned a favor," I said.

"Zeph and I haven't had a child," she informed me. Stroke, stroke, delicious stroke. "Though, almost every night…" Gestures with her free hand conveyed activities I dared not envision.

My waving hand mimicked hers. "To completion?"

"*Splendid* completion. Both of us. Every single time."

Far too much to think about. My own experience limited to

jaded professionals, I envied Zeph his perfect record, the lack of eventual issue notwithstanding. "You want a *gris-gris?*" I asked.

"Tried that," she said. Stroke, stroke, whimper, whimper.

"A doctor, then? A specialist?"

"Tried that too. Last season, while here selling oysters. Doc said Zeph's minnows never learned to swim." She took a deep breath. "Zeph really admired your daddy. Wanted to be just like him. Would want a child who'd be like him as much as possible, too."

Distracted as I was, it took me a moment to decipher her implication, long enough that she interpreted my silence as consent. To seal the deal, she kissed me so passionately I could hardly think, and what thinking I did was mostly about "splendid completions."

She unbuttoned my pants. "I'm too young to be a father," I protested.

"Going to find that out, aren't we?" she said.

Splendid indeed, as all the terrible things I'd done and the even more terrible things numerous parties were planning to do to me all disappeared under a grappling, clutching ecstasy that is one of God's truest miracles. When sonneteers pen their rhymes, love appears a thing immutable, lasting a lifetime or even longer, beyond the grave, through eternity. My seed planted, in those post-coital moments with Tellia I realized there is also love, equally deep, equally profound, whose destiny is to be not a fire but a flare. To burn intensely but just for an instant. And love lasting a moment need cede no measure of value to love that lasts forever. In the heavens there are stars, but there are also shooting stars, precious in their brevity.

Such a pretty speech. I imagined some man or woman caught philandering uttering it to their wronged spouse. Though maybe even true, it'd sound as hollow as an empty milk pail. The gumbo of love and lust and amity and ardor was as complicated as Mother had once warned. Though accomplished at the physical act, about the rest I still had much to learn.

~

At dawn I woke. Already wearing her threadbare fisherwoman dress, Tellia folded the gown and associated underthings Dixon had loaned her. Tidying the shabby room neater than we found it, she discovered the Bible that a couple of years back some religious order had begun placing in the nation's hotel rooms. I was surprised she picked it up because I didn't think she could read. I was more surprised when she sat on it and began wiggling her butt across it, periodically lifting it to her cheek to test its temperature.

As brightening sky crept through the curtains, I watched her press my pants with spit and a warm Bible and wondered what life would've been if Mother and I had actually caught that sternwheeler to Leeville after our first disappointing days in the city. Would I be an oysterman like Zeph? Have a wife like Tellia? Would I be happy?

I shuffled to the washstand. "I'm not sure I'm the man Zeph is."

"You did okay" she said. "Not splendid, but okay."

"No, I mean rising above my jealousy knowing that my wife…" More hand gestures.

Tellia seemed surprised. "Zeph can't ever know about what we did. If we made a baby last night, he has to think it's his. Otherwise, he'd kill you."

Heaven, help me. I didn't need any more mortal enemies. "Don't you think Philo will suspect? Tell Zeph. Taunt him with it."

"Philo?" She gave me a hard look. "Maybe I should collect Zeph without you, leave you figure out what to do about Mr. Dixon."

Not bad advice. I gathered my clothes. "It irks me I traded my best suit for these rags which for all I know were yard-lifted from the clothesline of some shark who'll recognize them."

A grin blossomed on her face. "You need a safer disguise?"

In the District, those whom the German progressive Dr.

Hirschfeld had recently labeled "transvestites," often, when they sang well, headlined in cabarets. Myself, I hadn't dressed as female since, well, since I'd last spent time with Tellia. As a child, I never got to the corset.

"You have to wear it," she insisted as she helped me into the outfit Ell lent her. "Else they'll think you're lewd and give you a closer look."

She was right. Though attitudes were finally changing, most city folk suspected any grown woman leaving home without a corset was either impoverished or immoral or both. Women complained of discomfort, restricted movement, the inconvenient fastenings, but really I had no idea what a torture device a corset actually was. As Tellia yanked my laces, my left kidney switched places with my spleen. With every cinch my gall bladder thrust itself like an impassioned lover into my liver. A stuffed-in pillow gave me a bosom but added nothing to my comfort. I doubted I could walk, wasn't sure I could breathe.

Nevertheless, every man should once in his life go promenading in drag just to see how the other half lives. Though I had no razor, the morning before I'd treated myself to an extra-close barbershop shave for the birthday celebration that never happened. While I never would've been recruited by a parlor house, there were uglier women strolling the French Quarter. Passing men admired me! At least admired my bosom. "A feather cushion!" I wanted to shout but didn't, the way respectable women never do. The fools pretended they weren't looking and I pretended I didn't notice they were. Like I'd formed some secret compact with every stranger on the sidewalk to let him ogle me and playact otherwise. If that happened to me, God help a truly attractive woman. How long for lingering eyes that at first feel like flattery to become a bore then a nuisance then a curse? I determined that the next man I met I'd let him know I was male and thereby expose the silliness of his fixation. But I didn't.

I didn't because the next man I met was Philo Leboeuf.

To passersby, our fight probably more resembled a

vaudeville routine than the earnest brawl it was. It almost didn't happen. I recognized him and dipped my head. Tellia's hat hid my face. It wasn't necessary. His eyes were on my bosom. "Mam, have you maybe seen a man and woman," and he went on to describe Tellia and me, height, weight, coloring, the works. There I was in the dress she wore yesterday, in the hat she wore every Sunday, in the face God gave me. He didn't notice any of it. The whole time his eyes explored the rise of my chest which no doubt symbolized the mother he'd lost or the wife he never had but in fact comprised a tattered settee cushion.

"Never seen them," I lied in falsetto, stepping around him. Would've got away clean except I muttered a hair too loudly, "You stupid ass."

It was an odd contest. The corset hobbled me. Philo possessed his own longstanding handicap. Our hopping and flailing drew stares but no intervention until there arrived several *descaderos*, those picturesque Sicilian dockworkers characteristic of New Orleans' port. With their wives and sweethearts, the half-dozen couples were just now returning from celebrating the 4th of July. Copious red wine had left them beached halfway between the waving palms of a fine drunk and the ferocious waves of a raging hangover. They paused to watch Philo and I trade blows. "Sometimes a wife needs a good beating," offered one of the descaderos who, off the sharp look from his sweetheart, added, "That's what my mama says."

Philo, who'd just hammered my gut, answered, "Wife? Ha! That's a laugh."

What Philo didn't realize was that by the *descadero* code, beating your wife is your own affair, but beating an unrelated woman demands punishment. The Sicilians began nudging their sweethearts out of harm's way. But Philo was wily, as scoundrels often are. "Not even a woman!" he announced. "A man dressing as one."

With murmurs of dismay the descaderos studied me. "A sissy! A woman-dressing sissy!" Philo was off the hook. As aberration against nature, I'd be beaten instead. The men would have a chance to show off for their gals and get a little exercise before their hangovers took firm root. Before the first blow fell, however, Tellia arrived.

"Don't hurt him! He saved my husband!"

Confusion bubbled among the Sicilians. Philo gave the pot another stir. "Saved the husband, bedded the wife." Tellia shot me an angry look, as if I, not Philo, had been indiscrete.

The descaderos huddled over this quandary like rabbis debating the Talmud. Did adultery with the wife of a stranger demand reprisal? Their sweethearts joined in, as opinionated as the men. One made goat horns with her fingers, symbol of the cuckold.

Events moved faster after Zeph, mummified in bloody bandages, hobbled up on crutches. Tellia dashed to him. "I was coming for you, *mon amour*!"

After more heated murmuring, the Sicilians' spokesman addressed Zeph. "We believe this crazy poof dishonored you. You must beat him. If necessary, we'll help."

Zeph, who'd been delirious and opiated the day before and hadn't otherwise seen me since I was eight, didn't know what to make of this. By that point I wasn't sure either. To clear the air, I peeled off the dress, but my un-poofing was perhaps a strategic error. I saw temper rise in Zeph's pale face.

"Don't be silly," Tellia answered his questioning glance. "He helped us, but you were all I thought of, you and only you, all day, all night." It was true. I'd been between her thighs but despite my pretensions never inside her heart. Willing to sell herself to strangers to save Zeph's leg, giving herself to me to get him the child he wanted was merely, as merchants say, *lagniappe*.

Then Tellia added: "If you have to thrash him, okay, just don't wear yourself out."

What?

Whoomp! Pain seared my shoulder. I saw Zeph winding up to swing his crutch again. Fighting back seemed unfair considering his condition. Running would've got me chased by the whole crowd. I'd been trying so hard to turn a new leaf this seemed unfair, but if a beating was unavoidable, it might as well serve good purpose.

"Don't take Philo home with you," I whispered.

Whoomp, the next blow fell. "What the hell are you talking about?"

"Your brother will betray you."

"You're crazy." *Whoomp,* crutch found flesh again.

"A wise owl," I squeaked." *Whoomp!* " — never lets a snake near the nest." *Whoomp!* "You can't trust him." *Whoomp!* "He wants your wife." *Whoomp!* "To scrutinize her bosom" *Whoomp!* "and probe her pom-pom." *Whoomp!*

Pausing to catch his breath, Zeph asked so only I could hear. "You see things like your mama did? Things nobody else sees?" So he did know who I was.

"Precisely," I lied.

Whoomp! "Fall, you mullet. I'll stop whacking you." A marvelous suggestion. I dropped to the pavement. Tellia stepped over me like I was driftwood on the beach.

After all that crutch swinging, Zeph had trouble walking. The descaderos lifted him onto their shoulders and carried him toward Lugger Landing as, one suspects, on feast days back in Sicily they carried to the sea the statue of their village's patron saint.

Philo hung back. His boot hit my ribs. Pain circuited ankles to eyebrows. "That's on account," he warned. "Still owe you a thumping of my own." He scratched his balls with his stump, then hurried after the others. I wondered if Mother would recognize my bruises as a courageous sacrifice that might save a marriage. That would impress her, wouldn't it?

While waiting for the world to stop swaying, multiple shadows fell across me. Slowly I was able to focus enough to realize who they were: Ell's thugs. Each dangled a sock, different styles, different colors, but all holding something heavy and round. Softballs maybe; in my experience never very soft. Receiving another, perhaps worse beating struck me as both excessive and unfair.

"Your lucky day," I said, trying to balance sounding both friendly and sufficiently damaged. "Someone already did your job for you. So you get the morning off. Can enjoy a bucket of beer. Recover from the 4th of July."

I saw them exchange looks, entertaining the idea, but a scar-faced fellow, apparently the platoon leader, said, "Not how it works. Mr. Dixon told us to thrash you. What happened previous don't matter."

"What if I told him it was y'all who gave me these bruises?"

"Wouldn't be honest," said Scar-Face.

He hit me full force with his sock. Alongside the pain came a tangy-sweet smell. Where did they grapefruit in July, I wondered as the goons closed in.

~

"Baroness, thinking only of your interests, if you sever my pecker your house will forever be notorious as the spot where… Well, where a man got his pecker severed. What respectable whore," I indicated the bawds listening from the staircase, "could do her best work in such an ill-reputed house of ill repute?"

With my manhood on the line, I should've resisted clever phrasing. After two wallopings, I had no struggle left if she actually intended to amputate my phallus, which is what she'd announced she would do the moment I'd staggered back into her parlor.

"Keep your skinny prick then," the Baroness decided, "though it nestles here only after full payment, no discounts. But that nine bucks you took was naked theft. I'm chopping off a finger like I promised to do if you ever stole."

"A just punishment," I admitted through loosened teeth. "However there, too, we find drawbacks. To keep your books until you find someone more trustworthy, I need all ten."

"You could scribble with nine."

"If that were the only issue I'd say grab your cleaver.

Unfortunately ten pennies comprise a dime, ten dimes a dollar. With nine digits, I'd miscalculate." I feigned counting on my fingers. She appeared dubious. As I considered which finger I could most readily do without, Elliot Dixon walked in. Mother hung on his arm, reminding me yet again of the infinite possibilities and dense complexities of inter-personal relations.

"Just who I need," the Baroness welcomed Ell. "Want to maim the boy here but ruled out his fingers or his cock. If we sliced off an ear, would I be scrubbing blood—"

"Not here for that," Dixon interrupted. "Just checking that my macs did no more than I ordered." He smiled at Mother. She nodded back. I wondered how Victorine liked Mother being so chummy with her fancy man. Or what Calypso thought, watching from the staircase.

Ell touched my bruised cheek. I flinched. "A most excellent beating," I said. "If you hit me too, you're just gilding the lily."

"You always were funny," he said without smiling. "Here's what: keep on keeping the Baroness' books. Bunk in her stable like you always done. You can hike to and from her door in a straight line across Basin Street, then go wherever the hell you want long as it's not in the District. That's my new rule. No rambling for you between Basin and Claiborne, downtown side of Canal to the uptown side of St Louis. Break that rule, next time my boys break bones."

"I'm banished from the District?"

"About sums it."

I was too foggy to contemplate such a life-changing restriction. "May I collapse now?"

I didn't wait for an answer. After a hard *thump*, the carpet felt soft.

The last thing I remember was Mother cradling my head, saying, "No woman ever had a son like you." I suspected it was not a compliment.

Tutorial IV

MISPLACED MOTIVATIONS

Enumerate a dozen reasons
(excluding love)
for winning someone's heart.

I healed. Caught up bookkeeping. Bought forgiveness from the Baroness, sold hoodoo to the girls. Purchased their favors — except Calypso, though she flirted with me incessantly, which upset Mother, the point I suppose. Mother never acknowledged my efforts to save Zeph's leg and marriage to be an act of grand, Achillian sacrifice. How could she not see it? "I'm a new man, Mother. Talk with Ell. Tell him to lift my house arrest. I miss my friends."

"What friends? When you need to bare your soul, who besides me is willing to listen?"

Ouch. "Acquaintances, then. The crooked barker at Marcet's shooting gallery. Patrolman Benton, whose nightly gratuity is never enough. I'd give anything for another boring story from the old steamboat captain who's probably walking his mangy dog outside our door right now."

"You have peculiar friendships."

"You're one to talk," I said.

"What's that mean?"

Uh-oh. "Doesn't mean anything."

She knew it did. We'd never discussed Calypso and I'd resolved to never, ever let her know what I'd seen through her window. Even so, in the weeks since my birthday their relationship had flowered. At meals they chatted like schoolgirls, holding hands, not caring who saw. After the last customers left, they'd have boisterous fights that the grumbling Baroness had to hike upstairs to quash so her other girls might sleep.

"You're talking about Calypso?" Mother asked, her voice as sharp as a woodman's ax. "Aren't I entitled to friends too?"

"Mother, naturally—"

"Don't I deserve happiness?"

"Of co—"

"Who are you to judge?"

"I'm not—"

"Calypso's like a daughter to me." I guess my astonishment showed. "Well, maybe not a daughter," Mother backtracked. "Still, a bond between women a man could never fathom."

Oh, well. Good a time to hash it out as any. At least we were alone, on her balcony watching violet clouds swirl on the first cool front of autumn. The air teased with drizzle, but not enough to chase us inside. I kept my voice calm. "I fathom more about you and Calypso than you give me credit for, Mother. At least I fathom the what. Not sure about the why."

She stared at me a good twenty seconds. Any anger evaporated. "I don't understand the why either. Does anyone ever? No matter whether a he or a she or a God-knows-what they stroll alongside. In a way I'm proud for trying something new at my age."

"You're not old."

"My mirror says different. Compared to the other girls—"

"*They're* prostitutes."

She ignored that. "Calypso makes me feel young. Reminds me of Clo. And when she's not making me terribly, terribly angry, she sometimes makes me very happy."

"Then I don't have anything to say about it."

"You aren't ashamed of me?"

"Never, Mother. Not once."

She smiled. "Even the time you wanted me to shave my head and wear a hood?"

"I do wonder what Father Groetsch might say about your present arrangement."

She chuckled. "He'd put me kneeling on rice and reciting 'Hail Marys.'"

"And me alongside you," I said. "But it'd be 'Our Fathers.' Under the circumstances, you praying to a looker like the Virgin would make him nervous." She laughed harder, I did too, feeding each other, unable to stop, until our sides hurt. She let me put an arm around her.

"You're so smart and loving," Mother said. "You deserve all the world can offer. Let's take away everything that gets in the way of that."

"Like my house arrest?"

"Honey, Ell lets you roam the whole rest of the city. Go out. Do things. Go to parties."

"What parties? I don't know anyone outside the District."

"Come on! You've got imagination. If low society's denied you, launch into high society. You're the stepson of Colonel Louis Bonreve."

"I'm also Assistant Madame of a brothel. You don't think there'd be whispers?"

"What gentleman would dare, when you can whisper louder? Whisper to their wives and daughters. Or complain to Ell Dixon."

"Who banned me from the District."

"Because thinks of you like a son."

"Ha!" Ell Dixon, a father figure. Lord! Now and then Mother lost touch with reality, yet, though it'd never be as easy as she thought, her launching-into-high-society idea was intriguing. "I'll think about it, but I have one more question. Promise you won't be angry, and promise to answer truthfully."

Curiosity and nervousness wrestled in her eyes. "I promise."

After years in the city we mostly spoke English, but for such a delicate inquiry I switched to French. "When customers go to your room, are you still only telling fortunes?"

I'm sure she saw me hanging on the answer. Her comforting hand found mine. "Of course. Whatever else would I be doing?"

~

It wasn't so difficult. In the Baroness' parlor I'd overhear complaints about the cost of an upcoming soiree. I'd commiserate until I had date and address. Arriving — not on the guest list — I'd thank so-and-so for his personal invitation. Even the gentlemen who knew I'd not simply misunderstood them dared not dispute me, fearing I'd refresh their memory about their visit to our brothel. It never came to that. Within weeks I was a regular, within months a fixture. I bribed a Carondelet Hotel clerk to reserve a mail slot for me so I'd have a respectable address to receive the legitimate invitations that started to arrive.

Mothers of debutantes loved me because I never took liberties. I didn't need to; my physical wants were amply quenched back at the Baroness'.

Fellows my age loved me because, privy as I was to the inner workings of women's minds, I could offer excellent advice. Which I must say they needed.

Fathers, well, fathers may not have loved me, but they relaxed once they realized I'd mind my manners, keep their secrets, and take over on piano once the band's contract expired, thus saving them considerable overtime when their daughters begged for another hour of music.

The girls themselves loved me because they sensed in me the confidence that only comes to a seventeen-year-old when he's being well sported several times weekly by ladies who know their business. Since my young masculine mind was not each waking moment ruled by an overfilled testicle sack, and since I knew that, despite what Mother hoped, my true circumstance would eventually doom any serious courtship of these girls, I was free to be ecumenical in my attentions. In an aesthetic mood, I danced with the beauties. When feeling intellectual, I sought the smartest girl in the room. If benevolence took hold, I offered myself to the wallflowers.

Usually I was the best dancer there, reflecting years of practice as the Baroness' girls used me and a Victrola to while away idle hours. I cannot count the dances I taught nor the young ladies I taught them to. Some girls were so hopeless that before I'd go out, I'd mix a batch of Make-Me-a-Great-Dancer powder to keep in the pocket of my evening jacket. When no one was looking, I'd sprinkle a little *gris-gris* over the feet of any mediocre dancers to give them one night when they might waltz like Irene Castle.

One dark cloud shadowed these splendid evenings: Pierce Douglas White. My nemesis, living in the city while studying at Tulane, had grown into the sort of fellow who loved to pontificate (frequently in front of the black help) on "the Negro problem." He'd proclaim his dedication to reforming society by fighting for temperance and segregation, and against "the Social Evil." He'd begun penning rants against "the Menace of Racial Equality" that, echoing the times, mainstream newspapers published.

When Pierce found out where I worked, I feared the game was up, that he'd tell the Judge who'd then find Mother.

Pierce never blabbed. I suppose he knew that if unmasked I'd be banned from these soirées and he loved having me around to humiliate.

At a coming out party on Coliseum Square, I was getting oyster salad for a homely miss when Pierce "accidentally" bumped me. Bivalves and mushrooms splattered his shoes. Pierce demanded I drop to my knees and clean his spats. Everyone watched to see if I'd kowtow to this bully who, a decade since I met him, still stood taller and more athletic than me.

"Of course I'll clean them," I said, disappointing Pierce who was spoiling for a fight. I crouched at his feet and gave him as good a shine as any corner bootblack. If his cronies snickered, I didn't mind. Swabbing olive juice from his patent leather, I quietly sprinkled an entire pouch of Make-Me-a-Great-Dancer powder over them.

After that, Piece couldn't hold a glass without sloshing punch. Couldn't chat without being asked why he fidgeted. Couldn't even enjoy a dance, since no girl had a prayer of keeping up. When he left — early — I hurried to the window to watch him Shim Sham Shimmy down the street in his sparkling shoes. Oh, how I gloated, but he got the next laugh.

Mid-April, 1912, with the States bannering stories about the awful Titanic disaster, a back-page notice hit me harder: Pierce White had become engaged to heiress Aralee Gueydan. That's right, heiress.

After the Flood of '03, Aralee's father attempted to rebuild family fortunes by buying cutover swampland on the cheap. He schemed to pump it dry and populate it with sharecroppers, but the soils proved thin and his levees fragile. As his acreage oozed back into swamp, Mr. Gueydan became the butt of local jokes. Aralee, despite blossoming loveliness, found herself sliding down the social ladder. Then arrived a ten-gallon-hatted Texan proposing to wildcat for oil in Gueydan's swamp. Better lucky than smart it's said. Mr. Gueydan proved extremely fortunate. Derricks sprouted like coco grass, neighbors traded ridicule for envy, and invitations again stuffed Aralee's postbox. To her beauty, charm, and petroleum fortune, her parents wished to attach prominence. How better than by marriage to Golden Boy Pierce White? That Judge Pike had a hand in arranging this union I had no doubt, though as best I knew he was in Cuba. I became anxious to run into Aralee when she next dipped a toe into the New Orleans social scene.

July 4th, 1912, I took the Railway & Light to Spanish Fort, hoping to hear Papa Célestin's Orchestra. I would've liked to invite Mother, but outside of business hours she and Calypso had become inseparable. I didn't need Calypso's taunting to reinforce Mother's fears about my future, especially on a date as full of portent as my eighteenth birthday.

Climbing off the Morris car, I waded into the holiday throng milling toward "the Coney Island of the South." My mood immediately soured. Standing atop a popcorn crate alongside soap box socialists and preachers spouting verse, Pierce White was extolling the virtues of "hygienic racism," proclaiming how octoroons, quadroons, mulattoes, etc., were obsolete concepts. People were either white or black, worthy or not, with no gradations in-between. He'd drawn a crowd. I suppose that a century after the Louisiana Purchase, the city's Creoles and their wiggly Latin attitudes toward race were losing their grip.

Unwilling to let Pierce ruin my birthday, I skirted past until I noticed Madame and Monsieur Gueydan in the crowd. If Pierce and her parents were here, Aralee probably was too. I found myself walking over, but as I got close, like a punch in the gut, every nerve seared raw, I saw who stood next to them: Judge Pike. No piano for me to hide in this time, no mask to conceal my identity. I felt the impulse to run, but the son of Achille Cheramie does not flee from enemies, nor bow before devils. I held myself straight and walked into the tiger's cage.

Judge Pike gripped my hand, studying me, I assume measuring the changes since that sorrowful night at Athena back in '07. Something about me seemed to surprise him. Perhaps it was how much hatred oozed from my every pore.

"How is Aralee?" I asked Madame Gueydan.

Before she could answer, her husband blustered, "The question is *where's* my daughter. I told her not to wander." He pulled his wife closer to the soapbox to better hear Pierce's diatribe. Judge Pike remained where he was.

"Is your Mother here?" I saw him hanging on my answer.

"The Colonel confided in you," I said. "He'd have wanted you to explain the legal ramifications before something big as suicide. You knew what he was considering. Possessed information that his fortune had been saved yet held it back. Waited. Probably watched his window from the trees. That's how you got there so fast after the gunshot."

"Is this your own theory?"

"I've had years to think it through. We aren't all as nimble of mind as you, Judge."

"He was my best friend."

"Makes it more heinous, don't you think? Makes you a cold-blooded murderer."

"Harsh judgment, considering you pulled the trigger."

"An accident. You know it. You knew then."

"Those years considering yourself in mortal battle with him, of wishing—"

"I was a child."

"How'd you phrase it? 'Wishing he'd go away and leave Athena to you and your mother'? Well, you managed the first part." I'd not spoken to the man in a half-dozen years yet it took him only moments to unwrap my core of guilt, insert a soup spoon into it, and stir it all around. "Where is your mother?" he continued.

"Cuba," I spat.

He chuckled. "No, not Cuba. I see you heard about my contribution to President Taft's 'Dollar Diplomacy.' What you don't know is I only went there to look for her. A wild goose chase that became a rare opportunity. My first year in Havana, three-quarters of a billion American dollars poured into the Cuban sugar industry. For a well-connected lawyer familiar with the sugar business—"

"Who was willing to ravage the poor for his rich and powerful cronies."

"The rich and powerful always ravage the poor. I simply provided mechanisms to accomplish it without brute force."

"A middle-man for corruption?"

"It's lucrative. If you hadn't killed Louis Bonreve, today I could buy him six times over."

"You're proud of what you are?"

"Discreet, but proud, yes. I allow the wealthy and ruthless to be respected captains of industry instead of blood-soaked warlords as in epochs past. One might consider me another modern marvel, saving lives, preventing undue suffering."

"A miracle invention, like surgical anesthesia?"

"Precisely," he answered, ignoring my sarcasm. "Now I'm back. Where's your Mother?"

"She still hates you."

"At least that means she's alive."

I hadn't meant to give him comfort. "Really hates you. Spits on your memory."

Though I wasn't entirely sure that was true, it felt good to poke him with it. It drew more blood that I expected. His smugness fell away like scaffolding collapsing. "I know I was cruel and petty and foolish. If there's a way to make up for that, I will."

"There's not."

"Shouldn't that be hers to decide?" He looked almost ill. Who would've guessed his obsession with Mother would last this long? "I heard she became a… After… After what happened with your stepfather. This cotton factor said it. He thought it was funny. I struck him with my walking stick. Numerous times. Cost a fortune to settle his lawsuit. It wasn't a subject people brought up around me after that."

"What did he say?" I asked. I was pretty sure I knew but wanted the Judge to voice it because it pained him so.

"He said she became a whore. No truth in it, is there? I thought I saw her at a hooker's ball once. Here in the city, before I left. That couldn't be, could it?"

Was it crueler to say yes, because it would hurt him to know he'd forced her to live in a whorehouse, even if she wasn't one herself? Or crueler to deny it? I wanted to be cruel as possible. I considered shouting, "She's become a lesbo!" but didn't. "She remarried. Moved to San Francisco." I almost said someplace farther, but doubted he'd swallow another foreign land.

"What's the name of the fellow she married?" He wasn't sure he believed me.

"Philip Hall. In the export business, transshipping dried

shrimp to Shanghai, but not Oriental himself, of course. They met when he came to Louisiana interviewing suppliers." I was becoming a very good liar.

"Do you have her address with you?"

"Wouldn't give it to you if I did."

"Is she happy?"

"I've said enough."

"It's good to know though it means she's far away. Married again? That's a shame. What I'd give to just once more see her glide into a room the way she did, carrying with her all the aerie eroticism of a Venezuelan waltz." He stared into space, no doubt picturing her. "Often, in a crowd like this, I look for her," he confessed.

The way I sometimes looked for Melpa and her child. How I hated this man, hated him more in this sorrowful puppy-dog mood than I did when he was a snarling pit bull. From the soapbox, Pierce's twaddle drew another round of applause. The Judge clapped too, though he hadn't been paying the speech any attention. "Pierce is an ass," I said.

The Judge chuckled at my vehemence. "Pierce clerks for me. Did you know that?" I didn't, but I refused him the satisfaction of an answer. "He can't stand to talk about you either. Employing a bigot like Pierce frees me of having to myself prattle all that supremacy of the white man claptrap."

"After what you did to Nat, you claim you're not racist?"

"As with most issues of deep conviction, I hold no firm opinion. Black or white strikes me as less important than whether someone's useful. Racism's a noisy distraction. Your friend Nat, a hapless bystander. Non-combatant casualty. The way things brew in Europe, you'll soon see more such victims than you can dream of..."

He could've been chanting the rosary for all I listened. My mind flew from my head, my heart fluttered out of my breast. Across the archipelago of hats turned toward Pierce, one face looked straight at me. Framed with crimson curls and sheltered by a sailor hat, it possessed beauty so classic it rendered fashion moot, with a smile so mischievous it made me beam. She was the most stunning woman I'd ever seen, excepting Mother.

She wagged her finger, beckoning. The Judge saw. I didn't care. Blindly as any moth sucked into a lantern pyre, I glided toward Aralee.

~

"Are you really idiot enough to marry Pierce?"

It sounded harsher than I intended and wasn't an ideal greeting after many years apart. Aralee drilled me with an angry stare, then, dimple by dimple, crinkle by crinkle, her smile crept back. Abruptly she skipped away. "I'm rich now. Had you heard?" she lobbed over her shoulder.

"I heard," I said, hurrying to catch up.

"Don't let it change how you act toward me. I hate that."

"I'll treat you like I found you in the gutter."

She laughed. "Let's hurry."

"Where to?"

"Away from my parents."

"From Pierce as well?"

"Absolutely from Pierce. Then to a grave around here, I heard it's romantic, like Romeo and Juliet."

"I know it," I said. "I'll take you there."

"And tell me the romantic story?"

"The very romantic story."

"Then you'll tell me what you've been doing all these years since I've seen you?"

Hmm. "The grave's this way."

~

"Her name was Owaissee, 'bluebird' in Choctaw. She liked to fish by moonlight on Lake Pontchartrain. One night a squall arose. Her pirogue was sinking, she was certain to drown. Except she was rescued by Sancho Pablo, commandant of the fort here."

"They fell in love?"

I shrugged. "A lively young woman, a handsome young man, a courageous rescue."

"Could be us."

"I haven't rescued you."

"Not yet," she said. Lord God above, Aralee was pretty. In the shade of those trees. Leaning on the cast iron rail surrounding the grave. Listening to me like nothing else in the whole wide world held interest. "What happened next?" she prodded.

"Her father, Chief Wahewawa—"

"You're making that up."

"I'm not. Wahewawa wasn't happy about Sancho Pablo. Sort of the way your own father—"

"I'll handle Papa." She wove her arm through mine. "Finish the story. I understand it ended badly."

"Hearing a bluebird call, you traipse into the woods expecting your beloved and get bludgeoned by a tomahawk..."

She held my arm tighter. Through layers of cloth and a rampart of corset stays, my upper arm pressed against her breast. "It doesn't always have to end badly, does it?" she said. "If two people care for each other?"

~

Angry when he found us, angrier still when Aralee refused to go back with him, Pierce divulged that I was a cadet, a procurer.

"I'm no such thing!" It was true. For all my varied duties at the brothel, I never recruited girls.

Pierce scoffed at my denial, upped the ante, calling me a pimp, a word considered offensive even among pimps. Aralee seemed, well, impressed. "My, at least one of us appreciates the seamy side."

"I'm an accountant," I protested. When Pierce hooted an ugly laugh, I couldn't resist clarifying: "Tallying dollars paid to fallen women by hypocritical gentlemen just like—"

I never finished. Always athletic, Pierce had somewhere learned to box. Fist hit nose, my world went white.

"Shame on you, Pierce!" Aralee said, though with altogether too much glee. "Shame, now go fetch a nurse!" He didn't move.

She lowered her voice. "Think I'd marry a brute who leaves a family friend bleeding onto the sod?"

His bluster dissolved. Aralee waited till he left earshot. "Let's hurry."

"Hurry where?"

"To fish upon the lake, you silly Sancho!"

I hadn't been on a boat since arriving in New Orleans, if indeed a beribboned goose, propelled by pedaling, entirely counts as a boat. We never left Bayou St. John. Though only sixty feet from a shore thronged by thousands enjoying the rides and casinos and 4th of July breezes, we were together without chaperone and I was thrilled.

Aralee chose the goose over the swan, the jolly sea serpent, and other fanciful choices because "when seasons change, geese fly so far away no hunter can find them." She dumped into my hands the considerable fortune tucked into her beaded silk purse. "Pay for the boat and hold the rest for whatever we do next. I insist on seeing how good an accountant you are."

I didn't argue. Though embarrassing to see myself as docile as Pierce in the face of her commands, I knew I was embarking not just on a goose boat but also on a day of adventurous possibilities. I didn't want that journey to end as quickly as my own meager funds would necessitate. Though I resolved to not steal a penny of her money, I admit I was already speculating how I might rob her of her virtue.

How could any fellow have felt otherwise? To start with, the way she sat: languid against the thwart, legs outstretched, her feet near mine with her creeping hem scandalously exposing her ankles. Sheer stockings over porcelain skin, in turn stretched taut over delicate bone, rose out of supple Cuban heels. I pedaled the boat faster, tried not to stare. She was gazing at the shore so I could hope she didn't notice me gawking, but in my heart I knew she did, of course she did, yet she made no move to tuck up her legs, or tug down her skirt, or face me so I'd have to look away. I fantasized unbuttoning her shoes, slipping them off her feet. Tugging on her toes, this little piggy, that little piggy. I felt my phallus rising and wondered if she noticed that too.

You might speculate why a fellow who lives in a whorehouse where inmates go about scarcely clad at all could get worked up over silk-covered ankles. You might speculate, but if you do, you don't understand eros. The breasts and thighs of a harlot can be yours for simple coin. A long, unfettered look at the ankles of a cloistered maiden usually requires a wedding ring. What was going on here? Did Pierce often get the eyeful I was enjoying? Was this a simple continuation of our childhood kissing on the dock and touching in the dark, of my painfully remembered witnessing of Pierce exploring her pre-pubescent body in the hay straw? Or had Aralee been corrupted and was now as wanton as the girls of Baroness von Kempe, only without the necessity to charge for it? I didn't think so, and I was as expert in such matters as anyone this side of Ell Dixon. My diagnosis was that this spirited young woman whose future was proscribed had decided to indulge before her wedding in a piece of precisely measured wickedness. I'd come to the right place at the right time to be cast as… What? Cad and seducer? No, more likely "old flame." Long-lost love conveniently/inconveniently reappearing out of the mist.

She'd leave her fiancé baffled on the shore, her parents merely baffled, and go for a goose boat ride, let me observe her ankles, perhaps hold her hand. Before we parted I'd be granted a kiss or two. She could go to the altar feeling like she'd tasted forbidden excitement before settling down. Since Pierce had spilled the beans, she'd ply me with questions about pimps and whores and the demi-monde. Ever after she'd secretly consider herself worldly. Aralee's exposed ankles implied no whorishness. On the contrary. She'd put money in my hand and expected services in return. I was the whore. Instead of ten minutes on my back I was to deliver a measured dose of the wild life that she could tuck away for future contemplation.

Well, if that's what this was, I'd give the girl her money's worth. And as I said, she'd handed over a great deal of money.

~

Leaving jacket, shoes, and the park nurse on the bank, Pierce dove into the bayou, *Splash!* His form was excellent, a perfect American crawl, as he cut through the water after us. It'd be worth it to win Aralee's heart if only to hear people snicker at Pierce over it. I pedaled harder, past a dozen wading sinners awaiting baptism from a wet-to-his-chest preacher. I thumbed at Pierce: "Reverend, there's a soul needs cleansing."

Our goose beached with a thump. I won another glimpse of those ankles as I helped Aralee out. Swimming after us, Pierce never saw the preacher's freckled hand until it thrust his head under the murky bayou, Praise the Lord! I didn't tarry to watch the scuffle which ensued.

At Over the Rhine beer garden, a crowd waited for tables. I scrunched low. "What next?" Aralee asked.

Wondering how far she'd let me go, how fast, and where might I take her to find out, I heard a voice ask, "*This* is what you do when Mommy lets you wander?"

I spun. Beer foam mustached Calypso's upper lip. I didn't see Mother. By cardinal rule, prostitutes never acknowledge a trick in public unless acknowledged first, but Calypso was a born rule-breaker and besides, our relationship was infinitely more byzantine than simply hooker and john. She pressed against my arm with sufficient wantonness to make a nearby mother hurry her children away. I was gratified to see Aralee react with ice-cold jealousy. "Introduce us," she growled.

"Yes," bubbled Calypso. "We might have lots in common." Her tongue snaked out and licked the suds off her lip. I pictured several ways this encounter might end, none good.

"Aralee, this is my mother's friend, Calypso. Calypso, this—"

"I'm his childhood sweetheart," Aralee claimed. "I gave him his first kiss."

"What a coincidence," Calypso smiled. "I gave him his first—"

"Isn't the park busy, what with 4th of July?" I interrupted, easing Calypso's grip off my arm. A moment before I'd been plotting to corrupt Aralee; now I wondered how to protect her from the corrupting influence of Calypso.

"You knew your son had a secret paramour?" Calypso asked Mother, who walked up carrying a box of spun sugar Fairy Floss.

"Mother, you remember Aralee. Her family stayed with us during the Flood of '03."

Aralee curtsied. "I see you still turn my son's head," Mother said.

"Oh, I hope so!" Aralee said, red curls bouncing. "He's such a fascinating fellow."

It was like a scene out of some other person's life. Aralee wore not a stitch that didn't scream respectability. Wealth. A ticket anywhere she wanted to go and evidently she wouldn't mind going with me. Watching Mother waving a pull of her cotton candy I saw that I'd finally impressed her. Hoping Pierce, or heaven forbid, the Judge, wouldn't arrive to ruin the moment, I forgot where closer danger lay.

"The four of us should spend the day together," cackled Calypso.

I panicked but needn't have. Mother, dearest Mother, said, "Don't be silly. Three's a crowd and four would be catastrophe. Take your ladyfriend and celebrate your birthday." As Mother leaned to kiss my cheek, she whispered in my ear, "Don't mess this up."

I silently swore to make Mother proud. I'd bring home this blushing bride — well, home being Basin Street, maybe we could meet at Galatoire's. Aralee could afford a wedding party there. Aralee could afford anything. As we walked away it dawned on me that, her charm and looks aside, marrying an heiress has advantages. I could afford gifts for Mother. Return to the lifestyle of my childhood. Own a proper library. Even buy Athena's library. Hell, we could buy Athena! I was speculating how many years the average oil well flows when Aralee tightened her grip. "Don't let them see us." Bless the winsome girl. While I'd been lost in reverie, she'd been on the look-out, spotting the predators before they spotted us: the Gueydans and the Judge were listening to soaking wet Pierce offering no doubt a scurrilous recap of our encounter.

"Let's ride the Ferris Wheel." I said. "Out of reach, a moving target."

"Papa will find us," Aralee objected. "And Pierce. He tracks like a beagle."

"Would you be willing to leave the park? Knowing how angry they'd be?"

Her eyes twinkled. "Angrier than they are already?"

My quandary: we could slip away, board the electric railway back to the city, continue reacquainting somewhere private. If we did, Pierce and the Gueydans and Judge Pike would scour the park. They'd not find Aralee but might spot Mother. Whom I'd forgotten to warn that Judge Pike was here! I needed a plan, a way to lure Pike from the park.

"Can you run?" I asked.

Aralee gave me a long look, put a hand on my shoulder to steady herself, bent one leg up, reached back and slipped off her shoe. The other foot, the same performance, drawing the eye of every male passer-by. She handed me her pumps. I longed to put them to my nose and sniff.

My scheme was to wait for a Morris car preparing to leave. We'd sprint past the Judge, Pierce, et al., get their attention, beat them to the streetcar, board as it pulled away, leaving them in the dust. They'd hop the next train, Judge Pike no doubt alongside the other hounds, with Mother free to enjoy her day at Spanish Fort.

Writing it down now, I realize how impossible my plan was, but somehow it worked. Hand in hand we dashed. I blew Pierce a raspberry, grabbed someone's spearmint shaved ice and pelted Judge Pike, painting his shirtwaist with a green bleeding heart. Aralee's Mother shrieked. Her father bolted after us. We bumped people, got shoved, squeezed past. "Excuse me, excuse me," I said. They'd get angry anyway and take it out on those coming up behind, slowing them down. We hopped the car as it pulled away. Pierce's shouts couldn't make the conductor stop. As we picked up speed, Aralee flashed her naughty grin, the one that kept tearing off chunks of my heart. We dropped into the farthest seat of the Whites Only section. On the varnished slats between us, Aralee's hand found mine.

"Take me to a cabaret," she whispered.

"Cabarets are disreputable."

She took her hand back and retrieved her shoes. "I want to see for myself. Pierce would never take me."

We couldn't be seen in a cabaret. They were too notorious for people of our social position. Well, her social position but one that over the last half-hour I'd begun to aspire to. A position which could be cemented by the right marriage.

"Aralee, in cabarets the food is foul, the liquor fouler, the entertainment—"

"But the waiter girls are pretty, aren't they? Prettier than me?"

"No girl's prettier than you. How about dinner at Antoine's?"

"Have you ever dallied with a cabaret waiter girl?"

"Never would without a gallon of disinfectant."

"You've had other dalliances though? You're a man of the world? Pierce, I'm almost certain, is still…" She lowered her voice to a whisper. "As am I." So their long-ago tryst in the Colonel's stables had not progressed much since? Interesting. In the District one doesn't often meet post-pubescent female virgins.

"Not till marriage," Aralee continued. "That's what Mama says, the whole and total I ever hear about sexual matters. Have *you* ever talked to a girl about sexual matters?"

"Maybe once or twice."

"See? You're more worldly than Pierce. And sweet. You were always the sweet one. If I remember, a good kisser too."

I suppose I blushed. She laughed. I'm a fool for any girl's laughter. Aralee's was spontaneous and uninhibited. I was falling in love with her, though I knew that was a mistake. My goal was to marry her. Losing my head wouldn't help.

"At a cabaret we could talk about anything," she said. "Even shocking sexual matters. We could hold hands. Kiss again. In public for all to see. I bet that's allowed."

I imagined savoring Aralee's lips but tried not to. Cabarets, any I knew, were in the District where I was banned, where if spotted by anyone allied to Ell Dixon — half the population — I'd be thrashed into pulp.

~

"Wooga chooga!" Aralee and I shouted in unison with four dozen other people. She'd never danced the Grizzly Bear before yet took to it like Goldilocks.

My strategy had backfired. I'd ruled out a cabaret, where we'd be tempted to tarry if the show was good. Instead I took her to a seedy dancehall a half-block into the low-rent side of the District, the sort of 'tonk where on off-nights they hosted cockfights or dogfights or old-style rat baitings when they could catch enough rats, which in that joint wouldn't have seemed difficult. I was sure that after one whiff, Aralee would refuse to set her dainty feet amongst the sawdust on its floor. We'd be out of the District again before Elliot Dixon could whistle.

Aralee loved the place.

Could've been worse. The crowded dance floor hid us fairly well. I was pretty sure it ran payoffs through Tom Anderson, not Ell Dixon. If a barkeep recognized me, he'd less likely turn me in. Besides, it was hard to be fearful while having such fun.

"None of the ladies are wearing corsets," Aralee observed as we finished a Bunny Hug.

"A corset's too restrictive."

"How would you know?" she chided.

I just gave her a goofy look. "Where might the powder room be?" she asked.

She was gone so long I fretted she'd left. When she returned, the porcelain doll I'd arrived with had been traded for an actual woman. "What did you do with your corset?"

"Left it hanging on the mirror," Aralee laughed. "Now we can really dance."

And we did. Freed of stays and lacing, Lord but that woman could move. As jazz music and reefer smoke poured off the bandstand, her pompadour came unpinned, liberating fiery red tresses. No need of Make-Me-A-Great-Dancer powder for her!

Something else was going on as well. Consciously or not, there's a certain female silhouette, engineered via substantial foundation undergarments, that I associated with uptown soirees where one enjoyed chaste dances and polite conversation. Another silhouette, the less fettered fashion familiar from the bagnio, usually meant the woman was available for sport. Aralee trading the former shape for the latter set my expectations a-jumble.

Then there was the sweat. Rivers of sweat that soaked us through until Aralee's chemise and blouse became nearly transparent. Her hardened nipples protruded like twin beacons. Delicious sweat mingled between us from her hand to my shoulder, my palm to her waist, sweat born of the steamy hall, the frenzied dancing, and yes I admit an uncharacteristic nervousness which stole upon me as desire swirled and congealed and finally articulated itself in my fevered mind: I wanted to fuck this girl and I wanted to do it soon. Sure, I wanted to marry her, but I wasn't going to wait for that.

"Let's get out of here."

"I like it here," Aralee protested.

"You can't say no. It's my birthday."

"I'd forgotten! You must have a birthday kiss."

Never a girl for half measures, Aralee kissed me full on the lips. I never enjoyed a kiss so much. She wasn't complaining either. Dancers began ribbing us, "Hey, you two, they rent rooms by the hour upstairs." We were too preoccupied to laugh.

"Let's get out of here," I said again when our kiss finally broke.

"Where to?" she asked. I felt I could've said "the moon" and she wouldn't have argued.

I didn't say "the moon." I said, "To a cabaret."

~

"Everyone can see," she said.

"Not clearly," I answered.

"We should close the curtain."

"If we do there'll be nothing to stop me."

"*I* could stop you."

"If you asked, I'd stop, but you won't."

She smiled at my confidence and sighed at my touch. It'd been lunchtime when I first spotted Aralee at the amusement park. Now it was dinner hour. We'd gorged on raw oysters and slaked our thirst with a number of Pimm's Cups. What a pleasant novelty not to worry what things cost. I got us a private booth on the mezzanine level. With solid wood walls on three sides, the fourth which overlooked the stage came equipped with a draw curtain for when the entertainment within the booth grew more interesting than the orchestra.

At noon in the goose boat I'd grown semi-erect from a glimpse of Aralee's ankles. Since arriving in the booth, I'd fondled those ankles, removed her shoes, and tickled her feet. From there I'd savored the firm musculature of her calves, allowing her ample time to feign resistance. It was a game I knew better than she, but we were enjoying it equally. With oysters and alcohol taking effect, my exploring fingers reached the hem of her bloomers. Aralee wiggled, legs spreading then closing again, tantalizing me. I feared we'd reached the limit of what she'd let me do exposed by the open curtain, but if I rose to close it, the interruption might prompt skittishness, perhaps regret for liberties already allowed. A delicate moment. Our waitress could close the curtain, but she seemed to have forgotten us, having probably supposed we were ready to be alone.

Nothing ventured, nothing gained. I slid my hand up Aralee's thigh, caressing her though the soft silk of her bloomers, bunching the hem of her skirt — which usually trailed the floor — up past her knees.

"Everyone across will see."

"Half of them have their own curtains closed."

"Half don't."

"What do you care? You won't run into your parents' friends in a place like this."

"Maybe not, but Judge Pike knows many people. It'll get back to him."

Judge Pike? My hand tickles inches from her maidenhead and she brings up Judge Pike? Well, let Judge Pike hear. Let him know whose hand has been where. I scooted my fingers up Aralee's thigh till there was no farther to go. Happy circumstance, her bloomers were the slit bottom type, not the ones with a buttoned back-flap. After hours of foreplay, she was soaking. I resisted the urge to plunge right in. Afternoons with my big sisters had taught me a thing or two. I feathered along her entrance to the spot most responsive. Aralee rolled her bottom against the seat cushion in matching rhythm. She forgot about the open curtain. She looked like she might not even remember her name. This was almost too easy.

Our waitress chose that moment to return. She pretended she saw nothing out of the ordinary. Considering where she worked, she probably didn't. "Should I close the curtain?"

"Should she?' I asked Aralee. I wanted it to be her decision.

"Yes," she sighed. Curtain rings rattled over the rod, then the waitress left us in privacy to do whatever we would.

I had no condom. Aralee carried no douche. Not until actual copulation was underway did I consider that from this encounter a child might ensue. I found myself liking the idea. I might've gotten Tellia pregnant but could never claim that kiddie. With Aralee it'd be different. A boy, for our first. I'd teach him to read, we'd play ball, watch from the levee as steamers left for Cairo and Calcutta and Caracas.

I tried to imagine Aralee's face in young male form, but even a moment studying her parted lips and half-closed eyes made me forget about the future. Beneath me writhed a lithe, stunning, willing young woman, an object of fantasy since I was eight. In some ironic way we'd returned to the innocence of childhood, except now we were grown. Affection and intimacy had different expression. Once I'd nudged through her maidenhead barrier, Aralee took to intercourse like a duck to water. She was vocal, vigorous, quick to follow my lead yet not shy about guiding me toward her own greater pleasure. What pleasure! Maybe I'd been misled by professional harlots. I'd never seen a woman so relish a rip-roaring fuck.

Temptation resides in the mind, Mother said. I guess I do sometimes think too much. Certainly I had that day. What Aralee and I were doing was not about her fortune nor my future social position. Not about marching her to the altar nor binding her to the birthing bed. Not about Pierce, nor the Judge, nor what Mother might think. Here, on my eighteenth birthday, I was for the first time in my life enjoying sex that didn't include some sort of transaction — even my tryst with Tellia involved a service rendered.

I'd not impregnate Aralee today, nor coerce her into any lifelong commitment. Our future would be however she wished it. This evening would bear no burden beyond the same ecstatic culmination of irresistible attraction enacted by so many couples in so many lands since Adam first fell head over heels for Eve. Now would only be about now.

Suddenly, now *was* now. My moment rushed upon me. Time to slide out of this maiden's warm sheath before my penis could erupt.

A hand gripped my shoulder. It was so unexpected I lost my place, missed my chance to withdraw, and felt the first jet fire into Aralee's womb from my spasming cock. Then, abruptly, I was wrenched out of her. My manhood flapped in the wind. Aralee began screaming — *not* in pleasure. His hand entwined in my collar, Pierce White twisted me to face him. The beagle had tracked his quarry down.

Certain processes, once begun, demand completion come what may. Thus, as Pierce yanked me from the loins of his fiancée, my erect, insistent maleness — ignoring its change in surroundings — fired a second jet of semen that hit Pierce in the left eye. Those poor sperm! And if Pierce was enraged before, that — if you'll pardon the metaphor — was the icing on the cake.

Tutorial V

WHEN INTEGRITY FALLS SHORT

Choose as essay topic
any of the following:
1) Rationalize abandonment
of a friend in need;
2) Describe a promise you kept,
but for self-serving reasons;
3) Justify blackmail. (Use as
many pages as required.)

Dark angels toted me to Hell. Perhaps what I deserve, I thought, then I recognized Chicken-Wing Charlie, the clarinetist. They weren't Negro demons grasping the corners of my burlap-sack stretcher; they were the cabaret's orchestra. It started to come back. Pierce punching me and punching me, breaking my nose. The proprietor arguing against involving police.

Blood pooled in my eye sockets. Where was Aralee? "I have to go back," I croaked.

"Hush," came a familiar voice: Mother, shepherding my porters. I passed out again.

The Baroness' carriage house became my hospital. At first, I did little but sleep. Whole weeks I cannot remember, missing like articles clipped from a newspaper. Forbidden, forgotten, or both, I saw none of my sisters. The Baroness dropped in occasionally but only with issues of bookkeeping when unpaid suppliers halted deliveries. Mother served me soup and emptied my bedpan and brought by Dr. Cazenac, who seemed genuinely impressed by my injuries. One afternoon, Calypso snuck in offering to suck my phallus for free. I wasn't even tempted.

Mother refused to discuss how she'd known to find me at the cabaret. Would Judge Pike find us? He'd said his clerk was loath to discuss me, and that before I'd cuckolded Pierce, so my rival might not reveal I worked in the District. I prayed the Judge believed my Mother-moved-to-San Francisco story.

Between bouts of coma, I wrote letters. Wooing Aralee. Proposing marriage. Strategizing elopement. Mother posted them, she said. I never received replies. I tried Come-To-Me spells. Decided to call on Aralee in person — halfway to the street I collapsed. Mother hid my clothes.

Slowly I mended, reading any newspaper I could induce someone to bring me. A <u>Times-Democrat</u> column submitted by Pierce showed he was growing broadminded: Negroes weren't the entire cause of the nation's ills; Jews and immigrants also shared blame.

In September I woke to find that morning's <u>L'Abeille</u> opened to page three....

Tyro attorney Pierce Douglas White
trades orations for sonnets
Elopes with fiancée Aralee Gueydan
Happy couple honeymoons
with year-long European tour

The cad had married her! And scammed a law degree though

only age eighteen! Curse you, Judge Pike, for your sinister hand in these evil machinations!

Out of the newspaper dropped an envelope, addressed to me, dated weeks past. It struck like an arrow, rending my soul:

Dear sweet man,

Pierce insists I never see you again. As do my parents, my friends, and Judge Pike. Therefore, goodbye forever — unless you break in to steal me away like I've been warned white slavers like you frequently do. If you don't, I understand.

Yours truly (with no regrets),
Aralee Gueydan

Break into her boudoir, sweep her up into my arms, leave by the window. I could've done it. I would've done it. Maybe it wasn't too late! I hobbled out the door. Made it to Rampart Street — of necessity, wearing only drawers. The beat cop, Benton, dragged me back. Mother tipped him and shooed him out. "I'm sailing for Europe," I announced.

"What I've wanted for you your whole life and you finally decide to go when you can barely walk to the street? Enough nonsense. I've got customers waiting."

I held up Aralee's letter. "But you find time to hide my mail?"

"I can't shoulder this madness anymore," she said, her voice dead. "Trying to spark with that girl nearly got you killed. I forbid you to—"

"Forbid? You forget I'm grown-up now."

She eyed me. The fight seemed to go out of her. "Maybe you are. Maybe it's time I grow up too, admit that what I've got is as good as I'll ever have. Enjoy Room 9 with its sagging wallpaper because it's all downhill from here. But I always hoped you, at least, could go the places I never went."

"I will. With Aralee."

She sighed. "'No regrets,' your letter says. Better than what's salvaged from most love affairs. At least you had one night."

"One night's not enough."

"One night's all *I* had." Mother started for the door, her shadow sweeping the wall like a bogeyman. Pain shot through my shoulder as I rose, too fast, to follow. I caught her, wrapped my arms around her. "I was wrong," she said. "I thought if you and Aralee… I thought it might put everything back in place for you. I thought…" A sob convulsed her. She spun to face me, clinging like we'd both die if she let go. "Doesn't matter what I thought because I was wrong. You finding her made things worse. Promise me you'll leave Aralee to that other fellow. Please. Promise."

I promised.

I lied.

Between persisting blackouts I began to obsess on sailing to Europe, following their trail, bludgeoning Pierce with my crutch like Zeph did me only worse. I scribbled plans. Then another blackout. Days. Weeks. When I'd reawaken, someone would've stolen my notes.

My sisters started visiting. I suspect Mother sent them. They were open for business. I wasn't. Sex was dangerous. Sex killed Achille Cheramie. I nearly paid the same price. One day, I came to from a stupor and found a weeping woman on my cot. Gladys, who'd always been nice to me, pretending I gave her orgasms when I hadn't. Over my shoulder the Baroness whispered, "She caught the Old Joe."

"You put a syphilitic whore in my bed?"

"Hush." To Gladys: "Don't cry, dearie. They got '606' now. We Germans invented it. You cure right up." Gladys buried her diseased head in my pillow.

"Where will *I* sleep?" I was sleeping most of the day, and since I wasn't buying sport, bed was also where I engaged in twice-daily self-abuse, so it was an important question.

The Baroness dragged me aside. "Get her on a train going somewhere far. I'll pay a one-way ticket but not first class, you hear? Don't get spongy."

"I won't get spongy, but I want ten dollars for my trouble."

"You're a thief!"

"You're a whore. Ten bucks or carry out your own trash."

"Must dishearten your mother how calloused you've grown."

After I took Gladys to the station, I burned my cot. I'd miss Gladys, but I'd never been fooled by her fake orgasms. And now I had ten dollars. Of course I no longer had a bed. Okay, I could sleep in the Baroness' carriage. Money, that was the answer. How I would defeat Pierce, and Judge Pike, and everybody like them. Money was power. I'd never have as much as the Judge, nor Pierce now that he controlled Aralee's fortune, but I only needed enough to hire a few brawny macs like Ell employed, thugs who'd maim or kill anyone as long as you paid enough. I would see to it I had enough. With them behind me I'd get revenge and rescue Aralee and become a folk hero among the do-wrong people.

I began to skim from the Baroness. If I wasn't too greedy, I doubted she'd notice. Lightening the envelopes Ell picked up was considerably more dangerous, but it was his fault. If it wasn't for my house arrest, there'd have been a thousand ways I could've hustled a crooked coin in the District. Though Mother occasionally wielded mysterious sway over Ell, about my continuing banishment she refused to intervene.

I squeezed harder in places I could reach. When I asked three dollars for a Make-the-Bitch's-Hair-Fall-Out candle, Ramona spewed venom. "You came to my bed a sniveling kid and I jazzed you into a Don Johnny. This how you pay me back?"

"You charge top dollar for tricks," I countered. "Why shouldn't I?" She threw a douche syringe at me.

I started loitering (taking the shortest, most direct path out of the District, as was Ell's requirement) outside Parish Prison. Over bottles of Old Heidelberg, a just-released con artist taught me the slick-tricks of his trade. For a platter of fried snapper, a burglar demonstrated how to pick a lock. If I was going to be a bad guy, I intended to be good at it.

One afternoon a drummer called to sell striped stockings and lace bloomers to the girls. With a brush mustache and hair parted down the middle, the salesman was quick to flatter, inventive with compliments, sharp at bargaining. His prices were high (including as they did a cut for the Baroness) but whores, often snubbed in conventional boutiques, preferred to shop this way.

Scantily clad already, the bawds showed no qualms undressing further to try on just-bought treasures. Calypso shook a rose-tipped breast in my direction. Mabeline (or Madeline; I never could tell the twins apart) offered to let me butter her biscuit for half-price. I declined and went to the carriage house. Tried to nap but couldn't sleep. Thought of taking myself in hand, though auto-eroticism was becoming an ever-feebler substitute for the real thing. Then had a wonderful idea: why not bully the lingerie peddler into paying *me* a sweetener? I hurried back to shake him down, but by then the only one left in the parlor was Estelle. She leaned back on the sofa and lifted both legs, each modeling a different stocking. "Does dip-dyed or ingrain flatter me more?"

I was already flying to catch the drummer, still hoping to cop a bribe. From our top step I saw him go into Maison de la Victoire. I trotted after him.

Halfway there I froze, realizing where I was, what I'd done, terrified I'd hear Ell's whistle. But…

If anyone could convince Ell to ease up, it was Victorine. Swallowing as much fear as I could make go down, I kept walking, rehearsing what I'd say, to be ready, but also to crowd out thoughts of the consequences if this gambit failed. Breezing past the doorman, I ballroomed through the parlor where a dozen dark-eyed beauties, each a different shade of cream or brown, were as eager to buy the drummer's wares as the Baroness' white girls had been. Forget squeezing him; I was playing for bigger stakes now.

I waved from Victorine's office doorway. Surprised, she set down her pen. "Does Ell know you're here?" she asked.

"No, but I have a *great* idea for you."

"If you believe it's worth another beating, I suppose I ought to listen." Frightening words, but she was smiling. So far, so good.

"Have the lingerie drummer come in the evening to auction his frills. Let *customers* buy for the girls, who'll goad them to higher prices. You could demand a larger percentage."

"Good idea. Why offer it to me instead of your employer?"

"I need a favor. As you know, Mr. Dixon banned me from wandering the District."

"An edict you violated by coming here."

"Everyone knows he's your fancy man."

"When it suits him."

"I hoped you might intercede on my behalf. I could be useful. Do you favors."

Her index finger began tapping the desktop. "Would you provide me a list of the Baroness' best customers, their sexual proclivities, and their addresses?"

"Favors *within reason.*"

"Your offer was vague. Now it's vague and limited."

I felt like a hooked catfish. "Ask anything that doesn't violate a trust others place in me."

"An *ethical* cadet. What's the world coming to?" She went back to sorting mail. "Ell thinks, in today's climate, it's dangerous for a white madame to lodge coloreds. In your reservoir of hoodoo and what-have-you, can you conjure a *gris-gris* to turn my girls white?"

She had to be toying with me, but then as always she was so hard to read. "You're joking, right?"

Her smile offered only further ambiguity. Maybe she was serious. Did she want it only for her girls or herself as well? I remembered Touloulou's claim that Victorine took pains to hide her perilous drop of Negro blood. Did she really believe hoodoo could eradicate it?

"You're asking things beyond my power." Coming around the desk, I kneeled before her. "Please. I'm at wit's end and you were almost my godmother."

Victorine paused, thought about it, then put a finger to my chin, tilting my face. "You do so resemble your father."

Her words spread over me like soft butter on toast. "Wouldn't Pa have wanted you to help me?"

She snickered. "Take off your shirt."

"Pardon?"

"You won't divulge secrets, won't do magic, yet claim you'll give me the shirt off your back. All right, hand it over."

An odd request, but she was an odd woman. I loosened my collar, unbuttoned my shirtwaist.

She examined me as if I was a painting she might buy. "Your father, as fishermen do, often went shirtless. I want to see how far your resemblance extends." I confess it meant a great deal to me that my physique live up to Father's.

"Achille always seemed to be carrying something," she said. "A basket of shrimp. A bushel of oysters. Try lifting that armchair over your head."

I did. It was heavy.

"Higher," she said. I shifted to avoid her chandelier and whimpered when her fingers slid across my ribs. Though a quarter-century older than I, she was still comely. My nipple sprang up at her touch.

"Rumors around the tenderloin say you haven't had a woman since that heiress. That why you want to roam? If so, you might not have to wander far, nights when Ell goes elsewhere for his pleasure."

"Victorine, you're as ravishing as Helen of Troy, but remember that Helen's dalliance cost both Greeks and Trojans dearly."

"All right, put your shirt back on," she said, uncharacteristically wistfully. I put the chair down with a grunt. She walked back to her desk. "Then you may leave." Without the least promise of assistance. My banishment might last forever. I put on my shirt.

Toulоulou had said she'd pined for my father. Evidently that was true. Touloulou also told me that other secret about her. Thin ice. I watched her letter opener slice an envelope.

"Interesting," I chose my words, "Ell worrying it's dangerous for a white madame to lodge colored girls." Looking up from her letter, she waited, unblinking, like I was talking to the Sphinx. "With Pierce White's crowd stirring up emotions, I see how it's perilous for a *white* woman to lodge colored prostitutes. But if the madame herself is colored—"

"You're saying I'm colored?"

"Doesn't matter to me whether you are or not."

"But you imply I'm only passing as white. Did your mother tell you I was colored?"

"No. Others from Chenière visit the city, though. Some live here."

"You swallow their age-old gossip?"

"As I said, it doesn't matter to me."

"Yet you bring it up." She wasn't making this easy. Why should she?

"It might matter to other people," I forced myself to say. "Associates. Intimates. I assume Mr. Dixon doesn't know."

I expected anger. She grew calmer. "Blackmail?"

"An ugly word."

"An ugly thing. Your society friends have been a bad influence." She stood, walked to the door. I wasn't sure if I'd won the game but knew I'd lost her respect. "I'll speak to Mr. Dixon," she said. "Time you come back to the District. It's where someone like you belongs."

In the parlor, the drummer was packing up and the girls showing off their purchases, too early yet for customers. "And we missed your birthday," Victorine continued, as if our chat had been purely social. "Your eighteenth, so important in a young man's life. Girls, who'll take this gentleman up for a belated birthday present?"

The offer surprised me. Generosity had never been Victorine's strong suit. If this was how she wished to seal our bargain, however, it was all right by me. Yes, I'd been celibate too long, but more than that, I'd never in my life lain with a colored. While the only evidence that some of these fair-skinned girls were in any degree *négresse* was that they lodged here instead of at Baroness von Kempe's, the mystique was there. I felt a brief pang over Aralee, but — months into a year-long honeymoon — why should she complain?

A pretty harlot perching cross-legged on an ottoman spoke. "I'll do him." Something rang familiar about the voice. Then she smiled and I saw her chipped tooth.

~

Melpa, who'd been Mother's dresser and my childhood friend. Melpa, whom Nat loved and Conquering John seduced. Melpa, who years ago carried a child of uncertain parentage, a child I'd sworn to provide for.

We made love.

At first she was reluctant to talk about Athena, but eventually we cried together for Nat and cursed Judge Pike.

We made love again.

Both of us wondered but neither knew what had become of Conquering John. Realizing we'd fallen to whispers as we spoke of him, we laughed at our fear. Melpa recounted how she'd survived as a laundress. Once her boy started school, to raise tuition she'd become a whore. The child, almost nine, was so fine and polite, Melpa said, that Victorine, normally strictest of madames, allowed him to sleep winters in her attic and during summer in the coal bin.

This third time we made love was even more sweet but evidently too leisurely because Victorine came knocking. "Hurry up. The girl has customers."

I floated downstairs, so lost to infatuation I nearly danced into Elliot Dixon. With the distance between us less than the throw of his muscular arm, he peered into my eyes as if looking for an incubus, then spat a clean shot that rattled a spittoon a full nine feet away. "Don't look scared," he said. "Victorine says you've marked enough time and she's no fool, so okay, you can carouse the District. But never cross me again."

I pumped his hand. "I won't," I said and almost believed it.

"And goodness' sake, steer clear of Judge Pike. He's nobody you want for an enemy."

"You know Judge Pike?"

"When I take collections to the capitol, who you think I hand them to?"

Judge Pike was bag man to the legislature? "Does he realize I'm bookkeeper at—"

"He doesn't ask who ladles me the grease as long as it comes regular." Ell cuffed me with his open palm, intended I think as affection because it only hurt a little. "For a smart fellow you're awfully slow sometimes."

I lit out, not wanting to witness the smile of Melpa's customer when he left her room. I was back the next day. The day after. Money I'd saved to hire thugs, I spent on Melpa. I saw Victorine calculating the leverage it gave her over me, but I didn't care. It was a strange way to keep my promise to Nat. I managed to make excuses to myself about that too.

What about Melpa turned my head? Her boudoir wiles? Those fabulous gluteal muscles? Association with a happier past?

All that but also something more. Before Melpa I'd been peering into madness. Losing track of hours, sometimes days. Melpa hauled me back from the brink by inviting me into her heart, into her thoughts, into her worries and common sense and boundless capacity for silliness whenever a good laugh was required. She accepted me as neither hero nor villain, just an ordinary man whose beard stubble scratched and farts smelled but who was also clumsily capable of kindness.

Of all she brought to my life, one thing in particular made me a better man. I encountered that gift one morning when Millie the laundress interrupted my bookkeeping to tell me I had a messenger. On the back stoop waited a solemn mulatto boy who shook my hand in a formal manner and said, "I understand you knew my father, whichever of the two he was."

Melpa's son had been born Christmas Day, 1903, several

weeks premature, in a mule shed near Paincourtville. No midwife to help her, Melpa was attended by three field hands who'd run from debts owed a plantation store near Belle Rose. Having seen the glow of her lantern they understood it to mean the Holy Spirit summoning them. That possible misapprehension notwithstanding, these three men were very wise. Though they'd never read Dr. Voorhies' famous paper, "The Care of Premature Babies in Incubators," through native cunning they adapted a chicken brooder warmed by decomposing hog manure and thus saved the tiny innocent, who was named Noël for the day on which he was born. He'd since grown into a shy, slender nine-year-old with coffee-colored skin and enormous, curious eyes. Nat was his father, not Conquering John; I was almost positive.

Noël led me across Basin and Rampart into the French Quarter. Across an overgrown courtyard behind a tumbledown townhouse sagged the apartment of a musician friend of Melpa's who was out of town on a gig. Melpa waited with a great big smile to go with her account of the tall tale she'd dropped on Victorine to get free for the afternoon.

We ate, the three of us, like a family. The jambalaya was simple yet tasty, but Noël was hungrier for stories of Athena, the place he'd been conceived but had never seen. I remembered how it frustrated me as a child that Mother chose to be closed-mouthed about her life before the plantation, so I was generous with details. Melpa said little. I saw her listening and imagined she was awash in those memories too. The boy, I know, appreciated my stories, because even before he ran out of questions he said, "You old folks must be tired. I'll pick up the kitchen."

"Well aren't you a jasmine by the window," Melpa said as she walked into the bedroom. My eyes followed her. Noël watched me. Did he know what I was thinking? Did he approve?

He offered me the crown of his head. I kissed it. "Go with Mama," he said, "and you two have a good rest."

You'd think a prostitute would have enough of sex, but Melpa seemed to need it even more than I, and that was a great deal. We huffed and puffed through a climax, then lay gathering our breath. She atop me. Me inside her.

"A woman could spoil to this," she sighed.

"A fellow, too," I answered.

A moment passed before she spoke again. "You've been throwed way down from that high horse you rode as a kid. Even so, nobody says you got to settle for a woman in the Life, who's a good few years older than you, a colored woman with no money put away and a son whose daddy she can't name for sure."

"Well, well. Never stopped to consider all that," I joked. She poked me in the ribs and rolled off. My body missed her weight, my shrunken penis her warmth.

"You might still got a shot at that Gueydan girl's looks and money if you work it right."

"*This* feels right," I whispered.

"Lordy," she said. "Lordy, lordy, I'm surely bound for trouble." She kissed circles on my chest that spiraled toward my groin. Things that woman did with her mouth I won't attempt to describe. After excitement, erection, and another eruption came a twilight of bliss which turned into a nap. When I woke, I slid my arm from under her sleeping head, dressed, and tiptoed out.

Noël sat on the kitchen floor surrounded by old, broken piano keys, pretending they were steamboats. "Play," he said. His inflection left it somewhere between question and command. Sitting on the floor, I picked up a black key, saying "Loose the sternline, loose the bow," the way I'd heard dockmen cry. I steamed the block of ebony into the boy's imaginary river.

By the time I noticed Melpa watching us from the bedroom door, Noël and I had instituted port improvements that would've made Mayor Behrman proud. "He started a ferry to Westwego, Mama," Noël said. Melpa rewarded me with a smile

I felt all the way to my toes.

That afternoon became the first of many. Sometimes we met in Melpa's room at the sporting house. Better were trysts in the carriage barn of Baroness von Kempe or, like that first magical day, when we secured a neutral hideaway. Noël always allowed us time to do what adults do. Playing in an outer room if there was one, or napping sprawled across a dresser, face to the wall, sleeping through our passion then waking the moment Melpa was ready for a nap herself, and I ready to play. I hoped that from Heaven Nat observed us with contentment.

Christmas Day, 1913, his birthday, I bought Noël a bicycle sized for a child, complete with horn and basket. Everyone except him and me considered it extravagant, my mother in particular. "I received expensive gifts at his age. Do I seem spoiled?"

"Yes," Mother said.

Foolishly I persisted. "Then it's amazing a woman as fine as Melpa puts up with me."

With a devastatingly non-committal grunt, she picked up her hairbrush.

"I realize Melpa isn't rich like Aralee," I snarled.

"What's that got to do with it? She's a woman. Women are not to be trusted."

"Mother, *you're* a woman."

"So I should know about it, shouldn't I?" Her brush ripped through tangles.

"What'd Calypso do now?"

The brush stopped. She hated it when I was perceptive. Would she have preferred a dim-witted son? "Says we've gotten too serious," Mother admitted. I felt badly for her but knew anything I said would make me the villain. She started back brushing. "It's because of the Life. If we could escape we'd be happy but it's not easy for a pair like us because outside the District people aren't so accommodating which you'd know if you weren't blinded by your little harlot."

"Her name's Melpa."

"Of course. Melpa. Used to play together. You always stood up for her. Well, I guess something else is standing up now and she sure seems to like playing with it."

"Mother, stop it. If Calypso makes you this crazy, get rid of the bitch."

Mother threw her hairbrush, *BAM*, dinging the striped wallpaper. That's when I realized this mood grew from more than just arguing with Calypso. Arguments with Calypso happened every day. "What'd you see, Mother?" She shot me a look. "You had a spell, I know by how you're acting. Tell me what you saw."

She picked through her cosmetics. "What's the point? You can't change what's to come."

"I don't believe that."

"Then you're a worse fool than your father, worse than your stepfather, worse even than Calypso. Go. I have to get ready for the evening trade." A dab of rouge became a blood-red smear until her fingers massaged it into something more pleasing. Thirty-six now, she could pass for twenty-six, younger by gaslight. Why'd she refuse to acknowledge how fine Melpa was? Something in my future? In Melpa's? Her own?

I walked to the door, tried one last time. "What did you see?"

Mother eyed me in her mirror. "How well do you swim?"

A funny question. "I used to make it across the bayou. Why?"

"They say God occasionally sends floods to destroy the wicked."

~

"Am I wicked?" I asked. "I mean really wicked. Deep down."

Victorine knew Melpa saw me on the side, so it pleased her to find me in her parlor with cash in hand. She shrugged. "All men do wicked things. Out of anger, carelessness, fear. For fellowship, when a brotherhood becomes a mob. Sometimes they simply want something and to get it steal or kill." She offered a cold smile. "Or blackmail." I blushed.

"Don't worry'" she said. "I keep no record of injuries done me. It'd be too long a list. I do tally whom I can trust, but that's a *very* short list and you were never on it. Now give me five dollars and go bed your whore."

Melpa was furious. "Your bucket must be overflowing to pay for it when you know I got tomorrow afternoon off." What annoyed Melpa was the waste of what we were coming to consider not *my* money and *her* money but rather *our* money.

When I burst into tears, her anger ebbed. "Don't seem fair me having to raise *two* little boys," Melpa joked as she stroked my back.

I knew my tears were justified. Melpa and Noël made me happy, but I'd seen how fragile happiness is. Something would screw it up, something my fault, born of my wickedness. The abyss remained close. How easy to tumble in. Mother, perhaps, had already seen it.

Despite such episodes of despair and my continuing occasional blackouts, through winter and spring Melpa and I grew closer. I bought her earrings. She composed me a silly poem. I mended her clothes. She trimmed my hair. I did my best to become as loving a spouse as Louis Bonreve tried to be, as exciting a lover as Achille Cheramie, as gentle as Nat Toussaint.

That summer I heard Pierce and Aralee had returned from abroad with trunks of exotic curiosities and a darling baby son. With a couple so prominent, I'm sure half the matrons in New Orleans did what I did, count months on their fingers, the arithmetic of gestation. It tallied, just, for a child conceived on his parents' honeymoon. If the boy was early to turn over, respond to voices, follow a moving finger, well, with parents like his, what did you expect?

Did I long to see if my features might be mirrored in that tiny face? Of course. But it'd serve no one, least of all the babe. I didn't contact Aralee. She didn't contact me.

I'd also heard Tellia had borne a child, which she and Zeph (whose leg had healed perfectly) christened Achille Leboeuf. My father would've liked that, I think. With the kid's April 1st birth date I suspected I might find resemblance there too, but again, what good would it do anyone? Parentage is sticky business.

July 4th, 1913, I turned 19. Melpa, Noël, and I celebrated by going to the flickers at the Orpheum. What a delight to live in an age when technology was so transforming the world. The automobile, the aeroplane, now moving pictures. In the last row of the balcony reserved for coloreds, my arm around Melpa and Noël in my lap, we watched Bronco Billy shoot the baddest bad men down. Never had wickedness seemed so capable of containment.

When school started in the fall, Noël was the nuns' favorite pupil. Evenings, skipping the newspaper's rhetoric of race and scorecard of which European state floated the most battleships, I sifted pages of a Beacon Reader, helping Noël with his phonics. Doing what I had promised Nat gladdened my heart. We kept house in the carriage barn. When the Baroness bought a showy Oldsmobile she kept her old coach in case autos turned out to be a passing fashion. The coachman's seat became Noël's bunk. Melpa and I enjoyed the enclosed cab's lush cushions. Her night's work done, Melpa would walk home via a back-alley route Noël had blazed. She'd kiss her sleeping child and her waiting man. Never offering brothel gossip, never mentioning customers. That world we kept apart.

~

June 28th, 1914, a week before my 20th birthday, at the bagnio's busiest hour a member of the legislature was romping with Lettie, an accomplished seductress from Ohio who stood a tad plump but had pretty eyes. They sent down for crème fraiche. It wasn't clear it was for eating. In any case we were out. Mindful that the quasi-legal status of prostitution required friends in the statehouse, Baroness von Kempe suggested I see if Madame de la Victoire could spare any cream.

Happy to abandon my accounting — a toothache was killing me — I hoped if I overpaid for the dessert Victorine might let me slip upstairs with Melpa a few moments. Carrying an empty bowl, I dodged sidewalk drunks, offered a cigar to Patrolman Benton, petted the old riverboat captain's scruffy dog. At the brothel, I got a nod from the Professor, but saw no sign of Melpa.

In the office, a man sat on Victorine's desk, his finger brushing her cheek. He wore an expensive lounge coat and trendy gaiters you'd expect on someone younger. When he turned, I dropped my bowl. Even on Victorine's plush carpet, the delicate china cracked in two.

"What a clumsy fellow," said Judge Pike.

Tutorial VI

STRATEGIES & TACTICS

The great militarist scholar, General Carl Philipp Gottfried von Clausewitz, postulated war's three foundations as 1) hateful rage, 2) blind luck, and 3) rational policy. For your essay, recount a conflict with a rival, co-worker, or loved one. Identify how each element of Clausewitz' unholy trinity came into play.

Possibilities bubbled. With a shard of broken bowl I could blind him. Or smash the Tiffany lamp across his brow. With the letter opener, pierce his vest, shirt, flesh, a mortal wound.

I was only bold in thought. My feet stayed riveted to Victorine's Samarkand carpet.

"Seems to have run of your office. Does his Mother lodge here?" The Judge caught himself. "No, a white woman, she couldn't." He stood, collecting himself before he asked, "Is she indeed a whore?"

"The boy claims she tells fortunes," Victorine answered.

The Judge laughed, harsh and bitter. "Where?"

"Miss Victorine, please."

"Baroness von Kempe's." Victorine appeared to take no joy in her betrayal but exhibited no hesitation either.

The Judge looked at me. "The problem with maneuvering amongst the powerful is that you forego all the ripe intrigue beneath you. You'd said you were an accountant. I never considered you might work in Storyville, and when Pierce comes around he won't discuss you at all." To Victorine, his vitality returning: "The gentlemen I brought by, extend them every courtesy."

Victorine nodded, ever the accommodating madame. Judge Pike picked up his homburg hat, setting me in motion. No doubt he thought I was running to warn Mother. Wrong. I was off to arrange an ambush.

~

Hitched to a pair of splendid geldings, the landau formerly belonging to Colonel Bonreve sat at the curb. I'd evidently walked past it earlier, only Melpa and an aching molar on my mind. I would need to be more wary. I'd also need a plan.

A gun could be purchased in the District, but I wasn't carrying enough cash.

Some gentleman's walking stick could bash Pike's head, but stealing one would mean battling its owner and maybe the police.

A Go-Away-Evil? I had no time to conjure.

Judge Pike stepped out the brothel's ornate door: dress impeccable, bearing regal, fiendish mind disguised by genteel demeanor. His was not a name the man on the street knew, yet every door at City Hall was open to him, most at the Baton Rouge statehouse, quite a few in faraway Washington. He made introductions, solved problems, arranged favors, and was rewarded handsomely. Fabulously rich, unflappably amoral, in the region's bastions of power he was undisputed king of the shadows. God, however, in His wisdom sets limits on mortal power. Rich or poor, humans are merely human. The most exalted king can never be so great that he does not share the biological necessities of the pauper, just as no steed is so magnificent that it doesn't need to take a good crap now and then, as proved true that very moment with the nearest gelding. My eye caught the telling lift of tail.

Poised on Victorine's stoop, the Judge in his smugness paused to install into his boutonniere a flower he'd no doubt plucked from the vase inside Victorine's door, a flower like Nat might have cut long ago. Judge Pike was taunting me.

The carriage horse, tail now vertical, yawned his anus into a perfect oval, like a human mouth poised to scream.

The Judge strolled down the brothel steps. No defensive posture. No fear. Unwise, Judge Pike, I thought, as with both hands I caught as it fell a steaming heap of well-digested oats.

A dozen hours earlier, across the world in the Austrian province of Herzegovina, a Bosnian-Serb revolutionary had attacked the carriage of the emperor's heir-apparent. He wielded a revolver. Some of his confederates carried bombs. All I had was a double handful of fresh horseshit, but it was heavy, warm, and fragrant. I hurled it. The strange meteor passing overhead startled gentlemen strolling the sidewalk. The Judge never saw it coming.

In Sarajevo, bullets pierced the body of Archduke Franz Ferdinand, kindling the Great War. On Basin Street, manure pelted the shirtwaist of Judge August Pike, starting a conflagration of its own. His nostrils quailed. His pupils flashed. He stank to high heaven. Best of all, bystanders pointed at him and laughed.

I'd needed time; I'd just bought some. Turning on his heel, the Judge marched back up the steps. I doubted he'd linger for a full bath. How long to borrow a shirt? I had to use the minutes wisely. Wiping my hands on the seat of his carriage, I pushed through the sidewalk throng, hurrying to warn Mother. We'd leave immediately. Like once before, with nothing but the clothes on our backs. This time, where? St. Louis? Baltimore?

Europe! Mother had always wanted to see Vienna. Melpa and Noël would love Vienna! We could —

Who was I kidding? I didn't have funds to get us to Vienna. I couldn't even afford a dentist. Where to go? Natchez? Biloxi? Would Mother leave if our destination was only Biloxi? Or might she use the Judge's attentions to make Calypso jealous? Or was it remotely possible that enough time had passed that she'd forgiven Judge Pike? That she might renounce her lesbianism and accept to be his wife? His mistress? It was dangerous to be certain she wouldn't. Her feelings toward him were complicated even back when.

If I must pick the moment I became an adult, it's when I decided I would do what was best for Mother whether Mother agreed it was best or not. In fact, knowing Mother, it would be better if I didn't even tell her what I decided. Maybe slip her laudanum and box her in a trunk on the Panama Limited to Chicago. Roll her into a carpet and load her on the Sunset to Los Angeles, freight C.O.D.

Clearly, this was not a caper I could dash off. How to restrain Judge Pike for a few days? Kidnapping presented too many hurdles. Hospital? A wound could lay him up while I devised a longer-range plan. Something painful, though not enough to get me hanged. I needed a weapon. This time dung wouldn't do. I remembered a loose brick on the curb near the Baroness'. It took a moment to find it, a moment longer to budge the old riverboat captain, standing on it, boring someone with tales of an ages-ago near-collision at Nine Mile Point. I fell to my knees. Shredded my fingers trying to dig out the brick. The steamboater's old hound kept trying to lick my ear. Men bumped into me, assuming, I suppose, that I was on my knees retching up excess liquor.

The dog barked in my face. His master jerked his leash. The cur came right back and nipped my ear. I drew back my head. That's when I saw…

He was trying to warn me. Judge Pike, in fresh shirt, was pushing through the crowd. The old dog began digging out the brick for me. Feeble paws scraped mortar. Together we got it. He barked at me not to dawdle. I slipped behind a Chevrolet parked by the curb, ready to spring out.

The man who'd condemned Nat and tricked Colonel Bonreve into suicide and who now intended to desecrate Mother was twenty feet away. Hefting my brick, I wondered where I should hit him. Despite his conceits, his head was a smallish target. The groin, good, not lethal but painful. The knee? Can't walk without a knee. He was ten feet away. I suppose I should've considered consequences, but I thought only of Mother. He must never reach her. Four feet. I was the man of the family, head of the household. Two feet. I dashed, brick in hand.

As a child at Athena, I would often spring out at Mother or Nat, sometimes the cook Yvonne, delighting myself with the fright I gave them. In the intervening years, however, my ambush technique had grown rusty. Thus I made several tactical errors. The first was to not notice Pierce White, buttoning his vest as he left Maison de la Victoire and pushed through the crowd to catch up to his mentor. After our last encounter, Pierce had scrubbed my sperm out of his eye so vigorously that he'd abraded its cornea and had since been forced to wear an eye-patch. Monocular vision notwithstanding, he again proved his athleticism by taking me down with a flying tackle before I got anywhere near the Judge. My brick skidded across the pavement. Pierce put his knee to my back and pinned me face-down to the sidewalk.

A more egregious error was to underestimate the vindictiveness of Judge Pike, who hissed, "Your duplicity cost me long, wasted years," as he prepared to kick me in the face. Disfiguring me seemed unlikely to endear him to Mother, but I didn't bother saying so. Passers-by paused to watch, yet none intervened. This was the District. If justice miscarried, Ell Dixon would settle it, or maybe the police. Where *had* Patrolman Benton gone?

About to have my head kicked in like a rotted pumpkin, my

erupting wisdom tooth suddenly seemed not a big deal. It'd be me in the hospital, not Judge Pike. I closed my eyes and waited to be scarred, blinded, or rendered simple.

And waited.

Heard thrashing that wasn't mine.

Cursing from the Judge, a positive sign.

I opened my eyes. The steamboat captain's dog had sunk his canines into the Judge's calf. Judge Pike tried to kick him off but the old hound was relentless. Pierce couldn't help without releasing me. The growing crowd laughed, further maddening the Judge.

I bucked, throwing Pierce over. Leapt to my feet. Pierce leapt too. He drew back to sock me. "What goes here?" thundered a voice. There, finally, came Patrolman Benton, with his drooping mustache, tall, domed hat, and knee-length, double-breasted coat. Pierce pulled his punch. I breathed again. Collections from the District might go from Elliot Dixon to Judge Pike to the honchos of City Hall, but a man like the Judge never soiled his hands greasing common coppers. That was my job. Still, I'd have to play it slick, and the dog, I noticed, had disappeared.

"Officer, arrest this man," the Judge spat as he inspected the punctures in his leg.

"Yes, by all means, arrest me," I seconded, knowing full well the patrolman would no sooner lock up the fellow who dispensed his gratuities than he'd cut off his own sticky fingers. "This gentlemen was seeking nothing more than routine sensualism when my bad manners so worked him up that the only thing for him now is to return another night once his distemper subsides." I straightened the Judge's lapel. He batted me away.

"Sounds reasonable," said Patrolman Benton.

"No, it does not," corrected the Judge. "I won't go anywhere except into Baroness von Kempe's where I intend to enjoy a certain lodger to the fullest." He eyed me, making sure I knew he meant Mother. "I'm a good friend of Mayor Behrman,

Patrolman."

I suspected Benton routinely encountered people claiming influence they didn't actually possess. Here was an opening. I took a bank note from my wallet — well, actually, it was the Judge's wallet I'd lifted while pretending to straighten his collar a moment before — my pickpocketing lessons had paid off. "To repair your torn pants." I offered the Judge his own money. He slapped it away, as I figured he might, which allowed me to tuck it into the cop's pocket more as casual gratuity than brazen bribe.

"Seems like an honest attempt at amends," Benton addressed the Judge. "Maybe you should get along home."

"I'm also a friend of Police Commissioner Eckert," the Judge hissed. "If I go home that's whom I ring first. I can't imagine he'd want his patrolmen to keep a gentleman from entering his own premises." What? "You see, like Maison de la Victoire and several other District palaces, I own the Baroness' building." The mystery of our landlord solved, the worst possible person, the worst possible moment. I didn't doubt it was true. Easy to imagine Pike using inside information to buy property cheap in the weeks before the Storyville ordinance passed.

Benton wavered. Pierce grinned. My wisdom tooth throbbed. I'd been outplayed. The Judge's path was clear. Luckily, he was too angry to settle for only Mother. "So I say again, arrest this young man. Shackle him to your precinct wall. Beat him. I won't have his mischief further disturb my pleasures."

"The charge would be?" I played for time.

The Judge grunted. "Assault. You sicced your dog on me."

"Patrolman, I don't own a dog. The Baroness would never allow it."

"Certainly he has a dog," Pike said. "Over there."

The crowd opened to clear our view. Next to the Chevrolet cringed a naked man of about fifty. Onlookers hummed at this new wrinkle. "Who are you, jay-bird?" asked Patrolman

Benton.

"Jerome Chabert," replied the naked man in a croaky, out-of-practice voice. The name sounded familiar but I couldn't place it. The fellow appeared as surprised as us to find himself standing there nude. I'd not have recognized him as the steamboat captain's dog except for the bit of the Judge's tweed snagged between his teeth.

"Of course, *my dog!*" I rolled my eyes for Patrolman Benton's benefit. "Let me get him to his doghouse." I sauntered toward Jerome, sliding off my jacket and slipping it onto his shoulders, "while you escort the mayor's *best pal* and prominent *whorehouse owner*" — I grinned and winked to plant all the doubt I could about those claims — "back to his carriage."

Benton's big mustache twitched. "Ain't no matter for police," he said. "Call Ell Dixon." He strolled away, twirling his billy, bribe in his pocket. Rubberneckers let him pass, three dozen conversations speculating on what would happen next. I was curious too. No matter how fond Ell might be of me, he wouldn't buck Judge Pike who possessed more leverage in the District than I'd known. On my side was only an arthritic hound who through some fluke of supernaturalism now seemed more like a lost lamb.

I saw the Judge whisper to Pierce, no doubt sending him to fetch Dixon. I had to move fast. "Who'd enjoy seeing a bout?" I bellowed, pointing at the Judge. "This, my friends, is Judge August Randolph Pike, whom I publicly challenge to…" The crowd waited. The King of the Shadows seethed at having his name shouted. "…to a dog fight." I dragged startled Jerome up the Baroness' stoop. "My pit bull here against the Judge's lap dog, Pierce." The crowd hooted. Pierce turned red. Foot traffic stopped, as it always did for a free show. Chauffeurs shooed off rounders climbing onto bumpers for a better view. Half-dressed girls peered from brothel windows. "Anyone to cover bets?" I asked. Fists went up, greenbacks protruding between fingers. "And to ensure this momentous contest is widely celebrated," I met Judge Pike's icy stare, "who promises to report its particulars in letters to the Mascot and Picayune? Judge August Randolph Pike" I enunciated each word, "deserves prominent mention for sponsoring this one-of-a-kind event!"

Despite his profound arrogance, the Judge could always recognize a skirmish lost. He strode away. Pierce followed, his single eye darting over the crowd. When they boarded their carriage, only too late did they notice that I'd wiped the horseshit off my hands onto its seat.

The disappointed crowd's hubbub faded to normal levels. I heard the old riverboat captain hollering, "Hurricane! Hurricane!" and remembered that's what he called his dog. Jerome pulled my jacket closer around him. "I can't go home like this," he said. Indeed. "Guess I got too worked up. Never dreamed it'd change me back after all these years."

This fellow clearly had a story to tell. Besides, I couldn't abandon him; he'd saved me.

The Judge wouldn't risk a second humiliation tonight. Sure, he could call any number of cronies, from Ell Dixon to the Police Commissioner, but that would entail insinuating questions and explanatory half-truths, maybe ribald asides, all liable to impugn his precious dignity. No, patience was the Judge's hallmark. He'd be all night plotting revenge. I probably had till we opened for business tomorrow afternoon. Meanwhile, my tooth hurt. My belly grumbled. A quick decision often turns out to be a disastrous one. Best let emotions settle before considering my options. "Let's grab a bite," I told Jerome.

"Got no money on me," the naked man confessed unnecessarily.

"I've plenty," I said, tapping the Judge's wallet. "We'll go to Antoine's."

"I'm not dressed for anyplace fancy."

A shape-shifter with a gift for understatement. Dinner would be interesting. I took him out back and lent him my old suit. He needed Noël's help to button it. I told the boy to warn his mother that in the morning we might all be going on a trip.

Noël appeared dubious.

~

Jerome rattled a tale of long-ago, waking up with feathers in his teeth and the social hardships of being a *rougarou*, little of which I followed as my mind wandered over how I'd defeat Judge Pike's designs on Mother. I'd asked for a quiet corner, assuming Jerome's table manners would be rusty. As he gobbled his *coq au vin*, I saw I hadn't been mistaken.

"Does it hurt to change between man and dog?" I asked.

"Meaningful change is always painful. That's why it's rare." Jerome picked up a chicken wing and sucked the meat right off it.

"How long had you been a dog?"

"Since '93."

Longer than I'd been alive. What does one say to that? "Did you like being a dog?"

He paused gnawing. "A dog's life holds certain satisfactions. For people, too often, the richer you are, the poorer you feel. The fuller each minute, the more bored you become. We awake promising we'll seize the day but spend it regretting the past or fretting the future. A dog lives moment by moment. Any morsel dropped off the table or impromptu scratch of the belly offers boundless joy." He went back to eating.

"Why'd you help me?" I asked. "Did I slip you a bone once?"

"No, but I bet you will now, if I change back," he said slyly. "Sentimental reasons. You look like your father." Only then did the name Jerome Chabert strike a chord from stories I'd heard. "Saved Achille's life too, once," Jerome continued. "He almost fell on a broken bottle. I caught him in time. He died the next day anyway — destiny's destiny I suppose — but I saved him long enough to enjoy his wedding night."

"Allowing me to be conceived."

"Guess I saved you twice then." He chewed the gristle off the end of a drumstick.

"What was my father like?"

"How do you mean?"

"What sort of man was he? How did he move? Talk? Think?"

"Think? Achille was more a man of action than thought."

Unlike me, plagued as I am by second guesses and third-rate intellectualism. "I've been told he was heroic."

Jerome considered. "I suppose."

How many people would call me heroic? Maybe Noël, but that had mostly to do with buying him a bicycle. Jerome cracked the drumstick to get at its marrow. "Your pa was the kind of man who was fun to be around. He filled a room. Gathered up life with both arms." Jerome attacked the bone with a loud sucking sound. "Now he did cheat at cards."

"Pardon?"

"Oh yeah, an awful cheat." Jerome moved on to a thigh.

"How can that be?" I sputtered. "Even Touloulou, who lost so much to Father, never accused—"

"Touloulou? Touloulou wouldn't have known he was cheated if your pa had stolen the trousers off his hips. Your pa had a way. Grinning, talking smooth. You wanted to give him all you had before he even asked. A way of leading people on and them following though they knew it wasn't smart, and afterward not blaming him. Like the store mistress—"

"Victorine?"

"The one running the cathouse now. Had her convinced he was going to marry her."

"I don't believe—"

"Some said he had your ma's little sister, the flirty one, thinking the same."

"My Tante Clo?"

Jerome shrugged. "Folks gossip. Even an outcast has ears."

I thought of all the things Mother and Tellia and Zeph and Tante Clo and Victorine ever told me about my father. None of it supported what Jerome was saying. None of it actually contradicted him either. "Zeph Leboeuf told me Father was quite musical," I said.

"Musical? Not that I knew."

"Zeph said he could sing like a mockingbird."

"Never heard Achille sing, not that I remember." As he picked through his plate looking for any morsels he'd missed, he chuckled at a memory. "Now, wasn't exactly music, but Achille Cheramie did fart louder than anybody you ever heard."

"Fart?"

"Loud enough to scare babies. Offer Achille a dish of navy beans, next morning he could out-blast the horn on the Southwest Pass lighthouse."

~

When the bill came, I realized I should've saved the money to get out of town. By then, Jerome was suffering a massive bellyache. Despite how he'd slandered Father, I felt guilty for involving him in my feud with the Judge, for spurring his re-transformation, for letting him gnaw chicken bones which everyone knows are dangerous for dogs. Leaving the restaurant, I helped him to a seat on a Studebaker's bumper. "I'll find a cab," I said.

On Canal Street I hired a scruffy caleche hitched to a half-lame mule. Returning to rue St. Louis, I didn't see Jerome until I spotted what I first thought was a discarded fur coat. He'd changed back. I didn't know what I should, or could, do about it. Scratching the scruff of his neck, I said, "A wise man once told me, 'A dog's life holds certain satisfactions.'" He licked my hand.

As the cab clip-clopped off, taking him home, the dog peered at me through its rear window. The sky was brightening in the east. Time to get Mother out, though I wasn't sure how I'd afford it or what lie I'd tell to convince her. Then there was the Calypso relationship, whatever its status at present. Melpa and Noël to arrange for. Tick tock, tick tock.

~

By the time I entered the brothel I had a plan, though granted, a plan mushy in the center and soft at the corners. I won't bother relating it. None of it came off anyway.

My first surprise was to find Calypso perched on a steamer trunk near the front door. I'd never seen her up this early. She wore a smart lavender-and-lace travel outfit. "The Baroness evicted me," she announced.

"Why?"

"I don't know."

"What's Mother say?"

"Good luck."

"What do you mean?"

"All she said: 'Good luck.' I know I'm not easy to love, but after three years pulling each other's strings, all I get is 'Good luck'?"

She was right, it didn't seem much, but I knew the hell she'd put Mother through. Smelling her perfume, I thought back to the day she took my virginity; remembered when I saw her take Mother; times she flirted with me and teased me, how she made Mother laugh, their boisterous fights. Like every comely whore who'd passed through these doors, done her time and moved on or was asked to leave, now it was her turn. I almost wished her "Good luck" but caught myself.

Bounding upstairs, at Room 9, I stopped; stopped bounding; even stopped breathing.

Any man who came of age in a brothel could not refute that he was hearing the sound of intercourse. The male groans weren't much different from Mother's fortune-telling sessions which I realized now had never been fortune-telling, that everyone had known it but had allowed me to pretend and probably chuckled over how silly I was. Silly. Witless. Idiotic. As Conquering John warned, stupid lasts a lifetime. Mother was a prostitute, no better than the other bawds here, though on account of me, more discreet.

And older, almost thirty-eight, attractive, but at her age most lewd women had sunk to a two-dollar house or more likely a crib. That Mother held Room 9 was because her presence secured an underpaid and (by and large) honest bookkeeper. As if I was Mother's pimp. Thank God Achille hadn't lived to see this.

I heard Mother moan and realized why this time was different from all the other times I'd stood outside this door and convinced myself that behind it she was only swirling tea leaves. She'd screwed *those* men in silence. To deceive me? Or to maintain her mystery and thus enflame their passion? If this morning she was quiet no longer, was it a cry for help? Or was Judge Pike — because that's the sadistic slime-dick levee-breaking ass-licking angel-raping monster I knew was in there with her — was he indeed the man she'd been waiting for? Waiting since that night under Athena's oaks. A man with whom her chance for happiness had been thwarted by her own hurt feelings and shock at the death of the Colonel though she hadn't much liked the Colonel anyway.

If help she cried for, I'd help her. If the other, well, her feelings be damned, I would murder the Judge regardless. If they executed me afterward, so be it. He'd tricked my stepfather into killing himself and arranged to have my dearest friend hanged and now he was screwing my mother and, worst of all, making a fool of me!

As mentioned earlier, a pro just out of prison had taught me how to quickly, quietly pick a lock. I slipped in. Mother was on her back, the Judge atop her thrusting with more vigor than I'd have expected from a man his age — he was in his fifties now. Mother made encouraging noises, her eyes squeezed closed, the Judge's face buried in her unbound hair. With the commotion they were making, neither heard me.

On the bedside table, beside a half-eaten brace of roast quail a bottle of Laurent-Perrier sat giving up bubbles. Two-thirds full, it'd be plenty heavy enough to cudgel Judge Pike. I pulled the bottle from its ice bucket like King Arthur drawing Excalibur from the stone. My dragon lay before me, gasping and hissing and humping my mother. I raised the bottle. Lift it high, I reminded myself. Aim it straight. Let its weight do the work.

Mother opened her eyes. "Don't!" she shouted.

Pike ceased all movement. "Did I hurt you, dear?" I'd never pegged him for a solicitous lover.

"I meant don't stop," Mother said. "Don't ever stop, August."

Don't ever stop, August? I wanted to retch. She pulled him close so that his face was once again buried in her hair. When he started back his vile thrusting, she nodded me toward the door. I was ready to bludgeon him anyway, I was, until I remembered her nursing me through yellow jack. Pretending she wasn't hungry in the tomb at St. Louis N°1 so I'd eat her share of Touloulou's gruel. Remembered she'd screwed a half-dozen men a night for years because *I* didn't fancy moving to Leeville. If she wanted the Judge, who was I to snuff his lamp?

I threw the champagne bottle against the wall. *Crash*, glass flew. A chunk hit the table sending a roasted quail flying. Judge Pike stilled his hips again.

"It's nothing," Mother urged her lover. "The bottle fell over. Don't stop, August."

That phrase! He went back to work. Again Mother nodded me toward the door, but I couldn't just walk away. Dropping to my knees, I pressed my forehead to the rug like a Mohammedan praying. I needed time to think, a place to do it…

I crawled under their bed. Perhaps I believed my presence might inhibit Mother enough that she'd send the Judge packing, but no. Above me his porcine grunting continued unabated. I listened and listened and listened until I had a plan.

Mother's red silk kimono lay discarded by the bed. I tore a strip off its hem; it was her favorite, but she shouldn't have left it lying about. With no needle for sewing, I decided folding would work equally well. As bed boards rattled and mattress springs clanged, I began to whisper.

God all-powerful and the saints and anybody else listening,
Let this mojo the color of Christ Jesus blood be your open hand.

From my pocket I contributed a silver dime; silver magnifies any charm. From the Judge's jacket draped on the chair, I snitched his pocket comb and harvested a single hair, enough to make the trick specific to him.

Deliver me and Mother too, Oh Lord, from his lying lips and deceitful tongue.
Footman, horsemen, I conjure you up from the Spirit World to keep him moving.

I scraped the soles of the Judge's shoes for specks of dust from myriad locations, each of which, if the charm worked, he'd be forced to return to.

Let him be vagabond, compelled to seek his bread in desolate places.
Let no man offer him a seat, or shelter him, or extend mercy unto him.

I cracked a wishbone from the half-eaten quail that had fallen to the floor and put the broken joint into the sachet.

Oh, dove who behind those feathers really is the Holy Ghost, add your power.
May the dead rise from the grave to be thine army and keep this sinner walking.

But the invisible spirits would never rise because I had no cemetery dust. It was the key ingredient lacking, the one necessity not within reach.

Once, years before, when I couldn't get cemetery dirt for a trick to ward off fever, I'd found that an alligator tooth made a workable substitute. I knew what I had to do.

My wisdom tooth, growing in crooked, had made the gum around it tender. To touch it with my tongue hurt, but that same touch told me that it didn't have a whole lot of wobble. If I wanted it, I'd have to work it loose which would hurt so much I wasn't sure I could be quiet about it. I put thumb and finger into my mouth. Grasped the molar. Pain roared through me and I hadn't gotten serious yet. No wonder dentists administer cocaine.

I can't believe I did this. As I wrenched the tooth left then right, I timed it to Judge Pike's thrusts as he fucked my mother inches above my head, thus camouflaging my grunts under his. Luckily — I suppose — they were being loud up there, Mother included. I thought of times as a child I worried about her noisy nightmares during those after-lunch naps with the Colonel. I flatter myself worldly, but I must be the boobiest naïf on the globe. Or maybe I'm quite ordinary. Who among us can look at their mother and see her as she really is?

The Judge was getting close. As he increased his pace, so did I. My mouth filled with blood. The pain was blinding. His moment came. The seed the Judge had hoped to plant in Mother for more than a decade now shot roaring out of him. He cried out and I did too; me in agony. If Mother joined our chorus, I don't want to know about it.

Wiping blood from my lips, I added my tooth to the red silk mojo and smashed the *gris-gris* flat. Ripping out the inner sole of one of the Judge's shoes, I placed the charm. Then an idea made me smile through my pain. I picked up Judge Pike's *other* shoe.

~

"That, I must say, was worth the wait," sighed the Judge. When I thought it impossible to feel worse, Mother giggled like a schoolgirl.

"Your son will not approve."

"My son ought to mind his own business," Mother said louder than necessary if only talking to Judge Pike.

"I lost my temper last night. Almost to the point of assaulting him," the Judge admitted.

"I lose my temper with him almost every night. I'd assault him too except he's grown too big to spank." Betrayal, betrayal, betrayal! To me and the memory of Achille.

"I've done things he'll never forgive," said Judge Pike. He was right about that.

"Don't we all sometimes do things beyond forgiveness?"

Mother replied with excess magnanimity. "If we don't let them slide into the past, how do we go on?"

Lying on the floor, periodically swallowing the blood accumulating in my mouth, I understood her words held wisdom, but I wasn't ready to hear them.

The satyr sated, Judge Pike sat up. Pulled on his pants. Reached for his shoes. I'd arranged them so that first-to-hand was the one dosed with the spell. As he slipped it on he paused, no doubt feeling a tingle he didn't recognize but which lent urgency to yanking on the second shoe where I'd prepared another surprise. Judge Pike yowled.

Mother examined his foot. "When the champagne bottle broke, a shard must have landed in your shoe. Went pretty deep, I'm afraid." Blood dripped from his foot like from a cracked faucet. I hoped it'd grow gangrenous. Now he'd be cursed with the Urge-To-Wander I'd concocted, and further cursed with a wound that would force him to hobble.

Mother escorted the Judge downstairs, careful as they left to keep his eyes from roaming under the bed. I climbed out to await her return. After a half-hour, I picked up her kimono, found a needle, re-hemmed it for her. After an hour, when she hadn't come back, I went down to the kitchen and salted a glass of water to gargle clean the hole in my jaw.

When finally I did see Mother late that afternoon, she wouldn't discuss what happened except to say I should expect to see more of the Judge and that she'd be cross if next time I didn't do a better job minding my manners. Next time!

The Baroness rejoiced over the leverage this new arrangement gave her with her landlord and thought that I, as bookkeeper, should cheer too. As far as the long-running fortune-telling hoax, she claimed, "We thought you knew but didn't want to discuss it. I mean, who'd actually believe a woman worked a half-dozen years in a whorehouse without getting screwed?"

Patrolman Benton got reassigned to the rowdiest precinct in town. Calypso landed in Chicago where, she'd been told, "men appreciate a talented lesbian."

Thanks to my spell, for weeks the Judge lived in motion. He even bought an automobile. Trouble was, it did not separate him from Mother. She went everywhere with him, his constant companion, returning to Room 9 only to change clothes. The Baroness bought Mother a second-hand nurse's uniform so she might engender less gossip when Judge Pike took her to important gatherings. Besides, a private nurse underscores a limping man's importance.

Melpa counseled calm. "A heart chooses who it chooses. Christ almighty, my foolish heart chose you."

July 4th, I turned twenty. The city celebrated. I didn't. Mother hardly came around anymore. Melpa had grown annoyed over my preoccupation with Judge Pike. I was having blackouts again. My steadiest companion was Noël. In idle moments rancid thoughts fester; Noël allowed me no idleness. His favorite tactic was to hand me a newspaper. "Read," he'd say. I'd read to him about the completion of the Panama Canal, due to open any day now, or about war brewing in Europe. August 4th, mighty Germany invaded little Belgium. A terrible thing but a world away. I didn't see how it could affect us.

~

The establishment was called a "French house" not because its inmates spoke French, though — as everywhere in the District, with its heavy Creole presence — many did. No, a French house meant the specialty was oral sex, a supposed proclivity of the Gallic nation. Its madame, Josette, was a native of Belgium. I suspect it was the morning's headlines that inspired Baroness von Kempe to stage her own invasion.

An envelope delivered, its contents read, Madame Josette hurried outside to where Judge Pike sat in his brand-new two-seater Lozier Meadowbrook, a fine, sporty automobile to satisfy the compulsion to wander with which I'd crossed him. As Mother waited by its fender, Madame Josette joined him in the car. What he told her — for it was reported she listened more than she spoke — is known only to them and God.

Meanwhile, in the proprietress' full view, Baroness von Kempe entered the brothel, exiting nine minutes later with its half-dozen choicest girls each burdened with carpet bags and hat boxes. Like a field marshal on parade, the Baroness led them to her bagnio. There, carpenters were already throwing up partitions to convert two bedrooms into eight, the nature of Frenching allowing a smaller floorplan than conventional copulation. I suspected the Baroness had cashed her chit for relinquishing Room 9's lodger to the exclusive enjoyment of Judge Pike, but confronting her, all I got were admonitions to "keep my grubby hands off the pretty new butterflies."

"Baroness, you know I see no woman but Melpa."

But the Baroness knew something I didn't. The sequel to her adventure I heard from Noël: how irate Elliot Dixon rose from Victorine's bed wearing a coverlet like a toga. Had fingers in mouth to whistle his battle call when interrupted by word the Judge waited outside. The two great men conferred in the Judge's car. Afterward, Ell tucked up his toga and went back in. "He looked mad but never whistled," recounted Noël. These revelations were only preamble. Noël had saved the worst for last. "That's why you can't see Mama no more."

"Who says I can't?"

"Mama does, and Miz Victorine, and Mr. Ell, and all the ladies were talking about it too. They say you're on the wrong side."

"I'm neutral!" Striding over to Maison de la Victoire, as Noël predicted I was denied entry. Though I hollered up at Melpa's room, she never came to the window.

The European war also had an Eastern front. There too things went badly for the allies. At a place called Tannenberg, the Kaiser's Prussians were whipping the butts of the Czar's Russians. After reading about it in the papers, Baroness von Kempe bullied a liquor dealer into sending Czarina Pavlova's brothel a notice of steep increase in the price of vodka. When the faux-Russian madame left to haggle, the Baroness pounced. Unfortunately, the day was sunny, and Madame Pavlova decided to return for her parasol. Caught by surprise with her coup in progress, the Baroness responded with brute force.

Fur being costly, Czarina Pavlova had stretched the fashion for feathered hats by trimming her garments with plumage. The effect was akin to encountering a five-foot-tall, half-plucked chicken, and that was *before* the Baroness got hold of her. Baroness von Kempe outweighed the slender Slav by a good forty pounds. After an uneven contest as ferocious as Tannenberg (albeit on a smaller scale) the Baroness returned disheveled but triumphant and followed by a troop of pseudo-Russian whores, most wearing only kimonos or knee-length chippies. Judge Pike did not appear involved in this incursion. Had he approved it?

The Baroness' boutique of sex was growing into a grand department store. Gentlemen flooded in, attracted by the unique amount of choice. All day long carpenters subdivided rooms till each boudoir could barely accommodate a bed and washstand. Only Room 9 seemed immune. The irony was Room 9 sat empty, but one rainy afternoon I finally found Mother in.

"Don't say another word," she began (I hadn't said anything) "or think you've the right to judge me" (never my intent) "or that you can stop me" (from doing what?)

Unmentionables fell into a spanking new suitcase. Now and then she'd cull a garment to the floor. The Judge's Urge-To-Wander should've been wearing off, but this seemed preparation for a voyage. "Where to, Mother?"

"I can't stop to talk. He hates when I make him wait."

"Where's he taking you? Certainly not to his Garden District mansion." She didn't answer. "The man abhors scandal. Gazing into the future, surely you see what everyone knows. You're a plaything to him. He'll never marry you."

A feral look came to her eyes. Her words hissed. "I debased myself with faceless men ten thousand times for your sake, but now I have a chance at, well, probably not happiness; still it's pleasant to run about in his automobile even though we only need it because you hexed him with craving to wander which I know you did so don't deny it and by the way how long till that spell wears off?"

"Mother—"

"Shut up. You won't tell me the truth anyway. The Judge washes more often than most men I've been obliged to know and his manners are perfection which makes it nice when he takes me by the lake to dine on trout amandine served on linen like it was at Athena instead of grabbing a quick supper in the kitchen between tricks while you playacted not knowing what happened in Room 9 because it made you feel better to pretend I read men's futures."

"But you *could* see the future!"

"I could see mine. It was bleak."

"You make it sound like you regret I was ever born."

"*That*, I did not say. We can't sort the events of our lives like potatoes, savor the good and toss the blemished to the hog. The night you were conceived was the happiest of my life so how could I regret you were born, but that doesn't mean there aren't moments, actually a number of moments, when you drive me stark, rampaging mad. Now kiss me and go. The Judge had me twice today so I'm tired and all right maybe a little cranky but I have to get packed because he's picking me up and like I told you he hates when I make him wait because he says I made him wait all those years so he shouldn't have to wait for me ever again."

"How romantic."

"Fuck you."

I flinched. *Those* words marked a line we'd never crossed. "Where's he taking you?"

"To the other side."

"Of the river?"

"Of the war, the war you started, because I know you put the idea in the Baroness' head."

"I never—"

"You're the only one clever enough and as a child you played with those toy warships and little lead soldiers and read all those books which I admit I encouraged but I'd have burned them had I known the mischief you'd cause with that knowledge and that because of it one day I'd have to move out of this room which has grown a bit shabby I admit but at least I'm used to it and now to move to who knows what they've got for me at Maison de la Victoire—"

"You can't lodge there!"

"I can, I will, and it's your fault."

"Mother, it's a colored house. The laws are strict and the police are starting to enforce them. You can't have the same brothel lodging colored whores and white wh—"

Her look froze me. I'd almost called my mother a whore. Aloud. To her face. Another line crossed. Silence fell, interrupted only by the *wheesh* of delicate fabrics flying into her valise. The quiet grew unbearable. She broke it first. "The Judge owns the building. He has every right to stay there."

"But you?"

"I'm his nurse."

"Since when have you been a nurse?"

"Since I stopped being a fortune teller. You'll pay for it, you know, because I've seen it, seen you in a great flood which for all I know you'll have caused yourself and you'll be fighting and flailing, swallowing water and going down—"

"You're confusing me with Father."

"I'm not."

"With how he died."

"No."

"You must be. Because I'm so like him."

"You're nothing like him. I could read your father like a book. *You* personify deceit, but that's not entirely bad because sometimes I read in your father things I'd have rather not known."

"Like what? Did he cheat at cards? Chase after Victorine?"

She eyed me. "The man's dead, his sins washed away, same as whatever sins you carry will drain away in a great flood like

Noah and whenever I have that vision, because I've had it more than once, it saddens me to watch you drown like your father drowned though in my heart I know you might deserve it more than he did."

"How did he deserve it?"

"I have to pack."

"Was it his fault he was lucky at cards?"

"I'm no longer listening."

"Or that women were attracted to him?"

"Can't hear a word."

How infuriating her grim, unfair, only partially accurate judgments of me and now Achille. If she was leaving, I wasn't going to be entirely sorry about it, though I suspected that with Judge Pike in the mix, things would somehow get worse.

"Apart from me battling a raging flood, what else do you see in the future?"

"Germany will try to invade France."

"The whole world knows that," I said. I didn't realize she wasn't talking about Europe.

Tutorial VII

STALEMATE & TRUCES

Retrieve your last essay. Chart the time since your tussle with that rival, co-worker, or loved one. Reference stress, melancholia, and continuing animosity as you re-examine your definitions of winning and losing.

Every day Baroness von Kempe looked more like Kaiser Wilhelm (except for his grand, upswept mustache, of course). One afternoon she caught me in the pantry with a spoonful of blackberry preserve halfway to my mouth. Ever since childhood, stress enflames my sweet tooth. The Baroness plucked up a Mason jar everyone in the house was supposed to contribute to if they snacked between meals. Obviously it was empty, but she put her monocle to it anyway, as if the clear glass might hide the penny or two I should've put in before indulging. I thought she was going to demand money; instead she announced, "I need a spell."

"No problem. I do require payment in advance."

She gave empty jar a shake. "As do I."

Touché. "Your credit's good," I offered. "Two bucks for love, three for luck, four buys a mojo that draws money."

She gave me a dead stare, asymmetrical due to her monocle. "Do I strike you as a woman who buys routine conjures?"

This could not be good. "What then?"

"Hoodoo to turn colored girls white."

The most extraordinary request I'd heard since Victorine requested the exact same thing. "You're planning to raid Maison de la Victoire, but the Jim Crow laws won't let you mix those bawds with your white ones here."

"So you're on board?"

"Absolutely not."

"Those girls would be better off here. Your little octoroon with the shapely bottom—"

"Her name is Melpa."

"Whatever you say. Melpa, so pretty. I'll let her read fortunes instead of turning tricks."

"I won't help you, Baroness."

"Then the law says house them separately. Means the carriage house. Means you sleep in the yard."

"You don't think I'd sacrifice my comfort for my principles?"

"I don't think you have principles. I can't count the promises you made me, or Ell, even your mother, that you didn't keep. One time or another, you convinced every girl upstairs, even the lesbos, that you'd be her one true fancy man, but soon as you copped twelve bits you bought a discount half-hour with one of her sisters."

"That's unfair!"

"Unfair you say with my blackberry jam smearing your lips. How about the bits of Spanish Fly you pilfered? The nine bucks you robbed from my cash box that time?"

"For a good cause!"

"Every cause can be claimed good if we're halfway clever when we lie to ourselves. You're a great liar. You think only of yourself. You're wicked and corrupt."

She was right. So was Mother. I was evil. I hadn't seen it because I'd looked for evil motives, but evil motives are as rare as black diamonds. We wicked do not set out to do bad things. No, we convince ourselves bad things are actually good. But what drew me into the Baroness' war was no epiphany, no revelation, nothing she said. I enlisted because of a single word uttered by Noël one Sunday night in early September after he'd woken me from a dreamless sleep. One word: "Come." I went. He led me through fissures in brick walls and loose fence palings, leaving me to stretch and scrunch and hurry to catch up. Somewhere behind Maison de la Victoire we came to an abandoned latrine. He swung the door and bid me in.

Disuse had left the place smelling more like cow barn than shit house. Spider webs spanned every corner. In the darkest nook huddled a figure I recognized from her sobs as Melpa. Moving slowly not to startle her, I pulled her into a shaft of moonlight and drew my own face into darkness so she couldn't see my reaction: accomplished liar I may be, but we all have limits.

I'd been beaten worse once or twice, but I doubt she ever had. She searched my face as if worried I wouldn't love her anymore. I saw my hand tremble, felt my heart race, and knew a crisp desire for revenge had just shot me through with adrenaline. Fight it, I told myself. This moment demands compassion.

Gently as I could, I took her in my arms. Told her I loved her, that we were a family, she and Noël and I. I promised to bathe her wounds and bring her broth and cool her brow. I never mentioned retribution. It remained foremost in my mind.

~

Pierce White had done it. She wasn't sure why. He'd had her first and seemed pleased with the sport. Afterward, studying her face, with no warning his fist slammed her jaw — *Crack!* — the first of many blows. Her cries brought the whole house. Half-dressed patrons broke down the door. By that point Melpa was semi-conscious. Sisters rushed to her. Victorine walked over to

Pierce, slapped his face, once, hard. "There are boundaries," she said.

I made Melpa as comfortable as I could in Baroness von Kempe's carriage house. It happened Dr. Cazenac was sampling our new inmates that night so I imposed on him — okay, threatened him — to prescribe medication. Near dawn, I closed my eyes, emotions bubbling. Noël cradled into my arms on the floor beside the carriage where Melpa fitfully slept. Three sleepless hours later I slipped from the boy's embrace, exhausted but with a plan. It was Labor Day. The holiday had been federalized the year I was born to mend fences with America's workingmen after the Pullman porters strike. It'd be working women beside me on the front line this day.

Across the Atlantic, the Battle of the Marne was in full swing. Every taxicab in Paris, 600 of them, was commandeered to carry reinforcements. Cannon would fire, men would die, and clearing smoke reveal the invincible German army in retreat, its plan to capture Paris abandoned. An omen if ever there was one.

Our battle plan was simple. I'd made an extra-large batch of Do-Not-Pass-Floor-Wash. With a four inch brush, I'd paint a blockade around Maison de la Victoire, leaving a single alley out till the end. The inmates, facing no income until enough rain fell to dilute my handiwork, were sure to take the Baroness' offer of a better situation down the street, with the promise of being freed of Negroism a substantial added benefit. Yes, I'd agreed to prepare a racial transformation charm, though I doubted it was possible. I know this sounds mad; I was mad. I wanted to strike at Victorine for letting Pierce run amok. For letting Judge Pike keep Mother as his willing captive. For thwarting my seeing Melpa when I might've protected her.

We marched out. To my surprise, an equivalent force sallied out of Maison de la Victoire. Leading them was Ell Dixon, Victorine, and still-limping Judge Pike. Mother was beside him. Pierce White had wisely stayed away. From every window on Basin Street, eyes peered. Across at the Southern Terminal, porters and pickpockets watched and waited. Thirty feet apart, both armies stopped. "Steady," intoned the Baroness.

The Judge wore one of his infuriating smiles, the kind that says I know what you're planning and have known it and prepared for it and didn't raise a sweat doing so. Then he and Mother stepped apart. Behind them was a man I hadn't seen in seven years, the most skillful hoodoo doctor I'd ever met, an authentic two-headed person. Beside him I was an amateur. An impostor. A terrified boy lost in the Quarters behind Athena.

My pail rattled in my trembling hand, for Conquering John the Doctor also held a pail.

He bolted toward me. His bucket sloshed. Shouted incantations scattered those around me. I wet myself, a little, but stood my ground. The hoodoo doctor dropped to his knees at my feet. He began painting the brick pavement. His Do-Not-Pass juice reeked like stale piss. A line became an arc that was turning into a circle — he meant to imprison me! I danced sideways out of his half-made trap. He immediately started over.

I didn't think. Couldn't think. Scooted out of his second circle. He started a third. I dropped to my knees. Dipped my brush. Began to paint, matching him stroke for stroke.

Conquering John saw the danger of being encircled himself. It distracted him. He lost his place. I caught up, inched ahead, but he was painting again, both of us frantic. I could imagine how onlookers were reacting but couldn't spare a glance.

As his fingers flew, Conquering John weighed the risk that I'd encircle him before he'd encircle me. I could smell his brew as he could surely smell mine, both powerful concoctions. Whoever let the circle close around him would be glued to this spot for days or weeks.

He blinked first. Backed out of the near-complete ring, hopped off the curb into the street, all while hardly missing a stroke on the circle he was painting around me.

I backed out too. Also hit the street. We both started new circles. It continued, each trying to flank the other, losing count of the attempts, the effect being a double squiggly line of concentrated Do-Not-Pass-Floor-Wash stretching midway across Basin Street.

Remember this was potent stuff and we each had lots of it. As the Do-Not-Pass properties permeated the cobblestones, the effect became apparent. Pedestrians froze. Horses shied. Automobiles stalled. One poor newsboy, ignoring shouted warnings, did a back flip, unable despite his considerable forward momentum to cross the double line of Do-Not-Pass.

At the far side of Basin stood the long sheds of the Southern line. Uniformed railroad men came running out, imploring us not to paint their tracks and thus disrupt the commerce of the entire Gulf South. I paused. So did Conquering John. "Smart, I guess, to leave a quick scoot out of town," he said. We rose, each on our side of the line.

In the weeks that followed the papers were full of the European war's "race to the sea" as trenches solidified the Western Front from the Aisne River to the English Channel. In the District, battle lines ossified just as immovably. Every day some arrogant local or ignorant tourist attempted to travel down Basin Street, most trying repeatedly, before surrendering to the invisible barrier and going the long way round.

It was bad for business, but I didn't mind. I gave myself to nursing Melpa and being father to Noël. Despite the Baroness carping about "the double agent Victorine tucked into my carriage house," once I made it clear that if Melpa left so would I, the Baroness contented herself deducting their board from my wages.

As Melpa healed we remained chaste, sleeping close but apart. When the season's new crop of pecans began showing up in the markets, I bought a sack. While the cook was out, I tapped the Baroness' molasses keg for a quart of heavy syrup. That evening, with the carriage house brisk with the first chill of autumn, I did my best to recreate one of my childhood sugar house visits. I played Nat, cracking pecans two nuts at a time and showing Noël how to pick their meat. Next I imitated the chemist, jiving the best Yankee accent I could as I'd "strike" the molasses warming in a jar beside the lantern. Noël and Melpa played their roles perfectly, except when we all burst into laughter. That night, Melpa and I once more became lovers, sweeter than ever because now I shared her with no other men.

It was a happy time, though Pierce White walked free. I knew that if I revenged myself on him the consequences would likely fall on Melpa.

Happy, except when across the invisible line I saw Judge Pike picking up Mother. Apart from her nurse's uniform, it seemed almost a proper courtship, as if the terrible things he'd done had never happened.

Happy, except when I remembered the Judge had installed Conquering John in the old latrine behind Maison de la Victoire as his personal, on-call hoodoo doctor.

Happy, except when Noël brought me a newspaper and said, "Read." I'd read about young men my age in Europe dying by the boxcar-load and pundits pondering when America would join the fray.

But those dreadful concerns faded to nothing when I held Melpa in my arms, until one night, when she asked, "How's the spell coming?"

"What spell?"

"The one you promised everybody, to turn coloreds white."

"Melpa, if that were possible, don't you think Conquering John would've conjured himself one by now?"

"You're smarter than him."

"What if I concoct a trick that turns me Negro?"

"You, Negro? With your sass? You'd be lynched by lunchtime."

~

October and November were dry, so what Conquering John and I did to Basin Street persisted longer than expected, but in early December, a 3" downpour washed our evil into the canals. From there the city pumped it into Lake Pontchartrain, where its lingering effects forced Antoine's to briefly take *crab meunière* off their menu.

On the European front, 1914 saw the famous "Christmas Truce." For one night the allies and their German enemies laid down arms, sang carols together, even left their trenches to exchange gifts across barbed wire. The holiday cease-fire on Basin Street was nearly as dramatic. Victorine had invitations printed to a Christmas Eve soiree for her neighbors in the District — allies, belligerents, and non-combatants alike — and the Baroness dared not deny attendance to her crowded inmates, especially around Christmas when mutiny always hung in the air.

Melpa wanted to show her friends she was okay. For Noël the soiree would be a birthday party — at midnight he'd turn eleven. I had my own reasons for going.

There's none so sentimental as a drunk whore on Christmas Eve. Fill a parlor with them and the floor lies slick with tears. I poured a glass of punch, sweet as candy to hide its spike of rum. "If that's courage you're building," said Victorine, putting her soft lips to my ear, "you won't need it. Pierce White had other plans."

"But you invited him? To an event where whites and colored mix?"

"I don't know what you mean. All my guests are white. My inmates are colored, but technically they're working. If a gentleman wants them, upstairs they go."

"Melpa will not—"

"Calm down. If necessary, we'll call Melpa a maid. Little Noël, a footman. Having black help at a white party doesn't break any prohibitions. And yes, I invited Pierce. I'd be a target for his mischief if I banned him."

"Mischief, when he beats a girl half to death?" I felt my bile rising.

"Mischief is the worst, the very worst, the police would call it, and you know that. You and I do not set the rules in this game, young man. We just wiggle around them best we can." Her hand found my back. The touch seemed more than conciliatory. "This would've been so much more interesting a party if I'd laced the tea-cakes with strychnine," Victorine said. She didn't appear to be kidding. Then I saw something that made my back stiffen. "Yes, Judge Pike is here," Victorine cooed. "You may insult him all you wish, as long as your barbs remain witty, your tone civil, and your fists unclenched."

"I'll try."

"Do it or you'll hear Ell's whistle. No joyous carol that." She gave my back one last caress and left to greet other guests. I watched the Judge chat with this person and that, no doubt saying just the right thing, but his eyes kept glancing up the staircase. Mother was making him wait. I decided to walk over and rub it in.

"Cooling your heels?"

He smiled. "Anticipation is part and parcel of Christmas Eve."

Across the room, Ell was eyeing me. I forced a smile. "How does Pierce's son fare? Spitting image of his father?" I asked, hoping to suggest my cuckoldry had been fruitful.

"Looks more like his old man every day," Judge Pike said, flaunting ambiguity. I felt like a novice fencing with a grand master.

"Dare I ask your intentions regarding my mother?"

"So you might prevent them? I don't enjoy being hexed."

"You once swore hoodoo was bunk, Judge."

"Occasionally I'm in error. Like everyone else, though perhaps less often. For instance, what I did to your flower gardener can never be justified. To say a spurned suitor suffered a monstrous temper may explain my actions but doesn't forgive them."

"You expect me to believe your repentance is sincere?" I fired back. "Or that your feelings for Mother were ever based on more than lust or envy?"

He eyeballed me a long moment. "I never know what she'll say or do, though I waste countless hours trying to predict. I rarely have a clue what she's thinking, though I spend inordinate time wondering. When I'm apart from her, it's difficult to consider anything else. When I'm with her, it's impossible. When I see her, or smell her perfume, or run across clothing she's left lying about, I feel my heart swell. That little crooked smile of hers, the way she walks across a room, and my swelling heart becomes a raging need that no levee can hold back." He took a breath and recaptured some of his composure. "A poet might call my condition love. Any competent physician would diagnose psychological obsession. Clear-eyed though I usually am, I don't dare name what I feel about her. I do admit that for a time I was too foolish to acknowledge it, then too afraid to pursue it, then too stubborn to let it take its time. Most embarrassing, too obtuse to find her, searching every banana tree in Cuba and mansion in San Francisco when actually you'd hidden her under my nose. Well, despite all that—"

"Do you love her enough to marry her?"

The question rattled him.

"Yes or no?" I pushed, though unsure which answer I wanted.

"Her husbands tend to expire prematurely."

"You're afraid of scandal," I said.

"Scandal would be distasteful, but you miss the mark. The problem's that the titans I arrange favors for must see me as predictable. If I lost my head, married a whore, even an exquisite, charming whore, they'd wonder what other silliness I might succumb to. A guilty conscience. Scruples even."

"So a mistress is all she'll be, and that only till you tire of her."

"More likely until she tires of me. Your mother's a woman of moods." He had a point. "Aren't I raising her out of the gutter as it is? Doesn't every whore dream of being a mistress?"

"I'll tell her you admitted you'll never marry her, one day toss her out like an old boot."

"Not what I said, but I suppose close enough for you to twist it that way. Of course I'll deny it, setting up a marvelous experiment. Which shall the good woman believe, my alluring lies or your unpleasant truth? Care to wager?"

I killed my father by distracting him. Killed my stepfather by bobbling confiscation of his firearm. Facing me was the fellow now sleeping in their bed. I wanted to murder him too, but this time with cold pre-mediation. I wanted it painful. Gory. I longed to snack on beignets dusted with sugar as I watched him bleed from jagged wounds. But he was correct. Mother would embrace his lies before she'd swallow my bitter truth. Hadn't I already tried to tell her? And if I killed the Judge while he seemed a shining knight, Mother would never forgive me. What I needed was for somebody else to kill him. As I said, I'd come to this party for a reason. With a plan. Time to put that plan into action.

I left the Judge as rudely as I could, waiting till he was mid-sentence. Petty, I know, but he had that effect on me. Weaving through the crowd, I sought Ell Dixon. "Happy Christmas," Ell said, dropping his voice to a confidential growl. "Ain't been baiting Judge Pike, have you? The man owns half the District. He chose your mama for his queen. If you stop picking fights with him, you could be a prince."

"I thought you and Tom Anderson were the only princes of the District."

"You could be one too," Elliot offered magnanimously. "Or be run off or beat dead, which is where you're heading. Don't seem a hard choice."

"Never does, because evil wears the most alluring robes."

He grunted. "You read too much. He's cheery, she's cheery. If he makes her happy…"

"But for how long?"

"How long? What foolishness. How long these girls get before men stop offering 'em coin? How long you and I or the Judge get 'fore some younger, stronger rooster spurs us off the fencepost? You want eternity, go be a priest. In the District, candles burn hot but they burn fast."

There was wisdom in what he said, but I hardly listened. Time had come to put my plan in place. It would take flawless execution, unwitting cooperation from several wary parties, and predictability from the human heart. Other than that I could see no barriers to its success. "Ell, I'm going upstairs to have a word with Mother. Would you come?"

He seemed tempted. "Think Victorine would prefer I stay with the festivities."

"I can tell you enjoy Mother's company."

"Christmas Eve ain't a night to get extra-curricular."

His statement suggested a clandestine amorous history that I didn't want to think about, though I hoped it laid a certain groundwork for what I was about to do. I launched in outlining to Ell a complex, elaborate, completely cockamamie scheme to halt the Baroness' war. I don't remember its flourishes, but it included bribes, brute force, and betrayals, elements a thug in an expensive suit would consider necessary. Desperate to end the Battle of Basin Street, Ell was willing to try anything. That's what I'd counted on. I nudged him toward the staircase.

Mother's role in the peace plan, I pointed out, was critical because she had a foot in both camps, but also because she was reasonable, even-tempered, intelligent, responsible, caring, sharing, loving, and every other positive adjective I could think of. Since this Christmas Truce was temporary, there was no time like the present to solidify our strategy with her.

Victorine snared us at the staircase. I remembered the old thief's admonition, "act like you belong there." "Ell asked me to help end this war between you and the Baroness. We're going upstairs to discuss with Mother the terms of an armistice."

"Am I invited?" Victorine asked.

"It'd be inappropriate," I said, oozing sincerity. "However much Ell shares with you later is his affair."

"Oh, I'm sure you're counting on all sorts of interesting pillow talk after this. Very well, play your games, my friend. Just remember, sometimes schemes go astray."

She let us by. Ell laughed as we walked upstairs. "If you do end this war, we'll ship you to Berlin, let you chat with the Kaiser." It was hard not to like this man, despite the brass knuckles in his pocket. He would make a fine stepfather.

You see, that was my design. I'd come with a powder to enhance Mother's beauty, lavender for attraction, sandalwood for magnetism, almond and bee's wings and purple petals of johnny-jump-ups. Ell would cross it, knock on Mother's door, he'd see her and fall in love. The next time the Judge approached her, King of the District or not, Ell would beat the crap out of him. Simple, right?

I was pretty sure Mother would deem her new suitor an improvement — as procurers go, Ell was a fine fellow. Younger, handsomer, more fit than the Judge. For decency's sake, I'd provide a consolation charm to Victorine, whose bed my scheme would leave empty. Unlikely she'd go mad and poison the whole neighborhood over it, right?

As we reached Mother's door, I feigned hesitation. "You go in first, Ell."

"Why's that?"

"I'd rather not run into Judge Pike."

"The Judge is downstairs."

"You never know."

"We just saw him," Ell said.

"The man's deceptive."

"Won't argue that." Ell stepped around me to knock on Mother's door. During this conversation, I'd been quietly sifting the Fall-Instantly-In-Love across the carpet. A body exhibits a slight, involuntary shudder when a spell takes hold, subtle, but recognizable to those who know what to look for. Ell ambled across my trick but exhibited no twitch. He was about to knock on Mother's door. I called him back. He crossed the spell *again.* "What?" he asked, looking me in the eye. Holy shit! Now he'd fall in love *with me*! Except he didn't. I couldn't imagine what had gone wrong.

"Good, you haven't gone in," I heard Victorine say. "Don't you know it's rude to call on a lady with your collar crooked?" Ell shuffled to where she'd crept up the carpeted stairs. As she straightened his collar, from his shirt came a red flannel charm that had been hanging hidden around his neck.

"What's that?" I blurted. But I knew. I recognized Conquering John's needlework.

"You gots to learn 'bout women, boy," Ell laughed. "Light of your life says straighten your collar, you bleat, 'Yes, mam.' She says wear a good luck charm, you drape the pouch round your stem and don't ask questions."

Victorine sprang the rest of her trap. "Come," she said. "Let me fix your collar too."

She was steps away, but between us lay a line of Fall-Instantly-In-Love.

"My collar's fine."

"A woman sees flaws a man doesn't," she countered. I didn't move.

"Damn it," laughed Ell, "come or I'll drag you."

Looking stupid, no doubt, I stood like a rock. If I crossed the invisible magic, I'd glance at Victorine and be smitten. Know it was artificial, but be unable to resist. For weeks, humiliation and longing would constitute my diet. I'd be her plaything, her poodle, thus a thorn to Elliot Dixon, who might have me tossed into the Mississippi for it.

"Guess I will drag you," Ell said with less humor than before.

Then the door across the hall swung open. Out came the heir to a local iron foundry. I'd seen him earlier, walking upstairs with Melpa's friend, Tess. Coming out of Tess' room, he exhibited all the good cheer of a fellow recently serviced by a skillful harlot.

"Excuse me," he said, stepping around me and across the invisible line. He meant to step around Victorine also, but as he gave her a polite nod their eyes met. I couldn't stand to watch.

"No, excuse *me*," I said, walking over the now-inert spell; then past the young man, frozen in his tracks; past Ell wondering what just went down; and past Victorine, already calculating the power I'd bequeathed her over this wealthy young man.

"What about your plan?" asked Ell.

"I think he's decided it won't work," said Victorine.

Mother's door opened. "That my boy? Where's he heading?"

"Who can follow the shifting moods of your son?" asked Victorine.

"Not I," answered Mother. "Each time he walks in I never know who I'll be talking to."

I found Melpa, told her I was ready to leave. "Go," she said. "Noël will see me back."

After the crowded room, the air outside was chill. I pulled my jacket around me and trotted down the steps. On the sidewalk, pedestrians were sparse; most gentlemen were home with their families, trimming trees and singing carols. It was strange to see a well-dressed woman walking, stopping, walking again, trying to peer into windows of the high-class brothels. Streetwalkers weren't tolerated in front of the parlor houses, but she didn't look like a whore anyway. As I approached I realized her black hair was a trick of the flickering gaslight. Up close, it was auburn. She heard my footsteps and turned. She was more gorgeous than ever.

"Aralee, what are you doing here?"

"Looking for my husband."

"He's not here. I heard he had other plans tonight."

My answer angered her. That extra fire took a loveliness that would already turn heads and made it intoxicating. Things I hadn't felt in a long time, thoughts I hadn't had — at least not about her — came flooding back. I'm sure that cocktail of longing and affection and lust was apparent in my gaze. "Have you no shame?" she demanded.

I wasn't sure I did but saw no percentage admitting it. "What do you mean?"

"Don't you realize how it hurts me to see my husband chasing whores?"

"It's not my doing."

She slapped me. Hard. A single discreet blow, no hysterics. It wasn't clear any anger lay behind it. Obviously Pierce's behavior was pushing her over the edge. The enchanting madwoman peered into my eyes. Waiting. I wasn't sure for what.

"I don't know what I'm supposed to say," I told her. She didn't know what to say either. "How are you?" I finally asked.

She laughed bitterly. "It's Christmas Eve. I'm trolling the red light district looking for my husband." She laughed again. Through her pain she saw the ridiculousness of the situation.

"Apart from that itty-bitty annoyance, how are you?"

"We've got a child at home," she answered, serious once more.

A child that might be mine. "Is Pierce a good father?"

That, she didn't answer. "Twenty months old. Forever making me smile, but running me ragged too. He can get up the stairs now, though coming down's harder."

"He sounds lovable."

"He is." Those two words carried an invitation, but I'd thought this through before. The child might be mine but, as awful as Pierce was, what good would it do the kiddie to have me in his life, confusing things, planting seeds of scandal by my presence?

"I've a son, too. Called Noël, because tomorrow's his birthday." Aralee blinked back tears. I decided to change the subject. "How'd you like Europe?"

Another rueful smile. "If I'd been with you instead of Pierce, it would've been wonderful."

What could I say? The woman was so desirable. I still had feelings for her, but my heart belonged to Melpa. "I should go," I said. "Gifts to wrap."

She nodded. "A Christmas kiss before we say goodbye." She didn't allow me time to think about it. I'm not sure I'd have refused if she had. Her lips were warm, full, electric. The hair on my arms stood. Desire infused me, blanking out the night's cold. If Aralee ever decided to work Basin Street what a fortune she could make. I was walking thin ice and knew I better turn back before I fell through. Easing her away took all my strength.

Aralee did not want to hit the brakes. She stepped forward again. I held her back.

"We could go to Europe," she said. "Live in Paris. You'd like that."

"Europe's at war."

"Some other place then. Buenos Aires. Montreal."

"I can't."

"Your mother? We could take her along. I have the money."

"No. No, Aralee. No."

She looked like she was going to say something else then decided against it. My hands fell from her shoulders, shoulders born for holding.

"Send Pierce back to me. I'd happily spend my life with the boy who led me through the amusement park on his birthday, and took me dancing, and taught me the mysteries of man and woman. But if I can't have him, I at least want my husband back."

A hack went by. She hailed it. I thought she'd give me a last look before climbing in, but she didn't. On the nearest stoop I sat and thought about my life, what it was and what it could've been and what it still might be. The granite was hard and the temperature falling. I picked myself up and walked home. Melpa, who'd taken the back alley route, was already brushing out her hair. "What took you so long?" she asked. As I stumbled through the start of a lie, she put a finger to my lips. "You don't remember, do you?" She thought I'd had another blackout. I let her believe it. Shifting so I could lay my head into her lap, she said, "If God lets, I'll make you whole, I swear." She began a lullaby, "*Fait dô-dô, mon p'tit bébé.*" Sleep, my little child. Wrapped in her arms, I wanted never to wake.

~

The new year saw stalemate in Europe, stalemate in the District.

On January 19th the Kaiser's Zeppelin Corps dropped bombs on Britain. The same day, walking down Customhouse Street, I was shat on by a pigeon.

On February 4th the German admiralty announced their U-boats would sink enemy shipping without warning; within hours I was torpedoed by a pepperoni being unloaded too vigorously to a grocer on Decatur.

On February 16th in France there was hard fighting in Champagne. In the French Quarter of New Orleans, there was hard drinking of champagne at the Anonymous Gentlemen of the Scarlet Venus ball, one of whose sponsors, Judge Pike, being somewhat less anonymous than in years past. Mother reigned as unofficial queen. I didn't go. Melpa couldn't have bought a ticket if she'd wished, Negro blood deemed a flaw a costume couldn't hide.

Next morning, Melpa went for ashes at the colored church, St. Augustine. I walked to the cathedral where I was greeted by the scent of myrrh. I chose to kneel in the section where Father Groetsch was performing the ritual. He stopped short when he recognized me. We hadn't seen each other since I'd stolen his poor box.

"Have you turned away from sin?" Though the standard question, he seemed particularly keen on my answer.

"Trying my best, Father."

He smudged a cross on my forehead. "Remember thou art dust and to dust thou shalt return." As he moved on I think he added, "And won't that be a happy day!" but his accent is thick so I couldn't be sure.

When I returned I found the brothel lively considering so many inmates were suffering hangovers. "Gents what came for the Mardi Gras," the Baroness explained, "Heard about our extra girls and all crave one last rock and roll before boarding their trains. Had to pull out the stops to satisfy them, even chipped in on my back myself. Hope you don't mind."

"Why should I mind?"

"No reason." But she was looking at me funny. "Can you sort the cash box?" She took my arm, prodding me toward her office.

"What's the urgency?"

"I want to buy gifts for the girls. Them hustling so hard."

I'm embarrassed it took that outlandish claim to raise my suspicions. I lost moments trying to badger the truth from her. The cook likewise kept mum. "To hell with y'all," I said, leaving to see if Melpa could shed light on what no one wanted to tell me. What happened next, I cannot justify.

~

Forrest Dunfee inherited a small agricultural equipment business in Snellville, Georgia. From there he expanded into guano, manure, and other fertilizers. Farmers appreciated his thoughtful inquiries after their families. In town they esteemed his work for the church and his helping bring to Snellville one of those new Rotary Clubs. Everyone loved how he'd joke about his business: "It's poo-poo to you, but it's my bread and butter." "My product stinks, but good things come out of it."

A spring wedding planned to a farmer's daughter, at a Rotary luncheon Dunfee was coaxed into joining a couple of other bachelors for one last fling, down to the Carnival in New Orleans. He left Georgia with a ten-dollar gold piece in his shoe and the Ten Commandments in his pocket, vowing to break neither. Alas, he wasn't the first whose good intentions pranced away in The City That Care Forgot.

All of which to say he probably didn't deserve the beating I gave him when I walked into the carriage house, heard noises from the coach, and found him parked between Melpa's thighs enjoying the service he'd spent his last dime for.

I bloodied my fists on his face. Melpa couldn't pull me off. Even Ell Dixon had a job of it after the Baroness had him fetched. Dunfee was taken to a hospital and missed his train.

"I was fucking him for us," Melpa spat, angry as I'd ever seen her. "To raise going-away money. Going away, the three of us, to some part of the country where Noël and I can pass for white so we can be a family."

Fucking him for us. I loved her so much it hurt.

Tutorial VIII

EVIL AS ABSENCE OF GOOD

Describe a moment when dire events banished your better nature. Confess your appalling thoughts and deeds while enslaved to anger and despair.

As that colonized far-shore of France across the Mediterranean is Algeria, so the part of New Orleans across the Mississippi is called Algiers. This quiet faubourg of well-kept homes seemed safely distant from the District. Melpa wanted to set up house someplace farther, but I had unfinished business separating Mother from the Judge.

I answered the ad of a boatyard which needed an accountant. Finding the position already filled, I wound up chatting with the owner, a convivial fellow who — with profuse apologies — offered me a less remunerative job as carpenter's helper. On impulse I took it.

Under a friendly crew of boatwrights — some white, some black, some in-between — I suffered good-natured ribbing until I learned the tools I was sent to fetch, the proper way to lift a heavy beam, to see tasks that needed doing before anyone asked. To fit in I'd go shirtless like the others. Soon I was darker than Melpa; by spring, nearly dark as Noël; so everyone forgot I'd been white when I arrived. I became just another of the city's legion of mixed-race Creole tradespeople, the sort Pierce called affronts to God. I'd never been happier. When the hired accountant proved unsatisfactory, I was offered his position. Without regret I turned it down.

Melpa wanted to work too. I penned a letter of recommendation from "Mrs. Elmire Bonreve Bourque, Athena Plantation." I'm sure Judge Pike forged Tante Elmire's name to weightier documents. Melpa was hired as maid by a kindly widow.

Every afternoon I'd finish at the yard, collect Noël from school, and walk home. As he played in the kitchen, I'd prepare supper. Chopping and searing done, as the stew bubbled we'd work on lessons. Footsteps on the porch would send us jumping to meet Melpa. In her gray and white uniform, she'd unwrap delicious scraps from her employer's table to compliment the rustic meal I'd cooked.

After we ate, Noël would help put away dishes and I would read to them. If there was no fresh newspaper, I'd take an old Picayune and make up stories, pretending they were real articles. How our tomcat had decided he'd challenge Mayor Behrman in the next election. How the boatyard where I worked had been commissioned to build a new S.S. Titanic, only this time of wood so it'd stay afloat. With the papers full of war in Europe and Jim Crow at home, Melpa and Noël enjoyed my invented tales better.

On Saturday, May 8th, 1915, at a chapel in Tremé, Melpa and I wed. Since white marrying colored was illegal, Father Groetsch took a risk performing the ceremony. He preached how a good wife can gentle even the worst ruffian. As whores threw rice, Melpa and I kissed, then she left to catch the ferry to prepare our Algiers love nest. I took Noël to visit Mother. She'd been invited but I wasn't surprised when she didn't come, what with her and Judge Pike now inseparable. No doubt

Conquering John was supplying the Judge with love charms.

At Maison de la Victoire, inmates gushed congratulations, but Mother was out. "Do the Judge's associates really believe she's a nurse?"

Victorine shrugged. "He explains he's helping the fallen widow of an old friend. Judge Pike excels at making people believe whatever he wants them to."

"Mother included, evidently."

"You think she's a fool in love but your mother's no fool."

"Is she in love?"

"We inhabit a world where even a white woman can't vote, isn't allowed opinions, has her morality questioned if she enjoys sex. Your mother's playing a pretty fair hand with the cards dealt her. Now go start your honeymoon. I have work to do."

In the parlor I decided to wait a bit longer but must've dozed off in the too-soft chair. Waking, realizing hours had passed but Mother hadn't returned, I gathered Noël and hurried out. Hiking toward the ferry landing, the boy found a States abandoned in the gutter. "Read," he said. The headline shouted: "Lusitania sunk by U-boat — 1300 drowned." Cold damp crept up my back, a sensation the sunny day could not explain.

~

An empty house creates its own sound, which can be soothing but may be ominous when one enters expecting laughter and bright greetings. Melpa should've been home long before us, but she was not. She could've left on an errand, but would she have gone to the grocer's in the dress in which she was married? And if not, why wasn't it hanging in her armoire?

We waited. Waited. Waited still and still she did not come home. Noël and I spoke little, afraid what fears we might voice. His eyes were a darker black than normal. Was he thinking what I was thinking? Had Melpa taken the ferry and in the excitement of her wedding day traipsed too close to the rail?

Had thugs robbed her for the coins in her pocket, gifts from Father Groetsch? Robbed her and killed her and threw her in the river?

Had some lustful stevedore, obsessed by her beauty, chased her along docks full of rotted boards and steel cleats and barriers of cordage until she tripped and fell and drowned, victim of her own fatal allure?

At half past nine I asked a neighbor to watch Noël so I could retrace Melpa's likely route from the chapel to our home. By the time I reached the landing, the public ferries had stopped running. I paid a water cab to row me across. By midnight I was a nuisance at police headquarters, asking too many questions, receiving too few answers. Finally I dozed on a hard bench next to a shackled pickpocket. Recognizing me from the District, he left my wallet alone.

~

Her corpse snagged a branch downriver. Teen-age brothers running a trotline discovered her. The police, since I'd hounded them all night, knew to find me. On a block of ice her body lay covered with a thin blanket. They'd only let me see her face but promised they were hiding no evidence, only protecting me from witnessing what crabs and catfish had done.

I picked up Noël from the neighbor. We walked home, his hand in mine. I collapsed onto the porch swing. Though I thought I had words ready, they failed me. Noël crawled into my lap, forcing me to look at him. "I know what hurts too much to tell me," he said. "I felt it in my heart before I saw it in your face." I hugged him and wept.

Later, when my sobs subsided, he remained dry-eyed. "I was the joy of her life," he explained, "and you the second joy. With the wedding, us, a family — plus her friends and that nice priest who talked funny — you made her last day her happiest. What a sweet memory for when the angels came fly her away. I'm little and haven't seen much, but I bet not many people ever get a gift as good as that." How did a child of eleven become so wise? Had I possessed Noël's wisdom, I probably wouldn't have done the things I subsequently did.

~

The investigation was brief. The tobacco-chewing detective

refused to question Pierce. When I threatened to go to the papers, he threatened to throw me in jail. When I begged, badgered, and finally wept on the shoulder of Ell Dixon, he had the detective look into it.

On the afternoon Melpa drowned, while I was downstairs at Maison de la Victoire napping and waiting for Mother, Pierce was upstairs screwing Negroes in a less public but more literal sense than his usual loud-mouthed race-baiting. Hard to miss with his eye-patch, his prolonged debauch meant it was impossible for him to have done the murder, so apologies were made and he was not interviewed further. The detective met me on the docks to say he was closing the case. To prove he wasn't heartless, he'd inscribed Melpa's death as "accidental mischance" instead of suicide so she could be buried in a proper cemetery. "But dimes'll get you dollars she jumped on her own," he said, spitting brown tobacco juice into the Mississippi. "Whores, especially coloreds, rarely flourish after leaving the Life."

He could decorate his police blotter with whatever lies he wished. My heart knew what it knew. Out there somewhere walked the beast who'd taken my wife.

I doubt the segregated cemetery had ever seen such a mixed group of mourners. Co-workers from the boatyard, their wives and children. Melpa's employer and her auction-bridge club who loved Melpa's deviled eggs. Octoroon inmates from Maison de la Victoire and the polyglot girls lodging with the Baroness. Ell Dixon, Victorine and, in wary truce, the Baroness herself. Mother showed the good grace to leave Judge Pike waiting around the corner. Walking from graveside, I found her beside me. "A terrible thing. Don't make it worse," she warned.

"How could it be worse?"

The lawn was fresh-mowed. Grass clippings clung to our shoes. Mother put a hand on my arm to make me pause. "You hurt so much you hate the whole world which includes me but I'm not offended 'cause I know exactly how that feels, so maybe along the way I should've prepared you for such hurt, which is probably what you think, or will think sooner or later and recriminate me for, but there's no way to prepare a child for hurt like that. I couldn't do it but nobody else could've either. It'll feel like having a tooth pulled if the tooth was the size of your whole body and I wish I could give you wisdom to soothe it but nobody on Earth is that wise so I'll simply say again, please, don't let it break you into littler and littler pieces, that's the worst danger, especially for you, because, let's face it, you barely hold together on a good day. Okay?"

Then she was gone.

More people came to the house than it could hold. They left more food than our ice box could fit and patted my shoulder and wept into my ear. Later I asked Noël what had been said.

"They're sorry and sad and ready to help."

"Help do what?"

He shrugged.

My blackouts returned, became frequent. Between them I pestered everyone, looking for leads. Was arrested once, punched twice. I'd show up at the docks, asking impertinent questions. Descaderos began fending me off with the evil eye.

Important people complained. Elliot Dixon exhibited more patience than he ever had, or so folks said, but I pushed too far. One night on my way to catch the boat to Algiers, his thugs cornered me. Frankly, I kind of looked forward to a good beating, but they were there just to warn me off, much to the regret of their newest recruit, Philo Leboeuf, who'd been abandoned in New Orleans by his brother, Zeph. "Let sleeping bitches lie, or else..." Philo advised, scratching his ear with the drop-forged cargo hook that had replaced his missing hand.

The ferry was near empty. As I watched the moon's reflection tear and reform in the ripples of our wake, a familiar mermaid rose up in the water. "Remember me?" she cooed. "Tante Clo, your mama's baby sister. I was the pretty one." She looked exactly the same as when I'd seen her last, breasts full, hair flowing, scales shiny gold. I suppose *sirènes* exhibit the permanence mortal women lack.

We caught up. She did most of the talking, recounting love affairs with a heartless barracuda, a porpoise who beat her with his snout, an unfaithful grouper. "What's a mermaid to do when she swims in a sea of bad choices?" She'd come upriver to escape males of any saltwater species. Half-listening, I wondered if it was possible Melpa had turned into such a nymph.

"Tante Clo, how'd you become a mermaid in the first place?"

"A terrifying ordeal! I fell into the drink. Went swirling out to sea. A shark came round."

"To eat you?"

"It's what sharks do. I had to choose, there and then, no time to think. Be devoured or change into something that could only ever be half a woman. It's a choice every girl faces when she falls into the ocean. Most let themselves be eaten."

"But you changed? Just like that?"

"I've always been clever."

"What happened with the shark?"

"He broke my heart." She disappeared underwater, but a moment later was back offering me a wiggling bluegill. When I shook my head, she ate the fish in three bites.

"I lost someone," I told her. "Here on the river. Might it be possible she became a mermaid like you?"

She flicked away the fish head. "Hard to say. This water's murky. Anything's possible, I guess." I could see that, though trying to be diplomatic, she didn't hold much hope. I was tempted to slip over the gunwale, drop into the welcoming gloom. My fate was to drown. Mother had pretty much said so. Why not pick the moment? Outwit sour destiny, cross out of life at my choosing. Noël would do all right without me. I wasn't his real father anyway. Besides, what use are fathers? They're never as dependable as we want them to be.

"Tante Clo, did my father cheat at cards?

She shrugged. "He played cards with his fishermen friends, not me."

"Did he cheat at other games?"

Cackling — this was, after all, Tante Clo — she peered left then right to make sure no one eavesdropped. "Wasn't actually cheating, but once, after I'd teased him all day, as I stood on a stool putting jars on a shelf he came up, reached under my skirt, an inch at a time, till his fingers visited places no hand but mine had ever gone."

"I don't believe you," I said.

"Hardly anything to believe. He only fiddled a moment 'cause we heard your mama coming. No harm done. No one ever knew." Tante Clo loved to talk naughty, but why make up such a story? "Don't look at me like that," she complained. "I never let him do it again. They were getting married in a week." I'd boarded this ferry thinking I couldn't feel worse. Now I did.

In the water beside my aunt arose a hundred-pound catfish with waxed whiskers. As he splayed his fins like a peacock, Tante Clo gleefully shrieked, "You again!" and dove for the bottom. The debonair cat chortled and followed her down. As the ferry reversed its engines to dock, I wondered how much of what I'd just heard and seen had really happened.

When fathomless loss fills one's breast, it offers portal to evil. Evil thoughts. Evil actions. Perhaps most common, evil *inaction.* After Melpa's death, I seldom went to work. Rarely bathed, forgot to bring home food. Friends helped but after a while only on account of the boy. They gave up on me. Weeks rolled by when I didn't speak to Mother, nor often thought of her.

July 4th, 1915, I turned twenty-one. The holiday dawned sunny, but it'd rained the night before, plumping the figs in our tree. Too heavy, they fell. Too ripe, they fermented in the heat. A flock of robins found them. Soon drunk robins staggered around the garden. I fed brioche to the boy then untied the bell from the cat's collar and turned the hunter loose. From the window we watched the slaughter, me with Noël on my lap. The carnage in the European trenches we kept reading about could hardly surpass what we witnessed that day among the inebriated songbirds. Feathers flying and flesh devoured, it dawned on me I enjoyed the spectacle.

July became August; August, September. September crowded October: what did it matter? The 29th dawned squally. September 30th we woke to a gale, rendering even more surprising a knock on the door, our first visitor in weeks. Greater surprise awaited when I saw who was there.

The purpose of her visit, explained Baroness von Kempe, was to have detailed to her a perplexing issue of accounting, but that was a lie and she didn't try hard to make me believe it. Her true motive, intimated with oblique references, concerned the mother of the boy. Noël had avoided the back yard since the great robin massacre but was content to play on the front porch with the wooden aeroplane I'd made for him. Even in the wind shadow of the house, fierce gusts made the propeller I'd carved spin like it had a motor.

"Why'd you cross the river in this weather, Baroness?" I asked when we were alone.

"I know who killed Melpa."

~

"Got to get back to my bawdy house," complained the Baroness.

"Ferries won't run in this. You're stuck anyway." I marched into the howling wind.

"Then how will you get across?" she hollered from the porch.

"Just mind the boy. There's ham in the ice box."

"Ham? Who gives an unholy fuck about ham? What if you don't come back?"

Noël's face held the same question. "I better hurry," I said, "before the weather worsens."

Rain was sheeting sideways by the time I reached the river. I lowered a lifeboat from an abandoned ferry. Moments later I was rowing through whitecaps on the Mississippi. Rain hid my beacon, St. Louis Cathedral, but gusts kept its bell tolling, guiding me toward I wasn't sure what.

Baroness von Kempe had never met Pierce; her whores were too pale for his tastes. But Madame Leni, who'd taken over Madame Pavlova's, had told her how Pierce — or at least a well-dressed, handsome young man of Pierce's complexion and build with a patch over his left eye — had visited her bagnio and chosen for his sport a lithe, pretty brunette named Becca Goldberg.

Later, leaving her room, he railed how Jews killed Christ and were infiltrating America's banks. "The crap you hear too often," the Baroness recounted, "but usually not so soon after the blowhard's been schtupped by a jewess."

Going up to investigate, Madame Leni found Becca distraught. The john had cuffed her around, but that was the least of it. What shook her was the tale he told while she fellated him, how he'd struck a blow against races mixing by eliminating an octoroon — crime enough that — who'd had the audacity to marry a white man. Drowned the bitch on her wedding day. Becca described how he relived the girl's pleas as he hammered her fingers clinging to the side of the boat; and how telling the story worked him into a frenzy until he climaxed into Becca's mouth.

I disliked Pierce since age eight. Today I would murder him, an act of evil whose accomplishment would achieve good.

~

At Lugger Landing I scurried over capsized hulls, slipping, falling, barnacles slicing me. Crossing the levee, I wove through the shuttered stalls of the French Market as awnings tore away. A loose barrel careened down Decatur Street. Cutting through Jackson Square, I drew near the cathedral just as the cupola on the adjacent Presbytière ricked off of the roof.

BOOM! The wooden dome exploded at my feet. Up high it'd seemed eternal; down close I saw it'd long needed paint. Had I been spared, or warned? I continued, past Royal Street, past Bourbon, empty, windswept. At the corner of St. Louis and Dauphine stood a grimacing black man. "Big dogs eat little dogs, always did, always gonna," hollered Conquering John.

"Out of my way."

"You ain't got strength enough for the fight you mean to pick."

Ever the seer, he knew where I was headed. "Where I lack strength I'll use guile," I said.

He laughed. In that weather it hinted madness. "'Spite the tricks you stole off me, inside, you still be itty-bitty. Think you toppling them what rule the world, always did, always gonna? You kill this boy what drowned your sweetheart — yeah, I knowed it; every black man with ears knowed it — you do him murder, then what? Slay Judge Pike, then what? You 'spect another serpent not go slither in, grab his nest? 'Nother 'risto-cat uncoiling rope to show other white 'risto-cats how tough he be on nigras?"

Everything he said was true. I wasn't strong enough. I possessed insufficient guile. If I did somehow win, the victory would be hollow. So be it. I moved to step around him. Saw his hand snake into the tote sack slung across his shoulder. Saw it come out clenched, powder sifting through his fingers. Smelled the familiar scent of cemetery dust.

I caught his hand. We grappled. Thunder peeled as lightning struck close. The flash blinded me, but when the brilliance dimmed it was replaced by a vision. Whether on account of Mother's blood in my veins or Thor's bolt landing nearby, for that one moment I had the sort of look-ahead Mother describes. I hope I never suffer another.

With the hurricane swirling around us, I saw the future. His future. Jeering men and boys piercing his body with pot shots from small caliber guns. Someone hauling up a can of coal oil to douse him. Conquering John the Doctor burning alive to appease the angry white mob.

I saw his future and knew he'd seen it too, long ago, that it'd hung like a weight above his every day and made him who he was. Why acknowledge a child he'd never see grow up? Why feel compassion for Nat who'd at least receive a proper hanging on a sturdy gallows?

What passed between us made us intimate as lovers, but as often with lovers, afterward there was little to say. "May God be with you, Conquering John."

"With me?" He smiled.

I noticed his open fist. Hex dust sprinkled over me. I felt it take hold, yet sensed no urge to wander. No sudden amour. No repulsion nor attraction nor surge of luck good or bad. In what manner had Conquering John crossed me? I had no idea but suspected I'd soon find out.

~

"Why bake pastries during a hurricane?"

"Why roam around in one?"

"I came to kill you."

That got Victorine's attention. She closed the door of her shiny Wedgewood oven. I'd found her alone in her brothel's kitchen, a room she did not frequent. Though surprised by my threat, she didn't appear fearful. "At least eat a slice of custard tart before you do me in."

"Don't you want to know why I came to kill you?" I asked.

"I assumed you'd explain. You're often rash but rarely impolite."

The wind howled. The building shook. "I know you lied to protect Pierce. Said he was here the day he murdered Melpa. Well, today evil loses. I'm going to kill Pierce and kill the people who sheltered him. Judge Pike. You."

"Quite the housecleaning." She stirred the viscous yellow liquid bubbling in a sauce pan. "Except I didn't lie. Pierce was here. For all his faults, he didn't kill your wife."

"Bull! You're trying to save yourself."

"I certainly am not." She sniffed her custard. "Hope I didn't put too much vanilla."

"If not Pierce, who? Who else with that much hatred wears a patch over his left eye?"

"A manure salesman, believe it or not. Dunwitty, Dunbar, a name like that." Something rang a bell but I couldn't place it. "Visiting for Carnival, he'd been beaten so badly he lost an eye and for some reason blamed Melpa for it." Breath stopped coming into my chest. The day in the carriage barn, my bloody fists. "Returned to Georgia, this Dun-what's-his-name. Quit the Rotary Club and helped re-start that Klu Klux Klan. Then came back for revenge."

To believe her would mean Melpa's death was my fault. Why was Victorine so serene? Like a housewife with flour dusting her brow. Ignoring the storm outside. "He visited again. Recently," she continued. "My doorman wouldn't let him in, but I heard he battered an inmate at Madame Leni's." She offered a spoonful of custard. "Can you taste this and—"

I knocked the spoon from her hand. It clattered to the floor. My fists clenched. "You said *nothing*? When you knew he'd killed Melpa?"

"Melpa was the name *you* gave that girl. She called herself Tallulah before that." That caught me off-guard, as Victorine knew it would. She retrieved her spoon and wiped up the yellow smear it left on the tile. "She was Creole well enough but came from Opelousas. Had never heard of Athena before you dropped around. Never been to Bayou Lafourche." In the toasty kitchen, Victorine's smile was like ice. "A pretty octoroon with a chipped tooth offered herself and you saw what you wanted."

"But Mother—"

"Your mother *let* you see what you wanted to see. What you needed to see."

"But if it wasn't Melpa…? Why would she…?"

"You promised to turn her white, for God's sake. Why wouldn't she hitch onto you? Even if it meant putting up with the rest of it."

There was more? "What do you mean, 'the rest'?"

"I thought you were off to kill Pierce," she said. "He deserves it. If he didn't murder Melpa or Tallulah or whatever her name was, even so, he and his kind have made this city, this whole region, no longer fit to live in for people like me. So kill him. Go ahead. You killing Pierce, that would be a thing to see."

I felt gut shot. Had Melpa really been some stranger who smooth-talked her way into my heart like Mother and I had once smooth-talked our way into an Irish funeral? I could hear the storm growing stronger outside but wondered if it was really just in my head, effects of Conquering John's spell. I'd seen him hex people with Confusion-And-Discord. If this was that, he'd conjured a heck of a potent trick today.

Victorine found a mitt, opened her oven, and slid out two golden crusts. "Never told you why I was baking. A going-away party."

"Is Ell coming? I need to talk to him about Dunfee."

"No, I threw Ell out."

They'd been a couple since I'd known them. I didn't know how many more surprises I could take. Victorine spooned custard into the pie shells. "The District needs Ell, but I'm done with men." She paused with ladle mid-air. "Unless *you'd* be my fancy man. You're damaged goods, but show me a fellow who isn't. And if you're half the lover your father was—" She smiled at my expression. "No? Too bad. Your father was a dazzling lover. That's why I always had hopes for you."

After all she'd thrown at me since I barged in, I don't know why this unsettled me the most. "You and my father never..."

"Oh, darling, we did, many, many times. He was insatiable. Whenever I caught scent of him, I admit it, so was I. We joked that each thrust of his great big cock was a penny of interest on the money I lent him. After he paid off his loan — by both methods of accounting — and announced his engagement, well, the trysts became more seldom, but they never stopped."

"I don't believe you."

"Even the morning of his wedding. Those laughing eyes, that face I could never turn away from. 'Pretty Miss Vic, help me out. Cure my marrying day jitters with a quick screw.'"

"You're lying!"

"Lifting me like I weighed nothing, setting me onto my butcher block, pushing into me on the table where in an hour I'd be rolling dough for custard tarts for his wedding party.

Tarts like these." She nodded at her just-baked pies. "*Almost* like these. Today I changed the recipe a little." Victorine began tidying her counter, returning to the cabinet a sack of flour, a cake of yeast, a red pasteboard box.

If Victorine (or Mother, for that matter) was condemned to go through life searching for another Achille Cheramie, she'd not find him in me. If she sought instead an idealized Achille, with charm and vigor magnified but less his farts and faults and casual betrayals, she'd find him in no living man. Painful to wish for what we cannot have, foolish to want what cannot be. Yet who among us is not often foolish?

"Did Mother know?"

Victorine shrugged. "Ask her."

Tutorial IX

WICKEDNESS DIVIDED

Describe the harshest truth you ever faced.

Back-o'town was flooding. Dogs, cats, snakes, rats, each in foulest temper, battled for flotsam. In even worse humor than them, I was on my way to murder Pierce for a crime I now knew he hadn't committed, and then, with my bare hands, to crush the Judge's throat to save Mother from a fate she chose with eyes wide open. Churning rage is rarely rational.

Skirting the encroaching shore, I found myself near St. Louis N°·1 and had the notion to use Touloulou's cottage door to raft across flooded Tremé. Though I knew the cemetery well, I became lost in its maze. The farther I went, the deeper the opaque brown water became, until I happened upon, despite the flood, despite the weather, a funeral in progress. A lackluster affair, it boasted neither altar boys nor mourners, unless you count squirming Touloulou waiting to bolt closed the tomb. The Fearless Funeral Friar's incense dust-deviled up past where Patrolmen Benton hovered atop the crypt. "What are y'all doing here?" I hollered.

Neither Groetsch nor Touloulou answered, but Benton pointed a crooked finger at me. "Here 'count of you. Thanks to your shenanigans, I got transferred, got shivved, got deaded." Another soul on my conscience. Guilt and floodwater gurgled up my thighs. This wouldn't make it easy to unhinge Touloulou's door, and who knew where the rise would stop? Certainly not Touloulou, who abruptly cast aside his wrench and scaled the tomb to perch beside the ghost he couldn't see. Abandoned Father Groetsch, censor in one hand, oversized crucifix in the other, had the devil of a time keeping the casket from floating away. I seized the opportunity.

With a corpse for ballast, the coffin proved reasonably seaworthy but, lying on my belly atop it, paddling with my hands didn't propel me fast enough. Groetsch swung the crucifix like a batter swatting a knuckle-ball. The left arm of Christ embedded in the coffin top, just missing my testacles. As Father tried to pry it free, I put a foot on his chest and shoved. He fell into the flood then came up spitting and shouting in German words priests aren't supposed to say. I worked loose his crucifix and started paddling with it.

"You are beyond redemption!" Groetsch yelled. He hoisted himself up beside Benton and Touloulou, who was busy negotiating with the Blessed Virgin. The cursing priest, the dead policeman, and the tomb-keeper I owed money to disappeared behind the curtain of rain.

The sea voyage to the Garden District encompassed many adventures. One in particular demands note. On the corner of Dryades and Terpsicore, a large rat swam toward me. At first I paid no mind, but the creature seemed determined to climb onto the coffin and was in fact not a rat but a rabbit.

Perhaps the entire genus *Sylvilagus* had it out for Papa and this specimen meant to eradicate Achille Cheramie's last remaining seed. Perhaps God in Heaven, who'd long ago sent a rabbit to smite a certain fisherman for philandering, had decided that the apple had indeed fallen too close to the tree. Poised with cross raised to bash the creature, I had second thoughts. What if Touloulou wasn't so far off, that one could indeed bargain down the wages of sin? Could I slay Pierce and kill the Judge, yet lighten my sentence by saving this innocent critter? I helped the shivering bunny aboard.

~

When I looked for Pierce at the Felicity Street palace that Aralee's money had bought, the house stood waterlogged and empty. Three blocks farther, floodwater already claimed the first floor of Judge Pike's Jackson Avenue residence, but from its upstairs balcony, as if awaiting me, the Judge braved sheeting rain to watch me paddle the coffin toward him. "Come into the house," I heard him call. "Come take shelter."

Steering into the calmer wind shadow of the columned mansion, I looped my arm around a crepe myrtle. "Where's Mother?"

"What do you want with her?"

What *did* I want? I couldn't entirely remember, but it'd taken great effort to get here so I must've come for something. Whatever Conquering John hexed me with had made me dopey. "To protect her," I hollered over the wind.

"That's what you always say before you worsen her pain."

Was that true? I scratched the rabbit's ears. "I'm also here to kill Pierce White."

"That would be something to see," shouted the Judge.

Why did people keep saying that? Was any murder worthy of watching, or was this one special? Or were Victorine, and now the Judge, implying I didn't have the nerve to go through with it?

Think of times you casually uttered, "I could kill (whomever)." No go back — be honest — did you ever take those dark thoughts further and plan that fantasy murder, step by step, detail by detail, as if you'd actually do it, which, being a decent person, you didn't?

Regarding the murder of Pierce White, I'd imagined it in general terms, contemplated it as a series of concrete steps, fantasized its gory enactment. I'd threatened it aloud numerous times, as recently as a moment before. The reason I never did it and probably wasn't going to now was not from sympathy for

Pierce nor fear of the legal consequences. No, the reason I hadn't murdered that blot on humanity was because I couldn't bear the thought that I would then, *ipso facto*, be a murderer. Not an accidental murderer, which I already was several times over; instead a cold, pre-meditated, dark-hearted murderer, confirmed as evil, castable as picture show villain. I refused to see myself that way, so Pierce breathed.

But during those murderous fantasies and moral qualms and Hamlet-esque indecision, what I never considered but should've was that Pierce White — less philosophically constrained — might be equally considering, equally plotting, equally anxious *to murder me.* Thus, what I saw next I should've seen coming for some time.

Pierce wielded a knife as large as a cutlass. With his eye-patch, it gave him the mien of a clever pirate who'd somehow boarded my vessel unobserved. That two grown men, a rabbit, and a corpse might be enough to sink the coffin was my first thought, but it shouldn't have been because it distracted me. His shiny blade cut through the rain and just missed my nose.

We grappled. The rabbit squirmed out from between us and, I think, fell overboard. My fingers closed around Pierce's wrists, trying to force him to drop the knife. Its freshly honed edge flashed sharp as a razor. Phantom pains toured my gut, looking for a place to make their home if the blade came sliding in.

Inches away loomed a face that, apart from the eye-patch, wasn't unlike my own. Haunted by rage. Desperate for love. Hungry for sensation to ease the hurt, the guilt, the heavy burden of blame that forever seeks an outside object. Was I deserving to live while he was not? Didn't he, like me, possess an overactive brain inside his head, an overeager dick between his legs? Yet, if I could take his knife away, I would kill him. Whether it made me murderer or not, I didn't care anymore. It was him or me. Moral philosophy only takes you so far.

The knife fell, clattering on the coffin top, sliding into the flood. The battle went hand to hand. A punch flew. My teeth rattled. Before I could raise my fists Pierce hit me again. My blood tasted saltier than the brackish water around us. Conquering John: what had I promised him? To fight with guile. Pierce jabbed with his left but this time I dodged. Before he could come back with his right, I grabbed the sodden crucifix and poked him in his good eye with Jesus' thorny crown. He roared. I whacked his lying mouth. He cried out again, a delightful sound. Still he swung at me, but his un-aimed blows were easy to escape. I repeatedly batted him with the wooded cross, backing him into a branch of wind-shredded myrtle.

Pow! Pierce landed a blind, lucky punch. My body flew back, capsizing the coffin. I swallowed gallons of water. Realized I'd lost the crucifix: stripped of weapon, forsaken by Jesus. I fought toward the surface. A barrier stopped me. I felt for what held me down: Pierce's hands around my throat. They started to squeeze. I struggled, but even blind, he was stronger.

If he killed me, Conquering John would say "I told you so," but I'd not be there to hear it. The Judge would gloat. Mother would mourn. But what good had my life ever done Mother? Wasn't she at this moment in the clutches of the most dangerous man I knew? Well, most dangerous next to Pierce, with his fingers squeezing my larynx. Darkness crept in from the corners of my vision. The need to breathe grew acute.

What good had my life done anyone? What good to my three fathers? Achille Cheramie with so much brawn yet evidently a scalding weakness of the flesh. Louis Bonreve with riches and attainments, tied in knots by whom he'd been taught he ought to be. Nat Toussaint: meek, gentle, generous, who died for those three sins. All I'd been to them was Charon, ferryman on the River Styx, escorting each to the afterworld. I felt light-headed. My thoughts jumbled. As my body grew ever more desperate for oxygen, a piece of flying debris hit Pierce in the face and stuck. He let me go so he could pry it off. I exploded out of the water, sucked in a double-lungful of air.

I saw what had attached itself to Pierce's face. Not debris. The rabbit. Pierce fought to tear the creature off, but the bunny hung on like a convict to a pardon. I grabbed hold of the crepe myrtle, caught my breath, watched the murder happen. A passing rabbit was smothering Pierce, not I. Thus the complex equation of guilt and innocence hops back into balance.

Pierce went limp, pirouetting on the whitecaps as if again overcooked with Make-Me-A-Great-Dancer powder, but his dancing days were over. As I wondered whether it'd be safe to take such a homicidal bunny home as a pet, I realized the creature had let go. Saved me and disappeared. I resolved that if I survived this awful day I'd never again order *lapin à la cocotte* off any menu.

"Pierce," I heard the Judge shout. "Come into the house, Pierce."

What was this? Hadn't he seen the rabbit murder Pierce? Didn't he see Pierce's corpse bobbing on— Wait. I didn't see Pierce's body either. Must've sunk.

"Swim toward the house, Pierce!" the Judge called. "What are you waiting for?"

Was he blind? Or gone mad? Mad from grief over his protégé's death or imbalanced from the drop in barometer that accompanies a hurricane or crazed for the loss of Mother who finally left him to go… Where was Mother, anyway?

"Come, Pierce. Come take shelter." This time the words stopped my heart because they didn't come from Pike. Mother fought the wind to cross the balcony. "Pierce!" Who was she talking to? The only fool in the flood was me. "Swim, Pierce," she said, looking right at me.

Damn Conquering John! He must've dusted me with Make-Everyone-Around-You-Crazy. "I'm not Pierce," I cried. "Pierce is dead!"

My words prompted a huddled conference, words I couldn't hear. Hugging a column, his other arm around Mother, the Judge barked, "No time for foolishness, Pierce."

"Why are you calling me Pierce?"

"Because it's your name. Now come into this house or I'll find a new clerk."

"My name's not Pierce!"

"Then what is it?"

My mouth flew open, but I had no reply. Couldn't for the life of me remember my name. All that came was "Pierce White." "Pierce Bonreve." "Pierce Cheramie." Had Conquering John actually dosed me with Let-The-Blind-Man-See-His-Shadow?

"How could I be Pierce? I've had countless conversations *with* Pierce."

"We all have conversations in our heads," shouted the Judge. "*Most of us* realize when we're doing it."

"If I'm Pierce, why'd it take you so long to find Mother?"

"My clerk — days he showed up — always claimed his Mother was dead."

My eighteenth birthday at Spanish Fort, as we listened to now-only-God-knows-who rant from the soapbox, the Judge *did* seem surprised to find out Mother lived. But if I was Pierce, who was me? The other guy?

Or was there another guy?

As kids, Aralee had said I seemed like two people in the same body. Well?

After the Flood of '03, Pierce and I had shared a bed, but thinking back, wasn't that cot barely big enough for one?

Was I Pierce and Pierce me, one of us good, the other evil? My God, what if *he* was the good one? That's how the city's finest would judge it, him preserving the white race while I screwed my way through the red light district. Had I penned those hate-filled letters to the Picayune? But I never hated Negroes. Some of my best friends…

Nat. Judge Pike twisted *my* testimony to condemn Nat. How hard had he needed to twist?

Melpa. I'd loved Melpa with my entire soul — even if Victorine spoke truth and Melpa wasn't really Melpa. But when she'd been beaten and I found her in the old latrine, she at first seemed afraid of my touch. Might she have let me care for her if it'd been me who assaulted her?

Of course she might. Women forgiving men who brutalized

them was a sad old story and not just among prostitutes. The way Noël distracted me with things to read, was it so I'd behave and not hurt his mother again? "There are boundaries," Victorine told Pierce, but I no longer had any clue where those boundaries lay. Bad enough to be a monster. Had I been *two* monsters?

"Who am I?" I cried out.

"You are my son," Mother answered, spreading her arms to invite me into them, invite me in with whatever flaws whichever one of me who showed up might possess. Even in this weather, in her open palms I could see her stigmata, stigmata like Jesus, who reputedly devoted his greatest efforts to sheep as lost as me.

"Where do I live?"

"Felicity Street."

Aralee's house. Where Pierce lived. No. No, no, no, no, no. "I live in a brothel!"

"You might as well live in a brothel," the Judge shot back, "for all the time you spend in them." Then his tone changed. "Sorry, dear. I'd not meant for you to hear that." He spoke to a woman in the doorway behind him, a lovely lass with fire-red hair and a two-year-old in her arms. The Judge turned back toward me. "Pierce, don't you see you're upsetting your wife?"

Aralee, my wife? I married a gorgeous heiress, heckuva dancer and tigress in bed, and *forgot*? Christmas Eve, what had Aralee said? "Don't you realize how it hurts to see my husband chasing whores?" Why would she tell me, not Pierce? Unless I was Pierce? The coma after my eighteenth birthday: had I in fact been away on honeymoon? Hell, I'd sure hate to have missed that!

Her letter: a desperate plea for the return of the more pleasing side of her husband-to-be? She'd married the Judge's promising law clerk to appease her parents, but loved his wilder mirror image. "It's not too late for us," Aralee called from the balcony. "I can make you better. Or if you prefer to keep having conversations and even fistfights with yourself, that's fine too.

But come into the house. A boy needs a father."

Undoubtedly the best offer I'd had for some time. The problem was that while I'd known I was wicked, to admit I was Pierce would mean I was also a vicious racist, a heartless philanderer, a woman-batterer, and not incidentally, entirely delusional. I'd hated what Pierce was, abhorred what he believed. If those horrors actually existed inside me, if his hate had come out of *my* mouth, if it was I who bruised Aralee's faith and Melpa's jaw, then, well, drowning in a hurricane might not be a bad alternative.

Suddenly the myrtle tossed me loose. It took a moment to realize what happened. The tree sprang up because wind no longer pushed it down. The warmth I felt was the sun. I basked in the eye of the storm. Though the air wafted balmy, I'd heard enough stories to know tranquility wouldn't last. The second half of the cyclone was coming. Whatever I had to do to face it, I had to do now. If I thought I could go on living with what I'd learned about myself, then I had to make some big decisions quickly.

Forty feet away stood the Judge's mansion. That opulent house would survive the tempest. Even if I wasn't Pierce, I did sort of look like him. I could swim in and climb the stairs to the dry second floor. There I'd find fashionable clothes that fit and a beauty who could be my more-or-less lawful wife and a gurgling baby boy whom none would dispute was my son. The Gueydans would go along; they'd want neither the scandal of calling me impostor nor to buck the Judge by saying he'd engineered a switch, especially if Aralee was on board which apparently she was. At worst we'd have to skip town awhile. Aralee had said Paris was nice.

When we came back, I could visit Mother every day, share meals, exchange advice. Christmas Eve, the Judge had said he wouldn't marry her but that was when she was the other fellow's mother, not Pierce's, not Aralee's mother-in-law, Aralee with her fat bank accounts. The Judge had no doubt figured this out, another of his bold, byzantine schemes. He was a monster, sure, but no worse than me it turned out, and clever and witty and interesting to talk to. Generous, at least with other people's money. It'd not be a bad life.

Except for one thing.

Somewhere in this flood floated the corpse of Pierce Douglas White. A carcass, a cadaver, separate from me. Maybe it would never be found, but it had to be out there. Whatever crimes I committed, his were worse. I refused to be responsible for them. Perhaps at some time in some mysterious manner my two selves cleaved apart. Well, if you sell your house, is it your fault if it subsequently becomes scene of a crime? If you give away your automobile, can you be blamed if later it runs over someone's dog? *If* Pierce was once part of me, the operative word is *was*. I vomited him out as a fever-stricken child. I cheered his murder-by-hare. I could be the rich, respected, woman-beating bigot, or the penniless, perhaps delusional sinner whose heart beat gray but at least not black. The choice was mine. I made it.

Rise up horsemen and footmen and creatures of this sea that floodeth Sodom,
Witnesseth I taketh not reward off the innocent nor my brother's wife.

Aralee might have the power to convince herself that the man she wanted was the one she married, but it hadn't played out that way. If we were to have a future we'd have to give it time and start from scratch.

Relieveth, oh, Lord, the fatherless and openeth the eyes of the blind.
Let mine enemy say, I have prevailed against him!

The Judge might have the power to change my name and thus my destiny, to pull strings and shuffle papers so everyone would believe it, or at least go along. Everyone except me.

Cast me out of my mother's womb that my soul knoweth so well.

Pierce is dead. I am me. If I survive this flood I shall be cleansed by it.

Mother might have the power to pretend she and I were who we were not, the way we pretended to be long-lost relatives of a newly dead Hibernian when we first arrived in this fragile metropolis. Stakes were higher now: not a free meal at an Irish wake but a Garden District mansion, servants, silk. Mother could pretend. I would not. Even in the eye of the storm, good and evil represent a choice.

I owned the power to make that choice, to reject any future the Judge ordained or Mother foresaw or anyone carved but me. I had the puissance to uncross myself, to reject the bad fucking hoodoo that Conquering John conjured to twist me into a monster named Pierce Douglas White, who might or might not have occasionally occupied my body, Hyde to my Jekyll. Well, whether he'd ever lived or not, now Pierce was dead. Who conquers today, Conquering John? Who won this case, Judge Pike?

I aimed a finger at the Judge. "I'm not his clerk. Nor, tempting though it is, that young woman's husband. Father of her child, well, another story, hard to be certain. One thing sure though is that I'm your son, Mother. Your wicked, wicked son but I can do better. Your son, not Pierce, and even a conjurer as powerful as Conquering John, with all the other-people's funds Judge Pike no doubt placed at his disposal, cannot make me into Pierce. I've taken him off like a corset. Finally I'm free. Lumpy and imperfect, but free."

The two-year-old started to cry. Before she took the boy inside Aralee met my gaze and mouthed the words, "I always liked you better." I almost told her I loved her but figured that should wait.

"Perhaps we should go inside as well," the Judge said to Mother. "Your boy's been in water too long. His brain's sodden beyond repair."

"He's my son."

"Who since childhood has been cracked like a pecan, and

now the two hemispheres of nut have finally split completely apart."

He may have had a point, but Mother wasn't willing to abandon me, so Judge Pike upped the ante. He took a jeweler's box from his pocket. "I was going to surprise you later, but… Darling, will you let me bathe you in luxury and love?" He dropped to one knee. I could see the gold ring gleam. So the cad was a closet romantic, willing to marry her after all.

Mother seemed afraid to touch the ring. "I've been a wife, a mother, a whore. What does a wedding band matter? Any fool can drill one out of a five-dollar coin. Five dollars, the price of a no-frills screw on Basin Street."

"This ring cost *considerably* more than five dollars," said Judge Pike, still on his knees. For all his pretense, he was smitten as ever, as primed to ride the zephyr of her affection or burn at the stake of her whim. He grabbed her hand to force the ring onto her finger. It wouldn't go. "I know it fits," he said. "I measured while you slept."

"Too tight," Mother said. "It'll always be too tight."

"I'll buy a larger one, a bigger house, a grander automobile. A church wedding, honeymoon to Europe. You always wanted to see Europe."

Mother shook her head. The Judge rose. "All right, we'll take your boy along. All three of us, to Vienna, with its museums and *sachertorte* and legendary doctors."

That gave Mother pause. "You mean it?"

"If it's what you wish, dear, of course. We'll have him psychoanalyzed by Dr. Freud." *That's* why Mother had always wanted us to visit Vienna? "And then," continued the Judge, "we'll find an excellent sanitarium to see to his long-term care."

Whoa! I might no longer claim full sanity, but I wasn't willing to be put away. Nor it seemed was Mother willing to put me away, bless her heart. "If I stay with you, marry you," she said to the Judge, "I'm not sure I could make you happy."

"You could," he said. "Of course, you could."

"But if I leave, I know it'll cause you suffering."

"It would!"

She touched his cheek with something resembling tenderness. "As regards that suffering..." Her tone changed. "August, don't ever stop."

Mother was standing on the balcony rail before the Judge could react. I suspect she meant to simply dive in and swim over, but at that moment the hurricane eye-wall arrived. The wind caught Mother, ballooning her skirts, carrying her to me like a heaven-sent angel, or perhaps like an osprey snatching a bass — with Mother, it's sometimes difficult to tell.

"Come back," hollered the Judge. "That wicked son of yours isn't worth it."

Rather than shout above the wind, Mother answered him with a gesture. It was the first time I ever saw her give anyone the finger. She used her whole arm to do it.

"I can't believe you dove in for me," I said. "Into this horrendous storm!"

She glanced around. "I've seen worse."

Tide swept us away from the Judge's mansion. Terrible sights assaulted our gaze. A dog or perhaps man-dog swimming pell-mell after a chicken. A pie pan bouncing over the waves holding a custard tart with one slice missing. Twisted around a thorn tree, a scarf Mother believed was Calypso's but that I knew belonged to Melpa.

Near the corner of Calliope and Prieur, where a half-submerged row of boxcars on the Illinois Central track offered shelter from the wind, a rowing skiff appeared. Pulling the oars was Elliot Dixon, renowned bag man and procurer, who'd rescued Mother and me, not from the sea but from sailors, upon our arrival in the city eight years earlier. "Victorine said you'd headed this way," he hollered, reminding me that, romantically speaking, this Prince of the District was newly unattached. He pulled Mother aboard as I hung on his gunwale.

Once he made her as comfortable as circumstances allowed, he crawled over to me. Hat gone, his hair whipped crazily. I didn't take his offered arm. "Ell, is my name Pierce?"

Probably not a question he expected in that weather. He eyed me a moment, turned to Mother. She nodded. Ell leaned close. "Sometimes you have me call you Pierce."

What I was afraid of.

"Then sometimes you ask me to call you Noël."

Hunh?

"Hell, sometimes you put on a dress and want me to call you Calypso."

What?

He wrung out his big mustache. "S'okay. In the District we try to live and let live."

"How many of me are there?"

"Tough to say with so many yous coming and going. The betting pool favors nine."

Betting pool? Everybody knew about this but me? Ell had to be kidding. He didn't appear to be, but it was hard to tell with hundred-knot gusts contorting his features.

I looked at Mother. Maybe blame the prism of horizontal rainfall, but I saw myself reflected nine times. Had I split into several selves and Mother played along, helping chop the world into bite-sized pieces for her son who couldn't swallow it as one big chunk? But why had everyone else put up with it? Well, why wouldn't they? Harlots were in the business of letting men pretend to be whomever they wanted. The Baroness would tolerate almost anything to keep the lowest-paid bookkeeper on Basin Street. Ell wouldn't object unless the skim stop flowing although, looking back, maybe my house arrest had something to do with my condition.

"Climb into the boat," Mother shouted. All those years I struggled to take care of her, she'd actually been taking care of me, carrying an unimaginable burden, greater than any mother should and never complaining. Well, hardly ever complaining.

"Into the boat," she hollered louder.

"No," I said. Through the rain I could tell she was trying to figure out to whom she spoke. I turned to Ell. "Fine woman, isn't she?"

"None finer," he agreed.

And twenty-one years of hell I'd put her through. "Ell, you've got money socked away. Why not hop off the fencepost before some young rooster pushes you? Enjoy your ill-gotten gains. Take Mother to Europe."

In such wind I don't know how much of that he actually heard but evidently the gist because he gazed for a long moment at Mother, looked back at me, and nodded.

"A grand tour. Show her everything. Except the war zones of course."

He smiled. "She'll have herself a time. We both will. I promise."

"Climb into the boat, Pierce," Mother said, but I shook my head.

"Climb into the boat, *Noël.*" Well, if I'd reshaped a completely different woman into Melpa, why couldn't my imagination create her a child? The son of Nat I'd sworn to protect. No wonder everyone reacted strangely when I bought a child-sized bicycle.

"Climb into the boat, *Calypso,*" Mother tested. Had it been me in those frilly dresses giggling with Mother at mealtimes? Having late-night rows the Baroness had to quell? I'm sure Mother never let me into her bed, but if I stumbled upon her with some brutish customer, maybe I created Calypso to explain what I'd seen, and Mother went along because she loved me. Besides, she genuinely enjoyed Calypso's company, probably more than mine.

Mother tried again: "Climb into the boat, *Philo.*"

My God! "Mama, stop it. I can't be Philo. Philo's a real person."

"—who drowned in the Hurricane of '09," she hollered.

"Who told you that?"

"You did. One of you."

I imagined a cargo hook in place of my left hand. If I squinted, I could almost see it. Squinted like I was wearing an eye-patch. "I can't get in the boat with you, Mother. Three's a crowd and as many as I am would definitely be catastrophe. There comes a point in the lives of every parent and child when the child is no longer helpless and the parent not yet feeble, a confusing stage, but people muddle through it every day. We will too. It's time we travel separate paths awhile."

She knew it was true. I saw it in her face. "Yesterday you were a baby in my arms," she said.

"Yesterday's flown away. Yesterdays always do." I felt with my feet until I had footing I could stand on. "I've found bottom," I said. "Wherever I go from here, no matter how far away you are, your love will always protect me." She nodded, knowing she could leave now, because I finally saw the world clearly. A bit fractured but clearly.

"Promise you'll be careful," she hollered.

"Push off, Ell," I said. "You two have places to go."

Ell put his paw on my forehead and used it to shove off his boat. Oars bit whitecaps. Mother waved goodbye. Maybe it was weather-born illusion, but I swear her stigmata had vanished. She and Ell disappeared into the rain. I felt… exhilaration. Yes, exhilaration. If I'd never fill the shoes of Achille Cheramie, at least I had a closetful of my own to choose from.

We are every one of us evil and corrupt, just as we're every one good and generous, each in our measure, each to the vagaries of every different day and situation. I could love a black woman yet harbor racism in my heart. My occasional surrenders to violence shamed me, but I knew I was capable of gentleness too. I was greedy and giving, hard-hearted and compassionate, wise and foolish. Just like you. If I split those aspects of myself into separate compartments, well, I'm sure I had a reason. We can no more entirely eradicate the wickedness within ourselves than we can cease breathing. No more unfailingly maintain goodness than we can stop time. There's no shame in failing to achieve saintliness. The shame's in failing to try.

Awash in these contemplations, suddenly I realized I was also simply awash. Floating free. Had lost my foothold and could no longer touch bottom. Maybe I'd been a tad too philosophical.

I searched for the rowboat but Mother and Ell were gone. Exhausted from the day's events, I knew I couldn't tread water long. If I didn't find something to climb upon, I would drown. I didn't want to die. None of my constituent personae wanted to die. We were all so looking forward to getting to know one another.

"Blessed Virgin," I prayed, "if you deliver me (or rather, us) from the flood I will repent my wickedness." Swirling tide carried me over the New Basin Canal; it might've been the open Atlantic with its choppy waves and bottomless depth. "And that's just for a start, Holy Mother. I'll help other people repent too, give them guidance, save their souls."

Choking, sputtering, I was pelted by debris but none that provided flotation.

"I'll put it in a book! I'll call it, Advice from the Wicked!"

No response. The Mother of God was apparently unimpressed by my literary aspirations.

"All right, two books. Save double the souls."

Still nothing. I began sliding under the waves.

"Three books then. Three, sold as a package, all for one low price!"

As water invaded my lungs, speech became impossible. I felt a flash of panic, but it passed as quickly as it came. Calm descended upon me. The road has to end somewhere. Twenty-one years was not so short a lifetime and evidently I'd had nine lifetimes. I'd done all I could. Tried my best. Mother would be fine. Let judgment come.

Apparently judgment would be rendered in the metaphorical yet simultaneously visceral terms so reminiscent of the Old Testament. I felt in one hand scales, as of a serpent; in the other the nurturing yet erotic delight of a woman's full breast. Then it hit me that what I had my hands on were two ends of a buxom mermaid. She rose up, lifting me out of the flood.

"Tante Clo?" I said, coughing fetid water.

"Understood you might need a lift, nephew."

Had the Virgin Mary sent her, or had Mother? Or was I asleep in my Algiers bed, where I would wake to Noël bringing me coffee, saying, "Papa, I believe that while you were dreaming, you finally started to heal."

Had it been true what Tante Clo said about my father? That a week before his nuptials, Achille Cheramie tried to seduce his bride's baby sister? Just as on his wedding day, he had a last go at Victorine on her butcher block table. Then the next morning planted in Mother a seed of corruption that would grow into a subsequent, equally wicked generation: me.

If so, he died for his sins.

Or maybe he was just unlucky.

I'm 21 years old, fit, and some say handsome. With a gift for gab and a way with the ladies. Astride a mermaid in the midst of a hurricane.

I'm interested to see how my own luck holds.

~~~

And then…
~~~

Acknowledgments

To the love of my life, Michelle, for everything.

To my brothers Hol, WeeNee, and BouLou, their wives and children, and to our parents: MeMinn, who always thought every word was perfect, and Scrap, who offered countless suggestions. And to Yvonne and Betty and their families, too.

To everybody down the bayou for so much support and inspiration on so many projects over so many years.

To my Los Angeles agent, Peter Turner, and my New York agent, John Ware, who both died while promoting my career. For some reason, it's been difficult to find a new agent since.

And to the generous colleagues who offered their time, advice, and sometimes commiseration on this project's long journey: Julie Smith, James Lee Burke, Campbell Robertson, Moira Crone, Rodger Kamenetz, Anneke Campbell, Jeremy Kagan, Bertrand Tavernier, Tina DeSalvo Callais, Ellen Lewis, Wes Harris, Kris Davidson, Helen Krieger, Jim Catano, Wendy Goldberg, Chris Cenac, Rosemary James, and last but never least, Allan Sprinky Durand.

If I missed anybody – and of course I did – don't let my poor memory detract from my profound gratitude.

About the Author

When not aboard the family's leaky shrimp boat, Glen Pitre grew up in the Cajun town of Cut Off, Louisiana, went to Harvard on scholarship, graduated with honors, then immediately scooted right back down the bayou. He has made his living as a storyteller pretty much ever since.

Best known as writer, producer, and director of big screen dramas, cable thrillers, PBS documentaries, and IMAX films, his movies have played in theaters and on TV worldwide, been lauded at festivals such as Sundance and Cannes, and won countless awards, even earning Pitre a knighthood from France, *Chevalier de l'Ordre des Arts et des Lettres.*

His other works include novels (none, of course, as good as this one) and non-fiction books, museum exhibits and sacred space design, multi-screen video installations and immersive experiences, still photography, radio programming, professional theater, on-stage storytelling, and miscellaneous other episodes of driving blind through the intersection of shaping a narrative and making a buck.

With wife and frequent collaborator Michelle Benoit, Pitre currently lives just 35 miles from where he grew up. He is happy.

For more info, samples, freebies, links, etc., to Glen's work, visit CajunMovies.com. Sign up for our email list (at the bottom of the site's first page) to know whenever he has a new book, movie, museum exhibit, etc. You can also follow Glen on Facebook or track him down with any half-decent bloodhound.

To read other
BOOKS,
see wonderful
MOVIES,
watch fascinating
DOCUMENTARIES,
and enjoy
OTHER COOL STUFF
by
Glen Pitre
visit
www.CajunMovies.com

www.ingramcontent.com/pod-product-compliance
Lightning Source LLC
LaVergne TN
LVHW050916080826
845145LV00001B/103

* 9 7 8 0 9 7 0 1 3 8 3 5 4 *